Lord and Master

First in The Master of Gray Trilogy

Nigel Tranter

CORONET BOOKS
Hodder and Stoughton

ISBN 0-340-17836-1

LORD AND MASTER

Here was a man of such elegance, superb
bearing, confidence, and extraordinary good
looks, as to draw all eyes, whether in admiration, envy or sheer malice, a man of such
sparkling attractiveness and at the same time
mature and easy dignity, that it was hardly
believable that he had barely reached his
twenty-first year. Dressed entirely in white
satin and gold lace – and seemingly the only
man in that salon to be so – save for a black
velet garter below one knee, a black dagger-
belt, and the black lining to the tiny cape
slung from one padded shoulder, his dark
gleaming hair swept down sheerly to his
shoulders in disciplined waves and unusual
style, curling back from neat jet-jewelled ears.

AUTHOR'S FOREWORD

WAS the Master of Gray a devil incarnate? The historians say so. They unanimously portray him in 'colours so odious that, to find his parallel as a master of unprincipled statecraft, we must search amongst the Machiavellian politicians of Italy'. He was, we read, 'a young man of singular beauty and no scruples'. Again, 'He carried a heart as black and treacherous as any in that profligate age.' And so on.

Yet he was admittedly the most successful and remarkable Scottish adventurer of his adventurous age – the age of Mary, Queen of Scots, of Elizabeth, and of James the Sixth; of Reformation Scotland, the Huguenot Wars and the Spanish Armada, in all of which he had his finger. Moreover, he was accepted to be the handsomest man of his day – it was said, of all Europe – as well as one of the most fascinating, talented and witty. None, apparently, could withstand his charm – and though it is claimed that he betrayed everyone with whom he had any dealings, the same folk continued to trust him to the end.

What sort of a man could this be? What lies behind a man like that? Could so black a traitor be yet a lover of beauty, a notable poet and one of the closest friends of the noble Sir Philip Sidney? Or have the historians all missed something? Was the Master of Gray as black as he was painted – or even blacker?

What follows here is no more than a novel. Mere fiction. One writer's notion of Patrick Gray as he might have been; one man's attempt to clothe the bare bones of history with warm human flesh, however erring. In the process many liberties have been taken with historical characters – and to a much lesser extent with dates. Probably I have been less than fair to Chancellor Maitland, for instance, an able man and apparently more honest than most.

I have invented the important character of David Gray, the Master's illegitimate half-brother, in order to provide the necessary reporter close enough to highlight and interpret the latter's extraordinary career – so much of which, of course, must have taken place in secret assignations and behind locked doors, many of them bedroom ones!

5

Castle Huntly still stands, high on its rock, frowning out over the fertile Carse of Gowrie. It is perhaps no more than poetic if ironic justice that it now serves the purpose of a house of correction for young men who have strayed from the broader paths of virtue – and been caught.

NIGEL TRANTER

Aberlady 1960

PRINCIPAL CHARACTERS

In order of appearance

(Fictional characters printed in *Italics*)

PATRICK, MASTER OF GRAY, son and heir of the 5th Lord Gray.

David Gray, illegitimate eldest son of the same.

PATRICK, 5TH LORD GRAY, twice an Extraordinary Lord of Session, and a close friend of Mary, Queen of Scots.

Andrew Davidson, an agile cleric, former Abbot of Holy Church, now reformed, and Principal of St. Mary's College, St. Andrews.

Mariota Davidson, his daughter, duly legitimated.

ELIZABETH LYON, eldest daughter of the 8th Lord Glamis, Chancellor of Scotland – first wife of the Master of Gray.

SIR THOMAS LYON, MASTER OF GLAMIS, brother to Lord Glamis, later Treasurer of Scotland.

JAMES DOUGLAS, 4TH EARL OF MORTON, Regent of Scotland for the child King James the Sixth.

Hortense, Countess de Verlac, paramour and protectress of the Master of Gray, in France.

ESMÉ STUART, SEIGNEUR D'AUBIGNY, a cousin of Darnley and therefore second cousin of King James, later Earl and Duke of Lennox, and Chancellor of Scotland.

JAMES STEWART OF OCHILTREE, Captain of the King's Guard, later Earl of Arran and Chancellor of Scotland.

KING JAMES THE SIXTH OF SCOTS, son of Mary, Queen of Scots.

ROBERT LOGAN OF RESTALRIG, adventurer, cousin of the Master of Gray.

LORD ROBERT STEWART, illegitimate half-brother of Mary the Queen, and later Earl of Orkney.

LADY MARIE STEWART, daughter of above, second wife of the Master of Gray.

LADY ELIZABETH STEWART, notorious courtesan, daughter of the Earl of Atholl, and wife successively to the Lord Lovat, the Earl of March and the Earl of Arran.

SIR FRANCIS WALSINGHAM, Chief Secretary of State to Queen Elizabeth.

SIR PHILIP SIDNEY, poet, diplomat and soldier.

QUEEN ELIZABETH OF ENGLAND.

MARY, QUEEN OF SCOTS, prisoner of Elizabeth.

SIR JOHN MAITLAND, Principal Secretary of State to King James, later Chancellor of Scotland.

SIR WILLIAM STEWART, brother to Arran, assistant to Secretary Maitland.

In addition to the above, amongst the many historical characters, prominent during the colourful twelve-year period covered by this story, are the following:

JOHN, 8TH LORD GLAMIS, Chancellor of Scotland.

HENRI, DUC DE GUISE, Marshal of France, cousin of Queen Mary, and instigator of the Massacre of St. Bartholomew's Eve.

LOUIS, CARDINAL OF LORRAINE, ARCHBISHOP OF RHEIMS, brother to the above, international plotter.

JAMES BEATON, ARCHBISHOP OF GLASGOW, exile, and Ambassador of Mary in France.

WILLIAM, 4TH LORD RUTHVEN, uncle to the Master of Gray, later first Earl of Gowrie and Treasurer of Scotland. Chief actor in the Raid of Ruthven.

ANDREW, 8TH EARL OF ERROLL, High Constable of Scotland and Chief of the Hays.

SIR THOMAS RANDOLPH, English Ambassador.

M. CLAUDE NAU, Secretary to Mary, Queen of Scots.

ROBERT DUDLEY, EARL OF LEICESTER, favourite of Queen Elizabeth.

WILLIAM CECIL, LORD BURLEIGH, former Chief Secretary, later Lord High Treasurer of England.

SIR WALTER RALEIGH, diplomat and explorer.

SIR RALPH SADLER, of Wingfield, jailer to Mary, Queen of Scots.

GEORGE, 6TH EARL OF HUNTLY, Chief of Clan Gordon.

Chapter One

THE two young men were boys enough still to have chosen to await the summons to the great Lord Gray out of doors and in a favourite haunt of their childhood days – a narrow grassy platform or terrace before a little cave in the cliff-face, a sunny, south-facing, secure place, divided by a steep and narrow little ravine from the fierce and sombre towering castle that challenged earth and sky from its taller soaring rock opposite. Here, always, they had found their own castle, where they could watch the comings and goings to that other arrogant pile, close enough to see all that was to be seen, and to be hailed when required, distant enough to be out of the way and, when necessary, hidden in the cave – which was equipped with its own secret stairway, like the many within the thick walls of Castle Huntly itself, out at the back by a climbing earthy passage, up into the bushes and trees that crowned their cliff, and away. They had come here almost automatically, and without discussing the matter, when they heard from Rob Powrie the steward that my lord of Gray was not yet back from Dundee town, though expected at any time – and was expecting to see *them* when he did come. If this repairing to their cave and ledge was a harking back to childhood custom, it did not strike either of them that way.

For young men they were, even though for the taller slender one it was actually only his sixteenth birthday. The other was six months older, though frequently he seemed the younger. Young men matured early in the Scotland of King Jamie Sixth – and as well that they did, since so few achieved any length of years, what with one thing and another. The King himself, of course, was but eight years old, and his unhappy and beautiful mother Mary was already six years a prisoner of Elizabeth of England, at thirty-two – which all had something to do with it.

The youths passed their time of waiting differently – as indeed they did most things differently, despite the closeness of their friendship. Patrick, the slender one, paced back and forth along the little grassy terrace – but not in any caged or heavy fashion; in fact he skipped lightly, almost danced, every now and again in his pacing, in tune with a song that he sang, a song

9

with a catchy jigging air and words that were almost as grossly indecent as they were dangerously sacrilegious, while he twanged at an imaginary lute with long delicate fingers and laughed and grimaced and gestured the while, at David, at the soaring sinister castle opposite, at all the wide-spreading green levels of the Carse of Gowrie and the blue estuary of the Tay that lay below their cliffs. Patrick Gray was like that, a born appreciator of life.

His companion, a stocky plain-faced youth, with level grey eyes where the other's were dancing and dark, sat hunched at the mouth of the cave, and, stubborn chin on hand, stared out across the fair carselands and over the sparkling firth beyond to the green hills of Fife. He did not join in any of the ribald verses of Patrick's song, nor even tap the toe of his worn and scuffed shoe to the lilt of it. He was not sulking, nor surly, however heavy his expression might seem in comparison with that of the gay and ebullient Patrick; merely thoughtful, quiet, reserved. His heavy brows and jutting chin perhaps did David Gray some small injustice.

Each very much in his own way was awaiting the fateful summons, on which, neither required to be told, so much depended.

'He takes a plaguey time – eh, Davy?' the younger interrupted – not his jigging but his singing – to remark. He laughed. 'No doubt the old lecher requires to fortify himself – with a sleep, perhaps – after the exhausting facilities of Dundee! I have heard that the Provost's wife is exceeding sportive – despite her bulk. Tiring, it may be, for a man of his years!' They had observed my Lord Gray's return from the town, with a small cavalcade, fully half-an-hour previously.

'Houts, Patrick man – what way is that to speak of your own father!' the other protested. 'My lord was in Dundee on the business of the Kirk, did not Rob Powrie say?'

'And you think that the two ploys wouldna mix? God's Body, Davy – and you living in godly Reformed St. Andrews these past two years! Faith, man – the holier the occasion, the fiercer the grapple!'

David Gray considered his companion with his level gaze, and said nothing. He had a great gift for silence, that young man – of which no-one was likely to accuse the other.

Patrick laughed again, tossing back the dark curling hair that framed his delicately handsome features, and resumed his song – only now he inserted the name of Patrick Lord Gray into the lewder parts of the ballad in place of the late lamented Cardinal Archbishop David Beaton, of notable memory. And the refrain he changed from 'Iram Coram Dago' to 'Frown, Davy, Frown-oh!'

Even if he did not laugh in sympathy, the other did not frown. Few people ever frowned on Patrick Gray – or if they did, not for long. He was much too good to look at for frowns, and his own scintillating and unfailing good humour, barbed as it generally might be, was apt to be infectious. Beautiful, Patrick had been called, in face and in figure, but there was a quality in both which saved that beauty from the taint of effeminacy. From waving black hair and high noble brows above flashing brilliant eyes, a straight finely-chiselled nose over a smiling mouth whose sweetness was balanced by a firm and so far beardless pointed chin, down past a body that was as lithe and slender and graceful as a rapier blade, to those neat dancing feet, Patrick, Master of Gray, was all shapely comely fascination and charm – and knew it. A pretty boy, yes – but a deal more than that. Not a few had found that out, of both sexes, for he was as good as a honeypot to men and women alike. It was all, perhaps, just a little hard on his brother David.

For they were brothers, these two, despite all the difference in build and feature and manner and voice, in dress even – and despite the paltry six months between their ages. There were times when it could be seen that they might be brothers, too, in the lift of their chins, their habit of shrugging a single shoulder, and so on – attributes these, presumably, passed on by the puissant and potent Patrick, fifth Lord Gray, to his firstborn David, as well as to his seven legitimate offspring, and his Maker only knew how many others. Nevertheless, where the one youth looked a thoroughbred and a delight to the eye, as became a son of the late Lady Barbara of the fierce and haughty breed of Ruthven, the other, rather, appeared a cob, serviceable but unexciting, as befitted the bastard of Nance Affleck, daughter of the miller of Inchture.

The diverting song was pierced by a shout from across the ravine – pierced but not halted. Patrick, as a matter of principle, finished the verse before he so much as glanced over to the fore-court of the castle. But David stood up, and waved a hand to the man with the bull-like voice who stood at the edge of the other cliff, and promptly began to make his way down the steep slope of the gully, using roots and rocks as handholds. After a suitable interval, his half-brother followed him.

The climb up to that beetling fortalice was a taxing business, even to young lungs – and a daunting one too, for any but these two, for the place all but overhung its precipice, and seemed to scowl down harshly, threateningly, in the process. Castle Huntly, as well as crowning an upthrusting rock that rose abruptly from the plain of Gowrie, was, and still is, perhaps the loftiest castle in a land of such, soaring at the cliffward side no fewer than seven storeys to its windy battlements, a tall stern dominating tower, rising on a plan of the letter L in walls of immensely thick red sandstone, past small iron-barred windows, to turrets and crowstepped gables and parapets, dwarfed by height, its base so grafted and grouted into different levels of the living rock as to leave almost indistinguishable where nature left off and man began.

Breathless, inevitably, the young men reached the level of the forecourt, where horses stood champing, a level which was already three storeys high on the cliffward side, and found Rob Powrie, the castle steward and major domo, awaiting them in a mixture of impatience and sympathy. He was a friend of theirs, though only too well aware that his master was not a man to be kept waiting, especially when aggrieved.

'Why could ye no' bide decently aboot the place, laddies, instead of ower in yon hole, there?' he complained. He was a big burly man, plainly dressed, more like a farmer than a noble-man's steward. 'My lord's shouting for you. You'd ha' done better to cosset him a wee, this day, than keep him waiting, you foolish loons. Up wi' you, now . . . '

'My father has plenty to cosset him, Rob – too many for his years, I think!' Patrick returned. 'The Provost's wife, for instance . . . '

'Wheesht, Master Patrick – wheesht, for sweet Mary's sake! Och, I mean for whoever's sake looks after us, these days!'

'Ha! Hark to the good Reformed steward of the Kirk's holy Lord Gray!'

'Wheesht, I say! Davy – can ye no' mak him see sense? Get him in a better frame o' mind than this? My lord's right hot against the pair o' you, I tell you. It will pay you to use him softly, I warrant.'

'Come on, Patrick – hurry, man,' David jerked. 'And for God's sake, have a care what you say.'

The other laughed. 'Never fear for me, Davy – look to your-self!' he said.

'Haste you both. My lord is in his own chamber . . . '

They continued their climb, first up a light outside timber stairway, which could be removed for security, to the only entrance to the keep proper, past the great dark stone-vaulted hall within, where a number of folk, lairds and officers and ministers in the sombre black of the Kirk, set about long tables of elm, and up the winding stone turnpike stair within the thickness of the tremendous walling, David leading. At the landing above the hall, before a studded door of oak, he halted, panting, and waited for Patrick to join him.

Before the latter could do so, the door was flung open, and their father stood there. He frowned at them both, heavily, the underhung jaw thrust forward, but said nothing.

'My lord!' David gulped.

'Good day to you, Father,' Patrick called, courteously.

The older man merely stared at them head sunk between massive shoulders, rather like a bull about to charge. Lord Gray was a bulky fleshy man, florid of face and spare of hair. Though only of early middle years he looked older, with the lines of dissipation heavy upon him, from sagging jowls to thrusting paunch. The little eyes in that gross face were shrewd, however, and the mouth tight enough. A more likely father, it would appear, for the stocky silent David than for the beautiful Patrick, Master of Gray, his heir.

Equally without a word, the former stood before him now, stiff, wary, waiting. The latter fetched an elaborate bow, that was only redeemed from being a mockery by the sweetness of the smile that accompanied it.

The Lord Gray jerked his head towards the inner room, and turning about, stamped inside, the spurs of his long leather riding-boots jingling. The young men followed, with Patrick now to the fore.

It was a comparatively small chamber, the stone floor, that was but the top of the hall vaulting, covered in skins of deer and sheep, the walls hung with arras save where two little wooden doors, one on either side of the room, hid the cunningly contrived ducts in the walling which led down to the deep window embrasures of the hall, and by which the castle's lord could listen, when so inclined, to most of what was said in the great room below. Despite its being late May, a fire of logs blazed in the stone fireplace with the heraldic overmantel bearing the graven rampant red lion on silver of Gray. It was very warm in that room.

To this fireplace Lord Gray limped, to turn and face his sons.

'Well?' he said. That was all.

'Very well, I thank you, sir,' Patrick answered lightly – but not too lightly. 'I trust that I see you equally so – and that your leg but little pains you?' That was solicitude itself, its sincerity not to be doubted.

The older man's frown seemed to melt a little as he looked at his namesake. Then swiftly he shook his head and his brows came down again, as he transferred his gaze to the other young man. 'You, sirrah!' he cried, and he shouted now, in reaction to that shameful moment of weakness. 'You, you graceless whelp, you spawn of the miller's bitch – you that I've cherished and supported in idleness all these years! What have you to say for yourself, a' God's name? What do you mean by permitting this to happen? Fine you ken that I only sent you to St. Andrews College to keep this simpering poppet here out o' mischief. D'you think I threw my siller away on a chance by-blow like yoursel', for nothing? Do you? Answer me! What a pox ha' you been doing, to fail me thus? Out with it, damn you!'

David Gray drew a long and uneven breath, but his level gaze was steady on his father's purpling congested face. 'My lord – I have worked at my studies, and waited on Patrick here, as you ordained.'

'Waited on him! Fiend seize me – held up the lassie's skirts for him, mair like!' the older man burst out coarsely. 'Is that it? Is that the way you carried out my charges? Speak, fool!'

'No, sir.' Heavily, almost tonelessly, the young man answered him. He was used to being the whipping-boy for the Master of Gray. It was so much easier to pour out wrath upon himself than upon his fascinating and talented brother. Not that he enjoyed the process. 'I have done as you ordained, to the best of my ability . . . '

'God's Passion – *your* ability! Your ability means that the pair o' you are sent down from the University as a stink, a disgrace to the name and honour of Gray . . . and Master Davidson's daughter with a bairn in her belly!'

David stared straight in front of him, and said nothing.

'Speak, man – don't stand there glowering like a stirk? Give me an answer – or I'll have the glower wiped off your face with a horse-whip!'

David could have pointed out that it was not really the pair of them that had been expelled from St. Mary's College, but only Patrick. Likewise, that Mariota Davidson's bairn had not been conceived as a joint operation of the brothers. But such objec-

14

tions, he knew, would be as profitless as they were irrelevant. He had no illusions as to his position and what was required of him. Inevitably there were handicaps in the privileged situation of being foster-brother, squire, bodyservant and conscience for the winsome Master of Gray. 'I am sorry,' he said simply, flatly – but less than humbly. David Gray was in fact no more humble at heart than any other Gray.

'Sorry. . . .' Lord Gray's face contorted and his fists clenched beneath his somewhat soiled ruffles.

Patrick, misliking the sight and the ugliness of it all, stared away out of the small window, and sought to dwell on pleasanter things.

David thought that his father was going to strike him, and steeled himself to stand the blow unflinching – as he had stood many another, when younger. But the head-turned stance of his other son seemed to affect the nobleman – possibly also the fact that he could thus look at him without having to meet the half-mocking, half-reproachful and wholly disarming glance of Patrick's fine dark eyes.

'You, you prinking ninny! You papingo! Does this not concern you, likewise, boy?' Lord Gray looked down as the younger man turned. 'And these clothes? These mummer's trappings? This fool's finery? Where did you get it? How come you dressed so – like a Popish whoremonger? Not with *my* siller, by God!' He gestured disgustedly at his heir's costume. 'How dare you show yoursel' in a godly household, so?'

Certainly Patrick was dressed very differently from his father. He wore a crimson velvet doublet with an upstanding collar piped in gold thread, reaching high at the back to set off a cascading lace ruff. The sleeves were slashed with yellow satin, and ended in lace ruffles. The shoulders were padded out into prominent epaulettes. The waist of the doublet reached down low in a V to emphasise the groin, and the breeches were short, ending above the knee, slashed also in yellow and padded out at the hips and thighs. The long hose were of yellow silk, and the shoes sported knots of crimson ribbon. Lord Gray, on the other hand, as became a pillar of the new Kirk, was soberly clad in dark broadcloth, the doublet fitting the body and skirted, in the old-fashioned way, with only a small collar, and the ruff a mere fringe of white. The breeches were unmodishly long enough to reach below his knees and disappear into the tops of his riding-boots. The only gesture towards richness was the heavy sword-belt of solid wrought gold. As for David, his patched doublet and breeches of plain brown homespun, darned woven hose and solid but worn shoes, were all clean enough and as neat as they might be – and that was about the best that could be said for them.

Patrick glanced down at himself with no indication of shame or dissatisfaction. 'An honest penny may always be earned in St. Andrews town, at a pinch,' he said. 'Learning, I have found, does not always damp out lesser delights. Even ministers of your Kirk, sir, can be generous, on occasion – and their ladies still more so, Heaven be praised!'

'Lord – what d'you mean, boy?' his father spluttered. 'What is this, now? Do not tell me that . . . '

'I shall tell you nothing, my lord, that would distress you – God forbid! Indeed, there is little to tell. Is there, Davy? My lord of Gray's son is inevitably welcome in many a house. You would not have him churlishly reject such . . . hospitality?'

The older man swallowed, all but choked, and almost thankfully, if viciously, turned back to David. 'This . . . this, then, is how you guided and looked after your brother! You'll pay for this – both of you! I'll not be used thus. To drag my name in the dirt . . . !'

'Never that, Father,' Patrick assured. 'The reverse, rather. Indeed, always your name meant a great deal to us, I vow. Is that not so, Davy? And your honour, sir, of value above, h'mm, rubies!'

The Lord Gray opened his mouth to speak, shut it again almost with a snap, and went limping over to a desk. He picked up a paper there, and brought it back to them, and waved it under the boys' faces.

'Here is how you valued my name and honour,' he exclaimed. 'A letter from Principal Davidson apprising me . . . *me*! . . . that he must banish you from his University by reason of your filthy lewdness, naming you as father of his daughter's unborn bairn, and hinting at a marriage. God's death – marriage! With Gray!'

Even Patrick faltered at that *cri de coeur*. 'Marriage . . . ?' he repeated. 'With Mariota? The old turkey-cock talks of *marriage*, i' faith! Lord – here is madness!'

'Madness? Aye, by the sweet Christ! But whose madness? With all the other trollops of St. Andrews to sport with, you had to go begetting a bastard on the worthy Principal's daughter! Why, man? Why?'

Patrick mustered a one-shouldered shrug. 'I have it on good

authority, sir, that the daughter herself was a bastard of the worthy Principal, until a few years syne – when he was the holy Lord Abbot of Inchaffray.'

'What of it, boy? Can we no' all make mistakes?' my lord asked, and then coughed.

'Quite, Father.'

'Aye – but there are mistakes and mistakes, Patrick. Mistakes o' the flesh can come upon us all unawares, at times. But mistakes o' the wits and the mind are another matter, boy.'

'Which was good Master Davidson's, Father?' Patrick wondered innocently.

'Tush – his mistakes are by with. Yours are not. Principal Davidson saw the bright light o' Reform in good time . . . and so wed a decent woman in place o' the Harlot o' Rome. So he now can decently own his lass, and call her legitimate. Moreover, he is a coming man in the Kirk, and wi' the ear o' the Regent and o' Master Buchanan, the King's Tutor. He is no' a man to offend, I tell you.'

'Must Gray go in fear and respect, then, of a jumped-up coat-turned cleric, my lord?'

'God's Splendour – no! But . . . laddie, you ken not what you say. My position is no' that secure. The country is in a steer, and Morton the Regent loves me not. He and the Kirk rule the land – and I am known as a friend o' Mary the Queen, whom the Kirk loves not. Where the Kirk is concerned, I maun watch my step . . .'

'But you yourself are one of the leaders of the Kirk party, are you not?'

'Aye . . . but I have my unfriends. In the same Kirk. Why did you bring the Kirk into this cantrip, boy? I'm no' so sure o' Davidson. You heard – the man hints at marriage. And if he talks that gait loud enough, it will surely come to the ear o' my lord of Glamis. And how will you fare then, jackanapes?'

'Glamis?'

'Aye, Glamis. I have, God aiding me, arranged a marriage contract between yoursel' and the Lady Elizabeth Lyon o' Glamis. After much labour, and but a few days past. What will my lord say when he hears o' this, then? Glamis is strong in the Kirk party. None shall shake *him*. 'Twas the best match in the land for you. And, now . . .'

Patrick was not listening. 'Glamis!' he repeated. 'Elizabeth Lyon of Glamis.' Those fine eyes had narrowed. The speaker leaned forward, suddenly urgent, his voice altered – indeed all

17

of him altered, as in a moment. 'This . . . this is different, I think,' he said slowly. 'My lord – I knew nothing of this.'

'Think you I must inform you, a stripling, of all I plan . . . ?'

'I am old enough for the injury of your plans, sir, it seems – so old enough to be told of them when they concern myself, surely? Old enough for marriage, too . . . '

'Aye. Marriage to a cleric's mischance in a college backyard – or marriage to the daughter of the Chancellor, one of the greatest lords of the land . . . and the richest!'

Patrick smiled, and swiftly, as in a flash, was all light and cheer and attraction again. 'Elizabeth Lyon, as I mind her, is very fair,' he said. 'And notably well endowed . . . in more than just her dowry!' And he laughed.

'Aye – she has big breasts, if that is what you like,' his forthright father agreed. 'A pity that you ha' thrown them away, and what goes wi' them, for this strumpet o' Davidson's. Devil damn it – I had set my heart on this union between our two houses . . . '

'She is no strumpet.' That was quietly, levelly said.

Both Patricks, senior and junior, turned on David who had so abruptly but simply made that announcement. The elder's glance was hot and angry, but the younger's was quick and very keen.

'Silence, sirrah!' Lord Gray said. 'Speak when you are spoken to.'

'Davy likes the gentle Mariota well enough, I think,' his brother observed, significantly.

'I carena who he likes or doesna like – or you, either,' their father declared, 'What I care for is the ruin o' my plans, and the welfare o' our house and name. That you have spat upon, and cast aside . . . '

'I think you do me wrong, Father,' Patrick said quietly.

'Eh? Wrong? A pox – you say so? You mincing jackdaw!' Lord Gray took a wrathful step forward.

Patrick held his ground. 'Only because I judge you to be misinformed, sir. Your plans are not ruined, yet.'

'How mean you . . . ?'

'I mean that it is not I that should be the object of Master Davidson's ambitions – but Davy, here! Heigho, Davy is the culprit, I fear!'

There was little of difference between the gasps of breath drawn by each of his hearers. David turned swiftly – and found Patrick's gaze urgent upon him.

'Is that not so, Davy? Dear Davy! You have hidden your

18

light under your bushel for long enough, eh? The bairn is yours – faith, all yours!'

'But . . . !'

'God be good – what is this?' Lord Gray looked from one to the other. 'Are you telling me, now . . . ?' Davidson says in his letter . . . '

'Master Davidson, no doubt, would liefer have the Master of Gray for possible good-son than just our Davy! But he will be disappointed. Mariota's bairn need not claim me for father.'

'You mean that it was Davy . . . ?'

'Just that. We both found her . . . friendly. But Davy, I swear, found her kindest! You heard him. He is a deep one, Davy. I did not mind bearing the honour of it, or the blame, to save him, when it mattered less than a groat. But now, with the name and honour of our house at stake, in the matter of the Glamis match . . . '

'Yes, yes. Aye, so. I' ph'mmm. This is . . . altogether different. I' faith, yes.' The older man looked at David, his shrewd little eyes busy, calculating. As the latter started to speak, his father held up his hand peremptorily. 'Here, now, is a different story, altogether. Why did you not tell me this, earlier? I see it all, now – the rascal Davidson saw his chance. He would catch a fine fish with his little trull. He would hook Gray, would he? We shall teach him different.'

'Ah, but do not name her trull, Father,' Patrick put in quickly, smiling. 'Davy's feelings are to be considered, are they not? He would not have her named strumpet, recollect!'

'Aye, aye.' The Lord Gray actually chuckled. It was extraordinary the change that has come over the man. 'Davy's feelings shall be considered – houts aye. Davy will have his reward – our right lusty eager Davy! Boy – maybe we will make a churchman o' you yet . . . with Principal o' St Andrews, and like to be one o' Morton's tulchan bishops, for goodfather! We will have two marriages – aye, ye shall both embrace the holy estate o' matrimony. Embrace it right firmly. What could be more suitable? I will write me a letter to Master Davidson. No, better – I will ride and see him tomorrow, myself. I would not miss seeing his godly countenance at the good tidings I bring! Ha!'

'My lord,' David managed to insert, at last. 'Have I no say in this?'

'None, boy. None,' his father assured promptly, finally, but almost genially. 'You have done your part – and done it right notably, it seems. The rest is my affair.' He actually patted

David's shoulder. 'Now, off with you. Away, the pair o' you. There are folk awaiting me, below.'

'Sir – the lassie. Mariota. She, at the least, must needs have her say . . .'

'Houts – off wi' you! The lassie will do what she's told. And lucky to be made into a middling honest woman, by God! Now – off wi' you, I say. And, Patrick – in the fiend's name, get out o' those magpie's clothes before any o' my sainted callers see you!'

'Yes, Father.'

As the two young men went down the stairs, David leading, it was the other who spoke first. 'Was that not featly done, Davy?' Patrick asked, laughing softly. 'Was not there the dexterous touch? The storm taken at its crest, and calmed! The bubble burst! I flatter myself I wrought that not unskilfully.'

The other neither looked at him nor answered.

'I saved the day for us both, did I not? It got us out of there with smiles instead of tears. You cannot deny that I spared you a horse-whipping, it may be – or worse, man?'

Still his brother did not reply, but went stolidly on down the winding stairs.

'Davy!' Patrick laid an urgent hand on his companion's arm. 'You are not hurt at me? Man, Davy – you did not take it amiss? I acted all for the best. For all of us. You saw how it was. It had to be so. The honour of our name – aye, and the safety of our house, even – demanded it. You heard what my father said. I could do no other.'

They had come to the bottom of the stairs, and hurried past the hall. At the little guard-room that flanked the castle doorway they found Gilbert and James, two of Patrick's legitimate brothers, and Barbara his eldest sister, and these, mere bairns of ten and twelve, they brushed aside despite their eager admiration of Patrick's costume. Down the outside timber steps they went. Their own room was in one of the smaller corner towers that guarded the enclosing courtyard of the great keep on the landward side. Instead of heading thereto, however, David, still in the lead, made straight across the cobbled yard, past the tethered horses and lounging men-at-arms, to the great arched entrance under its embattled gatehouse, Patrick, still explaining, at his side. At the gateway itself, however, the latter paused.

'Where are you going, Davy?' he said. 'Not out there – not yet. I must be out of these clothes.'

'Later,' the other jerked, and kept on walking.

'No. You heard what my father said. About taking them off. We have him in kindlier mood, now. We should not offend him more.'

They were through the gateway now, past the main guard-room, out of which a woman's skirls of laughing protest issued unsuitably. David strode on, unspeaking.

'You are being foolish, Davy – stupid,' Patrick declared. There was more than a hint of anxiety in his attractively modulated voice now. 'Where . . . where are you going?'

His brother had swung off the castle's approach road, to plunge down the gentle grassy slope to the west. Below were birch trees, open woodland, reaching round the sides of the towering rock to the level carseland.

'Down yonder,' David told him briefly. 'Where we can speak our minds.'

'No!' the other cried. 'Not there. We . . . we can speak in our room. Anywhere, Davy . . . '

His brother's hand reached out to grip his arm fiercely, jerking Patrick on. 'Come, you!'

Patrick looked back at the castle, glancing sidelong at his companion, bit his lip, but followed where he was led, silent now.

Slanting down through the trees they came presently to a grassy hollow hidden amongst the birches and the tall bracken, out of sight of castle and road and spreading fields below – a haunt of theirs less popular than their cave and ledge perhaps, but useful in its own way. There, roughly, David unhanded his brother, and faced him.

'Time we made a reckoning, I think,' he said levelly.

'No, Davy – no!' Patrick's fine eyes were wide. 'This is folly. No way to behave. To settle differences. We are men, now – not bairns. See you – I can explain it all. If you will but heed me, Davy. If you will but listen . . . '

'I listened,' the other interrupted him, harshly. 'You had your say back yonder. Now, I will have mine! You are a liar, Patrick Gray – a liar, and a cozener, and a cheat! Are you a coward too?'

His brother had lost a little of his colour. He drew a deep breath. 'No,' he said, and seemed to find difficulty in getting the word out.

'Good, I was feared you might be – along with the rest. And you can run faster than me, yet!'

Patrick's head lifted just a degree or two, and his chin with it – and for a moment they looked very much alike. 'No,' he repeated

21

quietly. 'I do not think I am a coward. But, Davy – my fine clothes?'

'The fiend take your fine clothes! This is for your lies!' And David Gray exploded into action, and hurled himself upon the other, head sunk into wide shoulders, fists flailing.

Patrick side-stepped agilely, leapt back light-footed, and lashed out in defence. Of the first fierce rain of blows only two grazed his cheek and shoulder. But David was possessed of a swift and rubbery fury of energy that there was no escaping, though the other was taller, with the longer reach, and hit out in return desperately, as hard as he knew. The driving, elementary, relentless savagery of the elder was just not to be withstood. Short of turning and running, there was no escape. Patrick knew it, from of old – and perhaps the knowledge further invalidated his defence. In less time than it takes to tell, his lip was split and his nose bleeding.

Panting, David leapt back, tossing the hair from his face. 'That for your lies!' he gasped. 'This, for your cozening!' And plunging into the attack again, he drove hard for the other's body in crouching battering-ram style. Despite himself, Patrick yelped with sudden pain, hunched himself up in an effort to protect his softer parts, and was driven staggering back with a great pile-driver, to sink on one knee, groaning.

'That for . . . the cozening! On your feet, man! This for . . . your cheating!' David swung a sideways upper-cut at Patrick's chin, which all but lifted the other off his unsteady feet, and sent him tottering back to crash all his length on the greensward, and there lie moaning.

Swaying over him, grey eyes blazing with a cold fire of their own, David suddenly stooped and wrenched up a turf of long grass and roots and earth. On to his brother's beautiful face he rubbed and ground and slapped this, back and forth, into mouth and nose and eyes, before casting it from him. 'And that . . . for Mariota Davidson!' he exclaimed.

Straightening up, then, he looked down upon the writhing disfigured victim, and the cold fire ebbed from him. Panting he stood there, for long moments, straddling the other, and then slowly he shook his head.

'Och, Patrick, Patrick!' he said, and turning away abruptly, went striding off through the further trees without a backward glance.

The Master of Gray lay where he had fallen, sobbing for breath.

Chapter Two

My lord of Gray was as good as his word, and allowed no grass
to grow under his feet, either. He rode to St. Andrews the next
morning, and was home again the same night – and in excellent
mood. He made no comment at all on Patrick's battered features
and gingerly held frame, nor questioned the young men further
on what apparently was now little business of theirs. A busy man
of affairs, of course, he was not in the habit of wasting much
time on any of his offspring. His orders, however, were explicit
and peremptory. He and Patrick would ride on the morrow for
Glamis Castle, to fix the date of the wedding, before the
Chancellor went off to Stirling for his monthly meeting with the
Regent. The other marriage date was already satisfactorily
fixed, it seemed – even the disillusioned Principal Davidson
agreeing, presumably, as to the need for some haste in this
matter. It only remained for David Gray to go and pay his
respects to his future father-in-law. The nuptials would be
celebrated, if that was the apt word, as discreetly and quickly
as possible before the month was out and before the lassie
became mountainous.

The brothers were to go their different ways, then, for almost
the first time in their lives.

So the day following, early, the two parties rode away from
Castle Huntly, in almost opposite directions and contrastingly
composed. My lord's jingling company of gentlemen, chaplain,
and score of men-at-arms were finely mounted, their weapons
gleaming, plumes tossing, the red lion standard of Gray fluttering bravely in front of father and son; both were soberly clad in
dark broadcloth but with rich black half-armour, inlaid with
gold, above. They headed north by west for the Newtongray
pass of the Sidlaw hills and Strathmore of the Lyons. David,
sitting his shaggy long-tailed Highland pony, and dressed still
as he had come from St. Andrews two days before, trotted
off alone eastwards for Dundee town and the ferry boat at
Broughty.

As they branched off on their different roads, David looked
back. He saw only the one head in that gallant cavalcade turned

towards him, as Patrick's steel-gauntleted arm was raised in valedictory salute. David lifted his own hand, and slowly waved it back and forth, before sighing and turning away. They were brothers, yet.

Five miles on, avoiding the climbing narrow streets of Dundee by keeping to the water-front and the boat-shore, David rode further to Broughty, another three miles eastwards, where the Firth narrowed to a bare mile across and a ferry plied. Here rose the soaring broken mass of another Gray castle, still proudly dominating land and sea despite being partly demolished after its bloody vicissitudes during the religious wars of a few years earlier. David sat waiting for the ferryboat beneath the frowning river walls, and cared nothing for the fact that his own great-grandfather had first built them, his grandfather had betrayed them to the English, and his father had gained his limp and almost lost his life in seeking to retake them.

The ferry eventually put him across the swift-running tide, at Ferry-Port-on-Craig, where still another castle glowered darkly on all but friends of Gray, and which, acting in conjunction with that of Broughty over the water, could in theory defend the estuary and Dundee from invasion by sea, and in practise levy toll on all shipping using the narrows – thereby greatly contributing to my lord's income.

A ride of no more than ten miles across the flat sandy links of North Fife brought David thereafter, by just after noon, to the grey city of St. Andrews, ecclesiastical metropolis of Scotland, with all its towers and spires and pinnacles adream by the white-flecked glittering sea. The young man viewed it with mixed feelings as he rode in by the Guard Bridge and the narrow massive gateway of the West Port. The blood of martyrs innumerable did not shout to him from the cobbles, nor did the sight of so many fair and handsome buildings in various stages of defacement and demolishment, eloquent witness to Reforming zeal, distress him overmuch; but here he had passed the two most free and happy years of his life, here he had studied and learned and laughed and sported, here he had met Mariota Davidson – and from here he had been expelled with ignominy, because he was the Master of Gray's shadow and dependent, but two days before.

He rode down the narrow kennel of South Street, where pigs rooted amongst the mounds of garbage that half-filled the causeway outside every door, squawking poultry flew up from his pony's hooves, and the wooden house gables that thrust out on either side all but met overhead, enabling wives to exchange gossip above him from one side to the other in their own windows. Many of these timber houses were being pulled down, and the new stone ones being built by the Reformers out of the convenient quarries of the Cathedral and a score of fine churches, priories, nunneries, seminaries and the like, were set further back from the cobbles, so that one day the street would be wider, undoubtedly. But meantime the transported stone-work lay about in heaps everywhere, along with defaced statues, smashed effigies and shattered marble, greatly adding to the congestion and difficulty of passage. The smells and the noises and the sights of St. Andrews, though all familiar, were not without their effect on the banished student.

David turned in at the arched entrance of St. Mary's College. He dismounted, left his pony loose amongst the cattle which grazed on the wide grassy square within, and made for the corner of the great quadrangle where was the Principal's house, a handsome edifice, formerly the college chapel. He approached the door, and rasped diffidently on the tirling-pin. Needless to say, he had never before used the front door of this august establishment, whatever he may have done at the back – but his instructions for the occasion, from his father, were positive.

An arrogant man-servant answered his summons – and would have sent him packing with a flea in his ear, as one more presumptuous and threadbare scholar, had not David declared that he sought Master Davidson on an errand from my lord of Gray. Grudgingly, suspiciously, he was admitted, and thrust into a dark and book-lined room to wait.

He had to wait, indeed. Though he could hear the Principal's sonorous and slightly nasal voice echoing, now from the room next door, now from the hall, it came no nearer than that as the minutes passed and lengthened into an hour. Undoubtedly Master Davidson had more important matters to attend to than such as he represented. David waited as patiently as he might. After a while, greatly daring, he glanced at some of the books on the shelves, and found them dull stuff, in Latin. He went to the window, and gazed out. He paced round and round the perimeter of the stone floor, avoiding treading on its precious covering, one of the fine new carpets such as even Castle Huntly could not boast. Sometimes he listened, ear to the crack of the door, not for the well advertised presence of the Principal, but for the possible sound of Mariota's voice. She must be somewhere in the house. He would have liked to see her before he

spoke with her father – though liked hardly was the word to use –
but he did not see how this was to be achieved.

It was nearer two hours than one before the door opened to
reveal the impressive figure of Principal Andrew Davidson. He
was less lean and hungry-looking, was less hairy, than the generality of the Reformed clergy, being amply and comfortably made,
and of an imposing presence. His beard, indeed, was only wispy
– which must have been a sore trial to him, with the Old
Testament prophet as the approved model – and it was said that
the large flat black velvet cap, which he was rumoured to keep
on his head even in bed, was to hide the tonsure which painfully
laggard nature was failing lamentably to cover up. He was
dressed in the full pulpit garb of black Geneva gown and plain
white bands, now as always – though once again scurrilous
student whisper had it that if the wind off the North Sea waxed
more than usually frolicsome around a St. Andrews street
corner, and the voluminous gown billowed up, much silken and
ungodly coloured apparel might be glimpsed beneath. He swept
into the room now, and the door slammed shut behind him.

'You are David Gray, for want of a true surname,' he declaimed, in his stride as it were, as though in continuation of a
previous discourse, hardly glancing at his visitor. 'A whore-
mongering idler and a trifler with women, whom it seems, God
pity me, I must accept as good-son because you have taken gross
and filthy advantage of my foolish daughter. I cannot and shall
not welcome you to this house that you have presumptuously
defiled and outraged. God is not mocked, and his righteous
wrath shall descend upon the heads of all such as yourself. Nor
shall any dowry come to you with my unhappy and ravaged
daughter, upon whom the Lord have mercy – think it not! Such
dowry as she had, you have already lasciviously possessed, in
fornicating shameful lust!' The resounding well-turned words
and phrases slid in sonorous procession off what almost seemed
to be an appreciatively savouring tongue. 'The carnal appetites
of the flesh shall not inherit the Kingdom of Heaven, nor any
goods and gear of mine. *Jacta est alea!* What provision has my
Lord Gray made for you both, boy?'

David was so overwhelmed by this flood of oratory and part
mesmerised by the ceaseless and remarkable perambulations of
the dignified speaker, that it was some moments before he
realised that a question had been flung at him, and that the last
sentence had not been merely one more rhetorical pearl on the
string of eloquence. He gulped, as he found the other's

imperious if somewhat protuberant eyes upon him, *en passant*, as it were.

'I . . . I do not know, sir,' he faltered.

'Almighty and Most Merciful – grant me patience! Grant a ravaged father restraint! Hark at him – he does not know! He knows how to steal a helpless lassie's maidenhead! He knows the sinful antics of the night! He knows the way to my door, with offers of marriage! But he does not know how to support the creature whom he hath got with child! What is my lord thinking of? He fobs me off with you, *you* – dolt, bastard and beggar – and sends no word of what he will pay! You have no letter, sirrah? No promissory token . . . ?'

'None,' David answered. 'My lord said that . . . that all was arranged.'

'Arranged! Aye – arranged is the word for it, I vow! Arranged to cheat and defraud me! All a plot, a trick! By the holy and blessed Saint Mar . . . h'mm . . . by the Sword of the Lord and His Kirk – does he esteem me a babe, a puling innocent to be foxed and duped? You are sure, knave, that there is no letter coming, no privy word?'

'I do not know,' David reiterated. 'All my lord told me was that all was arranged. That you would be satisfied – satisfied with me as good-son. And that the marriage was settled for ere the month's end, before, before . . . '

'Aye – before yon fond fool through there thrusts her belly's infamy in the face of all who walk St. Andrew's streets, to make me a laughing-stock and a by-word before all men!' The reverend Principal had noticeably increased the pace of his promenade, in his agitation, so that now his gown positively streamed behind him. 'Father in Heaven – was ever a humble servant of Thine so used! Was ever the foul fiend's work so blatantly . . . boy – you did say satisfied? Satisfied was the word? My lord did declare that I would be satisfied with you as good-son – God help me! Aye – it must be that. Mean that I should be satisfied . . . receive due and proper satisfaction. Aught else is unthinkable. Perhaps I have done my lord some slight injustice? 'Fore God I hope that I have! Tell you my lord, fellow, that I await his satisfaction eagerly. You have it? Eagerly. Aye. Now . . . weightier matters await me, boy. You may go.'

David gasped. 'Go?' he repeated. 'But, sir . . . that is not all, surely? That is not *all* I came to see you for?'

'All, fool? Enough and enough that I should have spared you

27

thus much of my time. I am a man with great and heavy tasks upon me. I have the care of hundreds of souls in this place on my hands and heart. I have to see that God's will is done in this University and city. How much more of my time would you have?'

'But the marriage, sir? What of that? When is it to be? My lord said that you would arrange all . . .'

'Arrange all? Arrange what, in the name of the good Lord? Think you that this unseemly union, devised under some back stair, should be ceremoniously celebrated with pomp and display? I vow not! A shamed and ungrateful wanton's mating to a nameless bastard! Faugh, sir – *me* arrange it?' Davidson had his hand on the door latch. 'Wed you where and how you will – so long as wed you are. And before due witnesses – but not before me, I warrant you!'

'I see, sir.' David's voice was level, set, now. 'And when? When is this to be?'

'Should I care, man? When you like. Today if you have the wherewithal to pay the chaplain's fee. Wed the baggage now if you wish – so long as you take her away out of my sight, out of this house and this my city of St. Andrews! But . . . see you have it lawfully witnessed . . .'

That last was tossed over a black-gowned shoulder, as the ornament of the Kirk, fount of learning, and one-time prince of the Holy Church strode out into the hallway and was gone, leaving the door wide behind him.

For long the young man stood in that dark room staring after the cleric with unseeing eyes.

At length, sighing, David went in search of Mariota Davidson. He moved warily through to the rear of the house to the great kitchen. A serving wench there greeted his appearance with sniggers and giggles, but in answer to his enquiry pointed to an inner door, leading to a pantry. Nodding, he moved over, and opened the door.

The girl sat by the window of the small room, her hands on her lap, staring straight before her. At sight of him she rose to her feet, and stood waiting, wordless, wide-eyed.

'Mariota!' he said, his voice thick. 'Och, lassie, lassie!'

She bit her lip, lowered her eyes, and drew a deep quivering breath.

Quietly David closed the door behind him.

Mariota Davidson was not notably mountainous, nor even

too obviously pregnant – only somewhat thicker about the middle than her usual. At fifteen, she was a well-built girl, almost as tall as David, a gentle fawn-eyed creature, bonny, auburn-haired, her burgeoning womanhood glowing for all to behold. Only, today those normally easily flushed and dimpled cheeks were pale and tear-stained, and the great hazel-brown eyes red-rimmed and a little swollen. Even so, she was bonny, warm, appealing – to David Gray perhaps the more so for her so evident distress. She was dressed in a short sleeveless homespun gown of dark green, almost black, as became a daughter of the Kirk, even an outcast one, the skirt split down the front and gathered back to show an underskirt of saffron linen, with a white linen sleeved sark or blouse above. She wore a brief apron also, at which she tugged and twisted.

David came near to her, but not too near. 'I . . . I am sorry, Mariota,' he said. 'You have been crying. I am sorry. Do not cry, lassie.'

She shook her capless head of reddish-brown curls, unspeaking.

'You are well enough?'

'Yes,' she said, small-voiced. 'Where is . . . where is Patrick?'

'He is not here. He is . . . he is with my lord.' David looked down at his feet. 'He sent you greetings. He wishes you very well,' he lied.

The girl did not answer. She was twisting and twisting that apron. 'Davy – oh, Davy – what is to become of me?' she exclaimed, her voice catching.

He swallowed. 'It is . . . we are . . . has your father not told you, Mariota?'

'He tells me nothing. He will not even speak with me. None must speak with me. None must deal with me at all, in this house. He has ordered it. No soul has spoken to me for three days. Oh, Davy . . . !' She choked.

He took a step forward, to touch her, to take her arm – and then hesitated, withdrew his hand. 'You know . . . you know nothing, then?'

'Only that I am lost, lost,' she wailed. 'God will not have me, nor man either. None . . . '

He clutched at that. 'I will,' he said. 'I will have you, Mariota.'

She did not seem to hear him. 'I would kill myself, if I knew how,' she went on, tonelessly. 'I have tried – but it is not so easy . . . '

'Och, hush you!' the young man cried, shocked. 'What way is

that to talk? Wicked, it is.'

'Aye – but I *am* wicked. I wish that I was dead, Davy.'

'Lord, lassie – never say that! Never. You will be happy yet. I swear it. I will see to it – believe me, lassie, I will.'

'You are kind, Davy. Always you were kind. But what can you do? It was kindly of you to come and see me . . . after what I have done. I wonder that you came. But there is nothing that you can do, you see . . . '

'I' faith, girl – I am to marry you!' Almost he shouted that, to get it out. 'Marry, d'you hear? I am to marry you!'

Her breath caught, as she stared at him. She put a hand to her high young bosom. She opened her lips, but found no words.

David took her arm this time, earnestly. 'I am sorry, Mariota. I should not have bawled at you, that way. Sorry for everything. Sorry about Patrick. He would . . . do not blame him too much, lass. My lord would not hear of it. He has other plans for Patrick. I . . . well, I am the best that you can do, I fear. I am not Patrick . . . but I like you, lassie. I like you very well.'

The girl seemed not so much to be listening as searching, searching his eyes with her own, huge, alight, but fearful. It was her turn to reach out, with both her hands, to grip him. 'Davy,' she whispered, 'you would not cozen me? You would not do that to me? Not now?'

'No,' he agreed. 'I would not do that, now or any time. See you, Mariota – it is best this way. The child shall be my child. Folk will not question it – not in the Gray country, anyway . . . '

He got no further. Mariota threw herself upon him, her arms around his neck, suddenly laughing and sobbing in one, and near to hysteria, her full weight upon him, head hard against his shoulder.

'Davy, Davy!' she cried, panting. 'My dear Davy! Is it true? True? You will marry me? *You* will! Oh, Davy lad . . . God be praised!'

All but choked, throttled, by the vehemence of her, the young man struggled for air, blinked – but patted her heaving back too. 'Och, mercy!' he exclaimed. 'There, there. Of course it is true. That is why I am here – why I came. But . . . och, wheesht, lassie. Do not cry. Wheesht, now – wheesht!'

The tears were welling up fast now – but they were tears of joy and thankfulness and relief. He put her a little way from him, and took the corner of her twisted apron gently to wipe and dab at her cheeks and nose, whilst shining-eyed, trembling, she gazed at him through the glistening curtain of them.

Then abruptly, her lower lip fell, her eyes clouded, her whole face seemed to crumple. 'My father . . . !' she quavered.

'I have seen your father,' he told her. 'I have just left him. It is all right. He will have me as good-son. He will have me – if you will . . . ?'

'Oh, Davy – he will?'

'Aye. He would liefer it was Patrick, mind – as I swear would you, lass. But . . . '

'Patrick!' she cried. 'Patrick – never! I think . . . I think that I hate Patrick, Davy!'

'Eh . . . ? Och, no – how could that be? After . . . after . . . ?'

'Aye – after what I did! With him!' The colour had come flooding back to Mariota's cheeks. 'Nevertheless, I hate him – for what he made me do. Do to you, Davy. Thank God it is not him that I am to marry.'

'But, lassie – I thought . . . ?' David floundered. 'Why did you let him do it, then?'

'Well may you ask, Davy! Sweet Jesu – how I have asked myself! For it was not Patrick that I liked. Och, I *liked* him well enough, sometimes – but not . . . ' She shook her head vigorously. 'It was *you*, Davy – always you. But Patrick is . . . Patrick is . . . well, he is Patrick!' She stopped, biting her lip.

'Aye – he is Patrick!' his brother said. But it was his eyes that were shining now. 'Och, my dear – forget Patrick!' he cried. 'Here's you saying that you like me, like me well enough to . . . och, Mariota lassie – here is a wonder! Here is joy – for I like you fine too! Just fine. And we are to be wed – you and me, just. Man and wife. Dear God – I just canna believe it!'

Laughing, if somewhat brokenly, unsteadily, he took her to him – and she came to his arms eagerly.

So they clutched and clung to each other in that pantry, her tears wetting his face, her urgent body pressed against his, the lips tight fused together. For them a blessed miracle had been wrought.

But at all the commotion the child within Mariota kicked, and when the girl could free her lips, it was tremulously to form that taxing question. 'The baby?' she faltered, her face turned away from him. 'The child? Patrick's child! Do you . . . can you . . . oh, Davy – what of the child?'

'I told you – it shall be *my* child. I care not, lass – you it is that I love. And I shall love your bairn. *Our* bairn. Call it Patrick's never again – do you hear? I . . . '

A sound from beyond the pantry door caused them both to

start, and jump apart, fearful, frightened, uncertain yet. They faced that door, hand in hand. But it did not open. There was no further sound. Probably it had been only the kitchen wench leaning close, to listen. The urgency, the anxiety, the sense of danger to their new-found joy did not leave them, however.

'Take me away, Davy,' Mariota jerked, breathlessly. 'Now – I beg of you. Away from here – from this house. Anywhere. Quickly. Before . . . before . . .'

'Aye – I will do that, lass, never fear. But first we will be wed. Here and now. At once. Yes, we can. We may. Your father himself said it. He would . . . he wishes you . . . och, well – he said it should be done swiftly, see you. He would have it so.'

'Davy – can we not do it some other where? Not here. Not before my father. He will change his mind. To punish me. He will not allow it . . .'

'He will, my dear. He will. The fact is, he wishes it done and over. And he will not be there himself, he said. He is . . . is busy, with affairs. We can be wed now, by the college chaplain. Before two witnesses, he said. And then we can go.'

'Are you sure? That it is no trick? That he will not stop us . . . ?'

'Never doubt it. See – I will go to find the chaplain. Go you and make ready. Whatever you have to do. Make a bundle of some clothes . . .'

'No – after. I will not leave you. Not until we are wed. Nor then, either.' She clung to his arm. 'Do not leave me, Davy. The clothes matter nothing.'

'Very well. We shall seek the chaplain together.'

'He will be in his house. I know where it is. He sleeps every afternoon. He is a dirty, foolish old man – but belike he will serve. Come, Davy – and pray that we do not meet my father!'

Hand in hand they went through to the kitchen and out of the back door of the house, into the lane beside the West Burn. And turning along this, whom should they meet but the shuffling unkempt figure of Master Grieve himself, chaplain domestic of St. Mary's College and pensioner of the Principal. Many were the rumours as to the reasons for Andrew Davidson's patronage of this curious broken-down scholar with the rheumy eyes and trembling hands – whispers even that he might be the Principal's own father – but these mattered not to the two young people now. Master Grieve, in fact, declared that he had been coming to seek them, the godly Principal apparently having actually called at his humble lodging and given instructions to that effect only a short while before.

This evident confirmation of David's confidence that her father would not interfere, greatly comforted and encouraged Mariota. They turned, with the dirty and shambling old man, back to the house which they had just left, impatient already that the chaplain must go so slowly.

So there, in the great kitchen of her home, before her father's bold-eyed bustling housekeeper and the arrogant man-servant, more scornful-seeming than ever, as witnesses, with the giggling maid thrown in as extra, Mariota and David were wed, with scant ceremony, no ring, a deal of gabbling, sniffing and long pauses – but at least somewhat according to the lesser rites of the Kirk – even with a certain kindliness on the old man's part also. Bride and groom had no complaint to make. Only the calling of the banns had been omitted – but it would be a bad business if a great man of the Kirk could not arrange a small matter like that, afterwards.

When all was over, and the fee settled, Mariota was persuaded to go to her room and make up her bundle. She took but a few minutes about it, and no doubt her father at least would have approved the scantiness of the dowry which she took away from his ravished establishment. With only the kitchen-maid bidding them God-speed, they left the house thankfully, collected the pony from amongst the cattle in the quadrangle, and with Mariota mounted pillion behind her husband, set out by back ways through the streets of St. Andrews. They made a fair burden for even the sturdy Highland garron.

'Where . . . where do we go, Davy?' the girl asked, at his ear, her voice uneven, throaty.

'Home,' he answered simply. 'Where else? To the castle – Castle Huntly.'

'Must we go there? To . . . to Patrick?'

'Patrick will not be there. Patrick is at Glamis, with my lord. But never heed for Patrick – never heed for anything now, lassie. You are safe. You are the Mistress David Gray!'

But still she faltered. 'You will keep me safe . . . from Patrick, Davy?'

'Aye,' he said – but he frowned as they turned out of the West Port, northwards.

Chapter Three

PATRICK'S nuptials were of a very different order, as befitted the linking of two of the greatest and noblest houses in all Scotland. The matter could not be rushed, of course, in any unseemly fashion – even though Lord Gray was somehow possessed of an urgent itch to see the said link swiftly and safely forged. The Lord Chancellor Glamis, being a busy man and much immersed in affairs of the state, was not averse to a certain amount of expedition in the matter, so long as a minimum of responsibility for the business, bother – and incidentally, expense – fell upon himself. His lordship, though reputed to be the wealthiest baron in Scotland, was the reverse of extravagant, and with two other daughters nearing marriageable age, was inclined to look twice at his silver pieces. Gray accordingly, and contrary to normal custom, suggested that the ceremony and festivities should on this occasion take place at Castle Huntly and at his expense – and Glamis, after only a token protest, agreed.

Father and son, therefore, came home after four days in Strathmore, with the matter more or less settled, and Lord Gray, at least, in excellent spirits. The wedding would be held in one month's time, three weeks being required for the calling of the banns, and since my lord looked for much as a result of this union – especially as, so far, Glamis had no son, and Elizabeth was his eldest daughter – the arrangements should be on a scale suitable to the occasion.

Patrick himself, however, was just a little less ebullient than might have been expected. He confided in David right away – and he allowed no shadow of their recent clash of interests and temperament to cloud their companionship; Patrick was like that – he confided that he was more than a little disappointed in Elizabeth Lyon. Her breasts were as good as he had remembered them, admittedly, and she was a handsome piece in a strong-featured statuesque fashion, undoubtedly; indeed, as a statue, Patrick declared, she would be magnificent. But somehow she seemed to him to lack warmth; he feared that she might well prove, in practice, to be distinctly on the cold side – though needless to say he had done his by no means negligible best to melt her, in such opportunity as had presented itself. She had shown him no actual hostility, or really repelled his advances – better, perhaps, if she had done, as a titillation and indication of spirit to overcome – but had just failed to respond satisfactorily, much less excitingly. This was a new experience for young Patrick Gray in his relations with the opposite sex, and he was a little piqued and concerned. He confessed to David, indeed, that he preferred the next sister, Jean, a more adventurous nymph, with whom he had tried a fling or two; even the third one, Sibilla, though ridiculously young, was more enthusiastic in her embraces, he had ascertained. He had gone the length of suggesting to his father, in fact, the third night, that they should transfer their assault to the Lady Jean, in the interests of effectiveness and posterity, but my lord would not hear of it – had been quite shocked, indeed. Elizabeth, at seventeen, was the elder by quite three years, and there would be no comparison between the scales of their marriage portions.

Even David was only briefly and superficially sympathetic, Patrick felt.

In contrast, Patrick was quite delighted, and demonstrably so, at unexpectedly finding Mariota already at Castle Huntly. He sought her out at once when he heard the news, in the sheltered walled garden where Meg Powrie, the steward's wife, had set her to the light work of household sewing and mending, at which she could sit – and promptly caught her up to kiss her long and comprehensively, laughing away her struggles and protests. He was genuinely amused at her tantrums of outraged modesty, when David came hurrying to her aid, vowed that her mock wrath became her mighty well, heightening her colour, and forgave her entirely the long scratch her nails had made down his own fair cheek.

'Davy! Davy!' she cried breathlessly, her great hazel-brown eyes wide with an unreasoning fear that verged on panic. 'He . . . he . . . you promised! You said that he would not . . . that you would not let him . . . '

'Och, lassie – do not take on so. He was but welcoming you to the castle, I doubt not.'

'No! No!'

'But yes, yes, my dear Mariota! Exactly!' Patrick assured genially. 'Here is a most happy occasion – my first good-sister. How would you have me greet you? Stiffly? Formally? I' faith, no. After all, we are old friends, are we not?'

She bit her red lip, looking from one young man to the other. Then, snatching up her needlework she turned about and went hurrying away up the path between the blossoming fruit trees.

'Wait, lass,' David called after her, starting forward. Then he paused, and looked back at his brother. 'She is not herself. The bairn, it is – but two months to go, she says. But . . . ' His brows came down, in a fashion that Patrick knew well. 'You will kindly keep your distance from her,' he said. 'It is her expressed wish – and mine!'

'Well, now – here is no kindly way to usher the lass into the family, Davy . . . '

But his brother had swung about, to go hurrying in pursuit of his wife. Patrick looked after them both, thoughtfully.

Lord Gray's reception of the news of Mariota's presence in his castle, thus early, was of a different nature. Indeed, he showed very little interest, having so many more vital matters to attend to. He did not, in fact, see her for a couple of days, by which time his affability over the successful progress of the Glamis business was wearing a trifle thin as the full realisation of the expense of his wedding plans was increasingly brought home to him. Consequently, the fact that he had acquired even one more unproductive mouth to feed seemed to strike him with a force at first glance unlooked for in a man who constantly employed a resident bodyguard of between twenty and thirty men-at-arms, with little better to do than quarrel and procreate, not to mention the unnumbered other hangers-on that the dignity of a nobleman's household seemed to demand. It was David, rather than Mariota, who bore the impact of this realisation, in an unsought meeting with his father in the castle courtyard on the second day – for that young man had long made a habit of keeping out of my lord's way as much as possible, a practice at which Patrick was almost equally proficient. The lecture that followed, on expense, idleness, irresponsibility and bastardy generally, encouraged David to put forward, albeit tentatively, a suggestion of his own. Might he not be allowed to earn his daily bread, and perhaps his wife's also, as tutor to the younger members of his lordship's household? He had never had any urgent desire to become a minister of the Kirk, as had been part of Gray's intention in sending him to St.Andrews with Patrick, but at least he had done reasonably well with his studies, and almost certainly would have graduated Master of Arts in a few months' time, had it not been for the unfortunate clash with the Principal. Consequently he felt himself quite fitted to teach the young – and indeed would like to do so. He suggested, moreover, that as well as the nine Gray children, he might instruct others; some of the neighbouring lairds might well be glad to have their offspring taught, and be prepared to pay for the privilege – thus lightening his lordship's burden.

His lordship saw the point of this without any great deal of persuasion, and ordered David to proceed with the matter forthwith – especially the enrolling of his neighbours' idle and ignorant progeny. He further agreed to the allocation of the little-used north-west flanking tower of the courtyard as school-room, where wretched children would be well out of the way of his own feet. This arranged, he was able to wash his hands of David, Mariota, and all bairns and brats soever, to his considerable satisfaction.

David, therefore, thankfully took possession of the little north-west tower, set aside the vaulted ground floor for a store-house and stable, the first floor as a schoolroom and the top storey as a home for Mariota and himself, and moved in with such plenishings as he could beg, borrow, or contrive.

Only Patrick appeared to find this arrangement not wholly to his taste. He and David had shared a room, and usually a bed, together all their lives, and though this proximity had its draw-backs in the realm of privacy on occasion, it had had many advantages also for someone of Patrick's sunny and congenial temperament. The addition, moreover, of an attractive young woman, pregnant or otherwise, to this pleasantly informal little sodality was an advantage so obvious as to call for no stressing. David's reminder that Patrick would very shortly have a wife of his own to bed down with, and be translated to a fine room in the main keep for the purpose, had an only lukewarm reception.

Not that Patrick moped or sulked, of course; he was not of that kidney. Never at any time short of friends, or at a loss for amusement, he now had leisure and freedom to make the most of life – and life, for the Master of Gray, in the Gray country of the Carse of Gowrie, could be full indeed. He left the marriage arrangements happily enough to his father, and wore out a succession of horses dashing about Perthshire and Angus, in the joyous freedom of a man about to become a husband. His only expresssed regret was that David was not with him to enjoy the sport and observe his triumphs – but he sought to make up for this by frequently invading his brother's room in the little tower, usually in the small hours of the morning, to deliver gay and uninhibited accounts of the day's and night's excitements to a sleepy and protesting David and a tense and shocked Mariota. When reproached that this was no way to behave on the eve of matrimony, he countered with the reverse assertion – that it was in fact of all times the most apt and essential for such recreation.

So the weeks passed. Mariota grew thicker and heavier, and a little less nervy and wary, the schooling progressed, and the preparations for the linking of Gray and Glamis went on apace.

For one reason or another, Patrick never managed to see Mariota alone throughout.

Castle Huntly was transformed for the wedding-day – and not only the castle but the entire countryside round about. Contrary to common supposition, the Scots are essentially a demonstrative, spectacle-loving and colourful race, with a distinct flair for extremes, however well they manage to disguise the fact under a screen of dour gravity and curtness. Given the opportunity, they will kick over the traces more wholeheartedly than any of your Latins or Irishry, and opportunities for such jollifications had been sadly lacking in sixteenth-century Scotland since the godly Kirk had successfully banished the old religion with all its disgraceful though colourful mummery and flummery. Consequently, any legitimate occasion for public holiday and celebration, that the ministers could not very well ban, was apt to be seized upon avidly by gentles and common folk alike, and made the most of. And undoubtedly this was such an occasion – and with both lords high in the Kirk party, the ministers, however much they might frown on principle, could hardly interfere.

From the battlements and each tower of the castle, banners, pennons and streamers fluttered; stern parapets and machicolations for the hurling down of boiling oil, lead, and the like, were hung with greenery, and snarling gunloops spouted flowers and blossom. On the topmost turret a beacon was erected, ready to blaze and to spark off a line of similar flares on all the other Gray castles and strengths on either side of Tay. On every hill around the Carse bonfires were built, and the chain of them would stretch right back across the Sidlaws to Strathmore, twenty miles away. The Castleton and the Milton were almost buried under fir-boughs, evergreens and gean-blossom, and the villages of Longforgan, Inchture, Abernyte, Fowlis and the rest were garlanded, walls whitewashed, and preparations made for the public roasting of bullocks and broaching of ale-barrels on greens and market-crosses that had so recently lost their crosses. Dundee itself was to have its Law ablaze, and the bells of the great four-churches-in-one, St. Mary's, St. Paul's. St. Clement's' and St. John's, were to ring out – by special gracious permission of the reverend Master Blair, who was indeed to officiate at the wedding – a thing they had not done even for the birth of an heir to the throne, who had a Popish mother of course.

It was all thoroughly inspiriting, and a mere month was all too short a time for proper arrangements.

The day dawned at last, and Patrick greeted the said dawn in an alehouse in the Seagate of Dundee, in riotous company – although the ride back to Castle Huntly through the fresh young morning cleared his head wondrously. Certain guests, with long distances to travel, had already reached the castle the previous night, and by mid-forenoon the stream of arrivals was resumed. There was no room for all, of course, in the fortalice itself, nor even within its courtyard, and pavilions and tents of coloured canvas had been erected on the grassy former tilt-yard before the main gatehouse, in a circle to enclose a wide arena. Here, to amuse the ~arlier comers and the crowding local folk during the long period of waiting until the actual nuptial ceremony in the early evening, sports and games, archery, trials of strength, and the like were organised. There were jugglers and tumblers and acrobats, too, musicians and dancing bears, horse-races on the level flats below the castle rock. Food and drink and comfits, in bulk rather than in variety or daintiness, were heaped on trestle-tables out-of-doors. My lord, once having taken the grievous decision to put his hand into his pocket, was reaching deep therein – he hoped, of course as a sound investment.

The castle staff, needless to say, were deeply involved in all this, and for once even the lounging loud-mouthed men-at-arms had plenty to do. David was allotted the highly responsible task of separating the sheep from the goats – that is, meeting and identifying the parties of guests as they arrived, well out in front of the tented area, and directing them to their due destinations. Only the great lords, powerful churchmen and notabilities, and certain relations, were conducted to the castle itself, where they were greeted by either their host or his heir, and their retinues led off. Lesser lairds and ministers and gentry were taken to the courtyard, where one of Lord Gray's brothers did the honours before sending them down to the tilt-yard. The rest were ushered straight to the tents and the food, to be welcomed by Rob Powrie, the steward. Obviously the initial separating was a duty where any mistake made could be serious in their repercussions, in the matter of injured pride, and where tact as well as a

39

quick wit was required. Perhaps my lord thought rather better of his first-born bastard than he was inclined to admit, in selecting him for the work.

David, dressed for the occasion in some of Patrick's cast-offs – that was always the source of his wardrobe, but today he did rather better than usual – required all his wits. One of the first problems that he had to cope with presented itself in no less august a shape than that of his own new father-in-law, Principal Davidson, who arrived in the company of half-a-dozen other divines and scholars from St. Andrews, and who undoubtedly would have completely ignored the existence of David had he not been supported by three or four men-at-arms, in the Gray colours, in the capacity of escorts and guides. It fell to David to point out that whilst Master Davidson himself was expected at the castle door, his companions should not proceed beyond the courtyard – a rather delicate division, especially as one of the ministers had only recently been his own tutor in elementary philosophy, a subject that might well have commended itself to the said professor there and then, but unfortunately did not. David's polite but firm instructions, indeed, were not very well received at all, and only the jingling and impatient retinue of James, Lord Ogilvy of Airlie, queuing up behind, got them on their way without unseemly dispute. Master Davidson had no questions to ask anent his daughter – not of David, at anyrate.

More than one thorny problem to be settled concerned the vital matter of prededence: as, for instance, when the Master of Crawford's party and that of my Lord Oliphant came clattering up to David's gateway precisely at the same moment, one from the east and the other from the west. Like lightning, the coincidence developed into a major crisis. The Master, as heir and representative of the Earl of Crawford, premier earl of the kingdom, demanded that he should be admitted before any upstart baron, Oliphant or otherwise, whereas the Lord Oliphant insisted that as a Lord of Parliament, and Sheriff of Forfar, he took precedence over the heir of Crawford or Heaven itself. Angry words were exchanged, and hands sought sword-hilts as supporting gentry pressed forward to uphold these important points of view, when David hurriedly declared, at the pitch of his young lungs and in the name of my Lord Gray, that of course both noblemen should ride side by side up to the castle, as was seemly and proper, their followings likewise. Heads high, and frowning bleakly in diametrically opposite directions, the guests thereupon spurred on in what quickly developed into a race for the gatehouse.

The bridal party arrived promptly at noon in an impressive cavalcade of over fifty horsemen and as many laden pack-horses. My Lord Glamis, stern and noble-featured, and his dark-browed and hot-tempered brother, the Master, led the company, under the proudly fluttering blue lion on silver of their house, and it was not until the rearward passed him at the trot that David perceived the women of the party. Which was the bride he could not tell, for the six or seven of them were all wrapped in their hooded travelling cloaks – indeed, only of their legs and hose did he gain any admiring view, since they rode astride and at a pace that made primness difficult to maintain.

It was well into the afternoon before the last of the important guests put in an appearance, by which time David was not only weary of the business but fretting to get down to the entertainments and sports, especially the wrestling at which he excelled. Nor was he alone in this anxiety to be finished; my lord himself, fine in black velvet slashed with scarlet, came down from the castle to limp about and gaze impatiently westwards. The pompously important but self-conscious contingent of the Provost and Bailies of Dundee had just come up, with the Provost's markedly non-pompous and substantial wife interrupting her husband's official speech of congratulation and greeting with chuckles and ribald stage-whispers from the background, when the high winding of horns and the growing beat of hooves turned all heads – and turned them westwards.

The glint of sun on steel flickered amongst woodland to that side. Then out into the open came pounding a tight-knit column of heavily armed men, all gleaming breastplates, helmets and tossing plumes, led by a herald in spectacularly coloured tabard, four trumpeters with their horns at the ready, and two standard-bearers with streaming banners.

'A Douglas! A Douglas!' The chanted savage cry came on ahead of the riders, a well-rehearsed and ominous litany in the land for three centuries and more. David's back hairs lifted, despite the occasion, at the sound of it. He noted that, of the two great flags, that slightly to the fore, the larger, and set on the longer pole, was the Bleeding Heart of Douglas; the other was merely the treasured Red Lion on gold of Scotland.

As this hard-riding cohort bore down upon the waiting throng at a full gallop, the Dundee burghers scattered right and left alarmedly, women skirling. Even Gray drew back involuntarily from his forward-paced position. Without the least slackening of pace, the phalanx came thundering on, still chanting, turfs flying from drumming hooves. Douglas indeed usually travelled thus. Past the shrinking assembly at the gate they swept. David had a brief vision of a hulking man in a flying crimson-lined cloak, red-faced, red-headed, red-bearded, hot-eyed, who glanced neither left nor right, hemmed in by steel-clad horsemen. Then they were past, the echo of the antiphon 'A Douglas! A Douglas!' floating back to the welcoming group, punctuated by the shrilly imperative summons of the horns' flourish.

My Lord Gray, left standing and staring after, spat out profanity, his face congested, his frown black. Never had he loved Douglas, nor Douglas him. Only because of Glamis would that man darken his doorway, he knew. Cursing, he went hastening on foot in the wake of the column. The Lord Regent, the Earl of Morton, ruler of Scotland in the name of the helpless boy King James, had deigned to honour the occasion. The marriage might go forward.

The success or otherwise of the afternoon depended upon the point of view. Counting heads, certainly, the vast majority found it entirely to their taste, whatever might be the case with the smaller group that centred round the host, Lord Glamis, and the Regent; or, again, the black-clad and numerous concentration of the professionally disapproving ministers. Patrick, for one, indubitably enjoyed himself, winning both the important horse-races, out-swording all competitors at the rapier-play – for gentlefolk only, this, of course, so that David for instance might not compete – coming third in the archery, friend of all, particularly those he defeated, laughing and talking his way into all hearts, the ladies' more especially. David did none so badly himself, coming second to his brother in one of the foot races, being worsted at the wrestling only by a blacksmith from Inchture of twice his own weight, and making a respectable showing at putting the cannon-ball. Even Mariota ventured shyly out amongst the crowd, from the cherished seclusion of her tower-room, found herself caught up in the good-humoured excitement, and was the better therefore. The bride, of course, did not show herself; her time would come.

Two broken heads and a growing animosity between the Douglas men-at-arms and Gray's own retainers, rather than the ill-concealed impatience of the ministers, at length caused my lord to bring this stage of events to a close, around six o'clock.

Trumpets sounded from the topmost battlements, and all the important guests flocked into the castle, while the lesser gentry, the men-at-arms, and the commonality disposed themselves about the many long trestle-tables laden with food and drink. The serious part of the proceedings was at hand.

In the great hall of the castle, order gradually emerged out of chaos, the ministers, harsh-voiced, autocratic but notably efficient, now taking charge. Guests were herded six deep around the arras-hung stone walls, and, God having no use for precedence, except presumably amongst those ordained to preach the Gospel, no nonsense about position or prominence was permitted for a moment. Save, that is, around the doorway, where Lord Gray, the Lady Glamis and the Master thereof, the Regent and one or two others were grouped, with rather more elbow room, facing into the cleared centre of the hall, where the solid body of ministers stood behind a simple table covered with a severe white cloth on which lay a massive Bible, and nothing else.

David, with the Gray children, peered down at the scene from an inner window of the circular stairway, just under the springing of the high vaulted ceiling.

The trumpets sounded again, and a hush fell upon all in the hall – not on those outside, unfortunately, though the ten-foot-thick walling helped to deaden the noise of uninhibited jollification. Pacing slowly through the lane opened for them came two figures: the stooping ungainly person of Master John Blair, High Kirk minister of Dundee, whose plain loose black gown only partially shrouded his twisted and torture-scarred frame, hirpling but strangely dignified; and a few yards behind, Patrick Gray, resplendent in white satin padded doublet and trunks, slashed with gold, a white velvet short cloak slung negligently over one shoulder, and long golden hose of fine silk. The gap of admiration that was almost a moan indeed, with which the women at least greeted his appearance, was fully merited, for never had he looked more handsome, more beautiful, and at the same time more lithely if slenderly virile. Never, also, were trunks cut so short, or shapely legs so long. His expression schooled to a suitable sweet gravity, his gait so infinitely more graceful than that of the hobbling man of God, he came slowly forward, glance downcast. Only once did his eyes lift, as, when he passed the family group, the Regent Morton turned to stare from his curiously round, pale and owl-like eyes, hawked strongly in his thick throat and almost seemed as though

43

he would spit – but restrained himself to swallow instead.
Patrick's dark eyes flashed and his step faltered, but both only
for an instant. Then he paced on to the table, at which Master
Blair had turned. The minister stood, eyes closed, hands
together, seemingly in prayer. Something like a shiver ran
through the crowded hall.

David caught sight of Master Davidson's face as he watched
Patrick, and did not like what he saw.

A new sound reached them, the thin melodious singing of
young voices, accompanied by the gentle twanging of a lute,
that ebbed and flowed as the singers obviously came down the
winding stairway of the castle. The chant was mere psalmody, a
simple canticle; nevertheless, an almost universal frown spread
over the faces of the waiting clergy at this dangerous toying with
Popish folly – spread and remained as into sight came a youth
with the lute, and six maidens, dressed all in white and singing
clearly, angelically – however venturesome and eager their
glances. These included the Ladies Jean and Sibilla Lyon, and
Patrick's elder sister Barbara. Behind them walked the sombre
stern-miened Lord Chancellor Glamis, in unrelieved black save
for the high white ruff and sword-belt of heavy linked gold, and
on his arm, his daughter.

The bride did not do her family or her groom injustice. A tall
well-favoured young woman, fair, high-coloured, and comely
rather than beautiful, she drew all eyes. She wore a handsome
gown of quilted palest yellow taffeta, wide-skirted and wired,
and overlaid by open silver lacework, beaded with pearls. The
bodice was tight, with a lengthy pointed stomacher reaching
low to her loins, but cut correspondingly low above, in a wide
square neck, to reveal much of the high and prominent breasts
that rumour had spoken of, and with a ruff, rimmed with pearls,
rising from either shoulder rather like incipient wings. Over her
long flaxen hair she wore a crescent-shaped jewelled coif of
silk. She drew all eyes, yes – but, strangely, not the gasping
tribute that had greeted the Master of Gray.

'What think you, Davy? Will she serve our Patrick?' young
James Gray whispered.

' 'Tis Patrick will do the serving, I warrant!' his senior,
Gilbert, crowed from the experience which twelve years had
brought. 'Have you no eyes, Jamie?'

'Hush, you,' David reproved. 'They're about to begin.'

This seemed to be so. The Lady Elizabeth stood beside
Patrick now, before the minister, with her father a pace behind.

44

Lord Gray had stepped forward alongside Glamis. The maids, under the battery of frowns from the divinity, had backed away into the mass of the congregation, the lute-boy vanishing quite. All waited. Master Blair, however, seemed in no hurry to commence. Or perhaps he had in fact commenced, and was already engaged in silent wrestling with his Maker. He stood, head bent, hands clasped, and if his lips stirred, that was all. People fidgeted, shuffled and whispered, and the Regent sniffed loudly, hawed and muttered in his red beard. At last the celebrant abruptly raised head and hands heavenwards, and launched immediately, strikingly, into the full fine flood of eloquent and passionate assault on God and man. In a voice harsh but extraordinarily strong for so meagre a body, declamation, exhortation and denunciation poured from his thin lips in a blistering, resounding, exciting stream. The fidgeting stopped – as well it might. The Kirk was getting into its stride.

This introductory invocation and overture – it soared far above the realms of mere prayer – on the rich themes of man's essential and basic wickedness, filthiness, lust and sinful pride; woman's inherent shallowness, worldly vanity and lewd blandishing cajolery; the Scots people's painful and inveterate proneness to backsliding and going a-whoring after strange gods; the blasphemous and idolatrous life of that wanton Mary Stuart, chamber-wench of the Pope, for the present, God be praised, safely immured within godly walls in the South – this with a sudden lowering of the eyes and a hard stare at Lord Gray – and strangely enough, the excellence and maidenly virtuousness of that daughter of the Lord, Elizabeth Tudor; this all led up to the sound and sublime allegory of God's true Kirk, as the Bride of Christ, vigorously trampling into the mire of damnation that other Harlot of Rome who had so long defiled the sanctity of the Marriage of the Lamb.

This emotional crescendo suitably prefaced the actual nuptials, into which Master Blair plunged after quarter-of-an-hour of impassioned harangue – a tribute surely to the undimmed spirit within the twisted body that the Cardinal Archbishop had racked for his faith twenty-five years ago. The slightly bemused and abstracted gathering was, in fact, not quite prepared for the sudden transition and change of level in the proceedings, taking a little while to adjust itself. As well that Patrick himself was quicker-witted, or he might not have had the ring out in time, for this central and less edifying, but of course necessary, part of the ceremony was got over at high speed and with an almost scornful brusqueness. Protesting fervour had so purified and pruned the unseemly mummery of the Old Faith's marriage rites that there was little left save the affirmation of the exchange of vows signified by the clasping of hands, the fitting of the ring, and the declaration of the pair as man and wife. That did not take long. On the exhortation to the newly wed, of course, a minister of the Word could spread himself rather. Master Blair did that, dwelling at some length and detail on the pitfalls of the flesh into which the unwary or wilfully disobedient couple might so easily fall.

Patrick listened to this with an access of interest, and out of the corner of his eye sought to observe the effect on his bride. She did not blush, he noted.

The celebrant paused, now. All this was merely the warming up, the ushering in of the vital business of the day. He walked round behind the white-clothed table, took a deep breath, put one hand on the Bible, raised the other on high, and commenced the Sermon.

It was a good sermon, too – that was evident, if by no other indication than the rapt attention and shining-eyed regard of the ranked and hypercritical divines at the preacher's back. Frail body or none, cracking vocal chords, sore throat, spells of dizziness where he had to hold himself up by the table, James Blair thundered and besought, blazed and wheedled, shouted and whispered and quavered, painting equally clear roads to salvatuon and to fiery and eternal torment. The increasing hubbub from outside, largely drunken singing and bawling now, only urged him on; swooning weakly females within the hall did not stop him – there was no seating for this multitude, of course; when the Lady Glamis collapsed and had to be carried out, he did not so much as pause, and only a scornful flashing eye acknowledged the fact that many of his hearers, even supposedly strong men, had felt themselves compelled to crouch down on the rush-strewn stone floor. With my lord of Morton snoring loudly from one of the few chairs available, and Patrick supporting his bride around the waist, one hour and ten minutes after commencing, the preacher brought the notable and inspiring discourse to a triumphant close, and croaked a perfunctory benediction.

The Master of Gray and the Lady Elizabeth Lyon had been well and truly wed, the houses of Gray and Glamis were united, and the Kirk had struck another blow against the forces of Babylon.

Dazed and stiff and glassy-eyed, bride and groom and relatives and guests staggered out, to order the trumpets to be blown, the fires and beacons lit, and the bells to be rung.

'Wine!' they shouted, 'wine, in the name of God! Possets, punch, purled ale, belly cheer, for sweet mercy's sake!'

The wedding feast thereafter was on as generous and memorable a scale as the religious contribution. In no time at all that hall was cleared, trestle tables were erected, one transversely at the top for the principals, and the others lengthwise, forms dragged in for seating, and the long procession of smoking meats, cold flesh, comestibles, cakes, confections, and flagons of every sort of liquid cheer, brought in at the run, while torches were lit and the musicians set about their business. Fortunately perhaps, clamorous stomachs outrumbled the usual difficult demands of precedency in most instances, and earls and barons, masters and lairds, elder sons and younger, and their ladies likewise, were prepared meantime to sit down almost anywhere, thus greatly easing David's task, who, under the steward, had been allotted this second unpopular duty of seating the guests.

There were some notable dishes, apart from the normal succession of roast ox quarters, gigots of mutton, haunches of venison seethed in wine because they were somewhat out-of-season, kippered and pickled salmon to encourage a thirst, howtowdies of fowl, herbs and mushrooms, cabbie-claw cod-fish, and so on; half-a-dozen peacocks made a brave show, roasted still in all the pride of their spread tails; swans swam in ponds of gravy, their long necks cunningly upheld by skewers; and the *pièce de résistance*, an enormous platter requiring six men to carry it in, containing a young sow in milk and her eight suckling piglets, cooked to a turn and all most naturally arranged at her roasted dugs.

To all this the assembly did ample and appreciative justice, the clergy by no means backward.

My lord allowed the banquet to proceed for rather longer than usual before calling for the toasts. He did this, with his eye on Morton, lolling on the bride's left. As Regent and most important man in the kingdom, he could not be overlooked for the principal toast of the bride and groom, without insult. Yet Gray knew not what he might say, and feared the worst. The red stirk had the name for speaking his mind, and unfortunately could afford to do so. Consequently, the host waited for two hours after they had sat down to eat, in the hope that the

Douglas would be too drunk to say anything. In this he was disappointed, however, for though Morton was indubitably drunk, he had by no means lost the use of his tongue; indeed he was growing ever more vocal, singing raucously, cursing the musicians because their tunes were not his, bellowing intimate appraisal or otherwise of all the women in sight, including the shrinking Elizabeth – who, being within arm's reach, received more than mere verbal compliments, to the sad disarray of her finery – and generally displaying the non-impairment of his judgment and faculties. Reluctantly, Gray at last rose, signed to a trumpeter to quell the din, and announced the noble representative of the house of Douglas, Lord High Admiral of Scotland and Viceroy of the Realm, to propose the health of the happy couple.

Morton clapped his high hat of the new mode more firmly on his red head, wiped beard, ostrich-plume and gravy-soiled ruff with the back of a ham-like hand, sought to rise, found it for the moment beyond him, and made his speech sitting down.

'My lords,' he said thickly, belching hugely, 'reverend sirs, masters all – aye, and ladies too, bonnie ones and, *hic*, the other kind – hear me, James Douglas. Here's a, *hic*, fine match, 'fore God! Glamis stooping to Gray! A bonnie sight. Hech, hech – not so fast, my lord. Keep your bottom on your seat! No' so hasty, man. Think you I'd spit in the face o' the provider o' all these goodly meats? Na, na. But stoop my friend Glamis here does in this matter . . . for Lyon was Thane o' Glamis when Gray, my lord, was but some scullion o' yon Norman butcher! A pox – you canna deny it, man – so why fash yoursel'? Eh – Douglas, did ye say? God's wounds – what said ye o' Douglas?' Suddenly the gross torso of the Regent was no longer lolling, but leaning forward over the board, crushing Elizabeth aside, glaring with those hot pale eyes along at his host, massive, menacing.

No sound was raised within the hall save only the hounds cracking bones beneath the tables, the hiss and splutter of the resinous reeking torches, and the deep open-mouthed breathing of the Earl of Morton.

'Aye.' He sank back as, tensely, Gray stared directly ahead of him, down the hall, his face a graven mask. 'Aye, then. Douglas, I'd remind all here, was lording Clydesdale before this Scotland knew a king, aye or a puling priest either! Forget it not, I charge you! Aye. But, hech me – here's the toast, my lords. Glamis stoops, aye – but then he'd stoop, *hic*, to you all! Have to, by God!' A stubby thick finger jabbed and pointed down and around the tables. 'All – save maybe Crawford, there . . . the fox! And none o' you the worse o' the stooping, I warrant! Even Gray! But what's a bit stoop amongst friends? We'd no' do well to keep the best blood in the land bottled up, when there's so many who could do with, *hic*, a droppie o' it! Och, keep your seat, my lord – like I do! The best's to come! I said it was a fine bonnie match, and it is. The realm o' this Scotland will be the better, maybe the safer, for it. I'm thinking – for we need leal and well-connected folk around the throne, godly men with no taint o' Popery, no stink o' the skirts o' that foresworn wanton Mary Stuart about them!'

Again the brittle silence.

Morton chuckled throatily. 'You'll all agree, I jalouse, that this match could strength further that goodly cause – the cause o' Christ's Kirk, forby. A bonnie union! The lassie's bonnie, none will con- controvert. Enough to make an auld man hot, hot – aye, and a young one scorch, heh? Aye, burn and blaze . . . if he's no' a prinking prancing ninny! If our pretty lad here canna bairn her this night, it's no' a toast he's in need of, but a horning! I'd teach him – eh, lass? Here's to their health, then – and may the blood joined tonight run for the weal o' this realm, for once! Aye – amen!'

Morton drained his heavy silver goblet in a great single draught, and hurled it from him vigorously, right down the lengthwise table that faced him, along which it went crashing, scattering and spilling flagons and broken meats.

After perhaps ten pulsating seconds, those who could rose to their feet and pledged the fortunate pair.

All eyes were now on Lord Gray, who had risen last of all and had not sat down again with the others. Patrick however jumped up, waving a jaunty hand for silence, and smiled disarmingly on all around, particularly on the sprawling Regent and on his father. Angelic, almost, he looked after the last speaker – but a gay and debonair angel.

'My lords and ladies, good friends all,' he called, 'my respected and noble sire undoubtedly should speak first – but I vow that you have all had so much eloquence of late that I misdoubt if you can digest more, however fine. Moreover, I would hasten to relieve my Lord Regent's mind that I am indeed impatient to exchange even this fair room and company for another, higher in the house! Hence, forgive, I pray you, this cutting short of . . . compliments! Heigh-ho!'

A gust of laughter swept the hall. Lord Gray sat down.

'I cannot go, of course, without, and in the name of my wife also, expressing profound gratitude to you all for your good wishes, and especially to the noble lord of Morton for the delicate and typically droll fashion in which he expressed his kindly sentiments in your name. Ah, happy Scotia, blessed to have such a paragon, such a mirror of wit and wisdom, to preside over her destinies, Christ's Kirk abetting . . . in the name of His gracious Majesty, of course, upon whom the good God have mercy!'

Only the very drunk saw fit to applaud that, and laughter had died on all faces save that of the speaker.

'I am overcome, my friends – overcome with gratitude, with appreciation. It ill becomes a sprig of so humble a house as Gray to raise his voice in the company of the head of the house of Glamis, not to mention that of an illustrious, though alas junior, branch of the house of Douglas . . . !'

The sudden indrawal of scores of breaths was like a gust of wind in the trees. Morton was not chief of his name; Douglas, Earl of Angus, a mere youth, held that honour – though few indeed would have mentioned it in the presence of the Regent.

'However, I am at least a male, a son, Gray or no – thanks to my worthy and potent father – an attribute which has its advantages, especially on occasions such as this, and in present company!'

What started as a laugh died abruptly, as listeners perceived that there was more here than pleasant bawdry. Neither Lords Morton nor Glamis had a legitimate son to their name.

Patrick's own laughter was of the enduring sort, and music itself. 'So, my friends, I now go, with your blessing, my Lord Regent's urging, and the envy of not a few, I swear, to prove the said attribute to this fair bride of mine! My love – your hand, I pray.'

A great uproar broke out. Men shouted, women skirled, goblets were banged and sword-hilts beaten on tables. The Earl of Morton, bellowing, sought to rise, but liquor and Glamis's restraining hand held him down. Older men plunged into hot discussion with their neighbours, but younger men and women, from the lower end of the hall, were more active. They know their cue, and took it promptly, to come surging up to the top table. This was the signal for the bedding – and they had waited for it overlong. A rush of men grabbed Patrick, and propelled him at a run down one side of the hall, already tugging and pulling off his splendid white satin, while at the other side squealing girls did the same, and only a shade less vigorously, with Elizabeth.

David, who had watched all from the doorway, and quaked in his borrowed shoes towards the end, stood aside to let the loud-tongued parties past. He noted that Patrick was still smiling – but his bride was not, was weeping, in fact.

Up the stairs the laughing clamorous coadjutors of holy matrimony stumbled, almost half their principals' clothing already off.

David followed on, doubtfully.

At the bridal chamber two storeys higher, the disrobing process went on a-pace, only hampered by too many fumbling hands at the task – though now it was noticeable that it was mainly the men who gave of their services to the bride and the women to Patrick. Soon, stark naked, Elizabeth was carried over sobbing to the great bed and tossed thereon, and a few moments later Patrick was steered and pushed on top of her.

Thus went the custom, hallowed by years.

In the midst of all the advice, guidance and encouragement that followed, David suddenly and angrily decided that the business had gone far enough, and quite fiercely turned on the company and drove them from the bedchamber. Despite protests, he insisted, and far from gently. His only gentleness was when he closed the door behind them and himself.

Below, part of the great hall was cleared for dancing, but those who preferred to go on eating – or, more popularly, drinking – could do so at the top end of the apartment. David, still acting as assistant to the steward, was kept very busy. Lords, overcome by wine, had to be guided or carried into convenient chambers set apart for this necessary purpose; fights required to be discouraged as tactfully as might be; ladies were to be escorted to retiring rooms – no light or simple task this, sometimes; and early leavers, such as most of the ministers, and the Dundee burgesses, had to be led out to their horses, not infrequently needing a deal of help. Outside, too, a certain amount of surveillance became ever more necessary, as unlimited ale, good fellowship and high spirits had a cumulative effect, and hilarious uproar reigned. The crackling of bonfires, the wild music of bagpipes, the mass lovemaking, the shouting and singing and screaming were all very well – but fires in the wrong places had to be quenched, unofficial horse-races by firelight, with visiting lords' mounts, had to be stopped, and the large amount of expensive tentage spared as far as possible from damage.

It was a spirited evening, but taxing on those with a responsibility for oversight. Never had my lord's men-at-arms been so busy – or so many of them missing or unfit for duty.

It would be nearing midnight when, in the pandemonium caused by some young bloods' introduction of the dancing bears into the capers of the castle hall, and the consequent driving out of the animals into the courtyard and beyond, David, weary and dishevelled, heard a silvery laugh which he thought that he recognised, followed by a high-pitched whinny of feminine giggling. It seemed to come from the open doorway of his own schoolroom tower. Frowning, he paused for a moment, and then hurried thereto, to peer in. In the vaulted basement chamber, only dimly illuminated by the reflection of torchlight and bonfire-light without, were two people in close embrace. One was undoubtedly Patrick Gray, no longer in his white satins, and the other almost certainly was the young Lady Jean Lyon, his wife's sportive second sister.

Shocked, hesitant, David stood in the doorway, toe tapping the ground. The girl's laugh rang out again, part protestingly, part encouragingly. It had a penetrating and distinctive quality. David was turning to sign away the two men-at-arms who were his faithful shadows that night, when he caught his breath. Three more men were there, close behind, and the tall gaunt one who raised his voice now was the quarrelsome and haughty Sir Thomas Lyon, Master of Glamis. He and Robert Douglas, Younger of Kilspindie, with another Douglas, a mere boy, had come out in the train of the bear-ejectors.

'That was young Jeannie's voice, I'll swear,' he cried. 'She neighs like a mare in heat, that niece o' mine! Let's see who is playing stallion, eh?' And the Master came lurching forward, two parts drunk.

Desperately, almost unthinkingly, David turned and plunged into the tower to warn his brother. The Master of Glamis, a difficult and dangerous man, was known not to have favoured the match in the first place, and was close to Morton and the Douglases, closer than his brother the Chancellor.

Patrick and Jean sprang apart, the former cursing, the latter all guilt and disarray.

'It's the Master! Of Glamis,' David gasped. 'Quick – up the stair, Patrick, out on to the wall . . . ' A door from the schoolroom above led out on to the parapet-walk that crowned the enclosing curtain-walls of the courtyard.

He turned back, to delay the oncoming trio. But they were

close up, pushing aside the men-at-arms, young Kilspindie having snatched a torch.

'Out of my way, fellow!' the older man ordered, curtly.

'No!' David cried. 'This is my place, sir – my tower. My wife . . . she lies upstairs. A-bed, awaiting a bairn. Wait, you . . . '

'Aside, fool!' the Master shouted, one hand on his sword, and thrusting David back with the other. 'Think you I do not know Jean Lyon's voice?'

David was pressed against the door-jamb as the three gentlemen pushed inside. The flaring torch revealed Patrick standing waiting in mid-floor, unmoving, dressed in that same crimson velvet which he had worn on the day that they were sent down from St. Andrews. It also revealed the Lady Jean crouching away in a corner, white-faced, biting her lip. It revealed something else, too; her gown was now torn open down the front, baring her small bosom – though it had not been that way a few moments before, David would have sworn.

For seconds on end no one moved in that stone-arched chamber. Then the Master of Glamis let flow a furious stream of oaths and obscenity.

The girl raised her cracking voice. 'He . . . he tried to force me. He dragged me in here. He did this!' She pointed a trembling finger at Patrick. 'He did, Uncle Thomas! He did!'

Patrick opened his mouth to speak, and shut it again.

Sir Thomas Lyon, the Master, breathing deep and unsteady, tugged his rapier out of its sheath – and made but a clumsy job of it. 'Devil burn you!' he roared. 'You foul lecherous blackguard! By God's eyes, you'll pay for this, Gray! With your worthless life!'

'No! Stop, sir – stop!' David exclaimed, and hurled himself on the Master's sword-arm.

'Off – a pox on you! Off, sirrah!' Lyon shouted, and sought to fling the younger man away, unsuccessfully.

The two Douglases were drawing their swords now. Recognising that he could achieve nothing thus against three armed men, however drunk, David loosed the Master and leapt for the doorway where the two astonished men-at-arms stood gaping. 'Your swords!' he yelled.

The men were slow. David knocked aside one fumbling hand and himself whipped out the fellow's weapon. As the other got his half out, David snatched it in his other hand, and turned.

Patrick was dodging about behind some of the stores kept in that vault, eluding the wild thrusts and pokes of the Master of

Glamis. Jean Lyon crouched further back, her hands over her face.

'Shut the door,' David commanded, to the men behind him. 'Patrick – here!' he called urgently, and as the other glanced towards him, he sent one of the swords spinning through the air, hilt first, to his hard-pressed brother.

Patrick tried to catch it, missed, and it fell with a clatter – fortunately behind an empty barrel. In a trice he had it picked up, and flickering wickedly in the torchlight. 'My thanks, Davy!' he sang out, above the imprecations of his assailants.

And now the entire situation was reversed, for though they were three to two, the three were all drink-taken, one held the torch, and the younger Douglas was obviously no sworder. Whereas, whatever else Patrick Gray had neglected at St. Andrews, it was not rapier-play; indeed, he had been reputed the swiftest and deadliest blade in the University and the city. And David had all along been his sparring partner and foil. These were no rapiers, but heavy cutting swords – but in the hands of experts they served very well. In almost less time than it takes to tell, Lyon was pinned against the stairway with Patrick's blade through the padding of his doublet, young Kilspindie was disarmed, and the other was pleading for mercy. The assistance of the men-at-arms was not required.

'You are impetuous, Sir Thomas,' Patrick declared, easily. 'And loud of mouth. You remind me grievously of my lord of Morton!'

David was panting. 'You are wrong, sirs,' he told them, eagerly. 'About that girl. The Lady Jean. Patrick was not forcing her. She was very willing. I saw them. You heard her laughing, yourselves. Did that sound like a forcing?'

'Foul fall you – what of that?' Lyon answered thickly. 'Willing or no, it was not Jean that this mincing daw married tonight! He is a filthy fornicator who has besmirched the honour of our house.'

'Not so, sir,' Patrick assured lightly. 'I merely found one member of your house exceeding cold and unrewarding. And listening to all of Scotland enjoying itself below me, thought why not I? It is *my* wedding, after all! So I came down discreetly – and lo, another of your good house was ... warmer! All, as it were, within the family, you see!'

David stared at his brother, biting his lip – though his swordpoint wove a constant pattern between the two Douglases.

The Master of Glamis cursed loud and long.

'What now, then, Patrick?' David asked, at length.

'A choice for our friends,' Patrick said readily. He corrected himself, bowing. 'Our guests. Either we can all march from here into the hall, as we are now – dear Jeannie with us – to explain the entire matter to the assembled company, with possibly another little demonstration of sword-play there! Or else our guests can retire from here quietly and suitably, their swords in their sheaths, their mouths shut. For their own sake, for Jean's sake – and Elizabeth's. For everybody's sake, indeed. And I will retire equally discreetly and quietly to my bedchamber . . . and see if my wife has missed me! None need know what has happened within this room – for I shall see that these two men of ours do not talk. How think you, Sir Thomas? The choice is yours.'

There was no choice, of course. Not there and then. The reputation of the three gentlemen and the fame of the house of Glamis demanded silence on this matter. Angrily, sourly, they gave their words, were given back their rapiers, and went stamping out into the fire-lit night. Jean Lyon slipped out after them, her clothing held tightly in place, none halting her. Patrick spoke strongly, significantly, to his father's men-at-arms, and sent them packing.

When all were gone, the two brothers eyed each other.

'Thank you, Davy,' Patrick laughed, clapping the other's shoulder. 'I vow I do not know what I would do without you!'

David was less quick with his tongue. At last he spoke. 'Sometimes, Patrick, I think that you are the Devil himself!' he said levelly.

'Tut, lad – you exaggerate!'

'That poor lassie – Elizabeth . . . !'

'Ah, yes. Thank you for reminding me. I will return to her. But . . . och, Davy, I'd liefer it was our Mariota! Goodnight to you!' And he ran light-foot up the stairs and out on to the battlements.

It was still some hours before David himself was able to mount those stairs finally that night. He did so a deal less light-footedly than had his brother, and with little lightness in his heart either. He stood at his own window for a minute or so, staring out at the red fires that crowned every hill in sight, dying down now, but still a stirring sight, flaming beacons near at hand, mere pinpoints of light away to the north. The Master of Gray was wed.

Sighing, David turned and tip-toed to the bed where Mariota lay.

Chapter Four

IF Patrick Gray did not know what he would do without his half-
brother, he very soon started to find out. Word of the affair in
the schoolroom tower was not long in reaching his father, who,
in a stormy interview, expressed himself forcibly and to some
purpose. He pointed out that not only had Patrick jeopardised
the entire accord between Gray and Glamis and risked undoing
all his father's careful work, but he had made for himself a
dangerous enemy in Thomas Lyon, whom all knew as a
vindictive and unforgiving man, and influential. Made enemies,
too, of the Douglases, which most in Scotland were heedful not
to do. And of the Regent himself, in his reply to that toast.
A notable achievement for one brief night's work! Morton,
drunk or sober, would not forget.

Patrick's contribution, though prompt, was of the light-
hearted sort. He observed that probably he should have been
more discreet – but that discretion had not been greatly in
evidence in anybody, that night. Must he be the only discreet
one – on his wedding day? And had his reply to the unseemly
toast not in fact preserved his noble sire himself from major
indiscretion? His lordship had looked distinctly as though he
might explode at Morton's insults.

Lord Gray was not to be sidetracked. The matter was serious.
Patrick's life, indeed, might be in danger, for the Master of
Glamis was not one to overlook a slight. Moreover the man need
fear no serious retribution to come from Morton. His castle of
Aldbar, at Brechin, was much too near for safety; the Douglases
were much too thick on the ground in this area, too, to be provoked with impunity. If Patrick could not show discretion at the
right time, he should show it now. He would be better out of the
Carse, out of this part of Scotland altogether – and as far away as
possible from that little jade Jean Lyon, at Glamis! He was to be
gone – and right away. This very day. To the south, to Berwick-
shire. That was the place for him – Fast Castle, where his Aunt
Agnes had married that ruffian Logan of Restalrig. He would be
safely out of trouble there for a while, till tempers cooled. It was
no unusual custom for the newly-wed to betake themselves off
to other parts, after all – though in this case, the more prolonged

the stay away, the better.

Patrick went, since he must – and cheerfully enough. It did not fail to occur to him that pastures new, and life out from under his father's eye, might have attractions. It was only a pity that he had to take Elizabeth too. She was not consulted in the matter. She preserved a frozen-faced silence, which my lord assured would doubtless thaw in time.

David, not being important enough to incur the hatred or vengeance of noblemen, stayed where he was, schooling the children and aiding Rob Powrie. He missed Patrick.

Mariota, curiously enough, blossomed out like a flower in the sun. Even my lord noticed it, for her lightsome singing was apt to be heard when anybody crossed the courtyard, and vowed that never had he known a wench that looked forward to her lying-in so blithely. He even visited her at times, in her turret, and once went so far as to inform David that he was a fortunate man. David did not deny it. But still he missed Patrick. They had never been apart for more than a few days before.

Three weeks later Mariota was brought to bed of a girl, tiny, dark-eyed, exquisite.

When my lord saw the child, his small eyes widened, he whistled soundlessly, glanced at David, and said nothing. He came back twice that same day to look at her.

Very quickly David came to love that bairn. It had never occurred to him that it would not be a boy. He had decided that he would be a good, a just and affectionate father to the boy. But this tiny jewel of a girl, lovely from birth, quite overwhelmed him. He found her utterly absorbing – which was strange, for he never had taken any notice of babies hitherto. Indeed, Mariota railed at him a little jealously, vowing that the child had him bewitched. He would have had her named Patricia had not Mariota burst into tears at the suggestion. They called her Mary in the end – curiously enough on Lord Gray's urging. He said that he had had a sister of that name of whom he had been fond, who had died young. David had never heard of this – and wondered, in fact, whether it was not the lovely imprisoned Queen whom my lord was remembering.

Gray, indeed, to the wonder of all, grew swiftly and marvellously enamoured of the infant – unlikely in one who had spawned infants unnumbered and betrayed but little interest in any of them. In the hot sunny days of that fine summer, it became a commonplace to see my lord sitting in his castle courtyard rocking the cradle, tickling the mite's chubby chin, even

57

carrying the creature about, pointing out flowers and bees and the strutting fantails from the doocote – a sight to make men-at-arms goggle and gape. Moreover, David was seldom behind-hand in the same silly business, so that not infrequently the two all but came to blows as to who should pat the brat for wind, or wipe her clean. Unseemly, Mariota called it – a shameful sight. The frowns which she bent on them, however, were scarcely black, and her reproofs dissolved in smiles. She smiled a lot those days, and sang a lot, and grew bonnier every week.

That was a good summer and autumn at Castle Huntly, the happiest that its grim walls had seen for many a year. If only Patrick had been there . . .

My lord, of course, was much from home, and when he came back he was apt to be black-browed and ill-tempered, until Mariota and Mary between them had him gentled again. For outside the castle, all was not so happy. Morton's hand was heavy on the land, and those who were not his friends must walk warily; the Kirk was squirming under the nominal bishops he had imposed upon her – Tulchans, or stuffed calves, they were called, to milk her of her revenues, most of which went straight into the Regent's bottomless pockets. Kirkcaldy of Grange, the best soldier in the land, and Mary the Queen's staunchest remaining supporter, was executed like a common criminal. Mary herself was moved by Queen Elizabeth to closer confinement in Sheffield Castle. And with all this, the south wind carried hints of Patrick's doings that set his father scowling. He was not confining himself wholly to Fast Castle and its cliff-girt surroundings on the Berwick coast, apparently. All the wide Borderland seemed to be learning the name of Gray.

The winter brought still darker clouds – storms, indeed. Morton was proving merciless to all who sought to thwart his ideas of government. He led an army to the Borders to impose his will upon the unruly clan chiefs there – and Logan of Restalrig, Gray's nephew, was no gentle dove, to do what he was told. Patrick perhaps would have been better at home, under his father's eye, after all. It looked as though full-scale civil war might break out once more in blood-stained Scotland, for the Kirk was gathering itself to resist Morton's harshness against its ministers, who were being banished the realm in large numbers – in order, it was believed, to assist the Regent's economical policy of one minister to four churches, which of course left the revenues of the other three available for confiscation. January brought word of Patrick being involved in no fewer than three duels in the closes and wynds of Edinburgh, in two of which his opponents were killed; and one of them was named Douglas. The next month, Elizabeth Gray arrived unexpectedly back at her home of Glamis Castle, and declared unequivocally that she had come for good. And when, a few days later, Sir Thomas Lyon, Master of Glamis, was appointed Lord High Treasurer of Scotland, and third most important man after the Regent and his brother the Chancellor, my lord saw the writing on the wall all too clearly. He sent for Patrick to come home, secretly but without delay.

It was in fact the first real morning of Spring, and the cradle was out in the courtyard in the March sunshine, sheltered from the east wind, when Patrick rode in under the gatehouse of Castle Huntly. He made a dazzling figure in white and scarlet, with cloak of chequered black and gold, and one of the new high-crowned hats with an enormous down-curling ostrich plume.

My lord, who had just helped David carry the cradle down the twisting turnpike stairway – for no servitor was to be trusted with its precious freight – turned to stare at this gallant sight. Even the mettlesome black mare was new.

'My God!' he burst out, interrupting Patrick's gay greeting. 'Look at him! What a Fiend's name is this? A pageant! A guizard, by the Rude! A posture-master!'

Patrick sketched a bow, from the saddle. 'On the contrary – your very devoted . . . !'

'Devil burn you – is this where my siller has gone? What way is that to travel, man, through the Kirk's Scotland? And Morton's? I told you to come secretly – and you ride here in broad daylight gauded to outshine the sun!'

His son laughed, dismounting, and pressed a hand on David's shoulder, who had hurried forward to welcome him. 'I' faith, my lord, you would not have your heir slink into Gray country like some whipped cur? Not so do I esteem your honour . . . and mine!'

'*Your* honour! God's passion – you talk of honour! You? I . . . I . . . ' His father gobbled, at a loss for words.

Not so Patrick. 'Heigh-ho!' he exclaimed. 'It is good to be home. My lord, you look uncommon well. Er, vigorous. Davy – you are getting fat, I vow! Fatherhood, it must be – eh? And this . . . ?' He gestured towards the cradle. 'This can be none other than the cause of it! My . . . h'm . . . niece!'

'I sent for you, sirrah, to come home in haste,' Gray said

angrily. 'Three weeks agone! And secretly. For good reason. And here you come, unhurried – and thus!'

But Patrick was not listening. He was bending over the cradle, gazing down at the dainty wide-eyed creature within, so brilliantly breath-takingly, like himself. And for the moment the smile had left his comely features, and his lips moved soundlessly.

'D'you hear me?' his father demanded. 'A pox on it, man – think you that my orders are to be thus lightly . . . ?' He gulped, and started forward, hands outstretched to the cradle. 'Keep your hands off the bairn!' he cried. 'Can you not see that she is new settled?' And he grabbed his side of the cradle, and jerked it away violently.

At the jolt, the child was thrown to the side, and bumped her head. The great dark eyes widened still further, filled with tears, and the rosebud lower lip trembled as a tiny wail arose.

'Sweet Jesu – look what you have done!' Patrick charged, and he reached inside to pick up the infant.

'I . . . *I* have done!' my lord spluttered. 'Put her down. Do not touch her, I tell you . . . ' He reached out to snatch back the baby.

Patrick swept the whimpering bundle out and away, stepping, almost dancing, backwards with it. He pressed the little face close to his own, and began to whisper in the shell-like curl-framed ear, backing further from his father the while. He chuckled and wrinkled his nose and grimaced – and, in only seconds Mary's whimpers had changed to fat little chuckles also. Pink diminutive fingers clutched his own dark curls, and crows of pleasure mingled with his nonsense.

At sight of the two smiling faces, so close, so lit with the same light, Lord Gray halted, tugging at his beard, muttering. David watched, still-faced.

Patrick skipped about that cobbled courtyard as though it was a dancing floor, crooning a melody to the laughing mite in his arms, beating time before them with the ostrich-plumed hat. Right round the circuit of it he went, and came back to the cradle. But still he held the child.

'Here is a joy, a delight, a darling, a very poppet!' he declared. 'Why did you not write to me that she was . . . so? I swear, this one is fairer than any that kept me in the tall wynds of Edinburgh! Or otherwhere! I' faith – a beauty! And a rogue, too, I'll warrant. With a . . . a strong family resemblance, eh?' Patrick held the creature at arm's length, examining her. 'Remarkable!

Who would have believed that . . . !' He paused. 'Her mother?' he said. 'Always I esteemed the fair Mariota as most worthy of, shall we say, acclaim? Now, as mother of this cosset, this sweetheart, I love her the more! Where is she – Mariota?'

He looked up. At the tower window two floors up, and looking down on them, Mariota stood, still, motionless, save that her features were working strangely.

Patrick bowed as best he might, laughing, and held up the babe towards her. 'Greetings, my dear – and felicitations!' he called. 'You have done well. Passing well. Here is a very fair achievement. I vow, if I had known that you had it in you . . . !' He smiled, and shrugged one shoulder. 'And you are bonnier than ever. Which of you is the bonnier, would be hard to say . . . '

He stopped. The girl had turned abruptly away from the window, out of sight. Then he laughed again, and set the infant gently down in its cradle, to turn towards the tower doorway. 'I must go pay my respects to my good-sister!' he said.

'That can wait,' his father announced, shortly, sternly. 'Bide you a wee, my mannie. *I* have waited your pleasure for long enough. You will hear me, now. You have disobeyed my orders. You have squandered my money. You have made the name of Gray a by-word, going whoring about the land so that the poor lassie your wife is away back to her father. You have killed men . . . '

'Only in fair fight, sir – who would have killed me, else.'

'Quiet! You have endangered not only your own life, but the safety and well-being o' my house. You have offended needlessly the highest men in the land, so that I, *I*, Gray, may not walk the streets o' Dundee or Perth for fear o' meeting a Lyon or a Douglas! Aye, or even a minister o' the Kirk! Foul fall you, boy – is it crazed you are?'

'I think not, sir. I left here, when you sent me, and came home when you recalled me . . . as soon as affairs permitted me. Is that disobeying your orders? Can I help it if women favour me? As for Elizabeth Lyon, she is as warm to lie with as a fish – and smells something similar! Her father is welcome to her. Davy got the better bargain, 'fore God!'

'Silence, sir! You are speaking of your wedded wife . . . and the Chancellor o' Scotland's daughter! And worse, the new Lord Treasurer's niece!'

'Does that make her a better bedfellow? I will not go begging to Glamis for her . . . '

61

'No, sir – that you will not! You will do quite other than that. You go to France!'

'France . . . ?'

'Aye. And at once. You are better out of this Scotland for a while. It is a dangerous place to play the fool in! Perhaps in France they may teach you some sense. At least you will be out o' the way o' Morton and the Douglases and the Master o' Glamis. And maybe the lassie Elizabeth will like you the better for a year or two's parting. It has happened that way, before.'

'God forbid!' Patrick said, piously. 'But . . . France! My lord, this is a surprise indeed. I do not know what to say . . . '

'What you say, Patrick, is immaterial. You are going, whether you like it or no. Until you are of age, you will do as I say. We sail tonight.'

'Tonight? And *we* – you are going, too?'

'Only to Dysart, in Fife. A shipman there sends a vessel, each fortnight, to Le Havre. You missed the last one, by your delay – you'll no' miss this one. Wednesday she sails, if I mind aright. We'll go by boat from Dundee – I'll have Geordie Laing put us round to Dysart. I'm chancing no riding through Fife with you, with the Lindsays so thick with Glamis.'

'France,' Patrick said slowly, thoughtfully. 'France should be interesting, I think.'

'Aye, I daresay,' his father observed, grimly. 'But it isna just for interest I'm sending you there, you'll understand! You've a deal to learn, boy, that they didna teach you at St. Andrews. One day you'll be Gray, and a Lord o' Parliament. The Kirk's all very well – but you'll no' learn statecraft in Scotland these days. And statecraft is going to be important, especially foreign concerns, with the Queen of England having no heir but our poor Mary and young Jamie. Which way the cat jumps, Catholic or Protestant, is but a toss o' the coin. It behoves a wise man to take precautions, to be ready for either. Myself, I am deep thirled to the Kirk, these days – but you, lad, are young enough to keep, shall we say, an open mind. Such might prove valuable in the next year or two – who knows?'

'I see.' Patrick smiled. 'So I will be more valuable to *you*, my lord, in France, should the wind blow from Rome . . . is that it?'

'Something o' the sort. They say that Elizabeth Tudor is sickly, these days. Certain it is she'll no' marry now. Philip o' Spain kens that, and is casting eyes on our Queen Mary again. If Elizabeth died – and there's a-many who might help her that road – England could turn Catholic again almost overnight.

And it would be Mary on the two thrones of Scotland and England then, not young Protestant Jamie. It would be an ill thing if both Grays were so deep on the wrong side that our house would gain no advantage, see you.'

'I do see, very well, sir.'

'It will be kittle touchy work, mind. Work for no preening jackdaw. You'll have to watch your every step – for we want no ill tales coming back to the Kirk's Scotland. Warily you'll have to tread, and with your ear well to the ground. I have a sort o' a cousin, one Friar Gray, a Jesuit, at Blois. You'll go to him first. It is near Orleans. He is a man of James Beaton's, that was Archbishop o' Glasgow, who is Mary's ambassador. They will see you on the right track . . . '

'And Davy? Does he come with me?'

'He does not. D'you think I am made o' siller, man? Davy is fine here.'

The brothers' eyes met.

'A pity,' Patrick said.

'Come away up to my room, now, and I'll tell you something of what you must know if you are going to walk in step with the Guises. I was in France myself, at the Scots College in Paris, mind. Come, you . . . '

Regretfully Patrick glanced up at Mariota's window, sighed, shrugged, and turned to follow his sire.

Chapter Five

DAVID GRAY stood in the soaring plunging bows of the *Leven Maid*, of Dumbarton, shading his eyes against the April sun's dazzle off the heaving waters of the Bay of Biscay as he gazed eastwards, landwards. A pity, Patrick had said that time, those many long months ago, when he heard that his half-brother was not to go to France with him. A pity it may have been – and even Lord Gray had come to admit as much, in time, with increasing rue and regret. A pity – and here was David coming to France at last, three full years after that Spring day of 1576, not to undo the pity of it, since that might not be, but at least to cut short the sorry course of my lord's travail. David had come to France to fetch Patrick home.

Lord Gray had, in fact, miscalculated, and was paying the price thereof. Elizabeth of England had not died, nor even maintained her sickliness, and was indeed most notably and upsettlingly alive – even though still husbandless; Mary Stuart, poor soul, was still a prisoner, and seemingly further from the throne than ever – and owing to a succession of fairly feeble plots in her name, some instigated it was said by Elizabeth herself, was even more harshly warded than before; Protestantism remained unshaken in Scotland as in England, with the Kirk stronger than ever, and though Morton had resigned the Regency as a gesture to still the increasing clamour of the ministers, he retained the young King Jamie secure in his hands and ruled the country as before. All of which meant that Patrick's apprenticeship in statecraft was being worked out on the wrong side.

It was not this, however, that had brought my lord to the point of desperation, so much as that unfailing and chronic preoccupation of all Scots lords, however powerful – money, or the lack of it. Patrick, in France, had proved to be a positive drain, a very sink and gulf, for money. What he did with it all, the Fiend only knew – he did not vouchsafe such details in his letters, only requests for more and more. Indeed, he gave little indication of what he was doing at all, in his deplorably light and frivolous writings, despatched from Rome and Florence and Cadiz and the like, as well as from various ducal courts all over France.

But they all ended with the inevitable demand for the due maintenance of the honour and dignity of Gray – money. My lord had ordered him home more than once – but in return Patrick had pointed out the extreme costliness of the voyage, and that he could not move without cash – as it would be a scandal to their name to leave a host of debts behind him. More money sent, and he still did not return. At length, at his wits' end, my lord had sent David to fetch him back, with the necessary silver and no uncertainty in his instructions.

The port of La Rochelle, protected by its screen of islands, lay ahead of the wallowing vessel. It was a far cry from Castle Huntly, and a long way round to reach Patrick at Rheims – but of late, with the increasingly savage treatment of the French Protestants, Queen Elizabeth's relations with France had deteriorated, and the English captains were so active in the narrow waters of the Channel that Scots ships were avoiding the northern French ports and taking the west coast route unless in convoy. So David had sailed from Dumbarton on the Clyde, the *Leven Maid* heading well out to sea around Ireland, to avoid Elizabeth's busy pirates. La Rochelle, being a Huguenot stronghold, was apt to be spared the latter's attentions.

David, now just past his twenty-first birthday, had attained very definitely to manhood in these last years. Still only of medium height, he had become broad of shoulder and stocky of build, though slender-hipped and light-footed as became a swordsman and a wrestler – not that he had partaken much of such sports since Patrick's departure. He had become a solid sober family man, indeed, and asked for no better. Leaving Mariota and the little Mary had been a wrench, greatly as some part of him longed to see Patrick again.

Impressed by the fortifications of La Rochelle, which had only a year or two before withstood successfully the attacking fury of the Catholic forces under the Constable and de Guise, and by the wider streets and fine buildings, which he esteemed as on the whole superior to Dundee, David made his farewells to the shipmaster at the busy quayside, and sought to learn the approximate frequency of vessels sailing back to the Clyde.

'You're no' feart, man, to ask that,' the other said. 'With all these fell Englishry scouring the seas like a pack o' hound-dogs, pirating who they will! The wonder is that any honest shippers put to sea at all – for no trading vessel's safe.'

'But there is no war between us,' David objected. 'No war with Scotland. Or with France, either.'

'Think you that matters, lad? They do it for the sport, they say, these fine English gentry – bloody murder and robbery. And their dried-up bastard of a queen knights them for the doing o' it, they say! Each voyage we make could be oor last. You'll just have to take your chance o' getting back, and that's a fact. You may be lucky, and you may not. It's Rheims you're making for, you say?'

'Yes. At least, that is where the Master of Gray was when last he wrote a letter. At the court of Guise.'

The seaman spat on the stones of the quay. 'Aye. I' ph'mm. It' a gey long road you have to ride, then – right across France. I've no' been to Rheims, mind, but I ken it's in the north-east o' the country. Calais would have been the port for it. Och, I ken, I ken – beggars canna be choosers. But, see – it's no' that far frae the Netherlands border, I'm thinking. If your friend's close to the Guises – foul fall them! – he'd likely get you a safe-conduct through the armies o' their friends the Spaniards in the Low Countries, and you could win through to Amsterdam, and home frae there. Better than coming back the long road here. But . . . certes, man, you have chosen an ill time to go traipsing alone across this Europe! God – you have! A brave man you must be – or a gey foolhardy one!'

David Gray, in the days that followed, came to appreciate something of the shipmaster's point of view. As he rode north by east, on the very ordinary nag that he had economically purchased in La Rochelle out of my lord's silver, it was through a land where few men rode alone, or rode openly at all, save in clattering dust-raising armed bands, a sunny fair fertile land, rich to his Scots eyes, that should have smiled indeed – but did not; a land that cowered and looked over its shoulder at ruined villages, deserted farms, burned castles, close-walled unwelcoming towns, neglected fields and rioting vineyards. When David had left Scotland the buds had just been beginning to open and the snow still streaked the hills; here the leaves were full out, blossom decked the land and flowers bloomed. But not only blossom burgeoned on the trees; men hung, and women and children too, from so many of the poplars and limes that lined the long straight roads, and no one was there to cut them down; almost every village, burned or no, had its fire and stake in the market-place; scarce a duck-pond or a mill-lade was not choked with bodies of men and beasts. The smell of death hung over a goodly land; the hand of tyranny, misgovernment and sheer savagery was everywhere evident. Over all these fair provinces, of Poitou, Touraine, Blois and Orleans, through which David rode, the tides of religious war had ebbed and flowed for years. The traveller had been used to religious intolerance in his own country, but nothing had prepared him for this. He was shocked. Patrick, in his infrequent letters, had not mentioned anything of it.

Poitou, the province of which La Rochelle was the port, was the worst, for it had been a strong Huguenot area. Possibly still was, though first impressions were that the land was now all but deserted, save for the walled towns; closer inspection, however, revealed that there were still people living in the devastated countryside – only they tended to keep out of sight of travellers, even lone ones, hiding in woods and copses, peering from behind ruined buildings. Some of them David hailed, trying on them his halting St. Andrews French, seeking directions and food – but with scant results. The first night, after looking in vain for an inn that still functioned, he spent in the barn of a deserted farmery near Niort – that was not, perhaps, quite so deserted as it seemed. He slept but fitfully, fully clad and with his sword at his hand, and was away again, hungry, with the dawn.

Thereafter he bought food in the towns, and always carried a supply with him, humble enough fare of bread and cheese and sausage and the light wine of the country; but then, David Gray was a humble man himself, and looked it, in his plain well-worn broadcloth doublet and trunks, dented breastplate, patched thigh-length riding-boots, and flat cap devoid of jewel or feather. As well, perhaps, that such was his aspect, for none were likely to suspect the store of Lord Gray's silver coin that he carried amongst the modest bundle of his gear and provender. Possibly the length and quality of his rather prominent sword helped to discourage the ambitious likewise – however ill it matched the rest of him, save it may be the level gaze of his grey eyes and the jut of his chin.

Not that his long journey across France lacked incident entirely. The third night out, on a low-browed inn under the Abbey church of St. Martin at Tours, he was eyed interestedly during the evening by a pair of out-at-elbow fellow-guests, probably temporarily unemployed men-at-arms, and approached more directly later in the night on his straw pallet in the communal sleeping-room; fortunately however, neither of them proved to be really swordsmen, daggers being their preference for this indoor interviewing, and David, a light sleeper when not in his own bed, had them out of the door in the space of a couple of active minutes, to the marked relief of the other sleepers – though, less happily, the offended landlord forced him to follow them shortly afterwards, lest he bring the hostelry into bad repute with the watch. Since the gates of Tours were not opened until sunrise the rest of the night had to be passed, in drizzling rain, wrapped in his cloak in the Abbey graveyard.

It was only the next afternoon, still in fair Touraine, that, riding up the fertile but war-ravaged vale of the Loire, David heard a drumming of hooves behind him, and turned to see a group of half-a-dozen horsemen pounding along the track at no great distance behind. They had not been in sight when he had looked back a few moments before, so that they must have emerged from woodland flanking the road on the north. France was theoretically at peace from her civil wars, since the Edict of Beaulieu a month or so earlier had provided for concessions to the Huguenots, but David recognised military-type urgency when he saw it, and prudently turned his horse aside from the road and rode down towards the river-bank, to be out of the way. The band, however, swung round and came after him, with loud cries, which though unintelligible to the Scot, had their own eloquence. Without awaiting interpretation, he drove his reluctant cob straight into the Loire. The beast proved to be a better swimmer than might have been expected from its bony appearance, but the Loire is one of France's greatest rivers and the current was powerful, carrying the struggling horse quickly away downstream. The pursuit presumably decided that this trick lay with the river, for they contented themselves with hurling a mixture of fist-shakes, catcalls and laughter after the swimmers, and turned away after a little to ride on eastwards. David fairly quickly perceived that French rivers were not like Scots ones, all splatter and foam, and turned his mount's snorting head back towards the northern bank, which he was perhaps fortunate to regain after a hard struggle and fully half-a-mile downstream.

Chastened and wet, he rode circumspectly towards Blois, deciding that probably a very fast horse, equally with a nimble sword, was a prerequisite for travel in Henri Third's France.

Two evenings later, David crossed the Seine at Melun, and the Marne a day afterwards at Château Thierry without further incident. Rheims, and, he hoped, journey's end, lay but ten leagues ahead.

*

David was much impressed, riding into Rheims. There had been but few signs of devastation or ruin in the rich Champagne country through which he approached it, for this was the territory of the aggressive and powerful family of Guise, that rivalled even the royal house in wealth and influence. Here were the dual courts of the Duke of Guise and of his brother, the Cardinal of Lorraine, Archbishop of Rheims.

It was a handsome city, dominated by the huge twin-towered cathedral, that some said was the most magnificent Gothic building in Europe. Great abbeys and monasteries and churches abounded – for here were no Protestants; splendid palaces and the handsome mansions of the nobility were everywhere, there was a university – not so large as the three colleges of St. Andrews, however – and even the merchants' houses were notably fine. David had never seen anything like it, though he imagined that Edinburgh might be of this sort. The streets of course were crowded – unfortunately with the usual swash-buckling hordes of idle men-at-arms and retainers that formed the inevitable train of the nobility, and the bold-eyed women who in turn could be guaranteed to follow the soldiery. It behoved a discreet traveller to ride warily and offer nothing that could be magnified into provocation.

After considerable searching, David found a very modest hostelry in a narrow back street, whose proprietress, after summing him up keen-eyed, agreed to squeeze him in – for the city was swarming like a hive of bees. As soon as he was cleaned and fed he began to ask about the Master of Gray. He might as well have asked for the man in the moon; Rheims was so full of dukes and marquises, bishops, abbots, counts and the like, that the whereabouts of a single Scots visitor was neither here nor there. The only *Ecossais* that the good lady knew of, was poor M. de Beaton, who called himself Archbishop of Somewhere-or-other. The unfortunate gentleman lodged in the Rue St. Etienne. If monsieur was to ask there . . . ? This advice was made with a nice admixture of sympathy and scorn, which made David wonder.

It was already evening as he made his way to Rue St. Etienne by no means one of the most handsome streets of Rheims. Not to put too fine a point on it, the district might almost have been described as mean, and the house pointed out, though fairly large, had seen better days and was in fact partly warehouse.

The door was opened by an elderly servitor in the worn relics of a fine livery. A single glance at the long sternly-disapproving

69

features and greying sandy hair established him as a Scot, and David forsook his halting French.

'This, I am told, is the house of the Archbishop of Glasgow?' he said. 'I seek the Master of Gray. Can I learn here where I may find him?'

'Ooh, aye,' the man answered, looking his caller up and down interestedly, critically. 'The Master, is it, my mannie? I' ph'mmm' He sounded as though he did not think much of the enquired-for, or of the looks of the enquirer either. 'Well – you'll no' find him here.'

'No, I had hardly expected that,' David admitted. 'But do you, or your master, know where he is?'

'I wouldna hae thought you'd hae needed to ask that!' the other rejoined, with a sniff. 'He used to bide here, aye. But no' now. Och, no' him!'

'Indeed? Where, then?'

'Man, you must be gey new to Rheims to ask that!'

'I am but new arrived from Scotland. Today.'

'Is that so? Wi' messages? Wi' word o' affairs?' That was suddenly eager.

'For the Master of Gray,' David said pointedly. 'Where may I find him?'

'Och, well – you better ask at yon bedizened hizzy's, the Countess de Verlac. Aye, you ask there.'

'The Countess de Verlac? Will I find him in this countess's house, then?'

'Mair'n that – in her bed, man! In her bed, the fine young gentleman!'

'Umm.' David blinked. 'And where do I look for the . . . the lady?'

'In the Hôtel de Verlac, of course – where else? D'you ken him, this young gamecock?'

'We are, h'm, related.'

'D'you tell me that?' The servitor pursed thin lips. 'Well, if you're in a hurry to see him, you might as well just go to the Cardinal's palace, right away. He'll be there. They'll all be there, all the bits o' lairds and counts and sik-like, wi' their painted women. It's the usual high jinks, a great ball and dancing, to celebrate one o' their outlandish saints. They're aye at it – any's the excuse will do. There's one near every other night.'

David smiled faintly. 'You sound, I'd say, but little like an archbishop's henchman!' he said.

The other snorted. 'He's awa' there himsel' – the auld fool!

I tell him he should have mair sense.' He made as though he would shut the door in disgust – and then turned back. 'What's . . . what's auld Scotland looking like, laddie?' he asked, almost shamefacedly. 'Where are you frae?'

'The Carse o' Gowrie, above Tay. And it was cold when I left.'

'Och, well – I'm frae Melrose, mysel'. Aye, Melrose, snug on the banks o' Tweed. Bonny, bonny it'll be yonder, now, wi' the yellow whins bleezing on every brae, and the bit lambs skipping. I've no' seen it in fifteen year, fifteen year – and I'll no' see it again this side o' the grave, either. No' me. Good night to you!'

The door all but slammed in David's face.

He went in search of the archiepiscopal palace.

It was not difficult to find, being near to the towering cathedral, a great and splendid edifice standing in formal gardens, with fountains playing in the forecourt, and statuary, naked and to David's mind surpassingly indelicate, scattered everywhere. The huge gates, though they were guarded by halberdiers in most gorgeous liveries, stood wide open, and David was surprised that no attempt was made to question his entry. Indeed, half of Rheims seemed to be passing in and out of the premises, grooms, personal servants, ladies' maids, men-at-arms, pages, even priests and monks. The sound of music drifted out from the great salons, but it had difficulty getting past the louder noises of laughter and shouting in the forecourt, a hubbub which centred round a couple of fountains there. Men, and women too, were pushing and jostling there, and drinking from cups and tankards and even scooped hands. It was only when looking at the second fountain that David perceived that the water was purplish-red in colour – that it was not in fact water at all, but wine, red wine in this, white in the other. Almost incredulously, he pressed forward, to reach out and dip a finger in the flood, and taste. It was real wine, as good as any that he had had the good fortune to taste. Amazed, he stared. Admittedly most of what was not drunk ran back into the cistern below and would be spouted up again through a dozen nymphs' breasts and worse – but even so, the quantity expended must have been enormous, and quite appalled David's economical Scots mind. And this, apparently, was for the servants, the soldiers, the hangers-on, some of whom already lay about on the ground, young as was the night.

The contrast of this de Guise munificence, as against the harried and war-torn want of the provinces through which he had come here, was rather more than David's stomach would take. He forbore to join the beneficiaries.

He moved forward to the palace itself. It was quite unlike any building that he had ever seen, not only in its vast extent but in the profusion of its terraces, balustrated galleries, pillared arcades and porticos, at various levels, merging with the far flung gardens, and with huge windows opening on to all these. David, brought up in a tall stone castle, noted that it would be an impossible place to defend.

No attempt was being made to bar anyone's entrance thereto this night, at any rate. Lavishly clad figures danced out on the terraces, embraced in every alcove, and strolled and made love in the formal gardens, so that it was a little difficult, in the creeping dusk, to distinguish coupling guests from the profusion of statuary. In and out amongst them all went servants bearing trays of viands, sweetmeats, goblets of wine, fruit and the like. David's fear had been that he might not gain access to the palace; now it was rather the problem of finding Patrick in the throng.

As it happened, that was not too difficult, either. Edging his way through one of the great windows that opened off the magnificent main salon, he stared in at the brilliant scene. Under the blaze of thousands of candles in huge hanging candelabra, a splendid concourse of dazzlingly dressed men and women stood and circulated and talked and laughed, watching a comparatively few couples who gyrated slowly in the stately but archly seductive measures of the pavane, at the farther end of the vast marbled room, to the music of players in a gallery. The clothing of these people took David's breath away. Never had he seen or conceived of such splendour and ostentation, such a scintillation of silks and satins and gems. Never had he seen so many long and graceful legs coming from such abbreviated trunks, so many white shoulders and bare bosoms, such fantastic headdressing and outrageous padding of sleeves and hips. Nor had his nostrils been assailed by such a battery of scents and perfumes, or his ears afflicted by such din of high-pitched clamour. For a while he could only gaze, benumbed.

It was the part-contemptuous, part-angry gesture of a handsome and statuesque woman who dominated a group quite near to David, and who kept drawing the latter's somewhat guiltily scandalised eyes by the cut of her all black jewel-encrusted gown, that eventually turned his glance whither she pointed. It was towards one especial pair of the dancers.

David's breath caught.

Though he could scarcely believe his eyes, there was no doubt that it was Patrick. But how different a Patrick. Gone was the beautiful youth, the fresh-faced if mocking-eyed stripling, even the dashing young galliard of his duelling days in Edinburgh. Instead, here was a man of such elegance, superb bearing, confidence, and extraordinary good looks, as to draw all eyes, whether in admiration, envy or sheer malice, a man of such sparkling attractiveness and at the same time mature and easy dignity, that it was hardly believable that he had barely reached his twenty-first year. Dressed entirely in white satin and gold lace – and seemingly the only man in that salon to be so – save for a black velvet garter below one knee, a black dagger-belt, and the black lining to the tiny cape slung from one padded shoulder, his dark gleaming hair swept down sheerly to his shoulders in disciplined waves and unusual style, curling back from neat jet-jewelled ears. He had grown a tiny pointed beard and thin scimitar of black moustache, outlining the curve of his lips. His hose were so long and his trunks so short as to verge on indecency, front and back, and he danced with a young woman of swarthy fiery beauty clad in flame-coloured velvet, with such languid grace albeit naked and unblushing intimacy and touch, as to infer that they might well have been alone in the lady's boudoir – no doubt the reason for the disgust of the statuesque woman in black.

David watched, biting his lip.

In a little, almost imperceptibly, Patrick steered his voluptuous partner towards one of the open windows at the top end of the salon. David saw the woman in black start as though to leave her companions and hurry in that direction, then shrug and change her mind. He himself, however, slipped back through his own window, and moved up the terrace. He was waiting within the topmost window when Patrick and the young woman in red came out, laughing. They would have pushed past him without a glance had David not put out a hand to the other's arm. 'Patrick!' he said.

His brother turned, haughtily, angrily shaking off the touch. Then his eyes widened and his lips parted. 'My God – Davy!' he gasped.

'Aye, Davy. None other.'

For a long moment they gazed at each other. Patrick's fine nostrils flared, almost like those of a high-spirited horse. His dark eyes darted glances right and left. David read more than mere joy and affection therein. He nibbled at his lower lip. Then, abruptly laughing again, he strode forward to fling his satin-padded arms around his brother's dull and well-worn broadcloth.

'Davy! Davy!' he cried. 'Here's a wonder! Here's joy indeed! My good dear Davy – here!'

David's own throat was sufficiently choked with emotion as to render him speechless.

'Patrick! Patrick! What, *tête Dieu*, is this?' The young woman had turned back, astonished. 'Have you taken leave of your senses?'

'Eh . . . ? No, no, Elissa. This . . . this is . . . my good friend, Davy. And secretary. From Scotland, you understand . . . '

'Friend?' That was as eloquent as the raised supercilious eyebrows, as the swarthy girl looked David up and down.

'It is . . . you could call us foster-brothers. It is a common relationship in my country. Foster-brothers . . . '

'I do not think that I congratulate you, *mon cher*!'

Patrick laughed. 'Elissa is jealous, I think, Davy!' he said lightly.

David looked at the young woman doubtfully – and hurriedly looked away again. Of all the low-cut gowns of that palace, that of this sultry ripe Italianate beauty was surely the lowest – so low indeed that the point of one thrusting prominent breast was showing. David's embarrassment stemmed not so much from the sight itself, for it might have been assumed that the dancing had disturbed the lady's attire, but from a second glance's perception that it was in fact painted flame-red to match the dress – and therefore that it was meant to be thus on view.

Keeping his eyes averted, he bowed perfunctorily. 'The Countess de Verlac,' he said, more to cover his discomposure than anything else. 'David Gray at your service, ma'am.'

'Lord!' Patrick exclaimed.

'*Dieu de Dieu!*' the lady cried. 'That old war-horse! That, that dragon! Fellow, you are insolent!'

'*Mort de Diable*, Davy – you mistake! The ladies are, h'm, otherwise. Quite otherwise! This is the Viscountess d'Ariège from Gascony.'

But his partner had swirled round, the Spanish verdingale under her billowing skirts buffeting David in the by-going. She swept on towards the steps that led down into the gardens. Patrick looked after her ruefully, and made a face that turned him momentarily into a boy again.

'Forgive me, Davy,' he said. 'Give me but ten minutes. Less. You trod on delicate ground, there! Wait for me here.' Smiling, and patting his brother's shoulder with his perfumed-gloved hand, he went after the Viscountess – but sauntering, not hurrying, a picture of exquisite masculine assurance.

David, frowning, and cursing his own blundering awkwardness by comparison, not for the first time but now more feelingly than ever before, withdrew into the shadows behind a pillar, to wait.

In much less than ten minutes Patrick was back, casually, unhurrying still. He took David by the arm. 'We cannot talk here,' he said. 'There is an ante-room that I know of, round here.'

Another terrace gave them access to a smaller room, full of cloaks, riding-boots, swords and the like, less brilliantly lit than the salons. One of the Cardinal's guards stood sentinel over it, but made no attempt to bar their entry. Patrick turned to consider his brother.

'*Pardieu*, Davy – the trouble I am to you, eh? Heigho – so you have been sent to fetch me home!'

David cleared his throat. This had seemed a simple enough errand back at Castle Huntly, however responsible, lengthy and expensive. But, now . . . ? Of old, when really necessary, he had always been able to impress his own personality and will upon this brilliant brother of his, by some means or other, even if it was only his fists, at least briefly and for a limited objective. Probably because he had seemed to be the elder. But now, this confident gallant in front of him had grown so far beyond him, had changed in these three years into a man, and a strong and determined man most obviously, whatever else he might be. What impression could he, David, the humble schoolmaster and rustic, hope to make on this dazzling nobleman now?

If David had perhaps considered well, in one of the many mirrors of that room, the man that he himself had grown into those three years, he might have looked a little less hopelessly on his chances. All he did, however, was to eye his brother with that level gaze of his, and sigh.

'Aye,' he said, 'I am sorry about the lady, Patrick.'

The other laughed with apparently genuine amusement. 'Say it not,' he declared. 'You showed me a side of Elissa that I had not seen before . . . difficult as one might think that to be! But . . . here is a surprise, Davy. You have a come a long road – which is the measure of our father's concern for me, is it? Or for his precious siller, eh? Our fond parent believes that he is not getting a sufficiently good return for his money – is that it?'

'Can you blame him, Patrick?' David asked briefly. His hand's gesture, to include all his brother's gorgeous appearance, and the magnificence of his surroundings, was eloquent enough.

'Fine, I can, Davy! Think you that his small grudging doles pay for . . . this? The Gray lands are wide, and my lord's treasure-chest less bare than he would have us think. As heir to one of the greatest lords in Scotland, I will not live like any starveling exile. He sent me here, did he not? But . . . enough of such talk, for the nonce. You look well, Davy . . . and very stern! An upright stubborn bear of a man – or should it be a lion? A lion of Judah, rather than of Gray, eh? You mind me of some of the stauncher pillars of the Kirk! I'll never dare cross you again, Davy – I'd be feared!'

The other shook his head. 'Man, Patrick – you've changed, your own self,' he said.

'You think so? It may be that I have had occasion to. But . . . och, Davy – it does my heart good to see you. Like a breath of fresh north wind you are, with the scent of heather and bog-myrtle to it.'

'Yet you prefer *this* scent, I think?' his brother said, and touched those elegant perfumed gloves.

Patrick laughed. 'In Rome, as they say, one lives like a Roman. In Rheims, likewise.'

'Aye – what *are* you doing here, Patrick? What keeps you here? Living thus. These women . . . ?'

'Women never keep Patrick Gray anywhere – however useful they may be!' he was assured lightly. 'I have affairs here, that is all. Affairs that are not yet completed.'

'What affairs?'

'The old Davy – ever blunt as a cudgel! Affairs of some moment, shall we say? When a man has a father such as mine, Davy, clearly he must make his own way in the world, if he would not live on bannocks and ale – for which, unlike yourself, I have but little taste. I . . . '

He stopped. An inner door had opened, and framed therein were three men. Patrick made a profound obeisance. David, after a quick look at his brother, bobbed a brief bow, and waited.

The first two gentlemen were very similar, in build, in appearance, in expression, tall hawk-faced exquisites, dressed in the height of extravagant fashion; they might well have been brothers. The third was very different, older, a plump but

76

sagging man, with a tired and heavy-jowled face, clad in the florid and flowing, if distinctly tarnished, splendours of a prince of Holy Church.

One of the pair in front, a spectacular thin figure garbed wholly in crimson – doublet, cloak, trunks, hose, jewelled cap, ostrich-feathers, even sword hilted and sheathed in crimson and rubies, spoke, crisp-voiced. 'Monsieur de Gray, I was told that you had come to this room with a stranger, obviously a messenger. Who, and whence, is he?' This was curt, with little attempt to disguise a hint of suspicion.

'No messenger, Your Eminence, but merely my, er, my secretary, new come from Scotland,' Patrick assured, quickly.

'Secretary?' The speaker looked sceptical. 'He seems no clerk, to me. Since when have you aspired to a secretary, Monsieur?'

Patrick smiled, brilliantly. 'Only since tonight, Eminence. Formerly, Davy was my close companion and body-servant. Indeed, we were foster-brothers. My father, the Lord Gray, has sent him to me now, believing that he will be useful. In the matters in which we are interested. Davy is very . . . discreet.'

'I trust so,' the other observed, bleakly. 'If he is direct from Scotland, at least he will have news for us? For us all. What has he to tell us?'

Patrick shot a glance at his brother. 'I have not asked him yet, sir – save only of family matters. David – here is His Eminence the Cardinal of Lorraine, Archbishop of Rheims. Also his brother, my lord Duke of Guise, Marshal of France. And my lord Archbishop of Glasgow. They would have news of Scotland – of affairs there.' David felt a dig at his side from Patrick's elbow.

He bowed again, but still not deeply. David could not bring himself to bow low to any man. 'My knowledge of affairs is slight,' he said, in his stilted French. 'But such as it is, it is at their lordships' disposal.'

'How is it with Morton, lad? Is his grip of the young King weakening?' That was the rich and fruity voice of James Beaton, exiled Archbishop of Glasgow, traces of his couthy Fife accent still evident beneath the French. 'What of Huntly and Herries, the Catholic lords? Are the people making clamour for the Queen's release, God pity her?'

'Not that I have heard of, sir. The Kirk is not so inclined, and teaches otherwise. My lord of Morton still rules, yes. He is no longer Regent, but . . . '

'We know that, fellow!' the Cardinal exclaimed, impatiently. '*Mortdieu* – we are not years old in our information! News we desire – not history, sirrah! We have sent good money to Scotland, to stir up the people to demand Mary Stuart my cousin's release. Do not you tell us that it has been wasted?'

'No, no, Your Eminence – not that, I am sure,' the other and lesser Archbishop put in hurriedly. 'It takes time for the leaven to work. This young man, belike, is not from Edinburgh or Stirling . . . '

'He comes from the Carse of Gowrie only,' Patrick amplified. 'A country district. Where the Kirk is strong. Your Eminence need not fear . . . '

'I hope not,' the Cardinal said, thin lips tight.

'You carry no messages from our friends at the court of your king?' This time it was Henri, Duke of Guise, as crisp as his brother but a shade less keenly shrewd in aspect, however intolerant of eye as befitted the man who had instigated the Massacre of St. Bartholomew's Eve.

'No, my lord duke. I have not been near the court, at all.'

'Then, *cordieu*, we are wasting our time, Louis!'

'Perhaps. Fellow – your blaspheming renegades of the Church, these heretics of the so-called Kirk,' the Cardinal went on. 'How fond are they of Morton, now? What say they to the doles he takes from Elizabeth of England? Are they still as much a league of the damned as ever – or does *our* gold begin to do its work there? Even a country clodhopper will know that, surely?'

David took a deep breath, and felt Patrick's urgent elbow in his side again. 'The Kirk, sir, is not concerned with gold, I think,' he said, as evenly as he might. 'The Lord Morton, I daresay, is otherwise. Certainly the Kirk and he are not the best of friends.'

'Ha! Relations are worsening between them?'

'Morton was never popular, sir – but he is strong. He has not sought to make the Kirk love him. It is its revenues he desires.'

'And the other heretic lords?' the Duke asked. 'Glamis? Ruthven? Crawford? Gowrie? Monsieur de Gray's father? They are ready to turn against Morton?'

'I cannot tell you, my lord. They do not honour me with their confidences!'

'Sir . . . !'

'My . . . my secretary's French, my lord duke, is but that of a St. Andrews tutor,' Patrick interposed hastily. 'He means no offence, no incivility . . . '

'*Mort de Diable* – he had better not!'

'Patrick is right, gentlemen,' the Archbishop of Glasgow agreed smoothly. 'There is little in looking for a silk purse out of this sow's ear! I think that we have had as much from him as we are likely to gain. Perhaps, hereafter, I may question him in his own tongue, and see if he knows aught else of interest to us.'

'Very well, Monsieur de Beaton,' the Cardinal of Lorraine said shortly. 'See you do it.' He glanced at Patrick. 'Monsieur de Gray, I conceive that Madame de Verlac will be quite desolated if she is deprived of your sparkling company for much longer. Which would be a pity, would it not?' And without a further look towards David, his crimson-clad Eminence turned and stalked out of the ante-room, his ducal brother following.

Patrick fetched a deep genuflection. David did not. He, however, caught the swift and significant glance that passed between his brother and James Beaton, before the latter quietly closed the door behind him.

David expelled a long breath, and looked at his companion. 'You have a deal of explaining to do, I think, Patrick,' he said.

'Perhaps. But not now, Davy, not now. You heard what His Eminence said? About the lady. And such, in Rheims, from its Cardinal-Archbishop, is no less than a royal command. I must go. Later, we will talk.'

'When? Where?'

'It, h'm, may be difficult tonight. Yes, a little difficult, Davy – much as I would wish to see you. It will have to be in the morning. Tomorrow – not too early, though, I pray you! Lord – do not frown so, man. In Rome, as I say . . . !'

'Your lodging, Patrick – shall I call there, then?'

'Er . . . no. No, that would be inadvisable, I think.'

'But I am your secretary, it seems . . . !'

'Och, Davy, what's in a word? No – I will call on you. Where are you lodging? Ah, yes – undistinguished, but it will serve well enough. I shall call on you there, then, at noon shall we say? Yes, yes – noon will be amply early. Till then, dear Davy, go with God!'

'And you?'

'I . . . I do not aspire so high!' Patrick laughed, touched his brother's shoulder, and slipped out through the same door as the others had used.

Brows knit, David Gray turned back to the open windows.

*

79

'And how is the Countess de Verlac this morning?' David asked. 'Or this noontide!'

'Somewhat smothering, I fear – distinctly overwhelming, for the time of day! Despite her years, she is a woman of great energy and determination, I find. Fine to look at, mind you – at a modest distance. But . . . demanding.'

'Then why in Heaven's name bed with her, man?'

'For three good and sufficient reasons, Davy. One – she esteems me highly, and has a delightful house. Two – she is the richest woman in Rheims, in all Champagne it may be. And three – her late husband was a Huguenot, and her own leanings towards the true faith are not considered to be quite whole-hearted.'

'And how should this concern you?'

'Ah, that shows how little you understand the French scene, Davy. The Guises are most anxious that the lady should remain devoted to Holy Church – in particular her resources. And I am of some small value to them, in this regard.'

'But why, in the name of mercy? What is it to you what her faith may be?'

'*Pardieu* – as a good adopted son of our universal Mother in Rome, I cannot remain unaffected – especially when my lord Cardinal is so concerned!'

'Patrick – you? Rome? You are a baptised Protestant. Received to the Breaking of Bread . . . '

'Ah – in Scotland, yes. But do not shout the glad tidings aloud, so, Davy, I beseech you! For this is not Scotland, see you – far from it. And I would remind you – in Rome, do as . . . !'

David stared at his brother. Today, he was dressed all in plum-coloured velvet, slashed with silver, the long plumes of his high-crowned hat falling down one side to balance the long thrusting rapier at the other. 'You . . . you have become a Catholic!'

'Only insofar as it was necessary. And only in France, my dearest Davy.'

'Only in France! Does God take note of borders, then?'

'I sometimes wonder! I wonder, too, whether the good Lord cares more for the Protestants who damn His Catholics, or for the Catholics who burn His Protestants! But . . . a pox, it matters not to me, either way. It was necessary, I tell you.'

'Necessary for what? Patrick – what deep game are you playing here in Rheims? With these arrogant Guises? All that questioning, last night? By the Cardinal. What does it mean?'

His brother glanced around him. They were in David's unsavoury tavern, but the only other customer, for the moment, snored in a far corner. 'Surely you can guess?' he said, still easily but his voice lower set. 'You know why my father sent me here, in the first place. Apart from getting me out of the way of the Douglases and Thomas Lyon – to learn statecraft and foreign affairs, you'll mind. Well, I am learning fast. To ensure that if so be the Catholics should triumph in this stramash, in Scotland and in England, both Grays should not be notably on the wrong side.'

'I heard him, yes – and liked it not. But surely my lord did not intend that you should go the length of turning Catholic yourself!'

'What he intended, Davy, is not of the first importance. To me! As I told you, I have my own way to make. I cannot live in my father's tight pocket – nor wish to. There are ample means for an agile and clear-headed man to make his way in this naughty world, and I see them palpably. Whilst most men are blinded by passion and prejudice, less handicapped souls may gain considerable advantages. Hence, the Guises, or good Beaton, and Mary Stuart.'

'What has Mary Stuart – what has the Queen to do with it?.'

'Everything, my dear brother. Don't you see – here is what our late lamented Master Knox called The Honeypot? She is that still. Even imprisoned in an English castle for years, she remains a honeypot, the lovely Mary; and the bees – and still more, the wasps – buzz around her everlastingly. There is, h'm, honey to be gleaned there in plenty . . . for the clear-headed beekeeper, don't you see – who is not frightened of a sting or two!'

'I cannot say that I do see, Patrick.' David's voice was more level even than usual, cold even. 'Mary the Queen, poor lady, is in dire need of the help of honest men, I think. I cannot see where your honey comes in.'

Patrick was quick to note that chilliness of tone. 'Of course, man – that is just it!' he exclaimed. 'She needs help. She needs friends who will work for her – who will guide affairs in the right direction. No harm if they better themselves in the process, is there? By using foresight and wit? That was my father's game, and it is mine likewise. Only, I play it rather more subtly, and for bigger stakes.'

'Your father was known as Mary's friend. Still is, even in the Kirk.'

'Precisely – a belief that has been of the greatest advantage to me, whatever it has been to him! See, Davy, I have made my way deep into the councils of the Marian party here in France. The Archbishop Beaton is Mary's personal representative – and he and I are close. The Guises are behind it – for Mary's mother was their aunt – and the ruling house of Valois against it. Or, at least, the woman Catherine de Medici and her nitwit son, King Henri. France and Spain together can get Mary out of Sheffield Castle if they will, and if Scotland plays her part in the north. Elizabeth dare not challenge all three at once.'

'Aye. But Scotland is Protestant – as is England. And France and Spain are Catholic – and would impose that faith on us.'

'That is the difficulty,' Patrick agreed. 'But not an insuperable one. Religion is not the only thing worth fighting over, Davy!'

'The Kirk, I think, will not agree with you. Nor Scotland itself . . . '

'That is where I believe you are wrong. Properly handled, suitably shall we say encouraged, in the right places, I think Scotland – even the Kirk – can be made to see where her advantage lies.'

'And yours?'

'And mine, yes.'

'You do not suffer from over-modesty, Patrick – not that you ever did, of course.'

'I do not. It is a fool's attribute – with all due respect to yourself, Davy! But I have good reasons for my hopefulness, I assure you. It is no mere day-dreaming. I am not, in fact, a day-dreamer at all, you know.'

The other sighed. 'I do not know, really, what you are,' he admitted. 'I . . . I sometimes fear for you, Patrick.'

'Save your fears, brother, for others who need them more.'

'I still do not see what you hope to gain?'

'Leave that to me, Davy. I can surely serve Scotland, and myself, at the same time?'

'Others have said as much – and forgotten Scotland in the end!'

'I will not forget Scotland, I think – not with you as my watchdog!'

'Aye – I think you will not forget Scotland yet awhile, at least!' David agreed grimly. 'Since I am to take you back there, forthwith.'

The other laughed. 'Poor dutiful Davy!' he said.

'They are my lord's sternest orders.'

'Poor my lord!'

'I tell you, he is deadly earnest in this. Moreover, Patrick, he has given the money wholly into *my* keeping, the silver you asked for, to pay your debts and bring you home. There is sufficient – but *I* spend it, not you! On my lord's strictest command.'

'My dear good fool – think you that carries any weight now? I have made other arrangements for such matters! I thought that I had explained that? Moreover, do not forget that I reach the notable age of twenty-one in but a month or two's time. Coming of age may not have made *you* your own master, Davy – but it will me, I assure you! And it is quite inconceivable that we should be able to tidy up our affairs and arrange the difficult business of travel to Scotland in a few brief weeks! No, no, I fear that you must reconcile yourself to a further stay in *la belle France*, Davy-lad.'

David's glowering set expression was more off-putting and determined than he himself knew.

'Not too long a stay, of course,' Patrick went on, quickly. 'Indeed, I have hopes that it may be quite brief. I have affairs in train, with Beaton, that should take our cause a great step forward – and soon. We only await word from Paris – we wait the arrival of the key, the golden key, that may well unlock Mary's prison doors eventually. Until then, of course, I cannot leave France. But when that does arrive – heighho, I am at your disposal, Davy. You will not be able to get me back to Scotland fast enough!'

'So, you refuse to obey your father's express orders, Patrick?'

'I do, Davy, since other people are relying on me, now. Father's own friend Queen Mary, it may be. And you can keep his precious silver. It will not take up a deal of space in your baggage, I warrant!'

'I have no means of forcing you, but I shall make it my endeavour to see that we do go, and very soon, nevertheless.'

'Do that, Davy – if you can! Meanwhile, we must find you somewhere better to live than this kennel.'

'I will not come and roost with you in your aged Countess's houes!' David told him stonily.

'*À merveille!* I had not planned that you should!' his brother laughed. '*Pardieu* – that would be most upsetting! I would not trust the old lady with you, and that's a fact. No – I think my former lodgings with Archbishop Beaton will be best – hardened Calvinist as you are! You will be able to talk theology and ethics with him, Davy, to your heart's content! Come you – the stink of this place offends my nostrils. *Allons!*'

Chapter Six

AND so David was installed in the house of the exiled Archbishop of Glasgow, at the very centre of the web of plot and
intrigue which was being assiduously spun around the future
and fate of the lovely and unfortunate Mary Stuart, Queen of
Scots. He came to look upon James Beaton as an old hypocrite
and inveterate schemer, but sincere in his love of his unhappy
mistress – and not nearly such a formidable character to deal
with, in fact, as his gloomy and lugubrious manservant and
mentor, Ebenezer Scott from Melrose, who ruled the seedy
establishment and disapproved of all comers.

David saw Patrick irregularly and less frequently than he
would have wished, but he saw a lot of others who frequented
the house in the Rue St Etienne at all hours of the day and night,
especially the night; largely English Jesuit priests and im-
proverished Scots adventurers, few of whom won his regard.
As a consequence of all this, he found himself to be adopting, at
times, a cloak-and-daggerish attitude, entirely out of character
and quite uncalled-for. He fretted and chafed at the waiting,
idleness, and delay – and could do nothing about it, that he
could see.

All Rheims, of course, lived in an atmosphere of intrigue,
suspicion and duplicity, under the surface splendour and gaiety.
The Guises seemed to attract plotters and schemers like
magnets; perhaps it was her Guise blood that was responsible
for Mary Stuart's fatal attraction for such folk. Only, the three
Guise brothers were themselves the most active plotters of all,
with a catholicity of interest, range and ambition that knew no
bounds. Beside this Stuart one, their schemes embraced the
Catholic League, their advancement in the Spanish Netherlands, the affairs of the Swiss Federation, even the destination of
the Crown of France itself – and well the Queen-Mother,
Catherine, knew it. Patrick had chosen richly troubled waters in
which to fish.

At least he seemed to enjoy his fishing. Without appearing to
be in the least secretive, he did not confide very deeply in David
as to his comings and goings, his plans and exchanges. He was
evidently adequately supplied with money, and his wardrobe

was as extensive as it was handsome; if he did not inform his brother as to the precise source of all this, neither did he once approach him for a penny of my lord's silver. He was always cheerful, if occasionally slightly rueful about Madame de Verlac's excessively exclusive demands, though admittedly he did not let such cramp him unduly. He talked happily of his growing intimacy with Charles, Duke of Mayenne, the third Guise brother, and where this might lead, and more than once referred confidently to the awaited arrival of the golden key that was to unlock Mary the Queen's prison doors. This latter much intrigued David, but being the character that he was, he could not bring himself to question his brother more urgently on the subject than Patrick was disposed to tell. It might indeed have seemed a moot point, sometimes, which was the prouder Gray – the heir to the title, or his bastard brother and supposed secretary.

This role of secretary appeared to David to be so ridiculous and obviously false as to arouse the immediate suspicions of all who heard of it. That no such doubts were in fact expressed, at least openly, may have been a tribute to Patrick's exalted friends, his known skill with a rapier, or merely the fact that Rheims was so full of curious flamboyant characters, furtive conspirators, and people who were fairly obviously not what they seemed, that one modest addition was quite unremarkable.

David had no gift for idleness, and found time to hang somewhat heavily, even though, as the weeks passed, Patrick took him about with him more and more, declaring him to be something of a protection from designing women, bores, and once – in a dark alley returning from a clandestine meeting with Leslie, Bishop of Ross, in Mayenne's palace – protection from unidentified masked bullies whose swords proved to be but a poor match for those of the two brothers.

To salve his conscience in some measure, David wrote a letter to Lord Gray, informing him that they both were well, that the difficulties of getting home from France were however formidable, that the financial situation was better than had been anticipated – a cunning note, that – and assuring my lord that they would be travelling back just as soon as it might be effected. That was true, in some degree, too. The shipmaster of the *Leven Maid* had not exaggerated. It was no easy matter to arrange a passage to Scotland. Elizabeth's gentlemen-adventurers, so-called, had more or less closed all the Channel ports, and were increasingly turning their attention to the trade of the west coast harbours, like Brest, Nantes and La Rochelle. Practically the only open route from France to Scotland now, save under strong convoy, was by the Low Countries and Amsterdam. With the Netherlands occupied by Philip of Spain's conquering armies, access to Amsterdam must be by their permission. The Guises undoubtedly could obtain that for whomsoever they would, but for the unprivileged traveller, the journey was next to impossible. David was wholly in Patrick's hand, in this. He wondered indeed how this letter would go, and how long it might take to reach its destination, but it seemed that Archbishop Beaton had his own curious channels of communication, and assured that, for a consideration, it would travel safe and fast along with more important missives. The writer's concern for its speedy delivery was, to tell the truth, mainly in the interests of getting news of his safety to Mariota his wife.

Patrick's twenty-first birthday was celebrated by a great entertainment and rout, given in his honour by the doting Countess de Verlac. All Rheims was invited that was worth inviting, and in the usual fashion of these affairs, it was practically open house. The Hôtel de Verlac was not so large and magnificent as the archiepiscopal palace, of course, but it was even more sumptuously equipped and plenished, and the Countess, for so important an occasion, stinted nothing. There were two score of musicians from Savoy; performing dwarfs from Bohemia; a curious creature that was both man and woman, very rare, borrowed from the Duke of Lorraine; and a series of tableaux, cunningly devised and most lavishly mounted, depicting classical scenes, with a climax of the Judgment of Paris, showing Patrick himself, clad only in a vine-leaf, in the name part, producing swoons of admiration amongst the women guests, and Hortense de Verlac, naturally, as Venus, even the most prejudiced having to admit that for her age her figure remained extraordinarily effective – though perhaps if more candles had been lit it would have been a different story.

It was just after this exciting interlude, with Patrick newly returned in a striking costume, wholly black on one side and pure white on the other, from the two sides of the ostrich plumes of his hat down to the buckles of his high-heeled shoes, that an alternative diversion developed, quite unscheduled. The dukes of Guise and Mayenne had been present from the start, but now their brother the Cardinal-Archbishop was announced, with the usual flourish of trumpets. Dressed as ever in crimson, but in the extreme of fashion, he stalked in, to the deep bows of all the assemblage save his brothers and David Gray – who was here merely as a sort of a supernumerary to Patrick and not really a guest at all. For once however, it was not His Eminence who drew all eyes, but the man who strolled smilingly in his austere wake.

Involuntarily, David looked from this newcomer to his brother. For, somehow, the two made a pair; were sib, as the Scots phrase has it; came from something of the same mould. Not that they were alike in feature. Where Patrick was darkly and sparkingly handsome, this man was goldenly fair, and glowed. Patrick was the more tall and slender, the more youthful; the other was a man nearing forty, perhaps. Though also dressed in the height of fashion, and richly, his costume did not challenge the eye as did the younger man's. But he had a similar personal magnetism, a similar smiling assurance, an ease of bearing and grace of manner that were the counterpart of Patrick's Gray's. David considered them both, thoughtfully – and was not the only person in that chamber so to do, for the affinity and similitude were such as must strike all but the least observant. Men so well-matched, so essentially alike apparently, do not always commend themselves to each other. The reverse is indeed the more likely.

Patrick showed no signs of anything but intense interest, however. David was standing close behind him, having brought in a lute on which his brother proposed to accompany himself while entertaining the company to a rendering of romantic Scots ballads. Patrick spoke out of the corner of his mouth to him, softly, without taking his eyes off the new arrival.

'It must be,' he said. 'It can be none other. Yonder, Davy – yonder is the key, I'll swear. The golden key I told you of. Yonder enters our fortune, if I mistake not. I had not known that he was . . . thus. So well favoured!'

The Cardinal held up his hand for silence. 'It is my pleasure to announce the Sieur d'Aubigny,' he said in his thin chill voice.

The visitor bowed gracefully all round as the buzz of comment and admiration rose, smiling with seeming great warmth on all, and came forward to meet his statuesque hostess, who had just appeared, rather more fully clad than heretofore, from her boudoir.

'Yes, it is he,' Patrick murmured. 'Esmé Stuart. Methinks I schemed even better than I knew! That one will open many doors, it strikes me – and smoothly. Heigho, Davy – I see us on our way home to Scotland soon enough even to please you!'

After a word or two with the Countess, the Cardinal brought the Sieur d'Aubigny over to Patrick. 'Here is your colleague-to-be, my friend – Monsieur de Gray, from whom we hope for much. The Sieur d'Aubigny, Patrick.'

The two men's eyes met, and held as they bowed. In that great room, indeed, there might have been only the two of them. Then Patrick laughed.

'Esmé Stuart is as peerless as is his fame!' he declared. 'I stand abashed. Scotland, I vow, like Patrick Gray, is to be esteemed fortunate indeed!'

The other's glance was very keen. 'I, too, believe that I have cause for congratulation,' he said, and his voice had a delightful throb of warmth, of patent sincerity. 'Indeed, yes. I also have heard of the Master of Gray – and am nowise disappointed.'

'I am happy, sir. Happy, too, that you have so nobly withdrawn yourself from the dazzling regard of Majesty, to come here!'

The other smiled faintly. 'Queen Catherine's embrace was ... warm!' he said, briefly.

'We heard as much – and honour you the more.'

The Cardinal, who had been joined by the two dukes, took each of the speakers by an elbow. 'We must find somewhere more private than this to talk, gentlemen,' he said. 'You will have much to say to each other. We all have. The Countess will excuse us for a little, I think, Come.'

All the room watched them go – and more than one figure slipped quietly out of that house thereafter. Here was news of which more than one source would pay well to have early word. David was left, with the lute in his hands.

He knew something of this man d'Aubigny, though not enough to account for all this interest. He was in fact one of the Lennox Stewarts, though he spelled his name in the French fashion, which had no letter W, as did Queen Mary. Nephew of the old Earl of Lennox, the former Regent, he was a cousin of Darnley, and therefore second cousin of King Jamie, who was Darnley's son by Mary the Queen. His father had succeeded to the French lordship of d'Aubigny, that had been in the family for five generations, had settled in France and married Anne de La Quelle. The son's reputation as a diplomat and statesman had of recent years grown with meteoric swiftness, and yet most people spoke well of him – no mean feat in such times. D'Aubigny was considered to be one of the most notable and adroit negotiators in an age when dynastic negotiation was involved and intricate as never before. He had only recently returned to Paris from a successful but particularly delicate embassage, in the name of the Estates of France, to the Duke d'Alençon. He was namely as a poet, as well.

Patrick was aiming high, undoubtedly – and presumably with at least some initial success.

David did not see his brother again that night, and the Countess's guests for his birthday party had to do without their ballads. The next morning, however, Patrick was round at Beaton's house in the Rue St Etienne most notably early for him, and was closeted thereafter with the Archbishop for over an hour. When he emerged, it was to summon David to ride with him to the Jesuit headquarters at Château St. Armand, a couple of leagues from the city. What his business was with the Jesuits, he did not divulge.

As they rode, Patrick waxed eloquent on Esmé Stuart. 'There is a man, for you!' he declared. 'Accomplished, witty, excellent company – but keen as a knife. I had not thought to be so fortunate when I proposed this project, Davy. The Devil assuredly, looks after his own!'

'Is it you that the Devil is looking after, Patrick – or Mary the Queen?' David asked.

The other laughed. 'As always, Davy, the doubter! Say, both of us! Perhaps it is his turn to do something for poor Mary – for the good God, you must admit, has not done much for her! Whichever it is, however, this time I think that there is some hope for her.'

'There have been projects and plots before, in plenty.'

'Aye, but this is no mere plot, man. This is a diplomatic campaign – statecraft, as my father would call it – a different matter altogether. I have put a deal of thought into it – and was not that what my lord sent me to France for?'

'Your golden key . . . ?' David prompted.

'Just that. See you – here it is. Morton is no longer Regent, though he still rules Scotland through young James, and the Privy Council which he dominates. But the difference is important, for whatever document has King Jamie's signature is now the law, whereas before it was Morton's signature that counted. Now, James is a sickly boy, and there is no accepted heir to the throne, save only his imprisoned mother – which means that the forces against Morton have no figure round which to rally. Provide that figure, and the country will round on the man who has battened on it for so long . . . with a little encouragement!'

'Provide an heir to the throne! A tall order that, surely?'

'Who better than d'Aubigny – Esmé Stuart? He is the King's cousin. First cousin to the late lamented Darnley.'

'But not of the royal house of Stewart. Of another branch, altogether. Henry Darnley was no true king – only given the Crown Matrimonial by Mary his wife.'

'Yet d'Aubigny is the King's near male relative. There is none nearer in Scotland, I think. And he has royal Stewart blood, too, for he is descended from a daughter of James the Second, on his father's side. He is legitimate – there are plenty otherwise, 'fore God! We could hardly do better, man.'

'You go too fast for me, Patrick,' his brother admitted. 'I do not take you, in this. What has it all to do with getting poor Mary the Queen out of Sheffield Castle, out of an English prison?'

'Plenty, man. Do you not see? Two things are necessary before Elizabeth can be made to release Mary. First, our Scotland must demand it, and seem at least to be prepared to back that demand with an army – Spain and France threatening the same. Scotland will never do that so long as Morton rules, for he is Elizabeth's tool, accepts her gold, and moreover hates Mary. Second, Elizabeth must no longer fear that Mary is planning to take her throne – that they do say is her constant dread, for Mary has more legitimate right to it than she has. But if Mary is no longer apparent heir to the Scottish throne – if our d'Aubigny becomes that – then she is no longer the same menace to Elizabeth. You must see that? Indeed, in order to keep Scotland divided, as is always her endeavour, Elizabeth might well agree to send Mary north to contest her rights against those of Esmé Stuart. If that could be arranged . . . !'

'Lord, Patrick – are you proposing that this d'Aubigny should rob Queen Mary of her right to her own throne, and England's too? For though she abdicated under threat, in favour of James, she is still in blood and before God and man, true Queen of Scots. A high price for her to pay, indeed, for opening her prison doors!'

'*Cordieu,* Davy – let me finish! That is not it, at all. There are more ways of getting past a stone wall than by butting your way through it with your head! Esmé Stuart has no wish to be King of Scots – or of England, either. Nor I to see him that. He is strong for Mary. It is all a device to bring down Morton, and to effect the Queen's release. Once that is gained, he will be Mary's loyalest subject. Think you that the Guises, Mary's cousins, would support my project otherwise?'

'Mmmm. As to that, I do not know,' David doubted. 'But ... how is all this to be brought about? I have not your nimble wits, Patrick. You must needs explain it.'

'Easily. We work on King Jamie, first. The boy has had an ill life of it – dragged this way and that between one ruffianly lord and another, Moray, Mar, Ruthven, Morton, without father or mother or true friend. Morton treats him no better than one of his own pages, they say. But they also say that the boy is affectionate, if shown a kindness. And shrewd, too, in a way, despite his quaking and drooling. Now, introduce Esmé Stuart, his own cousin, to his Court, to make much of him, flatter him, offer him the affection that he craves – Lord, Davy, don't you see? Jamie will be eating from his hand like a tamed bird, ere long, I'll warrant. We will see to that, the two of us!'

'And Morton?'

'Morton's grip is loosening. James is nearly fourteen. Morton will halt us if he can – but I have plans for that, too. Morton was deep implicated in Darnley's murder. Everyone knows that – but there was never any proof. In Edinburgh that winter, howbeit, I found a witness! Aye, I have a bone to pick with my lord of Morton, you'll mind! I think we can match him.'

'Faith, you fly a high hawk, Patrick! Is nothing too high for you?'

'I use my head, Davy. I told you – where most men are blinded by prejudice and passion, those who can preserve a nice judgment and a clear head may achieve much. Give Esmé Stuart – and your humble brother – a month or two with young Jamie, and we will have a declaration out of him nominating Esmé, his dear cousin, as his heir. And with that in our hands, the rest will follow as night follows day.'

'D'Aubigny is a Catholic, is he not? The Guises would never support him, were he not. Scotland – the Kirk – will never accept a Catholic as heir to the throne.'

'In the first instance, probably not. But we have considered that also. Esmé I am happy to say, is like myself – no fanatic in matters of religion! He is prepared to turn Protestant. This for your ear alone, of course, Davy – for our friends here might not like the sound of it too well!'

David looked with wondering eyes at his handsome brother, sitting his horse like a centaur. 'I do not know that I like it overmuch my own self!' he said.

'Shame on you, man – a good Calvinist like you! *Mortdieu*, you ought to rejoice at another brand like to be plucked from the burning – and such a notable brand, at that!'

The other did not reply to that.

'You will see now, Davy, why I could not just leave all and go home with you, at my father's whistle. Great things are toward, and since it was I who set them in train, I could not well abandon them to others.'

'So nothing now prevents us from going home to Scotland, with this d'Aubigny?'

'Nothing . . . save a letter. A scrap of paper. We cannot reach a king's Court, even such a king as our Jamie, without a royal summons. It is always so. And this has had to be sought with great secrecy, lest Morton get wind of it. We expect it any day now, however, for we have a friend at Court, who is privy to our project . . . and whom Morton himself appointed to be the King's watch-dog!'

'A gey slender thread that, I'd say, to hang your hopes on!'

'Not so. For James Stewart is an ambitious man, likewise – that is his name, a namesake of the King, James Stewart of Ochiltree, Captain of the King's Guard. He perceives that Morton is growing old and will not live for ever, and recognises that it is a wise man who makes due provision for the future! Moreover, he it is who was the witness that I spoke of, to Darnley's murder, and Morton's part therein. Why Morton advanced him, indeed! He was a page of Darnley's, then. A useful man, as I think you will agree.'

'And a traitor too, it seems!'

'The more useful for that, perhaps. But you are over-squeamish, Davy. We must use the weapons that come to our hands. Stewart has sent us word that he is confident of gaining the King's signature to our summons. We await it, daily.'

'So-o-o! You have been busy indeed, Patrick. I wonder how my lord will like it all?'

'My lord may like it, or otherwise, Davy – I care not. I am of age, and my own master now, do not forget.'

'And the siller?'

'Leave the siller to me, lad. I flatter myself that I have quite a nose for the stuff!' Patrick whistled a stave or two tunefully, and then turned to his companion. 'Dammit, Davy, you are a surly dog today! I vow you're no better than a crabbit auld wife.' Even so, he said it with a rueful smile.

David waited for a moment or two before he answered. 'Sorry I am if that is so, Patrick,' he said at length. 'I would not wish it that way – I would not. I daresay it is true. It is but . . . but my fondness for you, see you. You have started on a queer road, a gey queer road, that is like to be long and that we canna see the end of. I'd ask you to think well, Patrick, before you go further on it – out of the fondness that I have for you, I ask you. It is a road I'll not say that I like . . . '

'Whether you like it, or no, Davy, it is *my* road, and I am taking it. I am Master of Gray, thanks to our good father's curious tastes in women – not you! So be it – the Master of Gray will follow his own road. If you will follow it with him, so much the better – for we make a pair, Davy, and that's a fact. But if not, he takes it alone, and none shall stop him. Even you, brother! Is the matter clear?'

The other drew a long sigh, as he looked away from the brother that he loved so well, admired so greatly, and feared for so increasingly – and profoundly regretted, amongst other things, that the days when he could, as a last resort, drive some sense into that beautiful head with his two fists, were most patently gone for ever. 'Clear, aye,' he agreed, sad-voiced.

'Good. And do not sound so doleful, man. I promise you much diversion on our road – oh, a-plenty of it, 'fore God!'

'*Your* road, Patrick – not ours!' the other corrected, levelly, tonelessly. 'Is *that* clear?'

'I am sorry,' Patrick said, after a few moments.

They rode on in silence towards the Château St Armand.

Wherever their chosen roads were to diverge, at least the brothers' road home to Scotland was the same, and that road proved to be no smooth one. In the first place they had to wait for another two weeks before the hoped-for letter from Stewart of Ochiltree arrived. When it did, happily, it enclosed a not very impressive document, signed in an unformed hand by JAMES R, summoning his dear and well-beloved cousin Esmé, Lord of Aubigny, to his Court and Presence at Stirling, this fifteenth day of May in the fifteen hundred and seventy-ninth year of our Lord, together with his right trusty Patrick, Master of Gray, and such others as the said Esmé might bring in his train. Then, a further delay was caused by the non-arrival of six matched Barbary black horses, which the Guise brothers were contributing to the project as a gift for d'Aubigny to present to the young King, who was known to have a fondness for horseflesh, which no doubt he had found more to his taste in his short life than was the human sort. These brutes, though undoubtedly they would greatly help in producing a welcome reception at the Court of Scotland, were considered by the travellers as a major nuisance, not only for the delay, but because of the complications they must inevitably add to an already difficult journey.

Just how difficult it was to be, only began to dawn on David when, one day, Patrick informed him that they would be leaving the next afternoon. Not in any straightforward fashion, however. No farewells were to be taken, and their baggage was to be sent on secretly ahead of them. The Jesuits were looking after that; they apparently had their own efficient methods. Patrick and David would, in fact, ride almost due south, without d'Aubigny, supposedly on an evening visit to the château of the Duke of Mayenne, and only at dusk would they turn away north-eastwards towards the Meuse and Ardennes and the Low Countries. Meantime, d'Aubigny would have ridden, likewise without baggage, north-westwards towards Picardy, and would also turn east at dusk. Both parties would ride all night, changed into inconspicuous clothing, meeting at Sedan the next day, where their baggage would be waiting them. Sedan, on the border of France and the Netherlands, was in the centre of a Huguenot area, and so should be safe.

David thought all this was quite extraordinary, and taking the Guises' conspiratorial mentality altogether too far. Patrick explained, patiently. The Queen-Mother, Catherine, who still ruled France in the name of her feeble son Henri, was known to be against this project – and devilishly well-informed. She was automatically against any ambitious scheme of the Guises, though they were too strong for her to take open steps against them and she had to play them off against other divided forces in her kingdom. But in this instance she was particularly hostile, because of her abiding hatred of her former daughter-in-law Mary – and, it was suggested, of her personal predilection for Esmé Stuart's delightful company. At any rate, she had frowned on the entire Scottish proposal, forbidding d'Aubigny to leave her country. Catherine de Medici was not a woman to offend lightly, and Esmé was taking a serious risk in this matter. It was presumed that the Queen-Mother would not omit to take further steps to prevent him leaving France.

David thought that, surely, in this Guise country, an escort of the Duke's men would be sufficient to solve this problem?

It was not so easy as that, his brother assured. The Guises could not afford openly to challenge Catherine either. A clash between their soldiers and the royal forces was not to be considered at this stage. The Duke and the Cardinal were not going to embarrass their already delicate position over it – they had too many other irons in the fire. The start of the journey, they insisted, must be secret. That was one reason why the wretched horses were such a nuisance. Magnificent brutes, and six of them all matched, they would draw attention everywhere. So they must be split up. He and David would ride a pair; d'Aubigny and his man would take two more; and the remaining couple would be ridden separately by Guise minions to Sedan. Sedan had been chosen as the meeting-place because, being Protestant, the royal spies were less likely to infest it. Had it not been for the splendid horses, they might all have travelled as Jesuit priests, under the Spaniards' protection, right to Amsterdam.

God, forbid, David declared.

So, the following afternoon, nine weeks less a day after David's arrival at Rheims, he left it again, riding a very much more handsome and spirited mount, and only the Archbishop Beaton and his censorious servitor knew that their heretical guest would not be back again. With Patrick ridiculously overdressed for travelling, they rode southwards quite openly. Patrick indeed sang tunefully, and for once David joined in occasionally. Though heading in the wrong direction, they were on their way home.

At dusk, they hid in a wood, and Patrick changed out of his gaudy clothes into more suitable attire for riding, of excellent quality still but quiet and sober – David, of course, requiring no such metamorphosis. Thereafter, they rested their mounts for a while, and ate of the good fare provided by the kitchens of the Hôtel de Verlac.

'What does Madame the Countess say to the departure of her . . . her guest?' David asked, from a full mouth.

'Do you think I informed her?' his brother exclaimed. 'Lord, I would not wish to be in that house when she learns the truth, and that's a fact! Hortense is a woman of somewhat strong emotions, *tête Dieu*!'

'She has given you much, has she not?'

'Out of her plenty, yes,' he answered lightly. 'And I, for my part, have given her, of my modest store, more than I would!'

'I grieve for you,' David said.

They rode eastwards by north all that night, unchallenged,

through the low foothills of the Ardennes. It was more than twenty leagues, direct, from Rheims to Sedan, and by this route almost half as far again. Their horses were mettlesome and of fine stamina, however, and were not over-taxed. Patrick had had his route very carefully described for him, avoiding centres of population, choosing easy fords for the many rivers, and following roads which even in the summer dark they would be unlikely to lose. By sunrise they had crossed the Aisne, and by mid-forenoon were in Sedan, a strongly-defended city that allowed them entry as a pair of good Scots Protestants, Patrick's silver crucifix consigned to his pocket.

They found a modest tavern near the famous seminary that was already a place of pilgrimage for the Protestant world, and lay quietly there all day, resting themselves and their horses. In the late afternoon David slipped out on a reconnaissance, on foot, as the least conspicuous, and duly returned with the satisfactory information that he had located the Three Feathers Inn, that Aubigny and his man Raoul were there, with all four black horses. The city gates shut at sun-down, so they must all leave fairly soon, and by different gates. It was arranged that they should join up a couple of kilometres upstream where there was a passable ford over the Meuse during the dry summer months, that was not likely to be guarded. For this was the frontier. Once across the river, they were in the Netherlands.

Since to leave Sedan for open country immediately before the gates were shut might seem suspicious, they rode out, by the same gate through which they had entered, in the early evening, and turned southwards, unquestioned. There was considerable woodland along the riverside in that direction, in which they could wait until the shades of night made an approach to their ford as safe as might be.

While they waited thus, Patrick, after a certain amount of throat-clearing, came out with an intimation. 'Davy,' he said, his glance elsewhere, 'now that we are to be travelling in company with the Sieur d'Aubigny, I will have to ask you to address me with, h'm, less familiarity than is our usual, I fear. In his eyes, in the eyes of the world, you are but my secretary and . . . and attendant. I have told him that we are foster-brothers, but that is not a relationship that is much understood outside Scotland, I find. For the Master of Gray to be overfriendly with a . . . a retainer, might seem strange, you see . . . '

'You could always tell him the truth,' David mentioned, stiffly.

'I do not think that is necessary, or advisable.'

'I see. You do not wish me to call you my lord, or Excellency, by any chance?'

'Do not be stupid, Davy! Sir will be adequate. And another small matter. Since undoubtedly d'Aubigny's man will ride a little way behind him, not beside him, it will look a little strange if you do not do the same. So, hereafter, we shall ride two by two, myself with d'Aubigny, and you with his man. You understand?'

'Perfectly . . . sir!'

'It means nothing, Davy – between ourselves. You see that, surely? Just a . . . a convenience.'

'It means a deal, I think – the end of a chapter, brother. But so be it.'

When, a little later, they rode out of that woodland on their way through the gloaming, up-river, Patrick remarking that it looked like rain and a dark night, turned to find that his brother was not at his side. He was riding fully three lengths behind. When the former reined up, so did the latter.

'There is no need for this – yet,' Patrick said, frowning.

'Practice, they do say, makes for perfection,' the other observed. 'It would be a sorry matter, later, if through habit, I . . . inconvenienced you, sir.'

They rode on in silence thereafter.

It was David, however, who presently broke that silence. 'I think that they are behind us – the Lord d'Aubigny,' he said. 'I think that I heard the sound of hooves.'

They halted, and listened, but heard nothing save the murmur of the river and the rustle of leaves.

A little further, David again spoke. 'I heard it again. Or not so much heard, as sensed the beat of hooves. Many hooves.'

'It matters not,' Patrick decided, peering back into the gloom. A thin smirr of rain blew chill in their faces. 'The ford must be no more than a kilometre or so ahead. We will wait for them there. It may be that they are riding further inland.'

'Or others are,' David suggested.

However, when they reached the ford, easily identified by a ruined castle which had once guarded it on the French side, d'Aubigny and his servant were already there. They had all the baggage with them, loaded on the two extra blacks as well as on a pair of other beasts. D'Aubigny was a little anxious, for while waiting they had thought that they had heard the drumming of hooves, likewise. Patrick, however, was not of the anxious sort, and pointed out that there could be other parties than their own travelling war-torn France by night. But let them get across the ford, at once, by all means.

The crossing, in fact, was not difficult, for though the river was wide, the bed was of gravel, and the water never came higher than the horses' bellies.

At the far side there was a broad flood-belt of reedy level water-meadows, dotted with heavy foliaged trees that loomed monstrously out of the gloom. It was raining now fairly heavily, but there were no complaints on that score; the consequent darkness of the night was the more welcome. D'Aubigny, at least, let out a sigh of relief as they left the river behind.

'We are clear of the beloved France, at any rate!' he declared. 'Safe now, I think – if, *mort de diable*, there was ever any danger, in the first place!'

It was on the tip of David's tongue to remind him that what had been so easy for them to cross, was not likely to present any insuperable obstacle to possible pursuers – but he recollected his due place in the company, and kept silence.

It was only a few moments thereafter, however, before the Seigneur's satisfaction was rudely shattered. A rumbling pounding sound from over to their left turned all heads. The noise grew, and out of the mirk a dark solid mass seemed to thunder down upon them, across the grassland, on a broad front, the ground shaking under its approach.

'*Mortdieu* – back to the river!' d'Aubigny cried, tugging out his sword. 'It is an ambuscade!'

'No – forward!' Patrick shouted, 'This way!' and began to spur in the opposite direction.

David, behind with the man Raoul and the led-horses, peered, cursed, and then, straightening up in his saddle, laughed aloud.

'Mercy on us, it's just stirks!' he called out. 'Cattle-beasts, just. Come back, will you . . . sirs!'

Distinctly sheepishly the two noblemen reined in and returned, from their alternative directions. The meadowland, it seemed, was dotted with grazing cattle, and a group of them, as often happens at night, had come charging over inquisitively to inspect the new arrivals, and now stood a few yards off in a puffing, blowing, interested line.

In dignified silence the travellers moved on, David and the other attendant well in the rear, with an escort of lowing live-stock behind.

'Drive those brutes away,' Patrick shouted back. 'We do not want the whole world joining in!'

Beyond the meadows, the track eastwards rose up a gentle hillside through thick woodland. It was very dark in there.

After making a brief effort to discourage the cattle, David and the man Raoul were riding after their principals, when, mounting the first rise, David in the lead, abruptly drew rein. Before them, the track dipped down fairly steeply through a slight clearing, and this suddenly came alive with movement and noise and the clash of steel. Here were no cattle, but armed men assuredly, converging on both sides upon the two noblemen.

'Halt, in the name of the King!' rang out a peremptory command. 'Stand, I charge you!' The skriegh of drawn swords, many swords, was very audible.

David's hand flew to his own sword-hilt as Raoul came pressing forward.

'*Allons!*' the other cried. 'It is the Valois! *Peste* – come! Quickly!'

Almost David dug in his spurs to charge forward also – but on an instant's decision, his hand left his sword-hilt to grab at Raoul's arm instead. 'No!' he jerked. 'No – not now! It is useless. There are a dozen – a score. Too many for us. Better to wait. Wait, man! They will not see us here, in the trees. Wait, I say!'

'*Mon Dieu* – fool! They need us. Can you not see? Are you a coward? Come – *avant!*' And shaking off David's hand, the other spurred forward, drawing his sword.

Tight-lipped, David watched him go. But only for a moment. Then, tugging at his reins violently, and dragging his mount's head right round, he went clattering off whence he had just come, perforce pulling the four led beasts behind him.

Back down into the meadows he galloped, to the cattle which he had so lately driven off.

That main group was still fairly tightly bunched nearby, but many others were scattered in the vicinity. In a wide sweep David circled these, whooping, driving them inwards. Times innumerable, as a boy, he had herded my lord's cattle thus on pony-back, amongst the infinitely larger levels of the Carse of Gowrie. Skilfully he rounded up the startled snorting brutes, sword out to beat flatly against broad heaving rumps, the four led-horses by their very presence assisting. How many beasts he collected he did not know – possibly thirty or forty. There were more available, but he had no time to gather them. Back to the track through the woods he drove the protesting herd, and the steaming stench of them was like a wall before him.

Up the track between the tree-clad banks the cattle steamed, jostling, stumbling, half-mounting each other's backs, eyes gleaming redly, hooves pounding, and at their backs David Gray rode and beat his way and yelled.

At the top of the slope, he redoubled his efforts. Through the mirk and steam he could just make out the horsemen still clustered about the track below him, presumably staring up. Onwards down the hill he drove his plunging herd, in thundering confused momentum, and at the pitch of his lungs he bellowed in French, above their bellowing.

'God and the Right! God and the Right! A Bourbon! A Bourbon! A Condé!'

He kept it up as though his life depended upon it, straining his voice until it cracked. These were Huguenot slogans, he knew, heard on many a bloody field; the King's men below would know them all too well.

Whether indeed the soldiers down there were deceived into thinking that here was a large squadron of Huguenot cavalry bearing down upon them, in the darkness of the wood, or recognised it merely as a concentrated charge of many angry cattle, is not to be known. Either way, however, it was no pleasant thing to stand and await, in a narrow place. Right and left and backwards, the horsemen scattered, bolting in all directions to get out of the way. Shouts, vaguely heard above the thunder of hooves and the bellowing of beasts, sounded confused and incoherent, pistol-shots cracked out – but David's bawlings undoubtedly were the loudest, the most determined.

Down over the site of the ambush he came pounding, behind his irresistible battering-ram of stampeding cattle. 'To me! To me!' he shouted, now. 'Patrick! D'Aubigny! To me!' He yelled it in English, of course, in the excitement.

Peering urgently about him in the darkness and steam, David sought for his companions. He saw vaguely three horsemen struggling together part-way up the bank on his right, and glimpsed flashing steel. If they were indeed struggling, one of his own people must surely be included? Swinging his black off the track, and followed inevitably by the impressive tail of four laden pack-horses he headed up the bank, sword waving.

One horseman broke away from the little group as he came up, and went off higher, lashing his mount in patent anxiety to be elsewhere. The two remaining horses were very dark, and to his great relief, David discovered their riders to be d'Aubigny and his servant, the former supporting the latter who was evidently wounded. Both were disarmed.

'Quick – get down to the track! After the cattle!' David ordered. 'Hurry, before they rally. Where is Patrick?'

'I think that I saw him bolting – away in front,' d'Aubigny told him. 'In front of the cattle. Raoul's hurt. Run through the shoulder . . .'

'I . . . am . . . well enough,' the man gasped, clutching his shoulder.

'Can you ride? Without aid?' David demanded.

'Yes. I can . . . ride.'

'Quickly, then. After the cattle.'

Back down to the track they plunged, to go racing after the herd. Another horseman joined them almost immediately. In the gloom, assuming that it was Patrick, David was about to exclaim thankfully, when he perceived that the horse, though dark-coloured, had white markings. Thereafter, a slash of his sword in front of the newcomers' face was sufficient to discourage him as to the company he was keeping, and he hastily pulled out in consequence.

David began to shout Patrick's name, now, again and again, as they pounded along. His cries were answered, here and there, from the wooded banks – but none were in the voice for which he listened. It was not long before they made up on the cattle, the momentum of whose rush was beginning to flag.

The creatures slowed down still more notably as they came to an open glade, wide and comparatively level, where there were no banks to contain the track. Right and left many of the leading beasts swung off, others plunged on, others again wheeled and wavered, In a few moments all was a confusion of veering uncertain bullocks, snorting and panting, forward impetus lost. And at last, above the din, David's calling was answered. High and clear, from their right front, could be heard the cry 'Davy! Davy!' The cattle were not alone in pulling aside off that trench of a track, at first opportunity.

Swiftly David answered his brother's call, and, urging the others to follow him, pressed and beat a way into and through the milling mass of beasts.

Some few of the bullocks still went plunging before them, but the riders won through the main bulk of the bewildered animals – and there, in front of them, to the right, was a group of apparently four horsemen, waiting. Directly at these they charged – and the group was scarcely to be blamed for breaking up before them promptly, for though they were but three men, one armed and with one wounded, the others would be likely to perceive only a menacing mass of mixed cattle, horses and shouting men bearing down upon them. Moreover, Patrick, swordless, took a hand, kicking at other horses' flanks and lashing out with his fists.

Chaos seemed complete – but was not. The four re-united men, with the pack-horses, at least had purpose and a kind of order to them. David in the lead, they bored onwards through the trees unhalting, lashing their mounts, trending back towards the track and shedding their remaining bullocks, one by one, as they went. Thankfully they felt, presently, the beaten firmness of the roadway beneath their horses' hooves, and turned north-eastwards along it.

Only hard riding remained for them now – and they were almost certainly better mounted than would be any pursuers, on these Barbary blacks. The wounded Raoul was their weakness, but the sturdy Breton snarled that he was well enough, and would ride to hell if need be. Crouching low in their saddles, they settled down ot it.

Whether or no they were in fact pursued, they never knew. They had covered many kilometres of that road, and passed through a couple of either sleeping or deserted villages, before they deemed it safe to pull up, to attend to Raoul's wounded shoulder. About them, when they did halt, the night was wetly silent. Dismounting, David put his ear to the ground. No hint or throb of beating hooves came to him.

'*Dieu de Dieu* – we are safe, I think!' d'Aubigny panted. 'The King's men – or, rather, the Queen's – will not dare follow us far into this Namur, surely? *Peste*, but we were not so clever, Patrick!'

'I' faith, we were not!' Patrick agreed. 'Who would have thought that they would have followed down *this* side of the river? They must have known of our ruse, all along, but not dared to touch us near Sedan itself.'

'Or else got word of us in Sedan, and sent parties to watch the far sides of all the fords of the Meuse. It would be them we heard while waiting for you. *Pardieu*, Catherine is well-served, Patrick!'

'Aye – and so are we, I think! Davy – my thanks!'

David, examining the man Raoul's wound, shrugged. 'That

is unnecessary, your honour,' he said briefly. 'A mere exercise in farmyard tactics. I was, as it were, born to such!'

Patrick bit his lip.

David turned to d'Aubigny. 'My lord, I think that this hero of yours will survive. The bleeding is almost stopped. A clean thrust, I'd say – painful, but with no serious damage done.'

The Breton muttered something beneath his breath.

'Good. As well, praise the saints! Raoul, *mon ami*, it was a gallant attempt . . . though lacking in finesse, perhaps. Though who am I to judge, who did naught but lose my sword! Here is the paladin! Patrick, your Davy is a man of parts, I swear. That was notably done. He has a quick wit and a stout heart, damned Calvinist or none!'

'He is my brother,' the Master of Gray said slowly, deliberately. 'My elder brother.'

'But, of course!'

'No – not just my foster-brother, Esmé. My father's eldest son – only, conceived the wrong side of the blanket!.

'As though I did not guess as much, man! All Rheims, taking a look at the pair of you, said the same.'

Patrick's breath seemed to take the wrong route to his lungs, somehow, and all but choked him.

'He has my gratitude, at all events,' d'Aubigny went on. 'Here is my hand, Master Davy Gray. I shall not forget.'

'I thank you, sir. Do you not think that we should be riding on, nevertheless . . . if your lordships will forgive my presumption?'

'Davy, let it be, man!' Patrick all but pleaded. 'I am sorry.'

'He is right, Patrick. If Raoul is fit enough, we should no longer linger here. We cannot be sure that they will not follow us. This town, Montlierre, can be no more than a league or two ahead, where we are to place ourselves in the hands of one of Philip's captains. Until then, we cannot be assured of our safety.'

Getting started, thereafter, was difficult, with Patrick holding back so that his brother might ride alongside, and David doing likewise so that he should lie suitably behind – d'Aubigny looking on, eyebrows raised.

That, indeed, was to be the pattern of their subsequent journeying through the Low Countries to the sea at Amsterdam. The Guise letter of credentials, and the noble travellers' Catholic eminence and charm, might be sufficient to gain them safe conduct from Philip of Spain's occupying forces, but more than anything of the sort was necessary to soften entirely a stiff Gray neck.

Possibly the miller's daughter of Inchture had had almost as good a conceit of herself as had my lord of Gray.

The Scots are like that, of course.

Chapter Seven

THE brothers' long road homewards together finally parted at the port of Leith, in the estuary of the Forth and in sight of the great rock-girt castle of Edinburgh. Patrick, to the end, urged that David should stay with him, pleading the need, both of himself and d'Aubigny, for a secretary and esquire in their ambitious project. But David was adamant. His road was not Patrick's; he had to render the account of his stewardship to my lord, who had sent him; moreover, he had a wife and a bairn awaiting him at Castle Huntly, from whom he had been parted overlong already. He had no desire for a life of courts and cities and intrigue, anyway – his schoolroom and country affairs were amply to his taste. It was Castle Huntly for him, forthwith.

Patrick could have gone to Castle Huntly also, with d'Aubigny, and from there prosecuted the very necessary spying out of the land and enquiries before they descended upon the Court of King James at Stirling – for of course their appearance must be very carefully arranged and timed, with prior secrecy vital, lest Morton and his friends should take steps to nip all in the bud; but Patrick preferred to avoid his father's house meantime, and claimed with some reason that Castle Huntly was too remotely placed for gaining the essential gossip and information about the Court and the Douglases, and for making contact with the right people, to enable them to make their move at the best moment. He fancied rather his cousin Logan's house of Restalrig, between Leith and Edinburgh, for a start at least, where they could roost incognito meantime. Surely, never did two more incongruously and conspicuously eye-catching incognito-seekers land on a Scottish shore, Barbary blacks and all.

So David bade God-speed to his brother, with urgent but not very hopeful requests that Patrick watch his step for sweet mercy's sake, and offer as few cavalier challenges to fate as in him lay, and thereafter transferred himself to a coasting vessel which would sail for Dysart and Dundee at the next tide. He frowned a little as he went, for in his baggage he now carried an expensively handsome jewelled clasp for Mariota and a brilliantly dressed Flanders puppet for little Mary, just handed to him by Patrick, which must greatly outshine the length of cambric and the roll of ribbon that were to be his own humble gifts.

David rode on a very third-rate horse next day, after the Guise blacks, through fields of ripening corn in the fertile Carse, into a sinking golden early August sun, and his heart was full. Here was his own colourful matchless land, so much more beautiful and diversified than any that he had seen on his wanderings, with the blue estuary of the Tay, the green straths and yellow fields, the hills everywhere as background, rolling or rocky, cloaked in woods or decked in bracken and heather, and beyond all, the blue ramparts of the great mountains. He had scarcely realised how much he loved it all. Even the tall frowning castle on its jutting rock had its loveliness for him, the raw red stone-work mellowed by the sunset; or perhaps it was only what lay within its massive walls that made it beautiful for him.

He clattered into the courtyard, under the stern gatehouse, flung himself off his mount, and went racing up the stairway of the little schoolroom tower, to hurl open the door of Mariota's room – and find it empty, deserted. Not even their bed was there. As though an icy hand had clutched him, he ran back, down into the yard. A single man-at-arms sat in a sunny corner, cleaning harness. Of him he demanded where was his wife, his daughter?

'Och, they bide up in the main keep noo, Davy,' he was told. 'They're fine, man – fine. My lord's had them up there beside him a couple o' months syne, for the company, ye ken. Sakes – no' so fast, Davy. They're no' there, the noo. They're doon below – doon in the fruit garden, pulling berries . . .'

David was off hot-foot, through the postern-gate and down the steep stepped path cut in the side of the rock to the little hanging garden, dug out of a flaw in the cliff-face, with soil laboriously carried up from the plain below. The woman stooping over the berry-bushes, and the child at play beside her, made a pleasing picture in the chequered gold and shadow of the sunset.

Mariota heard him coming, and turning, stared. Then, with a cry, she dropped her basket, sadly spilling the fruit, and came running, arms wide. 'Davy! Davy my heart!' she sobbed.

Hungrily, joyfully, he took her to him, swinging her up off her feet, kissing away the tears of gladness, murmuring incoherent broken endearments, follies, questions. Tightly they clung, the man's fierce possessive strength a haven, a benison to her, the woman's warm rounded comeliness an exultation and a promise to him – until the insistent tugging at the top of his dusty riding-boot made David look down, to sweep up the child in one arm, laughing to her chuckle as she thrust a fat raspberry into his mouth. So they stood, under the towering walls, for the moment in bliss that the angels might envy.

Still holding the child, David put Mariota from him, a little. 'My dear,' he said, considering her. 'You are the fairest bonniest sight that my eyes have seen since I left this place, and that's a fact!'

'Not . . . not bonnier than the fine French ladies, Davy?'

He snorted. 'Them! The brazen painted hizzies! None of them had the looks of you.'

That was true. Mariota, at nineteen, was grown a very lovely young woman, fresh-coloured, gentle-eyed, tall and well-built, with nothing meagre or skimped about her. Something of this last, indeed, drew rueful comment from her husband now.

'At the least, lass, you have not dwined away for missing me! You are getting fat, I swear!'

She coloured, and dropped her glance. ' 'Tis . . . 'tis just that you . . . that Patrick is not the only . . . that you will be a father indeed, Davy . . . '

Here was further cause for embrace and joyful acclaim, more vehement on David's part, perhaps, than he realised. But in the midst of it, Mariota's gaze was over his shoulder, raised to scan the castle rock.

'Patrick?' she asked. 'Is he here? You have brought him?'

'No,' he told her briefly. 'He is at Edinburgh. My dear, my pigeon, my heart's darling – here is cheer indeed! Och, lassie – it's grand! I did not know . . . '

'He is not come, then – Patrick?' she said. 'But . . he is well? There is nothing wrong . . . ?'

He let go of her. 'Aye. He is well enough, never fear.' Rather abruptly he raised high the child whom he had still held within an arm. 'And see this fine lady! Is she not a fondling, an amoret? And as fat getting as her mother!'

Little Mary Gray was now four years old. She was a tiny laughing jewel of a creature, all lightness and beauty and dainty taking ways, and so uncannily like Patrick as to catch the breath. Though face and hands were stained with raspberry juice and her clothing was far from fine, she yet presented an extraordinary impression of grace and breeding and delicate enchantment. Emotions chased themselves across David's blunt features as he studied her.

'She is a cozener and a charmer, that one. Like . . . like her Uncle Patrick! Davy – why has he not come home with you? Is he coming soon? How does he look, now?'

'Older.'

'Aye, no doubt. It is three years and more since I have seen him.'

'And then, were you not only too glad to see the back of him?' David had not intended to say that.

'Yes, yes. Of course. I . . . I hate him!'

'You do not,' David said, heavily. 'Any more than do I? He sent you many good wishes – both of you. And gifts, too.'

'Ah – he did? Gifts, Davy? For me? For us?'

'Aye.' Her husband sighed. 'They are up there. Come you up, and get them.' A grey cloud seemed to have come over the face of the sun.

Up in the courtyard again, David handed over Patrick's jewel to Mariota and the doll to Mary – and neither having ever received such a present before, or dreamed of such a happening, their delight and excitement knew no bounds. In the circumstances, David let his own humbler gifts of cambric and ribbon more or less go in as make-weight, not even emphasising that they were from himself and not just more of Patrick's largesse. He was not good at this sort of thing.

The shadow passed, of course. Soon smiles and laughter were back.

David would have preferred to be back in their own little room in the corner-tower rather than in the fine chamber in which Lord Gray had installed the pair, but Mariota declared that it was a great improvement and that my lord had insisted on the move, saying that they must not be lonely whilst David was away. It was Mary, of course, who was at the bottom of it all. She and her grandfather were inseparables, and the child could do what she would with the irascible nobleman – which was more than could anyone else alive.

Lord Gray came back from Perth later in the evening, somewhat drunk, but loud in his demands to see his chicken, his little trout, his moppet Mary. The sight of David, however, especially minus Patrick, sobered him rapidly, and his son was haled into my lord's sanctum above the hall forthwith, the door shut, and questions hurled at him, thickly, incoherently, but with no lack of point or vehemence.

When he could make himself heard, David sought to explain.

He did his best for Patrick. 'He sends you all respectful duty and greetings, my lord – all reverence. But his affairs make it necessary for him to bide near to Edinburgh, for the nonce . . .'

'*His* affairs! A pox – *I* sent for him to come here, did I no'?'

'Aye, sir, but . . .'

'But nothing, man! I didna have him brought home to idle and bemischief himsel' in Edinburgh. You were to bring him here . . .'

'My lord, I brought him nowhere. Patrick is a man, now – of age, and, and his own counsellor. He came back to Scotland at your request, not at my bringing.'

'But with my siller, burn him!'

'Not even that.' David unbuckled the heavy money-belt that he had worn around his middle for so long, and put it down on his lordship's table, the solid weight of it thudding thereon significantly. 'There is your siller back, my lord – or the most of it. What has been spent of it was spent on *my* journeying – none on Patrick. He spends his own moneys now.'

'How may that be? Whence comes his siller – a young jackdaw with no penny to his name?'

David cleared his throat. 'He is that no longer, my lord. The years in France have changed him, almost beyond recognition. You will scarce know him. He has not wasted his time. You sent him to learn statecraft, and he has done it. He is very close to the Guises and Archbishop Beaton, and deep in their affairs. They trust him, wholly. He bears their despatches to the King, from the Duke and the Cardinal . . .'

'The more fools them, if they sink their money in Patrick, 'fore God!'

David did not comment on that.

'To the King, you said? To the Council, you mean, man?'

'Not so, sir – to the King. To young King Jamie, himself. And he has brought back with him the King's cousin. The Sieur d'Aubigny.'

He heard his father's breath catch. 'D'Aubigny? You mean . . . John Stewart's son, that was brother to old Lennox? Whe-e-ew!' All traces of intoxication were gone from Gray now. He stared at his informant. 'That man–some Frenchified outlandish name he has . . . aye, Esmé – that man, in Scotland, could be gunpowder, no less! He is ower near the throne, for safety.'

'I think that is why Patrick brought him. Patrick, I'd say,

finds gunpowder to his taste, my lord!' David told him, a little grimly.

His father took a limping turn or two about the room. 'I' faith, this requires thinking on, Davy,' he said. Then, swiftly, 'Does Morton know?'

'We hope . . . Patrick hopes not.'

'God's Body – *I* hope not, likewise! For if he does, he'll have the heads off both o' them! The young fool – to have brought that man here! It is as good as treason – or so Morton will have it! Don't you see it, man? This d'Aubigny, in Scotland, is like a dagger at James's throat . . . or a poison in his cup, more like! There is none nearer to the Crown's succession, in blood, save only that child Arabella in England. Morton will see him as a threat to his power over the King – and no man is that, in Scotland, and lives!'

David bit his lip. He had not realised what great danger Patrick had thrust himself into, with d'Aubigny. Put thus, he saw it clearly – and the picture of Morton that rose in his mind's eye, hurling that goblet smashing down the length of the table in the hall below, did nothing to soothe his new perception. 'He is as strong as ever – my lord of Morton?' he asked. 'Now that he is no longer Regent . . . ?'

'Foul fall him – of course he is! Who else, think you, rules? That slobbering thirteen-year-old boy, Jamie? Others who have tried are in their graves – Atholl, Mar, Lennox himself, Hamilton, even Moray. Morton's hand, if you look for it, you will find in the deaths of them all. He has the Council in his pocket still. Me, I havena dared show my face in the streets o' Edinburgh or Stirling for three years, man – no' since yon wedding-night. I never ride abroad with less than fifty men, for my life's sake. And I – *I* have done nothing against the man, save draw breath! And be a friend o' Mary the Queen, whom he hates. And now – this! Patrick hurt Morton sore, that night. Bringing this d'Aubigny to Scotland, I tell you, is as good as his death-warrant! The young fool!'

'I . . . I hope not, sir.' David shook his head. 'I misliked it, my own self. I said that he was flying too high a hawk . . . But I had not realised . . . Patrick believes, see you, that through d'Aubigny he may clip Morton's wings – aye, and gain Queen Mary's release also . . .'

'Precious soul o' God! Does the nestling clip the eagle's wings? What harebrained folly is this? What bairns' game have they been teaching him in France? Statecraft he was to learn . . . !'

'The plot seemed to be well worked out – with the Cardinal and the Duke and Beaton. The Jesuits, too, were in it, deep. They have sent money with him – much money, I believe . . .'

'Eh? Money? In Patrick's white hands? God be good – they must be lacking their wits!' But my lord's tone of voice had altered a little. He limped to the table, and picked up the heavy money-belt, weighing it in his hand, abstractedly. 'Jesuit money, you say? So that airt the wind blows! That is why he didna need his auld father's siller! Our Patrick's found bigger fools than himsel', eh?'

'Patrick is no fool, my lord, believe me. These years have done more for him than you realise . . .'

'Nevertheless, Davy, he has run his fool's head into a noose, here and now, by bringing this d'Aubigny to Scotland. Morton, with the power o' the Crown and the help o' Elizabeth's gold, holds the land fast.' Gray had dropped the money-belt and resumed his anxious pacing, and in that gesture David thought that he read proof that my lord, harsh-tongued and scornful as he might seem, was in fact fonder of Patrick than he cared to admit, more concerned for his gay and handsome son and heir than for the silver that he talked so much about.

'Morton has his enemies,' David said.

'Aye – in plenty. But they are powerless, disunited. That I ken to my cost.'

'That is one reason, I think, why Patrick has brought d'Aubigny – to give them someone to rally round . . .'

'A headless corpse will no' rally that many!' the older man declared, shortly. 'And that is what he'll be – and Patrick with him. As a threat to the Throne – treason . . .'

'Can Morton claim that? They have a letter from King James, summoning them to his Court.'

'They have?' Gray halted. 'Lord, how did they win that?'

'Through one, James Stewart of Ochiltree, Captain of the King's Guard – a friend of Patrick's.'

Unwilling admiration showed itself on Lord Gray's sagging face. 'So-o-o! Young Stewart? Old Ochiltree's son, and good-brother to John Knox! He is one o' Morton's own jackals.'

'One who is prepared to turn on the old lion, it seems.'

'Or to sell Patrick to him!'

'M'mmm. At least, he got the summons out of King Jamie.'

'For a price?'

'Presumably. Patrick did not inform me. But the summons to Court will make it difficult for Morton to accuse them of treason to the Crown, surely?'

'Maybe. But Morton has more than treason to his armoury. Poison, the dagger, a troop with swords, the cudgels o' a mob – it is all the same to Douglas. And there is no Glamis now, to lift a hand to help save Patrick, as Chancellor – even if yon business of his Elizabeth hadna scunnered him. He's dead. Slain, a year back. He left a new-born heir, thank God – so at the least the Master is no' the lord . . . '

'What is to be done, then? Patrick must be warned. I think that he does not understand all this, perhaps.'

'Warned, aye – if it isna too late. You must go to him at once, Davy. Bring him back here, secretly. Safer here, until we can make other plans.'

'And d'Aubigny with him?'

'A pox – no! Do you want us *all* brought low? Besieged in this castle? No – yon one must leave the country again, forthwith. Back where he came from, on the first ship for France. The only way for Master Esmé to come to Scotland is at the head o' five thousand French soldiers. God's name, I'd welcome him then!'

'I do not see them doing it, my lord – not after coming thus far . . . '

'Then you must convince them, Davy. Show them the truth. I think maybe this d'Aubigny will take heed for his own neck, if Patrick doesna. I will write you a letter for them.'

'Even so . . . '

'Davy, man, would you have your brother die, and no' lift a hand to save him?' It was not often that my lord referred to their brotherhood.

'No,' David sighed. 'As you will, sir.'

'Tomorrow, then. You'll be off in the morning. And pray sweet Jesu that you are in time.'

'And if they will not heed me? If Patrick will not come?'

'You will send me word at once, and bide with him to try to keep him out o' the worst trouble. Thank the good God that you at the least have a sensible level head on your shoulders, Davy.'

'Much good it does me!' that young man declared, sombrely, and went back to his wife. One night only, they were to have.

That was the homecoming for which David Gray had waited months.

Chapter Eight

'My lord is getting old, I think,' Patrick laughed. 'He was bolder once, if reports do not lie. Mary's friend in more than mere name! We must not encourage his unworthy fears, Davy. But we could nowise do as he says, in any case, for all is in train. Events move – they move. Or are moved! And, faith, we cannot turn them back, if we would!'

David turned heavily, determinedly, at his most levelly bull-like, to d'Aubigny. 'You, my lord – you have heard. My lord of Gray believes that you may have more regard to your own neck than perhaps has Patrick here. He bade me tell you that Morton is bound to win – and the penalty for losing will be your head. The heads of both of you. Morton still rules here – and kills.'

'Yes, Esmé, pay your due heed to our good sober councillor!' Patrick mocked.

D'Aubigny smiled. '*Mon cher* Davy, I appreciate your care and thought for us. And that of my lord of Gray. But we do not esteem your terrible Morton quite so terribly as do you. An angry vengeful savage, *vraiment* – like a bear. But even bears may be baited – when they provide sport for folk with more wits than themselves. I think Morton may well provide that sport. *Mortdieu,* even now, he begins to chase our ban-dogs, rather than ourselves!'

Patrick nodded. 'You see, we have not idled, Davy. We hope, before nightfall, to have a messenger from the Borders bring us the word that the bear has struck – at thin air. Then, heigho – it is Stirling for us, and the sunrise of youthful majesty!'

Mystified, David looked from one to the other. They were closeted in a room of the small but strong tower-house of Restalrig, the home of Patrick's cousin Logan, above its little loch, a mere mile from the royal but empty palace of Holyrood-house. From its windows they looked in one direction upon the long smoky skyline of Edinburgh, climbing up its spine of hill from palace to stern dominating castle; in the other, out over the smiling fields and woods and links of Lothian, down to the green cone of North Berwick Law and the scalloped sandy bays of the silver Forth. It was five days since their arrival from France, for it had taken David longer than he had hoped to make his return passage from Dundee.

Patrick explained. 'A well-lined pocket, I have found, will achieve much, Davy – especially in a land where so many men hate Morton. Two days ago, Cousin Rob Logan headed south for the Borders, where he has friends as you know – and Morton has both unfriends and lands. Lands in upper Teviotdale – Hawick and beyond. Around those parts are many Scotts and Turnbulls and the like – mere Border freebooters and rapscallions, but with a grudge against Morton for the Warden of the Marches he has set over them . . . and grievously short of siller, as ever. Last night, sundry houses of Morton's would be burning, I fear – so barbarous are the natives of those parts! This morning, at anyrate, Morton rode southwards hot-foot from his palace of Dalkeith – that we know from an eye-witness. Since it is his own Douglas lands that smoke, he has not just sent some underling. We but wait to hear that he is safely chasing Scotts and Turnbulls over the moss-hags south of Eildon – then Stirling and the King!'

'Our bear, Monsieur Davy, is decoyed, you see.'

'For how long?' David asked.

'Until, no doubt, he hears from the Master of Glamis, or other, that King Jamie has taken into his royal arms his dear cousin Esmé Stuart. Then, methinks he will come north again without undue delay! And by then, Davy, I hope that we will have a right royal reception awaiting the good Morton – with the aid of the Captain of the King's Guard. You see, we have not been entirely laggard, or as innocently witless, as our potent sire believes.'

David nodded slowly. 'I see,' he said. 'You will not give up your ploy, then, Patrick? You will not do as my lord says, this time either?'

'I fear not, Davy. Would you?'

'I do not know,' David admitted, honestly.

Patrick laughed, and jumped over to clap his brother on the back. 'Good for you, man – that from you is encouragement indeed! All will be well now, Esmé – for our Davy does not know! So usually, he knows all too clearly – and always against what I desire! It only remains for you to come with us, Davy, to Stirling, and our cause is as good as won! Be our secretary, guide, and mentor – aye, and our fervent intercessor with Scotland's Protestant God – and who can best us?'

David eyed his gay and beautiful brother steadily. These were my lord's own orders also, should he fail to get Patrick to abandon his project. It seemed that there was to be no connubial bliss for him at Castle Huntly yet awhile. 'I'll come with you if I must,' he said. 'Though, God knows, I'd rather be otherwhere.'

'Bravo! Esmé, you hear? The flagon, man. We'll drink to this, *tête dieu!* And now, Davy – what of the fair Mariota? And of that exquisite daughter of yours . . . ?'

D'Aubigny and David sat their mounts before the main gate-house of the great fortress of Stirling, with all the grey town in steps and stairs beneath them, the winding Forth, a mere serpent of a river here, coiling below, and the soaring ramparts of the Highland mountains filling the vista to north and west as though to make but doll's fortifications of these man-made ramparts nearer at hand. The six Barbary blacks, gallant, groomed and gleaming, sidled and stamped at their backs, for now, advisedly, the travellers bestrode less splendid beasts. The massive gates stood open before them, guarded by bored and insolent men-at-arms clad in the royal livery of Scotland – King Jamie's gaolers. The noon-day sun shone down on them, and on a fair scene. David wondered how many more such noons they might live to see.

At length Patrick came back down the cobbled roadway within the castle, strolling at ease and laughing, and with him a tall and resplendent figure, richly clad in gold-inlaid half-armour, with the red Lion Rampant enamelled on the breast-plate, and on his head a magnificent plumed helmet with the royal arms in gold embossed thereon. A handsome arrogant swaggering man this, a full head taller than Patrick and of a very different sort of good looks – bold, sanguine, aquiline, of age somewhere between Patrick and d'Aubigny. He looked the latter up and down, now, with undisguised interest if scant respect – and then his glance passed on to the horses behind, and more esteem was born.

'All is well, Esmé,' Patrick cried. 'Here is our good friend Captain Stewart of Ochiltree. The Sieur d'Aubigny, Captain. I suppose that, far enough back, you two are probably related?'

Stewart shrugged, but d'Aubigny was very gracious, assuring the other of his pleasure and satisfaction at the meeting.

'Our friend has arranged all,' Patrick went on. 'With notable effect. His Highness awaits us. He has arranged a formal audience, as being the safest plan in the circumstances – the more open our arrival at Court, now, the better. Not that there seems to be much danger . . . '

'None,' the newcomer announced curtly. 'I control the guard, and the King's person. My men are everywhere. No man in this castle will quarrel with James Stewart, and no message leaves but by my permission.' Stewart had strolled past d'Aubigny and David casually, and was stroking and running his eye over the black horses, but his fleeting glance flickered swiftly towards the two visitors. David, of course, he ignored entirely. 'A pair of these beasts will suit me very nicely,' he mentioned. 'This one, I think – and this!'

D'Aubigny stiffened, but Patrick caught his eye and an eloquent glance passed between them.

'His Highness may well so decide,' the latter said, quickly. 'It is most fortunate, is it not, Esmé – the Treasurer, my old friend the Master of Glamis, was at Court but two days agone, and is now returned to his castle in Angus. The Chamberlain is here, but he is elderly – next to a dotard, the Captain says. My Lord Ruthven is but new arrived from Perth – but happily, though one of Morton's men, he is also my mother's brother. The only other great lord in the castle is Glencairn, but he apparently is always drunk by this hour. So, allons!'

Sauntering with exasperating slowness, Stewart led them in under the gate-towers, up the cobbled roadway and through the inner walls, skirting the Douglas Tower and into the Palace quadrangle. At a strongly guarded doorway on the north side, the horsemen dismounted. Stewart was giving curt orders for the beasts to be led away and stalled, when Patrick intervened, explaining that they would prefer the blacks to be left where they were meantime.

Stewart frowned, but Patrick met his glare with an easy smiling firmness, and after a moment, the former shrugged again, and stalked on within. The three vistors followed.

Stewart was heading straight for great double doors, guarded by gorgeously apparelled men-at-arms, beyond the wide vestibule, and d'Aubigny realised with a shock that they were being taken directly into the presence chamber forthwith, just as they were. Hurriedly he protested, pointing out that they could not come before a monarch dressed thus, in riding attire, dishevelled and dust-covered after a forty-mile ride.

The Captain tossed a brief laugh over his shoulder. 'It matters nothing. He is but a laddie. There is no one here this day worth the dressing up for!' And he strolled on, to throw open the door.

D'Aubigny looked at Patrick, and then at David.

Stewart, with a perfunctory nod rather than an obeisance into the great room, spoke a few words to an elderly man stationed just within the doorway, and then beckoned forward the callers. For want of any instructions to the contrary, David moved onwards behind Patrick.

Their door opened half-way down a long high narrow chamber, somewhat dark because of the smallish windows of a fortress, the dusty arras-hung wood-panelling of the walls, and the smoky massive timbering of the lofty ceiling. To their left a number of people stood and talked and circulated in the lower end of the stone-flagged hall, at the base of which a wide fire-place held, even on this warm August day, a large fire of splutter-ing hissing logs – perhaps with reason, for it was a gloomy, chilly place within the thick stone walls. To their right were only three persons; two, halberdiers in royal livery and helmets, guarded two doors in the far wall; and near a raised dais bearing a throne of tarnished gilt with a sagging purple canopy, an ungainly youthful figure stood, in nondescript clothes, nibbling at a finger-nail and glancing nervously now towards the new-comers, now out of the nearest window.

The old man at the main door thumped with his staff on the stone floor. 'Your Highness,' he declared, in a high cracked voice. 'The Lord Esmé, Seigneur of Aubigny in France, to answer Your Grace's royal summons. The Master of Gray, likewise.' The Chamberlain looked doubtfully at David, sniffed, and added 'Aye.'

There was a pregnant silence, save for the spitting of the fire.

D'Aubigny and Patrick swept low in profound obeisance, graceful, elaborate. At their side, Captain Stewart grinned mockingly. Behind them David bowed as comprehensively as his stiff nature would permit.

The youth up near the throne made no move, other than to hang his head that was distinctly over-large for his mis-shapen body, and stare at the visitors from under lowered brows. He continued to bite his nails.

Straightening up, d'Aubigny and Patrick bowed once again, a little less low, but in unison, and then began to pace forward, Patrick a pace behind the other. David stayed where he was near the door.

James, by the grace of God, King, shambled over to the Chair of State, and sat uncomfortably on the very edge of it, where the stuffing was escaping from the torn purple cushion. At first glance he was quite the most unprepossessing boy that might be met with on a long day's journey, and the contrast with the two superlatively handsome, graceful and assured gallants advancing upon him was fantastic. Without being actually under-sized, he had a skimped twisted body, thin weak legs and no presence whatsoever. His mouth was large and slack, but even so it was not big enough for his tongue, which was apt to pro-trude and slobber. His nose was long and ill-shaped, his hair was thin and wispy; moreover, he did not smell altogether pleasantly. Only his eyes redeemed an otherwise repellent exterior – huge, liquid dark eyes, timorous, darting, expressive, but intelligent.

D'Aubigny went down on one knee before him, kissed the grubby nail-bitten hand that was jerkily extended towards him. Still kneeling, he looked up, and smiled, warmly, brilliantly, kindly.

'Your Majesty,' he said, low-voiced. 'Here is the greatest pleasure of my life – that I have travelled five hundred miles to enjoy. I am your very humble servitor, subject . . . and friend.'

'Ummm,' James mumbled. 'Oh, aye.'

Still d'Aubigny knelt and smiled, looking deep into those great frightened eyes. He saw therein the child who had been, a couple of months unborn, at the brutal murder of Rizzio; who a year later had screamed to the explosion at Kirk o' Field that blew up his father Darnley; who was taken from his mother the same dread year, when she ran off with Bothwell, and had not seen her since; who had known in this thirteen years no true friend, scarcely an honest associate or a kind action; the child who had been torn between ruthless greedy nobles, kidnapped, scorned, bullied, preached over, the pawn of power-seekers – yet the true heir of a line of kings that was the oldest in Europe, stretching back over a thousand years.

'May I rise, Cousin?' he asked, gently.

James had never been asked such a thing, before. He had never been spoken to in a voice so intriguing, so melodious, yet so friendly. He had never been smiled to, thus; he was used to being smiled *at*, mocked, when smiles came in his direction at all.

'Y-yes, my lord,' he said, jumping up himself.

'Do not call me that, Sire. I am your own true cousin, you know. Esmé. Esmé Stuart.'

'Aye. You are son of the Lord John who was brother to my grandfather Lennox.' That came out in a little gabbled rush.

Rising, d'Aubigny nodded. 'You have it exactly. I am much honoured, Cousin.'

'And you . . . you are legitimate. No' like the others.' Half-scared, half-defiantly, the boy blurted out. 'That's different, eh? You . . . you're no' after my crown, man?' A nervous snigger finished that.

The other's own eyes widened as he looked into those deep young-old brown eyes of the boy, and saw therein more than just intelligence. He raised a perfumed lace handkerchief to lips and nose, to give him a moment's grace. 'It is not your crown I seek, Cousin – only your love,' he said.

James stared at him – or rather, at the handkerchief. 'Yon's a right bonny smell,' he declared.

'Yours, Sire.' d'Aubigny said, and handed the trifle to him, bowing.

The boy put it to his big nose, and sniffed, and smiled over it, a fleeting smile at once acquisitive, cunning and simply pleased.

D'Aubigny turned. 'Here is my good friend and companion Patrick, Master of Gray, Highness,' he announced. Patrick, who had been standing back a little, sank down on one knee like-wise. 'Another who wishes you very well, and can serve you notably, I think.'

'Aye – he's bonny, too,' Majesty said, and thrust out the grubby hand again. 'You are both right bonny.'

'Your most humble subject, Sire – as was my father to your lady-mother,' Patrick murmured.

'Much good it did her!' the boy jerked, with a strange half-laugh. 'And you are Greysteil's nephew, are you no'?'

Rising, Patrick darted a quick glance at this strange youth, who was so uncommonly well-versed in genealogy. 'The Lord Ruthven was brother to my mother, yes, Highness – though I have not had word with him for years.' Something about the way that James had enunciated that ominous nickname of Greysteil, one of the men who had butchered Rizzio, warned him to go cautiously.

'Better no' let him see yon wee crucifix peeking out o' your doublet then, Master Patrick – for he's here in this room, mind! Or the godly Master Buchanan, either!' James said, low-voiced, giggling. 'Or they'll give you your paiks, I tell you!'

'H'mmm.' Patrick hastily moved a hand down the front of his doublet, which had opened slightly with his elaborate bowing, and tucked away the little silver cross that hung there. Only a tiny corner of it could have shown – which meant that those limpid dark eyes were as keen as they were expressive. He gave a little laugh. 'I am entirely grateful . . . and at Your Majesty's mercy now, more than ever!' he declared, but conspiratorially, almost below his breath. 'You can let me serve you – or tell the Kirk, to my sad ruin!'

He could not have chosen a surer road to the boy's heart and sympathy – and vanity. For James to hold power over someone was almost a unique experience, and delightful – especially over a handsome gentleman such as this – as was the thought of deceiving his dour Calvinist gaolers. 'I'll no' tell, Master Patrick – never fear!' he whispered. 'And I'm no' so much assured, mind, that the use o' symbols and sacred ornamentation is altogether contrary and displeasing to the mind o' Almighty God. For, see you, the Crown itsel' is a symbol, is it no', o' the divine authority here on earth. Aye.'

Both visitors blinked at this extraordinary pronouncement from the suddenly and pathetically eager youth, shifting from one foot to the other before them.

'Er . . . quite so,' d'Aubigny said, clearing his throat. 'Exactly, Your Highness.'

'I am greatly indebted to you, Sire,' Patrick declared, still in a suitably intriguing whisper.

Entering into the spirit of the thing, d'Aubigny murmured,
'*The fiery men of God's true Kirk, in ire,*
See in his Cross but timber for their fire!'

James stared, his eyes alight. 'You . . . you are a poet, sir?' he gasped.

'Say but a versifier, Cousin.

The name of Esmé, in the Halls of Fame
Shall ne'er be writ,
His Muse is lame
– and there's an end to it!'

'Och, man, that's grand!' the boy exclaimed, quite forgetting to whisper. 'I write poetry my own self,' he revealed. 'I . . . I canna just rattle it off like yon, mind. It takes me a whilie . . .

'True poetry comes only out of sweat and tears,' d'Aubigny nodded. 'That is where I fail, unlike yourself . . . '

He paused. The murmuring and whispering and stirring from the lower end of the chamber was growing very noticeable. Undoubtedly men there were becoming restive at this prolonged *tête a tête*. The elderly Chamberlain made no move to check the unseemly disturbance – indeed, his own glance at the trio up near the throne was distinctly suspicious as he strained his old ears to catch some hint of what was being said there. David, standing nearby, noted it all, perceived the hostility amongst the waiting throng – and also that the Captain of the Guard, for all his insolent-seeming lounging stance, was more tense than he appeared. As Patrick swept a glance around the room, and it met his own, David raised a hand, warning forefinger uplifted.

King James did not seem to notice; no doubt he was used to noise and hostility. 'I will write you a poem, Cousin Esmé,' he said. 'About you – aye, and Master Patrick here. Bonny men. And bonny France. The sun, they say, shines there a deal more than it does here?' He sighed a little. 'It will take me a whilie. I'm no' quick at it. And Master Buchanan gives me my paiks if I waste my time. Though poetry shouldna be a waste o' time, surely? You'll no' be gone, sir? You'll no' be away, that soon, before I get it done . . . ?'

'Indeed we will not, Your Majesty. We have come a long way, in answer to your royal summons. Until you send us away, we are at your disposal, Highness, and esteeem your Court to be our greatest joy.'

'Fine, fine. Give me but a day or two, sirs, and I'll have it ready. I vow I will. It will maybe be no' that fine, mind – no' in the French fashion . . .'

Patrick coughed, as James sought words for his over-large tongue. 'We must not weary His Highness, Esmé,' he said, almost imperceptibly jerking his head towards the other end of the presence chamber. 'We must not monopolise too much of his royal time. And there is yet the matter of the horses.'

'But, yes. Sire, we have brought a small gift for you from the illustrious Duke of Guise and the Cardinal his brother. A horse or two. They are without. If Your Majesty will deign to come inspect them . . . ?"

'Horses? For me?'

'Yes, Cousin – all the way from France. From Africa, indeed – from the Barbary coast.'

'Barbary! Eh, sirs – Barbary horses! For me!' The boy's excitement swelled up within him in slobbering incoherence. Then suddenly he began to chew at a slack lower lip. 'I canna,' he got out. 'I canna come. No' just now.' That was almost a wail.

'Cannot, Your Majesty . . . ?' d'Aubigny wondered.

'I'm no' allowed, man. I'm no' let to the stables until after my studies. Master Buchanan is right hot on that. He was hot against this audience, too. He wasna for letting me come – but Captain Jamie said he must.'

'I see. This Buchanan . . . ?'

'His Highness's tutor,' Patrick explained, one eye on the other end of the long apartment. 'The renowned scholar, Master George Buchanan, a pillar of the Kirk and lately Principal of Glasgow University.'

'And something of a tyrant, it seems?'

'He's a right hard man,' the royal student agreed, feelingly.

'Still, Sire, the audience is not yet over, is it?' Patrick asked. 'You can include therein the inspection of the presents that we have brought from the high and mighty princes of Guise, your mother's cousins, surely? It is a matter of state, I'd say.'

'I'm no' allowed, Master Patrick,' James repeated, miserably. 'I'd like it fine. But they'll no' let me out. I have to bow to them, and then go out the wee door at the back here. Master Buchanan's man is waiting for me behind there to take me back. I'm never allowed out the big doors.'

'*Mortdieu*, I think that you have not your Court entirely well arranged, Cousin!' d'Aubigny declared. 'I have visited many princes, and never have I seen it this wise!'

'Have you no', Cousin Esmé?'

'You are the King, Sire. You can do as you will,' Patrick put in.

'I wish I could, sir – but I canna . . .'

'I suggest, Esmé, that we prove to His Highness that his powers are greater than he thinks,' Patrick said, and laughed softly, easily, lest the boy be further affrighted.

'I agree. Sire, it is time that you asserted your royal self, I think. After all, you are nearly a man, now. You rule this Kingdom, for the Regency is at an end. Moreover, Cousin, I fear that their Graces of Guise might be much offended if they were to hear that you had not taken note of their gifts for hours.'

'Would they? Och, but . . . look – there's that Greysteil glowering at me, now! He aye glowers at me. He doesna like me, yon black Ruthven man. He'd no' let me past . . .'

Patrick laughed again. 'Leave you my uncle to me, Sire. Leave you it all to us. Just walk between us . . . and remember that you are the King of Scots in your castle of Stirling, and that fifty generations of your fathers have had their boots cleaned by the likes of William Ruthven!'

The King gulped, and looked from one to another, as they

took place on either side of him. Each lightly touched a bony elbow.

'We go look at your Barbary nags,' Patrick said. 'And there is no hurry, at all.'

So, together, the strangely assorted trio came pacing down the chamber, the two men at smiling ease, the boy in shambling lip-biting alarm. Great now was the stir at the fire end of the room. Men stared at each other, nonplussed – for there were no women present in this Court. The Chamberlain started forward, tugging at his beard and all but falling over his staff of office. Stewart of Ochiltree, all lounging past now glanced swiftly around, and especially over in the direction of one man at the front of the uncertain throng. That man did not look uncertain. Tall and lean, and hatchet-faced, in clothing more suitable for the hunt than a Court, of middle years, stooping a little, hawklike, he stepped forward determinedly. At the sight, the two escorts felt the boy between them falter and hold back.

Patrick spoke quickly. 'Sire – my uncle,' he declared loudly. 'We have not met with each other for years. Has the Lord Ruthven Your Highness's permission to greet me?'

Into the sudden hush that followed, the King's uncertain voice croaked. 'A-aye.'

'We are well met, my lord,' Patrick said immediately. 'His Highness has been speaking of you.'

'I am glad to hear it, Nephew,' Ruthven answered, in a voice like a rasp. 'I wouldna like to think that he would forget me! Nor you either, my cockerel! Where are you going?'

'The Sieur d'Aubigny, of the house of Lennox,' Patrick gestured. 'My mother's brother, the Lord Ruthven, one of the King's most faithful supporters, Esmé.'

D'Aubigny bowed, but Ruthven scarcely glanced at him.

'I said where are you going, Nephew?'

'His Highness is minded to inspect a gift of horseflesh sent to him by the Duke of Guise and the Cardinal of Lorraine. The suggestion is that you, Uncle, as a renowned judge of a horse, accompany the King and give him the benefit of your knowledge.'

There was a tense pause. Ruthven, who was a man of violent action rather than nimble wits, stared at his nephew from under beetling brows. Patrick gazed back, and meeting the other's fierce eye, lowered one eyelid gently but distinctly. Then, smiling, he turned again to James and pressed his elbow.

'Come, Sire,' he said. 'There is nothing that my lord does not know about horses.'

It was as easy as that. They moved on towards the door, and the terrible Greysteil, finding himself moving along behind, hastily strode forward to stalk alongside. The Chamberlain, at the sight of the four of them bearing down on him, hesitated and backed. Other men, with none of the great lords amongst them, stood irresolute. But Captain Stewart at least did not misjudge the situation. He raised his voice authoritatively.

'Way for His Grace!' he called. 'Aside, for the King's Highness!' And though on the face of it, his orders were for the guard at the door, none questioned the generality of their application. Men stood aside and bowed the quartet out.

David and Stewart fell in behind, and after a moment or two the flustered Chamberlain came bustling along also, to be followed by the entire throng.

Out in the quadrangle the horses stood where they had been left with the guard, the three nondescript saddled beasts and the six magnificent unsaddled blacks. At sight of them, James forgot his alarm, forgot the company he was in, forgot all save his delight in those splendid gleaming animals. He burst away from his companions and went running forward.

'Six!' he cried. 'Six o' them! Look – the bonny beasts! Och, they're bonny, bonny! And for me! You said they were all for me?'

Smiling, d'Abugny went strolling after the boy, calling reassurances.

Patrick elected to direct his attention upon Ruthven, however. 'A pleasant sight, is it not, Uncle?' he said. 'So much youthful enthusiasm! And enthusiasm in a prince, properly directed, can achieve much – can it not?'

Greysteil looked at him, broodingly. 'You're no' blate, Patrick – I'll say that for you!' he declared. 'You've a glib tongue in your head. But how long, think you, will you keep that head on your shoulders, man, playing this game?'

'I shall keep my head, never fear,' his nephew laughed. 'I use it, you see. As, I have no doubt, you are using yours. You know more than just horseflesh, I think?'

'I ken who rules Scotland, boy!'

'Who *ruled* it,' Patrick amended. He pointed. 'Yonder is the rule in Scotland, hereafter – the pair of them. The King and his cousin Esmé. Or shall we say Esmé and his cousin the King? It is a wise man who recognises a fact like that in good time!'

His uncle snorted. 'What think you Morton will say that that?'

'What he says is of small matter. What he *does* depends on who supports him!'

'The whole Council supports him, laddie.'

'Does it? Does Huntly support him? Does Erroll, the Constable? Does Herries, or Montrose, or Balmerino, or Sutherland . . . ?'

Ruthven spat on the cobble-stones. 'Papists!' he exclaimed.

'Are they? But still of the Council, even though they have not attended it of late! In letters to me, they indicate that they are thinking of taking a greater interest in their duties, Uncle!'

Greysteil said nothing to that.

'And the Kirk?' Patrick went on. 'Is the Kirk united in support of my lord of Morton?'

'The Kirk will no' support any Catholic Frenchie, I'll tell you that, boy!'

His nephew coughed. 'I have it on the best authority that Esmé Stuart has h'm, leanings towards Protestantism!' he said.

'God!' the older man commented, simply.

'The Guise brothers have been extraordinarily generous,' Patrick added, as though on another subject altogether. 'Not only in horses. They have entrusted me with considerable gold. As have . . . others. In the interests of amity and peace in Scotland, you understand. A noble cause, you will agree?'

Ruthven licked his thin lips.

'Elizabeth Tudor, I have heard, is finding her dole to Morton waxing unprofitable. She is thinking of cutting it off, they do say.' The younger man sighed. '*Pardieu* – the problems of steering the galley of state!'

His uncle was staring ahead of him, but not seemingly at the black horses. He appeared to be thinking very hard indeed.

Chapter Nine

THE conspirators could scarcely have chosen more effective means of gaining the young King's regard and confidence. He doted on horses, and hitherto had been allowed only a small stocky pony. He esteemed poetry as god-like, and d'Aubigny, no mean practitioner, had him enthralled. He was new enough to flattery, too, to be more than amenable to it; and Patrick never failed to remind him that, owing to the small matter of the crucifix, he held him as in the hollow of his royal hand. James was quite overwhelmed.

Indeed, the boy became almost embarrassing in his fondness, affection-starved as he was. He would scarcely allow either of them out of his sight – which had its disadvantages. He took a parallel delight in David also, whose plainness in appearance and manner no doubt came as something of a relief to the unprepossessing youth after the dazzling looks and scintillating converse of the other two.

But success for their plans depended on so much more than young James's reaction, vital as that was. On the whole, they were fortunate. In the absence of the youthful Earl of Mar, Hereditary Keeper of Stirling Castle, the Lieutenant-Governor, who might well have made difficulties, was not inclined to assert himself. He was a plain soldier, with no urge to meddle in politics or statecraft. He was undoubtedly impressed by the high birth of the visitors, and their authoritative manners. That he would not wish to offend Morton went without saying – but he was much under the influence of the strong-charactered Captain of the Guard, whom hitherto he had looked upon as a tool of Morton's. In the circumstances, he did not interfere.

The Chamberlain was actively hostile, but his duties were purely formal and gave him no executive power. The famous and scholarly George Buchanan, the King's tutor and Keeper of the Privy Seal, was crotchety and censorious, but at seventy-three, and ailing, was not in a position to challenge the new-comers. Moreover, he was known to hate Morton; their relations for long had been that of an uneasy truce.

As for Lord Ruthven, he disappeared from Court forthwith, with remarkable speed, discretion, almost stealth, for so spectacular a nobleman. There was no lack of suggestion as to where he had gone or what his errand might be. Patrick, however, was not greatly perturbed on that score.

It was, in fact, Stewart of Ochiltree who was the trouble. D'Aubigny disliked him from the first – which was scarcely to be wondered at, since the other made no attempt to be civil, much less respectful.

'That one is a surly dog, and too ambitious for our comfort. I think!' he told Patrick, whenever they were alone that first day. 'He has sold Morton – he will sell me, at the first opportunity . . . and yourself likewise, *mon ami.*'

'I would not deny it,' Patrick agreed. 'But not until it is to his advantage to do so. We must see to it that his interests lie with us – and suffer him meantime. Unfortunately, he is all-important to us. I like him as little as do you, Esmé – but we must have patience. We could not have done what we have done without him – nor do what we hope to do.'

'Then let us pray the Blessed Virgin that his manners improve!' the putative Protestant convert observed.

David, who was present, put in a word. 'Stewart is not just as he seems, I think. He is less confident, less sure of himself, than he would have you believe. I was watching him while you talked with the King. At the first, yon time. He was in a sweat, despite of his insolent airs. In especial, over the Lord Ruthven.'

'Say you so? That is worth knowing. Keep you your keen eye on him, Davy – watch him always.'

'If he is in a sweat over Ruthven, what will he be when Morton comes?' d'Aubigny wondered.

Always it came back to that – when Morton comes.

They were fortunate in being allowed five days of grace. Logan of Restalrig had done his work well – as indeed he might, considering the gold he had received. A courier from him reached Stirling the second day, saying that most of Teviotdale was alight, and the Armstrongs of Liddesdale had taken the opportunity to join in on their own account, as too good an opportunity for booty to miss. Morton was busy ranging the Border valleys, hanging men – ever his favourite pastime – though a little less spry about the ranging, if not the hanging, than in the past.

In Stirling no time was wasted. While d'Aubigny insinuated himself ever more deeply with James, Patrick wrote and despatched urgent letters, interviewed modestly retiring individuals in back-street taverns down in the grey town, and made one or two hurried visits further afield. David was sent secretly and in haste on the most important errand of all – across wide Perthshire indeed to the head of their own Carse of Gowrie. At Erroll he delivered a message to Andrew, eighth Earl of Erroll, head of the Hays and Hereditary High Constable of Scotland, and was closely questioned by that Catholic nobleman who, because of his religious convictions, had lived to some extent in retirement for years. David was less eloquent, undoubtedly, than were his brother's letters, for he had gained no noticeable enthusiasm for this entire project, and the thought of deliberately using his fellow-countrymen's religious beliefs against each other far from appealed to him; he had seen whither that could lead in France and the Low Countries. Thereafter, it was only with a real effort of will and no conviction at all that he turned southwards again, for Stirling; Castle Huntly and Mariota lay but a mere ten miles eastwards along the Carse.

The visitors from France were installed in a suite of rooms adjoining those of the King's own, in the half-empty palace wing of the fortress, where James could reach them and be reached at any time – gloomy old-fashioned quarters, of scant comfort, but the best available. They sent for their baggage from Restalrig, and even in their third-best French clothes made an enormous impression on the excessively dull Scots Court. D'Aubigny came to an arrangement with Master Buchanan whereby the royal studies were not to be too drastically interrupted; the tutor was grimly acquiescent, giving the impression that he found it hardly worth while to argue, when only a little waiting would resolve the matter.

Indeed, that was the general attitude, in Stirling. All men waited.

Then, on the fourth afternoon, Logan of Restalrig himself rode into the town at the gallop, with a score of tough Border mosstroopers at his heels. Only after a considerable clash of wills did Patrick prevail upon Stewart to allow this party, of what he named freebooters, within the castle precincts. Logan, a coarse, foul-mouthed, gorilla of a man, but namely as a fighter, brought the word that he had been racing Morton north from Teviotdale, and reckoned to have beaten the old sinner by half a day at least. The cat was out of the bag, at last. There would not be much more waiting.

There was no hiding the tension in the castle of Stirling that night. Patrick sent out hurried messages north and south.

According to Logan, Morton rode with his usual close escort of a hundred Douglases, only. He could raise a score of times that number if the occasion seemed to warrant it.

Despite the obvious need for closing the ranks, Stewart of Ochiltree was at his most arrogant and unco-operative. Perhaps he was merely frightened; perhaps he was beginning to doubt the wisdom of his change of sides? Even Patrick allowed himself to be a little put out by this. He came to James, down at the royal stables, where he was spending a deal of his time, with d'Aubigny, admiring, exclaiming over, even grooming, the six Barbary blacks.

'Your Grace,' he said, seeking to hide the urgency in his voice. 'I fear that it is necessary to make a gesture towards your Captain Jamie. To, h'm, bind him closer to your royal side. To indicate to him that your Highness's favour is . . . important.'

'Eh? Captain Jamie isna that much interested in my favour, Master Patrick.'

'He should be, He can be, Sire. It is essential . . . with my lord of Morton on his way here.'

At mention of that name, the boy seemed to shrink in on himself. 'He . . . he will send you away? The Lord Morton will no' have you here? He . . . he will give me knocks, again – hard knocks . . .'

'Knocks, Sire?' d'Aubigny raised his brows. 'Surely you cannot mean that Morton could strike you? Your royal person?'

'Aye, could he! Often he has done it. Hard knocks.'

'By the Mass, then he will do it no more, the ruffian! We shall see to that, Cousin.'

'And one way of seeing to it, Your Grace, is to ensure that Captain Jamie is your good friend, since he controls your guard. You should give him a present, Sire.'

'Eh? A present? What have I that Captain Jamie might want . . . ?'

'Plenty. For instance, Your Highness might give him a couple of these black horses. He has already expressed his admiration. for them.'

The boy's eyes widened, became huge. 'Eh? Give . . . my blacks! No! No – I'll no' do it!' The thick uncertain voice rose abruptly almost to a scream, as James started forward to the nearest horse. 'I'll no' give them!' he cried. 'They're mine, mine!'

Blinking, Patrick looked at d'Aubigny. 'Just two, Sire. You will still have four left.'

'No! Never! You'll no' take my bonny beasts! No, no, no!'

D'Aubigny hurried over to slip an arm around the boy's heaving shoulders. 'Never fear, Cousin,' he soothed. 'If they mean so much to you, no one will – no one *can* – take them from you. Forget it, Sire – it is all right. There are plenty of other gifts that you can make, after all.'

James had pressed his tear-wet face against the gleaming black flank of the horse. Sidelong, now, he peered up and round at his cousin. 'I'll no' give him my horses,' he declared, with tremulous stubbornness. 'But . . . but I havena anything else, Cousin Esmé. I've no other presents that I could give him.'

D'Aubigny laughed. 'You do not realise what you have to give, Cousin. You have more than anyone else. You are the King. You have lands and houses and castles and titles to give. Offices and privileges and honours. All yours, and yours only.'

'No' me. Yon the Lord Morton gives.'

'No more, Sire. He is no longer Regent. Nothing can be given without your signature. And anything given *with* your signature, stands.'

James turned round to stare at the speaker now, doubts, ideas, hopes chasing themselves across his ugly expressive face. 'Is that . . . true?' he asked. And he turned to Patrick to confirm it.

'Absolutely, Highness. All that is needed is Your Grace's signature on a paper, and the thing is done. Anything is done.'

'And . . . and I have lots o' . . . these things that I can give?'

'You have all Scotland.'

'Then . . . then, Cousin Esmé – I could give *you* a present!' That came out in a rush. 'Master Patrick, too. And Davy Gray, of course. What would you like, Cousin? Eh, man – what would you like?'

The two conspirators could not forebear to exchange glances. David, standing in a cobwebby corner by the hayforks, did not fail to read momentary naked triumph therein. But when d'Aubigny spoke, he shook his handsome head.

'No, no, James – nothing for me.' That was the first time that he had called the King merely James. 'Nor for Patrick either, I think. We are your true friends – we do not need gifts. Just for Stewart, the Captain. Give him something that will hold him fast.'

'I'd liefer give *you* something.'

'Another time, then. Later, perhaps . . . and thank you, James. Now – what for Stewart?'

Patrick spoke. 'The Master of Glamis,' he said, smiling brilliantly. 'The Treasurer. He has been amassing overmuch treasure of late, I hear. They tell me that he had Morton appoint him Commendator of the Priory of Prenmay, a year back, with all its fat lands and revenues. I suggest that you transfer the Commendatorship to Captain Stewart of Ochiltree, Your Grace.'

'C-can I do that?'

'Most certainly. It is all in your royal gift.'

'You wouldna like it for yoursel', Master Patrick?'

'I would much prefer, Sire, that Stewart had it. If I write you out a paper, will you sign it?'

'Aye.'

'Excellent, Your Highness. I think that we may rely upon Captain Jamie, hereafter!'

Late that night the uneasy fortress awoke to the clatter of horses and armed men, and shouts for admittance at the gatehouse. Patrick, fully dressed and unsleeping, was quickly down at the portcullis chamber – but only a few moments before the new Prior of Prenmay. They exchanged quick glances, in the gloom.

'Is that the Lord Morton?' Stewart demanded, of the guard. A large body of horsemen could be made out, beyond.

'No, sir. It is the High Constable, my lord of Erroll, demanding admittance to protect the person of the King's Highness. He says that it is his duty.'

'As so it is!' Patrick ejaculated, with rather more vehemence than was necessary. 'That is . . . well.' He sought to hide the relief in his voice.

Stewart turned to consider him, narrow-eyed. 'I had not known of this, Master of Gray,' he said slowly. 'I congratulate you. It seems that you have not idled.'

'Idleness has its delights – in due season, Master Prior. Time for that will come . . . for all of us,' the other answered lightly. 'Can I request you to have the drawbridge lowered?'

Stewart gave the order.

The Earl of Erroll, a grave middle-aged man of impressive appearance but few words, had brought with him seventy men and a dozen Haylairds. It was his hereditary privilege to keep the peace around the King's person, and so was the only man who might legitimately bring armed men into the near presence of the monarch – however many did so otherwise. His clinging to the old religion had cost him dear.

Patrick and Stewart, with David in attendance, had barely seen this contingent settled in quarters, when a further hullabaloo from the castle approaches brought them hurrying back to the gatehouse, wondering whether Erroll had arrived only just in time. It was not Morton yet, however, but the Lord Seton, with forty retainers, who had ridden hard from East Lothian on receipt of a message from Patrick. Seton was no Catholic, but he had fairly recently been ousted from the enjoyment of the revenues of the rich church lands of Pluscarden in favour of James Douglas, one of Morton's illegitimate sons. He was therefore in a mood for reprisals. He had been, of course, one of Mary the Queen's most staunch supporters, suffering banishment for her failing cause, and of late years living quietly at Seton Palace, taking no part in state affairs.

Stewart fingered his pointed beard as this company rode in under the portcullis. 'You cast a wide net, my friend,' he said to Patrick. 'I wonder at the diversity of your friends. Think you that they will make good bedfellows?'

'All unfriends of Morton are friends of mine, this night,' Patrick told him. 'And I would suggest that you consider not their diversity but that they come at all! Men who have not moved for years. Think you that they would be here if they believed that the tide ebbed against them?'

The Captain did not argue that. 'Are more to come?' he asked.

'One only, I think. There are others, but they lie too far off to reach here in time.'

'Your noble father?'

Patrick laughed. 'Where is my Lord Ochiltree?' he wondered. 'Fathers are safer kept in the background – do you not agree?' He did not require to amplify that, to point out that it was a short-sighted house which committed both chief and heir to the one side. 'what I wonder is . . . where is the Master of Glamis?'

Stewart frowned at that name – as he was meant to do.

It was a crisp autumn sunrise, however, before the red-eyed weary guardians of Stirling Castle saw the final company come climbing up the hill through the morning mists. No great cohort this, a mere score of riders perhaps – but the banner at their head widened Stewart's heavy eyes.

'So-o-o!' he declared. 'You fly yon carrion-crow, Gray! Beware that it does not peck your Frenchie's pretty eyes out!

It and its foul brood. They are nearer the blood, mind, than is your Monsieur.'

'My Frenchie is protected by a fine paper from such as these,' Patrick pointed out. 'The pen is mightier, as someone has said, than . . . h'm . . . than the implement that banner represents! What a blessed thing is holy matrimony, duly witnessed! Man, the Kirk and the Crown are united in love of it!'

The flag that they saw bore indeed the royal arms of Scotland – only with a black bar sinister slashing diagonally across it. Under it rode the Lord Robert Stewart, illegitimate son of King James Fifth, half-brother of Mary, uncle of the boy in the castle behind them. Rapacious, untrustworthy, fickle, he represented trouble. He was not long out of Morton's gaol, where he had been held by the Regency on a charge of treason, for years. He could bring no long tail of fighting men, since he had not the wherewithal to pay them, but he did his best with sons innumerable. Of the seventeen with him this morning, none were born in wedlock, and it was their father's boast that none claimed the same mother. They all required properties, lands, inheritances.

'A hungry ragged crew!' the other Stewart observed scornfully.

'Aye – but there is the witness to Elizabeth of England's doles, see you,' Patrick said. 'So the Guises assured me – and they are knowledgeable. He it was who brought them, at the first, they say. Heigho!' That was laugh and yawn mixed together. 'Now I am ready for the Douglas!'

They had plenty of warning – Logan's scouts saw to that. Morton had spent the night at Linlithgow Palace. The long presence-chamber, so much fuller of people than it had been for years, heard the distant echoes of the ominous cry, that had terrorised Scotland for so long, come drifting up from the town, and few there could repress a shiver at the sound. 'A Douglas! A Douglas!' the fell slogan rang out, and behind it the thunder of furious hooves throbbed on the warm air of noontide. In the long apartment hardly a man spoke.

Stiff, still, they waited as the noise grew and drew closer. Ears straining, they followed its progress, up out of the climbing streets, over the wide forecourt, drumming over the lowered drawbridge. Stewart the soldier had said keep the drawbridge up and the portcullis down – keep the man out; but the Master of Gray said rather let the man in, or he will turn at the closed gates, go and collect his thousands, and come back to batter them down. Doors open, therefore, they waited.

They heard the great clattering on the cobbles of the quadrangle outside, the shouts of men and the clash of steel. Patrick pressed a hand on the trembling shoulder of the boy on the Chair of State. No sound came from the entire room.

A hawking and a spitting came first. Then an angry bearlike growling, and heavy deliberate footsteps with the ring of spurs.

'Way for Douglas!' someone shouted outside, and from beyond scores of hoarse voices took up the refrain. 'A Douglas! A Douglas!'

Morton strode into the presence-chamber, scene of so many of his triumphs, took a few paces forward, and stopped dead, to stare around him. At his back came half-a-dozen Douglas lairds, and the Master of Glamis. No Lord Ruthven.

Quietly David and Stewart closed the double doors at their backs.

Morton had grown stouter, even more gross, since last David and Patrick had seen him, but lost nothing of his appearance of bull-like vigour. Clad carelessly in tarnished half-armour and dusty broadcloth he stood wide-legged, straddling, stertorously panting. If there was silver amongst the red of his flaming bushy beard, it did not show, nor in the untidy hair that stuck out from under his tall black hat. He glared about him, head and chin forward.

'Davy, request my lord of Morton to uncover, in the presence of the King's Grace.' Patrick's voice rang out clearly, pleasantly – the first words spoken in that room for some time.

David, needless to say, did not take that seriously, but as a gesture. He stood where he was, being a man of common sense. Morton emitted a sort of choking roar, and reaching up both hands, wrenched down the hat more firmly.

'A stink for the King's Grace!' he said, and spat on the stone flags.

Round all the great chamber he glowered – as well he might. Never before had he seen it thus. Armed men lined every inch of its lower walling, so that no space for another remained there, right round the throne-half of the chamber as well as the fire end. Some were in the royal livery of the guard – well spaced out, these, for Patrick did not altogether trust them – some in the red and white colours of the High Constable, the red and gold of Seton, others in the nondescript rusty morions and bucklers of Logan's mosstroopers, two hundred men at least. Silent, tense, armed to the teeth, they stood, their hostility like a palisade.

Morton's little pig's eyes darted on, ignoring the people at the lower end of the chamber, over those nearer to the throne – Erroll, Seton, Oliphant, Logan. At sight of the Lord Robert Stewart, they paused, and then passed on to where James, cloaked specially in the royal purple and wearing a chaplet of gold for crown, sat on the Chair of State and quaked. With an open sneer, he jerked his red head, to bring his lowering stare finally to the two brilliantly clad gallants who stood one on either side of the throne. Dressed in the lavish height of the French mode, d'Aubigny in golden satin, Patrick in white velvet with black, they looked like a couple of birds of paradise in a rookery.

Morton hooted, belched coarsely, deliberately, and then turned right round to look at Stewart, near the door. 'Clear me this rabble!' he snapped.

Stewart gazed straight ahead of him, motionless, wordless.

It was Patrick who spoke. 'Lord of Morton,' he said clearly. 'You have come unbidden into the King's presence – and remained covered deliberately. As a former Viceroy of the Realm you know the penalty for such. The Lord Constable is here to enforce His Grace's royal commands . . .'

'I do not talk with pap-suckers, nor yet prancing clothes-horses!' the other interrupted harshly. 'Erroll, you Pope's bottom-licker – this is rebellion!'

The Constable stared through and past him, and said never a word.

'Seton, you crawling louse – I ha' better things than you in my body hair! Is it banishment again for you – or the clasp o' my fair Maiden at the Tolbooth o' Edinburgh? Eh, creature?'

Silence.

'Robbie Stewart – whoreson! Fool's get! Beggar at my table! Was my last cell no' deep enough for you? Is it below ground you'd be?'

There was no answer.

'Precious soul o' God!' the Earl roared, and the entire room vibrated to the volume and the fury of it. 'Think you that you may remain dumb when Douglas bespeaks you? A fiend – I've plenty steel outby there to loosen the tongues o' you! Aye, a plenty. Will I have my lads in – eh?'

'Earl Morton, is that a threat of force in the presence of the King's Grace? Force and fear?' Patrick enquired, even-voiced.

'If so, you must know that it carries the punishment of immediate death, without formality of trial. And here is ample power and authority to enforce sentence – at once. Twice as many as your Douglas bullyrooks without!'

Morton drew a long quivering breath – but muttered only into his beard.

'Do we take it, then, that no threat was intended?' Patrick pressed, silkily.

'Not to Jamie, damn you – not to the King!' the older man spluttered.

'Ah! Good! Excellent, my lord. Nevertheless, I would counsel you to be more careful in your speech, in the royal presence, lest an unfortunate mistake is made – too late to be rectified!'

'Misbegotten whelp . . . !' the Earl began, when Patrick held up his hand.

'Silence, in the King's name!' he cried authoritatively, 'His Highness has something other against the Lord Morton than mere threats.' He drew a folded paper out of his doublet. 'Sire, is it your royal wish that I read this indictment?'

Dumbly James nodded.

'Hear you, then – by the command of the gracious and high prince James, King of Scots, King of Man, High Steward of Scotland, Lord of the Isles, Protector of Christ's Kirk – this! It has come to our royal knowledge that James Douglas, Earl of Morton, formerly our Viceroy and regent of our Realm of Scotland, has on occasions many received from our excellent sister, the well-beloved princess Elizabeth, Queen of England, certain moneys and treasure intended for the comfort and well-being of our royal self and person, it being inconceivable that the said princess should treat with and constantly enrich a subject not her own. And that the said James Douglas has wrongfully and treasonably retained the said moneys and treasure unto his own use and keeping . . .'

'It's a lie! A barefaced lie!' Morton bellowed. 'Jamie, they cozen you! It is lies – all lies!'

'. . . thereby grievously injuring both our sister Elizabeth and our royal self,' Patrick read on, without change of voice. 'Whereof we have witness in the person of our right trusty and well-beloved Lord Robert, Sheriff and Bishop of Orkney, who will testify . . .'

'Aye, I will!' the Lord Robert cried, stepping forward. Though dissipated, he had the typical Stewart good looks that had so woefully escaped his royal nephew. 'It is all true.'

'You forsworn lying bastard!'

'I was twice the courier who conveyed these moneys from Queen Elizabeth. Believing them for His Highness's Treasury . . . '

'Judas! Such as didna stick to your own accursed fingers!'

Patrick signed to the Lord Robert not to answer. 'This treasure, ofttimes repeated, amounting to many thousands of gold crowns, is therefore required at the hands of the said James Douglas, to be delivered without delay into the hands of our Lord Treasurer . . . '

'God's Passion! Are you all crazy-mad . . . ?'

'Furthermore, it being evident and assured that such ill measures against our comfort could not have been taken lacking the knowledge and agreement of our Realm's Treasurer, the said Treasurer, Sir Thomas Lyon, called Master of Glamis, is hereby indicted as being art and part in the said mischievous conspiracy . . . '

' 'Fore God – it is not true!' the Master of Glamis exclaimed, from behind Morton. 'I swear I know nothing of the matter, Your Grace!'

'Silence, sir! This is in the King's name. Accordingly it is our royal will and declaration that until such time as this indictment is duly and lawfully examined by our Privy Council, the said James Douglas, Earl of Morton, shall hold himself in close ward in his own house, nor enter our royal presence, under pain of treason, forthwith. Also that the said Sir Thomas Lyon, Master of Glamis, shall do the same, and is moreover hereby relieved of the office of Treasurer of this our Realm. Signed this day at this our Court of Stirling. James.'

For a few moments Morton's furious mouthings and trumpetings were quite incoherent, however alarming. At length he won consecutive words out of the chaos of his wrath. 'Jamie – Your Grace!' he cried. 'I demand speech with *you*. With your royal sel' – no' this fribbling babbler, this scented ape! It is my right – as an earl o' this realm . . . '

Patrick stooped, to whisper something in James's ear.

In a high-pitched nervous voice, the boy spoke. 'We cannot have speech with our royal . . . with any who remain covered in our royal presence.'

Cursing foully, Morton reached up and snatched off his hat, hurling it to the floor. 'It's lies about the money, Jamie,' he cried. 'It wasna for you, at all – never think it. A wheen gold pieces Elizabeth has sent me, now and again – but only for friendship's sake, see you. I did her a service once. Write and ask her yoursel', Jamie . . . '

Patrick was whispering again.

James stood up, having to hold on to the arms of his throne to keep himself upright. 'To accept doles from a foreign prince . . . within our Realm is in itsel' a, a treason,' he squeaked. Patrick prompted. 'Our Council shall debate o' it. Meantime our . . . our royal will is declared. You are in ward. Both o' you. You will leave our presence . . . no' to return. This . . . this audience is over.'

'God save the King's Grace!' Patrick called.

There was an answering vociferation from hundreds of throats. 'God save the King's Grace! God save the King's Grace!'

'Jamie . . . !' Morton exclaimed as the surge of sound died away – and there was pleading in that thick voice, for once.

Patrick, touching the boy's arm, James turned right about, to present his back to the room. 'My Lord Erroll,' he shrilled. 'Your duty!'

The Lord High Constable raised his baton of office. 'Earl of Morton . . . ' he began, deep-voiced – and at the sign every armed man in the great room took a jangling pace forward. It was not a very exact manoeuvre, for so close were they placed together already that the contraction in the ranks inevitably resulted in jostling and stumbling. But the effect was forceful and significant enough. The very walls of the presence-chamber seemed to contract upon the threatened figures.

Morton darted swift glances all around from red-fringed eyes. Already Patrick and d'Aubigny, their arms linked with the King's, were strolling towards the farther doors. 'Christ!' he said, and whirled abruptly around, almost knocked over the Master of Glamis, elbowed aside his gaping Douglas lairds, and went striding to the double doors. Captain Stewart opened them for him – and was rewarded by a stream of spittle full in his face. The Earl stormed out, shouting for his horses, shouting for many things.

When he and his had passed from view, all men in that room as it were froze in their places, silent again, listening. They heard a great confusion of voices, the well-known bull-like roaring, but no shouting of the name of Douglas. Then they heard the clatter of hooves, many hooves.

A great sigh of relief escaped from throats innumerable.

'*Magnifique! Splendide!* My congratulations, Patrick!' d'Aubigny exclaimed, laughing a little unevenly. 'You were quite impressive. Most dramatic, I swear. Our bear is baited . . . and retires to lick his wounds. Personally however, *mon ami*, I would have preferred our bear to be locked up – or better still, despatched forthwith. I would have had him on my cousin Darnley's business, right away. And saved time.'

Patrick shook his head. 'We are scarcely ready for that. Time is needed, there. Moreover – whisper it – I was not sure that our two hundred stalwarts would be so sure a match for his Douglases out there! Patience, Esmé – little by little is the way with bears. Anyhow, I vow he will never be the same bear again! Ah – but what is this, Sire . . . ?'

Majesty, between them, had burst into blubbering tears.

Chapter Ten

MORTON was not beaten yet, of course; it was not so easy as that. But he found it expedient to retire to his own great palace at Dalkeith – The Lion's Den, as it was called. And all Scotland rang with the word of it, in a surprisingly short time; all Scotland indeed, in consequence, seemed to flock to Stirling – or, at least, all that counted in Scotland – to see the new star that had arisen in the land, to test out the new dispensation, and to try to gauge for how long it might last.

A sort of hectic gaiety reigned in the grey old town under its grim fortress.

King James was by no means overwhelmed by this gaiety. Perhaps, having been dominated all his young life by the red shadow of Morton, he could not conceive of it being ever removed. Morton, and the fear of his vengeance, was at the boy's narrow shoulder day and night. Many of those who now thronged Stirling Castle had been Morton's friends, he swore – and doubtless still were. They were only spying out the land for the Douglas's return.

Only d'Aubigny could sooth him – Cousin Esmé, dear bonny Cousin Esmé, whom he had grown to love with a feverish and frightened and rather sickeningly demonstrative affection that caused titters, sniggers and nudging leers on all hands, but which David Gray, at least, found heart-wringing.

It was Patrick's idea, but Cousin Esmé's suggestion and advice, that a move would be the thing – a change of scene and air and company, a clean sweep. Let His Grace get out of this gloomy ghost-ridden prison of a fortress. Let him go to Edinburgh, to his capital. Let him set up his Court, a real Court, in his Palace of Holyroodhouse. Let him start to reign, call a Parliament, be king indeed. Let them all go to Edinburgh.

'Edinburgh . . . !' James quavered. He had never been to Edinburgh since he was a babe in arms, never been more than a few miles from this rock of Stirling. Clearly the notion was a profoundly radical one for him, full of doubts and fears as well as of intriguing possibilities and excitements. He stared. 'Edinburgh . . . Edinburgh is near to Dalkeith, where my Lord Morton lives, Esmé!' he got out.

'A fig for the Lord Morton, James! He will be the nearer, to keep an eye upon, *mon cher*. Edinburgh is the heart of your kingdom. If you will reign, it must be from there.'

'*Must* I reign, Cousin Esmé? Yet, I mean? Would you not reign for me . . . as my Lord Morton did?'

D'Aubigny moistened his lips, and could not resist a flashed glance at Patrick. 'Never, Sire,' he said. 'I am but your most devoted and humble servant . . . and friend.'

'But you could serve me best thus, could you no'? I wish that you would, Cousin Esmé.'

'How could that be, Your Majesty? I am but a lowly French seigneur – think you that your great Scots lords would bear with your rule through such as myself?'

'I could make you a great lord also, could I no'? I could, I could! I'd like to, Esmé.' Urgently, James came shambling over, to put an arm around the other's neck, and stare wistfully at his friend. 'I'd *like* to give you something – I would that! You said yon time that I had lots to give – titles and lands and honours. Will you no' let me give you a present, Esmé? I could make you a lord.'

'You are kind, James. But a title without lands and revenues to maintain it is but a barren honour. I am better as your humble d'Aubigny . . .'

'I could give you an earldom . . . wi' the lands and revenues. Could I no'?'

'Dear boy! But . . . ah, me . . . though I am humbly placed, I have my foolish pride, James. I come of a lofty line, all unworthily – your own father's line, the House of Lennox. Some new-made earldom might well suit many. But for me – ah, no! Leave me as I am, Sire.'

Those great liquid eyes lit with shrewder gleam. 'It is the earldom o' Lennox that you want, then, Esmé?'

'H'mmm. That would be . . . interesting. But . . . ah, no! Too much!'

'Unfortunately, there is already an Earl of Lennox,' Patrick mentioned, level-voiced for him. 'Esmé's uncle Robert, to whom Your Highness gave the earldom but last year.'

'Yon was my Lord Morton's doing, no' mine, Master Patrick. I but signed the paper . . .'

'A pity. Though, I suppose that a paper could be unsigned?' D'Aubigny yawned delicately. 'Not that it is a matter of any importance.'

'Aye, I could – could I no'? Unsign it? He is but a donnert

auld man, my great-uncle Rob. If I gave him something else...'

'I daresay that another earldom would serve him just as well,' d'Aubigny admitted, judicially. 'But ... *il ne fait rien*. It is a trouble for you, Jamie.'

'No, no. I would *like* to do it – fine I would, Cousin. You shall be Earl o' Lennox, I swear it.'

Again Patrick spoke, in the same cool tone. 'Parliament's agreement would be required to revoke an earldom already held, I think, Your Grace. It is not the same as making a new creation.'

'We were suggesting a Parliament, anyway, you will recollect, *mon cher* Patrick. In Edinburgh,' d'Aubigny mentioned lightly. 'Though the issue is hardly vital.'

'But it is, it is, Esmé. It is the first thing that I have ever done for you – you that have done so much for me. We shall do it. It ... it is our royal will!' James darted glances around like a dog that has barked out of turn. 'And then you can really rule for me!'

David Gray, from his corner, saw his brother consider the Stewart cousins long and thoughtfully.

And so, since Cousin Esmé, who was to be Earl of Lennox, advised it, the Court of the King of Scots was moved to Holyroodhouse.

David would have taken the opportunity to return to his own life at Castle Huntly, but Patrick was urgent that he should stay with them. He needed him, he said, more than ever, for the good Esmé was beginning to grow just a little bit lofty and difficult, and someone close to himself Patrick must have. David insisted on at least returning home to inform their father on the situation, since he considered himself still to be Lord Gray's servant, not Patrick's.

At Castle Huntly, however, my lord was just as determined as was his heir that David should remain at the Court; he did not for a moment believe that Morton had shot his bolt; he believed that Patrick needed his brother's level head more than he had ever done; moreover, it appeared to Lord Gray that the cause of the unhappy Queen Mary was tending to be lost sight of – and David should keep the urgency of that matter before his brother constantly.

After only a couple of halcyon autumn days with his Mariota and the little Mary, therefore, David turned his nag's head reluctantly westwards again for Stirling. A more unwilling courtier would have been hard to find.

The first snows were whitening the tops of the distant blue

mountains to the north when, on October the twentieth, the royal cavalcade approached the capital from the west. A dazzling company, for Scotland, they had passed the night at Linlithgow and now, thankful that, despite their escort of three hundred miscellaneous mounted men-at-arms, no assault by massed Douglases had materialised, they looked at the crowded roofs and spires and towers of Edinburgh, out of the blue smoke-pall of which the fierce and frowning castle, one of the most famous and blood-stained in all the world, reared itself like a leviathan about to strike. King James was staring goggle-eyed at this, declaring fearfully that it was still greater and more threatening than that of Stirling, when a crash as of thunder shattered the crisp autumn air, and set the horses rearing, all but unseating the boy on the spirited black, who cowered, terrified, as the crash was succeeded by another and another.

'Fear nothing, Sire,' Patrick called out, above the reverberating din, laughing. 'Those are but the castle guns saluting you in right royal fashion.'

'It's no' . . . no' my Lord Morton . . . ?'

'No, no. Those are *your* cannon.'

'But . . . but who are they shooting at, then?' James demanded, clinging to his saddle. 'Where go the cannon-balls?'

'No balls today, Highness – only noise. Blank shot.'

'A barbarous din,' d'Aubigny declared. 'But fear nothing, James – here is no danger, save to our ear-drums! But, see – folk await us before the gate, there.'

Pacing out from the archway of the West Port, and dwarfed by the soaring Castle-rock, came a procession of the Provost and magistrates of the Capital, bare-headed and bearing a great canopy of purple velvet and gold lace, under which Majesty, after listening as patiently as he might to a long speech of welcome, rode into the walled city. Crowds lined the narrow streets to see this strange sight – a king in Edinburgh again, after all these years. But they did not cheer. Edinburgh's crowds have never been good at cheering. The guns up at the Castle continued to make din enough for all, however – to the confusion and distress of the two ladies who, in allegory, contended for an unfortunate child before this youthful royal Solomon, who had to shout his judgment at them in between bangs. At the West Bow, a great globe of polished brass was suspended from the archway, and out of this descended a shivering child, as Cupid, naked but for sprouting wings, to present the keys of the city to the King. The infant's chattering teeth, fortunately or otherwise, prevented any speech, and the royal cavalcade pressed on. At the Tolbooth, in the long sloping High Street, however, Peace, Plenty and Justice issued forth, and sought to address the monarch suitably in Latin, Greek and Scots respectively, to the accompaniment of the incessant gunfire – which greatly upset James, who desired to answer back in the appropriate languages, and even, later, in Hebrew, when Religion, personified by a graver matron, followed on; for James, King of Scots, curiously enough, in bookish matters at least, was possibly the best educated youth in Christendom, thanks to the good if stern Master George Buchanan. There being no apparent means of stopping the loyal cannonry, frustrated, the royal scholar had to move on to the High Kirk of Saint Giles, where at least thick walls slightly deadened the enthusiastic concussions – though, before the ninety minutes sermon by Master Lawson the minister was finished, explaining, demanding and emphatically setting forth the royal duty of protecting the reformed religion of Christ Jesus, with thumps and bangs on the Bible to underline his points, James and his entourage were almost grateful for the explosive punctuations from the Castle.

Dazed and with splitting heads, the glittering company staggered out of church, to be led to the Market Cross, where a leering Bacchus in painted garments and crowned with garlands askew, sat on a gilded hogshead distributing slopping goblets of exceedingly bad wine, and an orchestra seemingly and necessarily composed largely of drums and cymbals, competed with the clamour of gunpowder. Almost in hysterics, James was conducted from these down the packed High Street again to the Netherbow Port, or east gate, where a pageant representing the sovereign's birth and genealogy, right back to the supposed Fergus the First at the beginning of the Fifth Century, was presented – and took some time, naturally, since each monarch in a thousand years was represented. The cannonade stopped abruptly, after some six hours of it, in the middle of the reign of Kenneth MacAlpine – presumably having at last mercifully run out of powder; though the entire city seemed to go on pulsing and throbbing to the echo of it for long thereafter.

At last, with sunset past and the figures of history becoming indistinct in the gloom, genealogy died a sort of natural death about the times of James the Second, and the bemused and battered and benumbed Court – or such of it as had not been able to escape long since – lurched and tottered in torchlight procession down the Canongate to the Palace of Holyroodhouse, and presumably a meal. Edinburgh had done its loyal best.

'My God!' d'Aubigny gasped, as he collapsed into a great chair in the banqueting hall, that happened to be the royal throne. 'My God, *c'est incroyable! Détraqué!* What a country . . . !'

'Would you prefer to return to France?' Patrick wondered.

'No! No – never that!' James cried. 'Och, Esmé – are you tired, man?'

'Our good Esmé is paying for his earldom!' Patrick observed.

Life at the great Palace of Holyroodhouse, under the green pyramid and red crags of tall Arthur's Seat, was very different from that in the cramped quarters of Stirling Castle. There was room and opportunity here for men to spread themselves, and Esmé Stuart, already being called Earl of Lennox though not officially so by ratification of the Council, saw to it that they did. He had James appoint him Lord Great Chamberlain and a member of the Privy Council, the former an office long out of use but which raised him above the elderly Court Chamberlain and put him in complete charge of the entire Court. And this was a very different Court from that of Stirling. Only those might attend who were specifically summoned – and the summons were made out by the Lord Great Chamberlain. Until the Council agreed to the appointment of a new Lord Treasurer, that vital office was in the hands of a deputy, a mere nobody, who did what he was told in the King's name; therefore the Treasury, such as remained of it, was available. Balls, masques, routs and banquets succeeded each other in dizzy procession – if not on the French scale, at least after the French pattern. Women appeared at Court in ever greater numbers, not just as the appendages of their lords, but in their own right, and frequently unaccompanied, a thing that caused considerable scandal and set the Kirk railing. The ladies all loved Esmé and Patrick, whatever they thought of the slobber-mouthed James – and Esmé and Patrick loved the ladies, but of course.

Patrick, however, in all this stirring Court reformation and improvement, devoted most of his efforts elsewhere. To Esmé's motto of 'a fig for Morton, *mon cher*,' he did not wholly subscribe; and he spent the majoirty of his time and energy at this stage seeking to circumvent and forestall any move on the part of the Douglas faction. Considerable funds were required for this purpose, since major persuasion was necessary in more directions than one; for while it was one thing to attend the new Court and enjoy the King's hospitality, as dispensed by the new Lennox, it was altogether another actively and publicly to turn against Morton, who sat like a lion ready to pounce from his den at Dalkeith six short miles away. Certain of the most essential personages in Patrick's plans demanded very substantial inducement indeed to throw in their lot with a régime which, on the face of it seemed unlikely to last overlong. The moneys which he had brought from France dwindled away like snow off a dyke – more especially as a gentleman at Court had to be adequately clad and appointed. Yet d'Aubigny – or my Lord of Lennox, as he preferred now to be called – was markedly unsympathetic, not to say niggardly, in this matter, making light of Patrick's fears and failing to put before the King the necessary papers for signature that would have opened the royal Treasury to his friend.

The fact was that now, Patrick – nor David either, for that matter – never saw James alone. Always Cousin Esmé was with him, delightful, amusing, friendly, inescapable. Both Esmé and Patrick had been appointed Gentlemen of the Bedchamber; but while the former's room adjoined, indeed opened into the King's bedchamber, Patrick found that he and David had been allotted rooms in the opposite wing of the palace, ostensibly on the King's command.

David not infrequently smiled grimly at the situation, and suggested to his brother that both of them would be safer and happier back at Castle Huntly.

Patrick and Esmé never quarrelled; they both needed each other and understood each other too thoroughly for that. It was rather that they seemed to be moving in different directions, their sights set at different targets, perhaps.

Patrick accordingly wrote urgent letters to the Guises, Archbishop Beaton, the Jesuits. Money he wrote about, but not only money.

More than once David spoke to his brother about the imprisoned Queen. Was poor Mary any nearer to her release, for their coming, or for all this expenditure of money? *Her* money – for it was largely the Queen's own French revenues that were being disbursed thus generously. Had Patrick not planned this entire project with a view to convincing Queen Elizabeth that Mary was no longer a menace to her throne and life, that Esmé Stuart was to be James's heir-apparent instead of his mother – at least on the face of it? Patrick admitted all that, and declared that it still stood. Only, Esmé now felt that it would be more practical to gain power in Scotland first, real power, which would make any announcement about the succession the more telling. This was not an issue that could be rushed . . .

The projected meeting of the Estates of Parliament was summoned at last, and on the eve of it Esmé Stuart arranged a great ball at Holyroodhouse, to which all those summoned to the Parliament were invited. No effort or expense was spared on this occasion, for it was important that all concerned should feel beholden to and enamoured of the young King and his new Earl of Lennox, in view of the nature of the enactments which the said Parliament was expected to pass the next day. Esmé, with Patrick's co-operation, excelled himself, and it is probably true that Scotland had never seen the like before. Nothing was stinted; decorations, illuminations, fireworks, musicians, entertainers, tableaux – at some of which the Kirk's representatives present all but had apoplexy – viands, wines, and bed-chamber delights for those so inclined. In imitation of the archiepiscopal palace at Rheims, Mary the Queen's fountain in the forecourt spouted wine – and good wine at that, even though such as men-at-arms, grooms and ladies' maids were not made free of it. The Treasury lid had been opened wide, this time.

The evening was well into its high-stepping stride, and the tableau which had been such a success at the Hôtel de Verlac, The Judgment of Paris, was just breaking up after a noisy reception composed almost equally of rapturous appreciation and howls of offended modesty, when there was an unlooked-for interlude. Patrick, in his brief and rather shrivelled vine-leaf, as Paris, was laughingly strolling off, with an arm round the delectable middle of Venus, and a hand cupping one of her fair breasts – suitably or otherwise, according to the point of view; Venus was not quite so authentically undraped as had been Hortense de Verlac – but on the other hand she was very much younger, and of a figure more slender and only slightly less magnificent. A Stewart, the Lady Elizabeth, daughter of the Earl of Atholl and new widow of the Lord Lovat, she was almost certainly the ripest plum yet to grace the remodelled Court, a bold-eyed, high-coloured voluptuous piece.

Down upon this charming couple strode a tall, handsome, and angry figure, unceremoniously cleaving his way through the cheering throng. It was the Captain James Stewart, of the King's Guard, and Commendator-Prior of Prenmay. Reaching them, he smote down Patrick's pleasantly engaged arm in most ungallant fashion.

'Unhand this lady, Gray!' he barked. 'Here is an outrage!'

All innocent amaze, Patrick stared at him. 'Eh?' he exclaimed. 'I' faith, Stewart – what's to do?' That was said into a sudden hush.

'Damn you – keep away from her!' the other jerked. And abruptly whipping off his short cloak which he wore in the fasionable style hanging from one padded shoulder, he cast it around Venus's upper parts.

Patrick gazed from him, downwards, and gulped. '*Mon Dieu* – you . . . you have turned her into a pretty trollop now, at any rate! Venus into . . . into Messalina lacking her skirts!' he gurgled. 'Oh, dear Lord!'

There was some truth in that. Venus's round pink hips, even with their wisp of net, and her long white legs projecting beneath the waistlength crimson velvet, somehow did indeed look supremely indecent.

The banqueting-hall rang to comment, delighted or scandalised, but all was outdone by the loud peals of clear laughter from the lady herself.

'Och, Jamie!' she cried. 'What a fool you are! Do you . . . do you think me cold? If so, you are wrong, I vow!' And she laughed again.

'You see,' Patrick said. 'You have mistaken the lady's requirements, Captain! She merits your apologies, rather than your cloak, I think!'

Wrathfully Stewart's hand fell to his rapier-hilt. 'Foul fall you, Gray, you Frenchified monkey!' he raged. 'Mind your tongue.'

At sight of that dropping sword-hand, David Gray, from his discreet corner in one of the great window-embrasures, started forward – to be restrained unexpectedly by a hand that clutched his sleeve quite firmly.

'Let them be, sir,' a cool quiet voice advised, at his side. 'Let them be. I know yon tall lad – and he is dangerous.'

'So I think!' David tossed back, jerking his arm free. He took two or three more paces, and then paused. Esmé and the King were hurrying over to the curiously clad trio in mid-floor, and everywhere men were bowing and women curtseying. David stayed where he was, meantime.

At the sight of the King, Stewart pulled himself together, and bowed stiffly, though his face still worked with passion.

149

Patrick sketched a graceful but capering obeisance suitable for a Greek hero, and the Lady Lovat, starting to curtsey, glanced downwards at her so spectacularly vulnerable lower parts, and then at the blushing faltering monarch, and tossing off the cloak, struck an attitude. James gobbled.

'Captain Stewart,' Esmé said coldly. 'I think that you forget yourself. Your duties in His Grace's protection do not require such dramatics!'

Stewart looked only at the King. 'I was carried away, Sire, by what seemed . . . offensive before Your Highness.'

'Och, it was naught but mumming, Captain Jamie,' James mumbled, keeping his thin shoulder turned on Venus. 'Master Patrick wasna meaning anything . . . '

'Besides, the Lady Lovat is affianced to my lord of, h'm March, is she not?' Well might the former d'Aubigny hesitate over that title. The earldom of March, like his own, was not yet ratified by Parliament; it was one of things to be done tomorrow. The lady's betrothed was indeed the elderly uncle of Esmé's, Robert Stewart, up till now Earl of Lennox, who had been persuaded to resign Lennox in exchange for this other title of March. 'What is she to you, *Monsieur?*'

The other did not answer that, though the lady giggled. He sketched another bow to the King, 'Have I your permission to retire, Sire?'

'Och, aye, Captain Jamie – but no' that far away, mind.' Majesty flickered his eternally anxious gaze around the crowded hall. 'You'll keep us safe guarded from the Lord Morton . . . ?'

Back at his window, David looked interestedly at the young woman who stood there alone, and who had sought to restrain him. She was dressed much less impressively than were most of the ladies present, but simply, tastefully, in ash-grey taffeta embroidered in silver, that went very well with her level grey eyes and sheer heavy golden hair.

'Your pardon, lady,' he said. 'I intended no discourtesy.'

'And I no presumption, sir,' she answered gravely. 'I but feared that, unarmed as you are, you might have fared but poorly with that long fellow. He is Captain of the Guard and an ill man to cross. And . . . and the Master of Gray can look after himself very well, I think!'

'He was not, h'm, clad for such encounter!' David mentioned.

She smiled, fleetingly. 'Perhaps not. Yet I think that the Master is fairly well appointed, however he is clad!'

'Umm.' He considered what that might mean. Both of them

had the same sort of level grey eyes.

'I was watching you, during yonder fool's-play,' she went on. 'I saw that you were concerned – and not for Captain Stewart, I think. Can it be that you are a friend of the beautiful Master Patrick?' Her glance, encompassing his own severely plain and inexpensive attire, seemed to question the possibility of such a thing.'

'Aye,' David said briefly. 'You could call me that.'

'Then, I think, my estimation of Master Patrick rises a piece,' the strange young woman declared.

Warily David eyed her. He had not seen her before, he thought. By her dress she might be a daughter of one of the country lairds attending the Parilament, or even the attendant of one of the great ladies; yet not in her style and manner, which was calm, assured, and spoke of breeding. He could not deny liking what he saw, whoever she was, and the cloak of secrecy and restraint, which he had come to wear like a second skin, drooped a little.

'I should not call myself his friend,' he amended then, rather stiffly. 'He names me his secretary. His servant would be more true, for I am no clerk.'

'Yet you do not look like a servant – nor sound one!'

'I am the Master of Gray's half-brother – but in bastardy. David Gray is the name.' He could not have stated why he told her.

'I see,' she said slowly. 'That accounts . . . for much.'

Mistaking her tone and pause, he flushed a little. 'I am sorry,' he said tartly. 'You should not be talking, Mistress, with a servant and a bastard. I . . .'

'And something of a fool!' she interrupted calmly. 'Who am I to look askance at bastardy or poverty, Master David Gray? Not Marie Stewart – even with her Queen's name.'

'Stewart? Another . . . ?'

'Aye. We are a prolific clan. In especial my branch of it! And not always over-particular – like yonder naked hizzy whom Master Patrick and Captain Jamie seem to find to their taste! I am the daughter of Robert Stewart, who tomorrow, for some reason that I have not divined, is to be made Earl of Orkney.'

David swallowed. 'You mean . . . the Lord Robert? The Bishop of Orkney? The . . . the King's uncle . . . ?'

'In bastardy!' she reminded, smiling.

'And you, you . . . ?'

'No,' she told him, gravely. 'By some chance I was born in

151

wedlock. One of the few! But that makes me no better – nor richer – than my bastard brothers and sisters.' She snapped slender fingers. 'So much for legitimacy! And now, Master David, since you are so close to the dazzling and all-conquering Patrick Gray, perhaps you will tell me why my peculiar father is being given an earldom tomorrow?'

'I . . . m'mm . . . I do not rightly know, lady. Save, it may be, that he testified against the Lord of Morton over the English bribes.'

'Rich recompense for biting the hand that once fed him!' she observed dispassionately. 'I believe that there must be more to it than that. Could it be that, bastard as he is, my father is near enough to the throne to rival . . . someone else? And so has to be bought off?'

David moistened his lips, uncomfortably. 'I do not know, your ladyship. I cannot think it.'

'There is talk,' she went on, 'of someone being named successor to our sorry young King – someone who has none of the royal Stewart blood. Could it be that since my father has the blood, even though illegitimate, he is to bought off with this earldom?'

'I do not know,' David repeated.

'And tell me, sir, should such indeed be true – about the succession – how long is my poor feckless cousin the King likely to live, think you?'

Shocked, David stared at her. 'You do not mean . . . ? You are not saying . . . ?'

'I but asked a question. I thought that the Master of Gray's secretary might have been able to answer it.'

This alarming conversation was interrupted by the arrival of the Master of Gray himself. Patrick, clad now in his silver-gilt satin, came sauntering up, smiling brilliantly right and left – but David knew, from something about his bearing, that he was upset.

'Davy,' he said, low-voiced. 'Where is Stewart? The Captain? I cannot see him. I must have word with him.'

'I would have thought that you had had words enough with him . . .' David began.

'Tush – this is serious. Stewart is too important a man to us to quarrel with – yet. And he is aggrieved already.' Suddenly Patrick became aware of the young woman at David's far side. He bowed, all smiles again. 'Ah, fair lady,' he said. 'Here is Beauty herself! And I am ever Beauty's most humble servant.'

'I doubt it, sir,' Beauty said briefly.

'Eh . . . ? You flyte me, madame. Beware how you flyte Patrick Gray!'

'I do not flyte you, sir. I do nothing for you – save prevent you seeking the Captain! He passed through yonder door into the ante-room, not long since.'

'Oh. Indeed. I see. Thank you. As I say, your servant. Come, Davy.'

'Fare you well, Master David,' she said. 'Though I doubt it . . . in the company that you keep! And trust not my father, earl or no earl!'

David shook a worried head, and hurried after his brother.

'Who was yon sharp-tongued jade?' Patrick wondered, making for the ante-room.

'The Lady Marie Stewart, daughter to Lord Robert, that's to be Earl of Orkney.'

'So-o-o! The beggar-man's brat – or one of them! So that is who she is? But she's handsome – I'll admit she's handsome.'

'May be. But I do not think that she likes you, Patrick.'

'Say you so? We'll see about that! You wait, Davy – wait and see!'

The Captain was not in the ante-room. They sought him in the long corridor.

'You said that Stewart was aggrieved?' David mentioned. 'Other than over the woman. What meant you by that?'

'There is bad blood between him and Esmé – our noble lord Earl of Lennox! You know that. Tomorrow Parliament is to assign the forfeited Hamilton lands that Morton has been enjoying, to Esmé, and h'm, in a small way, to my humble self. It seems that the Captain is something of a Hamilton himself – his mother was daughter to the Earl of Arran – an unlovely scoundrel to claim as grandparent! So now our warrior mislikes the dear Esmé the more!'

'With some reason, perhaps?'

'Reason, Davy, and the game of statecraft, are not related. Come, we must find our friend and soothe him with good words. Possibly even with some small Hamilton property somewhere. A pity – but we cannot afford an open rift. Not yet. Tonight's affair was folly – quite stupid. Over that strumpet! Already I have heard people whisper. We walk too delicately to seem to fall out. Or all is lost.'

'All being . . . ?'

'Why, Davy – the cause of the Queen. And the Master of Gray! What else?'

'I am happy that you remembered the Queen!'

'But of course, lad. Now, you take yonder stair, and I'll take this. We must find him, and quickly. He is a headstrong fellow . . .'

'*You* find him, Patrick – not I. Do your own soothing. I have better things to do, I think.'

'You have? You are going back to that wench of Orkney's?'

'Not so. To my bed. And I would to God that bed was at Castle Huntly!'

The next day, after a record short sitting, the Estates passed some godly business of the Kirk, redistribution of the Hamilton lands, ratification of the three earldoms of Lennox, March and Orkney, and the appointment to the Privy Council of the Lord Great Chamberlain and the Master of Gray. The Lord Ruthven, Greysteil, had arrived at Court unbidden, but coming to his nephew, attained entry – if not an enthusiastic welcome. He was a reformed man, it appeared. Now, most suitably, the Council appointed him Treasurer – a man with a good sound respect for money. Patrick, who undoubtedly arranged the nomination, declared that he lent the new régime both respectability and continuity, as well as a sound Protestant flavour – even though James and Cousin Esmé were less impressed. Morton, even if his shadow flickered constantly across the proceedings, was not once mentioned by name, even by Ruthven.

In a day or two, David did indeed return to Castle Huntly, to see his wife delivered of a fine boy. Almost without discussion and by mutual consent, they named him Patrick. In due course, even though he had promised himself otherwise, the proud father returned to the Court. He could not help himself, it seemed.

Chapter Eleven

MORTON was ill. Morton was dying. Morton was shamming ill, seeking to lull his enemies to carelessness. Alternatively, Morton was not ill but was planning to depart secretly to England, there to raise an army with Elizabeth's help, and return on its swords to power in Scotland. Morton planned to kidnap the King, send him to join his mother in an English prison, and rule as Regent again. Morton had attempted to poison the Earl of Lennox, who had the stomach-ache. The English Lord Hunsdon had arrived at Berwick-on-Tweed to organise the invasion of Scotland, to put Morton back into power . . .

So the rumours swept Scotland in the months that followed. Men did not know where they stood, where to place their allegiance. In the hectic gaiety of the Court at Edinburgh, uncertainty, fear, doubt, were always just below the surface. Yet Morton made no open move, lying omniously quiet at his Lion's Den at nearby Dalkeith. He *must* be ill. Or just waiting for his supplanters to destroy each other, or themselves, for him?'

The Earl of Lennox still claimed to care not a fig for Morton – but he had special secure quarters made ready for himself and the King in Edinburgh Castle, and the fortress stocked up to withstand a siege, plus a carefully worked out and secret method of escape from palace to castle, should the need arise. Moreover, a ship was kept in readiness at Leith, provided and crewed. That was the background to as brilliant a season as the old palace of Holyroodhouse had yet experienced.

The Master of Gray was somewhat better informed than most on the subject of Morton – as he ought to have been, considering the French moneys he disbursed for the purpose. He admitted once, of all people, to the Lady Marie Stewart, that the Douglas had indeed been ill, confined to his bed – to the young woman's prompt query of poison he made no comment. He admitted also that Morton had been sending couriers to Elizabeth, certain of whom had apparently called *en route* at a discreet house both going and coming back, with nteresting revelations. He agreed that Hunsdon had arrived at Berwick, and troops were being levied from the North Country English lords, for purposes unspecified. But when the Lady Marie had asked where all this was leading, Patrick only laughed, and advised her not to be over anxious – indeed, to leave anxiety to others, to whom it would do most good.

These confidences to the grey-eyed and calm Marie Stewart were not isolated, and represented an unforeseen but notable development. They coincided with a distinct and continuous cooling of relationships between Patrick and Esmé Stuart, also, with a parallel divergence of sympathies on the part of his brother David. Patrick, in fact, had to have a confidant always, and where one failed another had to be found. Why he should have chosen the Lady Marie is debatable; certainly she did not encourage him. Indeed, from the first she kept him at arm's length, not attempting to hide her hostility, distrust, and cool mockery – and obviously much preferred David's company. Perhaps that was part of her attraction: she represented a challenge, in her unaccustomed antagonism, and her curious partiality for his brother. Moreover, she was intelligent, discreet, and of a highly unusual quiet magnetism that served her better than the more obvious and spectacular charms of other of the Court beauties. And, because of her father's comparative penury, with the revenues of the Orkney Isles not yet fully organised, he and at least some of his multitudinous family had been granted quarters in the palace itself, and so she was fairly readily available.

Patrick appeared to feel himself compelled to lay siege to her, which might seem strange, since he not infrequently referred to her to David as 'the beggar man's brat' and 'that woman Stewart.'

David, for his part, liked her very well, and came to consider her simply as his friend – which, curiously enough, provoked Patrick into mocking mirth and barbed wit. He declared that simple friendship between a man and an attractive woman was a fable – and what would Mariota say?

Patrick did more than rail and confide and hint and laugh, of course. He was very busy, though even David knew but a tithe of all that he did. Especially in the vital matters of the Earl of Morton. A new subsidy from the Guises enabled him to subvert many who were very close to the Douglas himself – and Patrick had an undoubted nose for traitors. It was said that he had more spies in and around Dalkeith Palace than Morton had men-at-arms there – and many of these also were said to be bought, though rumour could lie. He enrolled large numbers of men to increase the size of the Guard, Captain Stewart co-operating – possibly with his own ideas as to their ultimate usefulness. This was before the days of standing national armies, but Patrick, by judicious friendships, favours and promises, provided at least the nucleus of an army, theoretically at call, from the armed bands of selected lords in Lothian and the borders – in the King's name, of course. He said – whatever he believed – that within twenty-four hours he could assemble four thousand men in Edinburgh . . . or to surround Dalkeith.

Esmé, Earl of Lennox, was busy too, though in rather different directions. He wooed the Kirk, publicly announcing his conversion to Protestantism, and humbly asked the Assembly to appoint one of their ministers to instruct him fully in the true and reformed Evangel of Christ Jesus. Master Lindsay, of Leith, was nominated for this important task. He hunted with James – well escorted – hawked with James, and wrote poetry with James. He produced masques from the compositions that he encouraged James to concoct, refurnished and refurbished the palace, personally designed the King's clothes and stocked the King's wardrobe. Nothing was too good for James, nor too much trouble – nor did the cost matter, for what else was the Treasury for?

As a consequence, James's love for his cousin grew and deepened, until it was the greatest factor in his life. Nothing could be done without Esmé, nothing decided, nothing even contemplated. And curiously, inconveniently, undoubtedly, if unforeseen, the accomplished elegant man grew fond of the shambling awkward boy. The lovers, they became known as – and tongues wagged unkindly, inevitably. Patrick was not concerned for James's morals, leaving that to others; but he was concerned for Lennox's usefulness to himself and his projects. He spoke to the other about the dangers of this so obviously burgeoning affection between man and boy, more than once – and earned no access of affection for himself thereby. To him the matter spelt complications, trouble – and he said so.

Incidentally, as another consequence of affection, Esmé gathered unto himself the rich abbacy of Arbroath, sundry royal and Hamilton estates in Lothian, Lanark and Carrick, the revenues from harbour dues at Leith, and the Keepership of Dumbarton Castle, most powerful stronghold in the West.

Not all of Scotland greeted these tokens of affection with acclaim.

Captain James Stewart, in especial, found the royal generosity excessive. His dislike of the Earl of Lennox waxed even stronger and more apparent – not that he ever had attempted to hide it. Scarcely a day passed without some incident between them – much to the King's distress, for he seemed to have some regard for his brusque and soldierly Captain Jamie also. Nevertheless, the latter would have lost his appointment and been banished from the Court long since had not Patrick insisted otherwise, that until the threat of Morton was finally removed, one way or another, Stewart's adherence was vital for them. After that, it might be different. The Captain, with great reluctance on Lennox's part, had been granted the Hamilton property of Kinneil, near Linlithgow. It markedly failed to satisfy him.

In the handsome new tennis-court at Holyrood which Esmé had installed for summer amusement, on the first sunny day of a wet July, a curiously mixed company sat in scattered groups watching a foursome in which Lennox partnered the King against Patrick and the Earl of Orkney – the former winning consistently, of course, for James did not like to lose. David was there, new back from a journey into the Highlands on the King's behalf, sitting on a bench beside the Lady Marie. Her elder legitimate brother, the Master of Orkney and Abbot of Kirkwall, sat with the Master of Mar, Keeper of Edinburgh Castle, waiting to play the winners. The Reverend Lindsay, Esmé's chaplain and preceptor, uncertain whether or not to disapprove of tennis, talked with Mr Bowes, Queen Elizabeth's new resident ambassador. And over in a far corner, part hidden by the shrubbery, Captain James was fondling the Countess of March – once Venus and Lady Lovat – whom marriage in no way incommoded.

'So you have come back, after all, Davy,' the Lady Marie was saying. 'You did not go home to your Mariota, as you threatened?'

'I had letters to bring back to the King,' David said, sighing. 'But I will go – and soon.'

'If Patrick will let you.'

'Patrick shall not, cannot, stop me.'

'Patrick can do most things that he sets his mind to, I think.'

'Most, perhaps – not all. As you yourself have shown him, my lady!'

She looked at him, in her grave way. 'No – I suppose that I

am the only woman at Court that he has not bedded with . . . as yet!' At David's frown, she smiled a little, 'You do not like the Court, the life of it, or the people at it, do you, Davy?'

'No,' he admitted, simply. 'Only you, of them all.'

'Thank you, sir – I am flattered! But you would be away from me to your Mariota, like a hawk released!'

He did not answer.

'You do not like what Patrick is doing, either, do you?'

'I do not.'

'And yet you love your brother, I believe.'

'Aye, I daresay. But that does not make me love his works.'

'No.' She paused. 'I do not think that you should go home yet awhile, Davy,' she said, at length. 'Even for your Mariota's sake. I think that you should stay – for Patrick's sake, for Scotland's sake, may be.'

'Eh . . . ?'

'Aye – if you love Patrick. If you love Scotland. I have watched you both, Davy, and I believe that you alone have any influence with Patrick. For he loves you also, you know. He is an extra-ordinary man, our Patrick. He is capable of great things – for evil or for good. He will do great things – already he is doing them. He is two men in one – and I fear that the evil may triumph. To the hurt of himself, and many.'

David turned to stare at her. 'You . . . you see deep, lady,' he said, trouble in his voice. Often, often, had he thought the same thoughts.

'I see a great responsibility on the broad shoulders of one Davy Gray!'

'What can I do?' he demanded. 'Patrick will not change his course one step, for me! Think you that I have not tried, reasoned with him? All my life . . .'

'And achieved more than you think, belike.'

'Achieved mockery and laughter . . .'

'Look, Davy, here is not time for small thoughts, small offence. Patrick is not engaged in small things – that is clear. He needs you at his shoulder. You may keep him from . . . from great wickedness. You may save him, as none other can.

'I . . . ? I am a mere servant, a humble attendant, no more . . .'

'Spare us the humbleness, Davy, for you are no humbler than I am! Less, I think. They say that we cannot escape our destiny.' She pointed into the tennis-court. 'Yonder is yours, is it not? Stay with him, and help him, Davy.'

He glowered straight before him, from under frowning brows.

'You . . . ,' he said. 'You have a great interest in him, in Patrick!' That was roughly said, accusatory.

'Say that I have a fondness for his brother,' the Lady Marie declared, even-voiced, and rising, moved over to speak to her brother.

David sat still, biting his lip.

The Earl of March came bustling into the garden, a foolish red lobster of a man. At sight of him, though his Countess did not still her squealing laughter, Captain Stewart arose, and came sauntering from the shrubberies. Seeing David alone on his bench, he came over and sat beside him.

'The Master of Gray plays a losing game out yonder,' he said, after a moment or two. 'If he takes not care, I think he may play a losing game elsewhere also!' That was ever the Captain James, blunt, scornfully to the point.

David made no reply.

'He rides the wrong horse,' Stewart went on. 'Yon prancing jennet is due for a fall – and will pull your fine brother down with him, man. He rears high, the Frenchman – over high. Your brother would be wise to bridle him . . . or find another mount!'

'You should tell that to the Master of Gray, sir, not to me,' David said.

'I will, never fear. And he would do well to heed me!' Stewart sat still, stretching out his long legs, and yawning.

The game was over shortly, in a handsome win for the cousins, and Patrick, after congratulating the King, came strolling over to David's bench, mopping his brow with a perfumed handkerchief – at which Stewart sniffed crudely. He sat down between them.

'Lord, it is warm!' he said. 'You look devilish cool, the pair of you. You should be warmer in His Grace's service – and play tennis!'

The Captain snorted. 'I like to win my games, Gray!' he jerked. 'Not play second to a French mountebank!'

'Hush, Captain! Can it be that you speak of my lord of Lennox, High Chamberlain of Scotland, Abbot of Arbroath, Keeper of Dumbarton?'

'Aye, none other. Mountebank, I said, and mountebank I mean! What else is his play with the King? What else is his trifling with the Kirk? He is no more a Protestant than is the Pope of Rome! He plays the part of a convert – but all the time, privily, he is bending the King towards Rome and France. I know – I have heard him at it.'

'Is that so? You must have good ears, then!'

'Aye, almost as good as your own, Gray! But maybe the Kirk's ears will grow sharper, too!'

'You mean – you might tell them? Enlighten them?' That was entirely easy, casually conversational.

'I did not say so – though the man makes me spew!'

'It might do no harm,' Patrick observed, smothering a yawn. '*Pardieu* – this heat! A little gossip amongst the fathers and brethren might enliven even the chill bones of the Kirk … to our dear land's benefit!'

Both his hearers looked sharply at the lounging elegant speaker, who now produced a comb to discipline his damp dark curls.

'*You* say that?' Stewart, the explicit ever, asked. 'How strong is your own zeal for the Protestant faith, Gray?'

'Need you ask, friend? Here at the grey heart of reformed Scotland, it all but eats me up!' Patrick assured, but lazily.

The Captain frowned. 'I doubt if I understand you, man,' he said.

'I am desolated.' Patrick gestured with his comb towards the tennis-players, who were commencing the second game. 'Dear Esmé – he is indefatigable. I hope that … he may not do himself an injury, with it all!'

Again the sharp glance. 'He well may!' Stewart said, grimly. 'He offends all the old nobility. He intends to rule Scotland – all can see that. Observe if he does not soon displace Argyll as Chancellor! Then he will make us all Catholic again – for I believe him to be, in fact, a Jesuit agent. I think that he plans an alliance with Spain and France … which means war with England.'

'So? You … er … think quite a deal, Captain, do you not? For a soldier!'

'Aye. And so do you, Gray. I do not believe that any of these thoughts of mine are new to *you*!'

Patrick smiled, and nodded towards a corner of the palace garden. 'A picture of connubial bliss are they not? The Lady March and her husband!'

The other did not rise to that. 'This is not what I aided your return from France, to the Court, for, Master of Gray,' he said heavily. 'As I understood it, you planned that Queen Elizabeth should hear of a new successor-designate to the Scots throne, and so fear our Queen Mary no longer – not that this Frenchman should take Scotland for his own!'

'Something of the sort,' Patrick agreed.

'If Elizabeth should come to hear of what is indeed toward, here,' Stewart went on, slowly. 'I think that she would take steps to set it otherwise.'

'That is possible. Then . . . why not tell her, Captain?'

'Eh . . . ?' Stewart looked not only at Patrick this time, but round at David also, as though seeking confirmation that his ears had not deceived him. 'Tell Elizabeth . . . *tell* her?'

'Why not? Her Mr Bowes does not strike me as a very intelligent man. It would be a pity if the good Protestant lady was misinformed, would it not? If the position concerns you, write to her, man. There is a great traffic of letters to her from these parts, anyhow!'

'And d'Aubigny – your Lennox?'

'A little . . . correction would no doubt be a kindness to him. As a bridle gentles too spirited a steed! A touch of the knee here; a pull on the bit, there – and a straight and useful course results for all, does it not?'

'God, Gray – you astonish me!'

'Why? 'Tis but common sense, my friend. When your mount veers to one side, you tug to the other, do you not?'

'But . . . why not write to Elizabeth yourself, then?'

'Ah, no. That would be unwise. Her Grace of England knows well, I am sure, that our Esmé and myself are close, that together we set this course. In any letter from me she would assuredly smell . . . jesuitry! Which would be unfortunate, would it not? No, no – you wield the pen instead of the sword, for once, Captain . . . in the good Esmé's best interests!' Stretching, Patrick rose to his feet. 'Now – I see the Lady Marie Stewart wasting her favours on her reprobate of a father! That will never do. Your servant, sir.' And with a bow of pure mockery, he sauntered off.

The Captain stared after him. 'Yon is a strange man, I vow!' he said. 'Deep. Deep as the Nor' Loch – and with as little knowing what is at the bottom!'

'Yes,' David said, level-voiced.

'Aye, an unchancy brother to have, I'd say!' Stewart rose, and stalked away abruptly, without farewell, as though he had just recollected something that he required to do.

David sat still, unmoving. The Lady Marie was right, it seemed – dear God, how right! He had not realised that it could go this far. The Queen of England, now . . . ! Troubled, seeing nothing of the gay and colourful scene about him, David gazed ahead. Almost, he was saying goodbye to Mariota and little Mary and Castle Huntly.

Chapter Twelve

'THE Douglas has played into our very hands, I tell you, Davy!' Patrick declared. 'A Yuletide gift, in truth! My waiting game is proved the right game. Here is the proof of it.'

Seldom had David seen his brother so openly, undisguisedly elated – indication, if such was needed, of the weight of menace that had hung over all about the King for so long, however lightly Patrick, for one, had seemed to bear the burden.

'He is coming to attend the Council next week, unbidden. My information is sure. He has decided that the time is ripe to move – that with most of the lords offended in Esmé, he can sway the Council, and with a few hundred Douglases around the Parliament Hall and a street mob worked up to yell against Popish Frenchmen, the day will be his.'

'As may not he be right?'

'I think not, Davy. Something on this sort is what I have waited for. There is more than my Lord Morton can make plans!'

The meeting of the Privy Council, an important one, was to be held on the afternoon of Hogmanay, the last day of 1580. Only an hour before it was due to start, the venue was changed from Parliament Hall, up near St Giles, to a room in the Palace of Holyroodhouse itself, at the King's command. When the Councillors – or such as had not already been warned – thereafter came riding down the long High Street and Canongate, on a chill dark day of driving rain, jostled by a clattering escort of hundreds of Douglas men-at-arms, it was to leave the No Popery crowd behind, their ardour notably damped. And at the great forecourt of Holyrood, and all around the palace, rank upon rank of armed men stood, mounted and afoot, pikemen, hagbutters, mosstroopers, Highland broadswordsmen, waiting silent, motionless in the rain, five or six times outnumbering the Douglases. No lord might bring with him more than ten men into the palace precincts, the Captain of the Guard declared – by the royal command. Morton, who obviously had expected to be forbidden to enter anyway, snorted a scornful if somewhat disappointed laugh, and strode within.

He was still smiling grimly amongst his red whiskers when he stalked into the Council Chamber. Men greeted him uncertainly, but there was nothing uncertain about James Douglas. He marched straight for his accustomed place at the right of the empty throne, where he had been wont to sit as Regent, and sat down at once. He produced from a pocket the small Regent's baton – to which of course he had not been entitled for two years, but which made a potent symbol nevertheless – and rapped it sharply on the great table.

'Sit ye down, my lords,' he commanded, in the sudden silence. 'Let's to business, Argyll, you are still Chancellor, are you no'? We'll have the sederunt.'

At the other end of the table, the Earl of Argyll, dark, thin-lipped, fox-faced, still stood. 'We await the King's Grace, my lord,' he said.

'The laddie can come in and signify the royal assent when we're done, man,' Morton snapped. 'Here's no bairn's work!'

'His Grace has intimated his intention of presiding in person.'

'Has he, 'fore God! Then let word be sent him that we are ready.'

David, sitting at another table at the far bottom end of the room, along with other secretaries and clerks, took in all the scene – the uneasy hesitant lords, the watchful Chancellor, and the assured dominant Morton. He was perhaps a little thinner than when David had last seen him, but had lost nothing of his truculent authority and sheer animal power. David noted that, though summoned, his father, the Lord Gray, was not present.

A fanfare of trumpets marked the royal approach. Preceded by heralds in the blazing colours of their tabards, the Lord Lyon King of Arms, and the Earl of Erroll as Constable, King James came in, robed in magnificence, but anxious-eyed and chewing his lip. He looked both older and younger than his fourteen years. At his right and left paced the Earl of Lennox and the Master of Gray.

Such as were seated, rose to their feet, bowing. Even Morton, sniffing and hawking loudly at all this display, perforce raised his posterior some way off his chair in a mocking crouch.

'We bid you all welcome to our Council, my lords,' James got out thickly, as he sat down in the throne, beside Morton unavoidably, but not looking at him. 'Pray be seated.'

As Morton, still crouching, opened his mouth to speak, Argyll the Chancellor banged loudly on the other end of the table. 'Is it Your Highness's declaration that this Council is duly constitute?' he asked quickly.

'Aye, it is. But . . . but first I . . . we oursel' would, would make announcement anent our dear cousin Elizabeth . . . Her Grace of England.' James was trembling almost uncontrollably, continually glancing over his shoulder and upward, where Lennox stood behind the chair which Morton had appropriated. 'I . . . we do hereby declare . . . '

He was interrupted by a loud rat-a-tat from without. The doors were thrown open, and the Captain of the Guard strode in, in full armour, plumed helmet, hand on sword-hilt. Straight for the King he hastened, an imposing martial urgent figure.

'Sire,' he cried. 'Your life is endangered!'

'Eh . . . ?'

'Sirrah – what means this unseemly entry?' the Chancellor croaked but with little conviction.

'Treason!' Stewart exclaimed, and sank down on one knee at the side of the throne. 'Sire – I say treason!'

At that dread word fully half the men in the great chamber were on their feet.

Two distinct table bangers beat for quiet, the Chancellor's gavel and Morton's baton. 'Silence!' the latter bellowed – and no voice could be more effective. 'What fool's cantrip is this?'

He got his silence and his answer. 'Sire, take heed!' Stewart declared. 'As Your Grace's guard, I charge you – take heed! This man at your side, the lord of Morton, has designs upon your royal person.'

'Belly-wind!' Morton scoffed.

'I . . . we will hear of our trusty Captain of the Guard,' James quavered. 'What is this, of treason, Captain Jamie?'

Still kneeling, and pointing directly at Morton, Stewart cried, 'Treason I said – high treason it is! I accuse James Douglas, before Your Grace and this whole Council, of the cruel slaying of Your Grace's royal father, King Henry Darnley!'

Uproar followed. A dozen lords were shouting at once. No amount of baton banging would still it. Not that Morton was trying. He was on his feet, in towering rage, roaring his loudest.

Terrified, James cringed on his throne, with Cousin Esmé's arm protectively around his shoulders. Patrick signed to Stewart to rise to his feet, and together they interposed themselves between the wrathful Morton and the boy. Stewart part drew his sword; he was the only man who might lawfully wear arms in the presence of the monarch.

Morton raved on for minutes on end, a furious foul-mouthed

tirade of such sustained violence and vibrant force as to set the nerves of every man in the room aquiver. Only when speechless through sheer lack of breath, was there a pause, and Stewart was able to resume.

'Such denials abate nothing of my charge, Sire. I charge this Council, for the King's safety, to bring the Lord Morton to his assize, when I will testify on oath that all is truth. I was but a page then, but I bore the confidences between this lord and his cousin and familiar, Archibald Douglas of Morham – whose was the hand that slew the King. The same whom this Earl Morton made a Lord of Session and judge of this realm, for reward!'

'You snivelling puppy . . . !'

'Where is Archie Douglas?' somebody demanded. 'Produce him, to testify. Produce Archie Douglas!'

'Aye!'

'The Senator Archibald Douglas fled last night, south of the Border and into England!' Stewart announced grimly.

That clinched the matter. When Argyll, perceiving his moment, demanded whether or no they, as the Council, would heed the plea of the King's Captain, there were a score of ayes. Any who thought to say no, looked hastily around them, and discreetly held their tongues.

Morton himself almost seemed to be stunned – or it may have been the first stages of apoplexy. He mouthed and all but choked, staring. 'Lindsay!' he managed to get out, at last. 'Ruthven! Glamis! Glencairn!'

But the aged Lord Lindsay gazed at the floor, and twisted his claw-like hands; Ruthven, the once terrible Greysteil, now considering events afresh, and in consequence the new Treasurer, looked out of the window at the beating rain; the Lord Glamis, that sober man, was dead, killed in, of all things, a brawl in Stirling street, and his brother the Master was banished the Court and sulking in the north; Glencairn indeed was there, but drunk, as ever – only, maudlin drunk where once he had been fiery drunk. The fact was, the old lion had outlived his jackals.

'God's curse on you all, for puling dotards and tit-sucking babes!' Morton almost whispered. He spat. 'That for you – each and all! I will see you in hell . . . '

'Captain Stewart,' Erroll said stiffly. 'You will see the Lord Morton warded securely. In this palace until late tonight. Then you will convey him straitly to the Castle of Edinburgh, where you, Master of Mar, will answer for him with your life. In the

King's name! Take him away.'

Stewart signed forward guards from the doorway.

Morton, of a sudden, assumed a great dignity. 'No man's hand shall touch Douglas!' he declared quietly, finally, and without a glance or a word to anyone, passed from the chamber, surrounded by the soldiers, Stewart following.

'The Council will resume,' the Chancellor called out, before chatter could begin, his gavel now unchallenged on the table. 'Silence for the King's Grace.'

James, however, was too overcome to do more than blink and wag his head. Argyll nodded.

'In the matter of Her Grace of England her letter to His Highness . . .'

So fell James Douglas, harshest tyrant that even Scotland had known in a thousand years, who had waited too long in the waiting game. Neither the Earl of Lennox nor the Master of Gray had so much as said a word, throughout.

Morton was taken after dark, by devious ways, to Edinburgh Castle, and though his leaderless men-at-arms rioted throughout the city and did immense damage, they could neither assail the palace or storm the castle to free their lord. In due course he was removed to Lennox's distant castle of Dumbarton, for greater security.

It was six months before the red Earl was brought to trial – if trial it could be called. One thousand men, no less, were sent to convoy him back to Edinburgh, and a Douglas attempt at rescue *en route* failed. By a jury of his peers, all his enemies, he was tried on June the second, and on the testimony of Stewart, Sir James Balfour, one of his own Douglases turned renegade, and letters from the imprisoned Queen Mary, was found guilty of being art and part in the murder of Henry Stewart, Lord Darnley, the King, fourteen years before. No one witnessed in his defence; those who might have done were either dead or had ill consciences and no desire to swim against the tide. He was condemned to die that same day.

The Maiden, set up at the Market Cross, outside St Giles, was Morton's own invention, and had long given him a great deal of pleasure and satisfaction. It was a somewhat clumsy contrivance, of a great knife counterbalanced by a heavy weight, all set within an upright frame, that was designed to whisk off heads with mere fingertip control – a forerunner of the guillotine, in fact. Now the Maiden took her begetter to herself right lovingly, to his own grim jests as to her well-tried efficiency. He faced her mockingly, declared as his last testament that none should know what so many wished to hear – where his vast accumulated treasure was hidden, since he had let none into his secret and made sure that the servants who had helped him stow it away had not lived to reveal its whereabouts; and as his dying prayer, mentioned, grinning, that if he had served his God as well as he had served his King he might not have come to this pass. Then, puffing, he got down on his thick knees, to lay his red head in what he called his Maiden's bosom – and the knife fell.

Set on a spike on the topmost pinnacle of the Tolbooth thereafter, the said head grinned out for long over all the capital that its owner had so long dominated. James the King trembled every time that he passed beneath.

Chapter Thirteen

'Is it not as good as a puppet show, Davey?' the Lady Marie asked, nodding her coifed golden head forward. 'An entertainment, no less. Even here, on the high top of Lomond, they're at their mumming . . . with Patrick pulling the strings.'

'Aye,' David said briefly. 'I see them.'

'One day, Patrick is going to get his strings entangled!' she added.

He companion made no comment, but shook his horse into a trot, to keep pace with their leaders. The young woman did likewise.

They were high on the green roof of Fife, on a crest of the long ridge of the Lomond Hills, far above the tree-level, with the land dropping away below them on either side in great brackeny sweeps, northwards into the strath of the Eden, wherein Falkland nestled amongst its woods, and southwards over rolling foothills and slanting fields to the sandy shores and great glittering estuary of Forth, beyond which Lothian smiled in the noonday sun and Edinburgh was discernible only because of its soaring castle. They had been hunting, from the Palace of Falkland, almost since sunrise – for James loved hunting, and was but a poor sleeper into the bargain. They had raised and killed three times in the forested foothills of Pitlour and Drumdreel, and then had put up a notable fourteen-point woodland stag, and all else was forgotten – at least by the King. For two hours they had run it, as it twisted and turned and sought sanctuary ever higher up out of the glades and thickets of the wood, up through the birch scrub and the whins, on to this high bare ridge where the larks sang and the curlews called, James and Lennox ever in front because of the fine Barbary blacks which they alone rode. And on the very crest they had found the hunted brute dead, its poor heart burst – for woodland life makes a stag heavy if nobly headed – and James had wept in vexation, for he had thought to shoot the killing bolt himself. Now they rode back along the heights, seeking a spot where they might water the horses and eat their picnic meal, a colourful and gallant company – though not all of them as fond of this sort of thing as was their monarch.

It was extraordinary how James had changed in the months since Morton's death. He was a different youth altogether, like some plant long hidden under an obstruction which blossoms up and swiftly spreads itself whenever the obstruction is removed. Not that all held that the transformation was for the better. He had taken to asserting himself, erratically rather than consistently; he would have no more of Master Buchanan; he indulged in sly tricks and devised cunning traps for all but his beloved Esmé; he sought to spend as much of his time as he might in the saddle, where undoubtedly he made a better showing than on his spindly knock-kneed legs. Morton's shadow had been potent indeed.

More than James burgeoned, of course, under the smiling sun that the Douglas's lowering threat had for so long obscured – in particular Esmé Stuart, Captain James, and the lady who had been Venus, the Lady Lovat, and Countess of March, and now was none of them. Unfortunately, to a large extent their burgeoning was mutually antagonistic. The Captain had blossomed to best effect, most assuredly. He was now James, Earl of Arran, Privy Councillor and Gentleman of the Bedchamber. He had known the price to ask – and when to ask it. On the very day before Morton's trial he had announced his terms: the Hamilton Earldom of Arran and the rest, or he would not testify. Since all depended upon his impeachment, at that late hour there could be no denial, Patrick had pointed out – though Lennox would have risked disaster fighting him. So the legitimate holder of the title had been hastily and judicially declared to be insane, and the honours and lands transferred to his illegitimate third cousin. And on the same happy day that his patent of nobility was signed, the Captain had the Court of Session declare the Earl of March to be frigid and incapable of procreating children, with the fortunate consequence that his marriage of less than a year earlier to the Lady Lovat was esteemed to be null and void. The pair were married the very next day – which enabled the lady's child by the Captain to be born legitimate a couple of weeks later – excellent timing, as all had to admit. The Earl and Countess of Arran were riding high – and would ride higher.

And yet, the Lady Marie Stewart suggested that it was Patrick Gray who pulled the strings.

Esmé, Earl of Lennox had not looked on entirely idly, of course. James, with a little prompting, had gladly created him Duke of Lennox, almost the first non-royal Scottish dukedom in history; moreover he had convinced Argyll that he was getting too old for the tiresome duties of the Chancellorship, and could well transfer these to the elegant shoulders of the new Duke. So now dear Esmé was Chancellor of the Realm, President of the Council, and first Minister of State. Also, he had taken over Morton's magnificent palace at Dalkeith.

David, for one, doubted whether these were strings of Patrick's pulling.

Such were the puppets that the Lady Marie exclaimed over on West Lomond Hill.

Admittedly they had been behaving ridiculously in front there, all morning, Lennox and Arran bickering with each other when they thought that James was not looking, very civil before the King's face and aiming slights and insults behind his back, ever jockeying for position, seeking to pull the boy this way and that. And the Lady Arran made her own contribution, ogling the King – and indeed all others so long as they were male – managing to have her riding-habit slip aside with marked frequency to reveal great lengths of hosed, gartered and well-turned leg, fetching a lace handkerchief regularly in and out of the cleft of her remarkable bosom with much effect, and laughing in silvery peals the while.

The Master of Gray, smiling, debonair, equable, but watchful always, rode beside and amongst them, occasionally coming back to where the Lady Marie chose to ride with David, but never leaving the principals for long.

An entertainment, that young woman called it; she had, perhaps, a mordaunt sense of humour.

The chief huntsman had found a suitable hollow, with a bubbling spring, and had come back to guide the royal party thereto, when the drumming of hooves drew all eyes northwards. Up out of the low ground rode a single horseman on a gasping foam-flecked mount. It was Logan of Restalrig, redfaced, rough, untidy as usual. He doffed his bonnet perfunctorily to the King, but it was at Patrick that he looked.

'Sire two embassages have arrived at Falkland, for Your Majesty, misliking each other exceedingly! One is from Her Grace the Queen, your mother. The other from Her Grace Elizabeth of England. I left them nigh at blows!'

'My, my mother . . . ?' James faltered, biting his lip.

'From Elizabeth!' Arran cried. 'An embassage you said, man – not a courier?'

'Sir Thomas Randolph himself – one o' the Queen's ministers.

Yon one who was once ambassador to our Queen Mary. Talking exceeding high and hot.'

Arran glanced sidelong at Patrick.

'And the other? From Queen Mary?' Lennox demanded. 'How comes it that she can send . . . that she . . . ?' He paused. 'She is not released? From her prison?'

'I think not,' Logan answered. 'It is Monsoor Nau, Her Highness's secretary. But he has my Lord Herries with him, and a troop o' Catholic Maxwells. They have ridden neck and neck frae Edinburgh – and are no' speaking love to each other!'

'Sire, with your permission, I shall ride fast to Falkland to welcome these, er, notable visitors,' Patrick proposed. 'To see to their entertainment until such time as Your Grace is pleased to receive them.'

'Aye. Very well, Master Patrick . . .'

'I will come with you,' Arran announced briefly.

'As Chancellor, it is meet, surely, that *I* should greet the Queen of England's envoy, James,' Lennox put in. 'Ascertain his business . . .'

'No need,' Arran interrupted. 'I am acquaint with Randolph.'

'I rather feared so . . .'

'Let us all go, Your Highness,' Patrick said quickly. 'You can outride us all, anyway, I doubt not.'

'Ever the one who minds his mark,' the Lady Marie mentioned, low-voiced to David. 'Observe how much attention poor Queen Mary's embassy receives! I wonder why Arran is so anxious to see the Englishman first?'

David did not put forward any suggestions.

So they all rode hot-foot, without stopping for a meal, down through the miles of woodland to Falkland, that most remotely rural of the royal palaces. James this time did not attempt to outdo his supporters. Always the mention of his mother's name set him in fear and alarm.

In the end, all three contestants for the duty saw the two ambassadors together in the great hall of Falkland, prior to the formal interview with the King – and for makeweight Patrick invited a fourth, his Uncle William, the Treasurer, never now called Greysteil, Lord Ruthven no longer, but Earl of Gowrie, so created by a grateful monarch who still feared the sight and sound of him. William Ruthven was another who had burgeoned and blossomed since the fall of his old colleague Morton; having once chosen the right course, he pursued it single-mindedly, and being the darling of the Kirk and idol of the godly, his nephew found him exceedingly useful on occasion. The fact that neither Lennox nor Arran liked nor trusted him by no means always invalidated his usefulness. As now.

The two ambassadors, with their trains, were already waiting at opposite corners of the hall, eyeing each other like packs of angry dogs, when James's representatives filed in. Immediately there was an unseemly scramble as to which should be first received. Monsieur Nau, small, dapper, excitable, claimed the right as his, as representing the sovereign lady of this realm of Scotland approaching her own son. Sir Thomas Randolph tall, dyspeptic, disapproving, asserted that as representing the reigning Queen of England, he took precedence over all others soever, especially one whose principal was a mere guest of his lady.

'Her prisoner, shamefully, monstrously held, you mean, *nom de Dieu*!' the Frenchman cried.

'Watch your words, sirrah, when you speak of my lady!' Randolph exclaimed.

'Your lady is a . . .'

'Your Excellencies,' Patrick intervened, smiling. 'My lord Duke of Lennox, my lord Earl of Arran, my lord Earl of Gowrie, and your humble servant, bid you both welcome in the King's name, I am sure that matters of precedence may readily be resolved by receiving you both at the same time. Then . . .'

'Not so, by the Mass – not so!' Nau contradicted. 'The Queen of Scots shares place with none, in Scotland!'

'The Queen of Scots is abdicate,' the Earl of Gowrie said bluntly. He certainly should have known, for he had been one of those who put the abdication papers so forcibly before the hapless Queen at Loch Leven, seventeen years before.

'*Jamais*! Never!' Nau declared. 'That was done by force. It is of none avail. My mistress is Queen of Scots, yet.'

'Then what is her son, man?' Gowrie demanded.

'He is the Prince James, Her Grace's heir and successor in the thrones of Scotland and England both, and . . .'

'My God!' Randolph burst out.

'Och, you're clean gyte, man!' Gowrie asserted.

'Fool!' Arran muttered. 'Does he take us all for bairns?'

Even Lennox looked alarmed and uneasy, and glanced swiftly along at Patrick.

'Monsieur Nau,' that young man said courteously. 'These are matters for debate, are they not? How are your credentials addressed, may I ask?'

'To James, Prince and Duke of Rothesay, from his Sovereign Lady Mary, Queen of Scots,' the other answered promptly.

'Then, Monsieur, I fear that they are in error. I would respectfully advise that you withdraw to yonder chamber and amend them. Amend them, Monsieur to James, by God's grace, King of Scots.'

'*Tête Dieu*, that I will never do, sir! Never! By Her Grace's command.'

Patrick shrugged one shoulder, sighed, and nodded along the line. Lennox took him up.

'Then, Monsieur Nau, I regret that you cannot be received,' he said firmly. 'It is impossible.'

'But Monsieur . . . my lord Duke! *C'est impropre!* The Prince's own mother . . . !'

'It is impossible,' Lennox repeated. 'If James is not King, then, then . . . No, no, Monsieur, you leave us no choice. Sir Thomas Randolph, you are accredited to King James, I take it?'

'Naturally, Your Grace.'

Lennox bowed. Nobody in Scotland had yet been brought to term him Your Grace, which here was awarded only to the monarch or his regent. 'And have you aught that you would say, h'm, privately, before you see His Highness?'

'No, sir.' . .

'Very well.' Lennox signed to the hastily summoned herald, who threw open the double doors and cried,

'His Excellency the Ambassador of Her Grace of England, to the high and mighty James, King of this Realm and of the Scots. God save the King!'

'You failed the Queen – Queen Mary,' David repeated heavily, stubbornly. 'The Queen whose cause you came to uphold – and for which you have received moneys in plenty! Failed her just as surely and as openly as though you had slapped her face!'

'Tush, man, I told you! Do you not see? I could do no other. She is foolish, headstrong, the beautiful Mary – always has been. To have accredited her envoy only to *Prince* James . . . for us to have accepted that, in front of the English Ambassador, would have been to accept her as sovereign still, and her son as no King. And if he is not King, then nothing that has been done or signed in his name since his crowning is lawful and true. I am not of the Privy Council, Lennox is no duke, Arran

175

no earl!' That would signify little – but what of greater affairs? What would the Kirk say? What would Elizabeth say?'

'I have not thought, of late, that you cared deeply what the Kirk said, Patrick! And should Elizabeth of England shape Scotland's policies!?'

'Lord, but she does, man! There's the rub – she does. So long as she holds in her hand the gift of the succession to the English throne, with Mary and James as the first heirs, so long can she take a part in shaping Scotland's policy. There is no avoiding it.'

'Tell me, Patrick,' his brother said quietly, deliberately. 'Would you rather see James on Elizabeth's throne, and you, his minister, wielding the power of England – or Mary released from her bondage and back in her own country as the Queen she rightly is?'

Patrick frowned – and he did not often frown. The brothers were standing on the parapet-walk outside Patrick's room in the south round tower of Falkland, on the evening of the ambassadors' arrival. 'Fiend take you, Davy – that is no question! You talk nonsense. I am pledged to the Queen's interests – but her best interests, not such folly as this. Besides,' he laughed again, 'I see Elizabeth's cunning hand in all this, anyway!'

'Elizabeth . . . ?'

'Aye. Elizabeth's hand. Or the heads of her two minions, Burleigh and Walsingham, the two cleverest brains in Christendom! How think you Monsieur Nau comes here in open embassage? Hitherto, Mary has been able to send to her son only letters smuggled secretly out of Sheffield Castle, these thirteen years. But now her secretary is permitted to leave her openly, to travel to Scotland. Elizabeth knew what his errand was, that is why – and wished it accomplished, I swear.'

'M'mmm. And you know what that errand was?'

'Aye. I saw Nau later, privately – and soothed him somewhat. Though he is not to see the King – that we cannot permit. He has come to propose an Association – a sharing of the Crown between Mary and her son. That they should rule as King and Queen together – or rather, as Queen and King, for she will grant the honour and be the senior.'

'As is only right and proper,' David said. 'An excellent purpose, I would say.'

'Aye,' his brother commented dryly. 'I daresay you would!'

'But . . . what of the religious differences? What is purposed there?'

'That the Kirk remains supreme, with James as its head –

as now. But that Mary remains Catholic, and there shall be full freedom of worship.'

'As there should be. Surely these are good proposals – if Elizabeth can be made to release the Queen. You say that you think that Elizabeth knows of this, and would have it so?'

'I did not say that – quite. Knows, yes, I think – and would have Scotland consider and desire it. So, heigho – she sends Randolph at the same time, threatening war!'

'Eh . . . ? War, do you say? War with England?'

'Just that. Such is Randolph's embassy. Threats of war, fierce railing over Morton's death, thunderings of vengeance. She does not like losing money, does Elizabeth – and she invested much in Morton, I fear!'

David shook his head. 'I do not understand. You have just said . . . How can she both approve of Nau's errand, and also threaten us with war?'

'We are dealing with clever folk, Davey – folk who understand statecraft as yon tranter down there understands falconry. They want James, and Scotland, to grasp at this Association with Mary, and the threats of war are to frighten him into doing it.'

'But why?'

'Why does Elizabeth hold Mary prisoner? For a good purpose, you may be sure – all that woman does is for good reason. It is to have a hold over Scotland. To prevent Scotland joining her ancient ally, France, or Spain either, against England. Her nightmare – Burleigh's nightmare – is a war on two fronts: Scotland in the north and France in the south. This proposed Association would play into her hands, so long as she holds Mary. Scotland would want something from her, must woo her, to get Mary back. She would dangle promises before us, and the hope of the ultimate succession – but that is all. Mary she will hold on to – and Scotland will not align herself with France. We beg our Queen back from her, and while we beg, Elizabeth and England are safe.'

'What then if *we* made the war? To get our Queen back.'

'Elizabeth is no fool, Davy. And she is well served with spies. She knows that we are in no case to invade England. We could mount a sally over the Border, yes – in conjunction with a French invasion across the narrow seas and perhaps a Spanish attack from the Low Countries and Ireland. But war, by ourselves, no. And would not the first Scot to fall be Mary the Queen?'

David shook his head. 'It is too deep, too murky for me,' he declared. 'Who may resolve such a tangle, the deil knows!'

Patrick bowed mockingly. 'Why, your younger brother may, Davy!' he said, smiling, 'if only Esmé Stuart will keep his meddling fingers out of it, and the gallant Arran confine his undoubted abilities to his bedchamber . . . and if perhaps Davy Gray does not carp and cavil quite so determinedly!'

'You . . . *you* would set yourself up against Elizabeth of England? And Burleigh and Walsingham? At your years, Patrick?'

'Why not? What have years to do with it? In such a case, a clear head, a nimble wit and a sure goal are worth many grey hairs!'

'And you believe that you have all these in sufficiency?'

'Thanks to God – and none at all, I think, to our esteemed father – yes! Have I failed hitherto?'

'Failed . . . whom?'

The two looked each other directly in the eye.

'I think that you can be too nice, too delicate, brother!' Patrick said softly.

'And I that you can be too clever . . . and too much forsworn!'

'So-o-o!' Then, at the least, we know where we stand, Davy. I thank you for all your somewhat negative advice. Meanwhile, I fear, we must send the ambassadors home – both of them . . .'

'Saying . . . ?'

'Ah, me – Nau telling his mistress that *King* James will consider her proposals fully, dutifully, and, h'm, at length. And Randolph, Randolph telling *his* that we shall do no such thing, that James alone rules Scotland, and that his mother is very well where she is . . . and that threats of war ill become so gracious a princess – who dares not carry them out anyway!'

'So it is out, damn you, Patrick – you admit it! Mary is very well where she is! There is our Queen's doom pronounced!'

'To your mind, it may be. To mine, it is the speediest way to win her home – if Elizabeth thinks that we do not want her. Go sleep on it, man!'

Chapter Fourteen

THREE people strolled by the sylvan banks of the River Eden, the noise of the chase long lost in the far-flung woodlands. Only the sounds of the forest were there; the river gurgled and chuckled, the finches chirped, cuckoos called hauntingly, endlessly, from far and near, and now and again a mallard duck would go quacking off in over-done alarm, seeking to draw attention away from her brood. For it was Spring again, the late and lovely short Spring of Scotland, and King James had returned to his beloved Falkland, where, even though the stags were not yet out of velvet, none could say that the King must not hunt them.

Of the three strollers, only David Gray, leading the horses, appeared ill at ease. The other two sauntered on ahead in apparent content – but only a very little way ahead, for the Lady Marie kept hanging back to include David in the desultory conversation. Nor did Patrick give any sign that he was otherwise minded, laughing, humming snatches of song, rallying them both, at his gayest, most relaxed, most charming.

David realised now, however, that Patrick had deliberately contrived this interlude – and presumably not for *his* benefit – urging Marie Stewart to take a shortcut with him to head off the stag, away from the main hunt, but soon finding themselves at the river and slowing down unhurriedly to proceed thus along its banks, dismounted. David had automatically followed his brother, since that seemed to be his destiny. Now he could have wished himself elsewhere, for he enjoyed acting neither groom nor gooseberry – though neither of the others gave the least indication that they considered him as such; indeed, it might well be that Marie was glad enough of his presence.

The three of them bore a strange relationship. Marie and David were now very good friends in their rather difficult situation, understanding and trusting each other, looking at many things in the same way. With Patrick the young woman was very different – provocative, highly critical, often downright unkind. Yet her interest in him was as undisguised as her frequent hostility. As for Patrick himself, he had pursued her in a casual and intermittent sort of way since that first meeting at Holyroodhouse, without letting it interfere with more urgent conquests or politic wooings. Something always seemed to bring him back to her – perhaps the fact that she refused to succumb to his wiles. David, for his part, recognised that she could be an excellent influence with Patrick, but liked her too well to wish to see her just another of his brother's playthings.

A faint call, rather different from that of the cuckoos, reached them from afar – the winding of a hunting-horn.

'Another kill,' the Lady Marie observed. 'Majesty is insatiable for blood. I suppose that we should be thankful that it is only deer's blood. Myself, I quickly have enough of it!'

'Aye, men's blood may come later!' Patrick said. 'James, God help him, has much to wipe out in his twisted mind. Kings often do such, bloodily.'

'He is a strange youth,' she agreed. 'He could scarce be otherwise. He will not thank us for deserting his beloved chase.'

'There are better things to chase than out-of-season deer!'

'Meaning, sir?'

'Meaning that the company of a beautiful woman is to me the more potent lure.'

'I have noticed that,' she said coolly. 'Many times.'

'Do you condemn me for that, Marie? In every sport does not practice make for perfection?'

'A comfort for those practised upon!' she returned. 'Like the King's poor stags!'

Patrick shook his dark head over her, ruefully. 'She has a curst quick tongue, has she not, Davy? She speaks *you* a deal more kindly, I've noted! How do you do it?'

'Davy does not practise on me. Or on every other woman that he sets eyes on!'

'I should say not! He has no need, you see. For our Davy is a practised galliard already. He has a most faithful wife . . . and two bairns born most undoubtedly in holy wedlock! Eh, Davy?'

'And you? You have the Lady Elizabeth Gray, once Lyon, have you not?'

A shadow, like a tiny cloud passing over the sun, darkened Patrick's face – but only for a moment. 'Have is scarce the word, I think,' he answered, lightly. 'A marriage to a painted picture or a marble statue would reward as well! I have not so much spoken to her for three years.'

'Yet she is your wife.'

'Wife! Is that a wife? Does marriage mean so much to the daughter of Robert Stewart!'

Steadily she looked at him. 'I wondered when that would out,' she said.

Patrick bit his lip. 'I am sorry,' he declared. 'That was ill said. Unworthy. You – you cause me to act the fool, always. It is those grey steadfast eyes of yours, I think. Accusing. So like Davy's. Always accusing. Christ God – you make a pair! It is not that . . .' He stopped. 'But why do I babble so – to you?'

Neither of them answered him.

They walked on along the riverside path, in silence, and the cuckoos came into their own again. Marie had fallen back alongside David, to take her own horse's head.

Abruptly Patrick turned. 'A plague on you both!' he exclaimed. 'You . . . you have spoiled a bonny day, a bonny lightsome day!'

David moistened his lips to speak. That was not like Patrick. But the young woman forestalled him.

'I am sorry, Patrick,' she said, gravely. 'I would not have wished that.'

He looked at her searchingly, at all the slender, riding-habited, coifed grace of her, and then at his brother – for him broodingly. Then, jerking a laugh at them, he turned forward once more to his pacing.

So they continued, beneath the young green canopy of the trees, in their strange walk, thinking their own thoughts to the mocking murmur of the river. Presently the surprising Patrick was singing again, an Italian air of pathos and pride and poignancy, the notes and words dropping singly like pebbles into a deep pool, a sad thing but somehow gallant. The girl behind him nibbled at her lower lip.

Coming to a grassy bluebell-painted bank at a bend of the stream, loud with the hum of bees and the heady scent of the wild hyacinths, Patrick suddenly sat down. 'Sit here,' he invited, indeed commanded. 'These bluebells, mayhap, will warm those eyes of yours, for me. Tell me, Marie – will you come with us to France?'

In the act of sitting down, she stared at him. 'France . . . ?' she repeated. David still standing, had turned to look as sharply.

'Aye, France – fair and sunny France. I find that I must needs go there. Come you with us, Marie. You would bloom richly there, I vow!'

'But – I cannot do that, Patrick . . .'

'If it is your reputation that concerns you, my dear, bring your father with you. A sister likewise, if you wish. But Davy will be there . . . to look after you, never fear!'

'I think not,' David said, from the background. 'I have had sufficient of France. Why go you there again, Patrick? This is sudden, is it not?'

'I go because affairs require it.'

'Your affairs? The Queen's?'

'Shall we say Scotland's affairs!?'..

'You go on the King's business? As ambassador?' Marie asked.

'Not exactly. Though something of the sort may be arranged, no doubt.'

'I cannot think that the Master of Gray would be a very welcome ambassador at the Court of France, of Catherine de Medici!' David mentioned. 'Not after our last hours on French soil! I'd jalouse that his errand is rather to the Duke of Guise and the Archbishop of Glasgow? Though, to be sure, I had thought that with his increased closeness to Scotland's Treasurer, my Lord Gowrie, he would have but little need of the gentry at Rheims!'

Lazily, Patrick turned to survey the brother who spoke so formally. 'Do I detect more accusation there, Davy? Man — you are so righteous, I wonder it doesna choke you! A painful affliction, it must be. Be warned, Marie — or you may grow as bad as Davy, scenting wickedness in my every move!'

'You will be spared my troubling you in France, at the least!'

'Not so, Davy. You must come. Life w'thout you would lack all savour, I vow! Besides, Marie, I feel sure, will desire your sober guardianship . . .'

'Patrick, do not be foolish!' the young woman said, almost sharply. 'I cannot go to France with you — even if I would.'

'Why, my dear? What keeps you here? This Court is plaguey dull getting, you must admit. Nothing but Esmé posturing and duking, Arran strutting and quarrelling, and deer being chased! Even Elizabeth Tudor has decided, it seems, that we are too dull and harmless for her concern. I' faith, Scotland will be a good place to be furth of, this hunting season, I swear.'

'Even so, I cannot go with you, Patrick.'

'Ah, me — your womanly repute wins the day, eh?' He sighed, gustily. 'Then there is nothing for it — I must marry you!'

The young woman's intake of breath was sharp enough to be audible. David's shock was almost as great. Together they gazed at the elegantly lounging speaker, wordless.

'Come — it is not so ill a thought as that, is it?' Patrick went on, smiling. 'It has been done before!'

'You . . . you are not serious?' Marie got out, at last.

'But, yes. Why not? For Patrick Gray to propose matrimony, after his former experiences, is serious indeed. As a last resort, you will understand! Will you not be the Mistress of Gray, my dear Marie, if you will not be my mistress otherwise?'

Marie turned to look at David, as though for aid, where he stood with the horses. That young man shook his head helplessly. This was quite beyond him. With Patrick, one never knew what might be in his mind; but surely he would not have made the suggestion thus, in front of David, if he had not been in earnest?

Presumably Marie thought along the same lines. 'And your wife?' she faltered. 'Elizabeth Lyon . . . ?'

'There is the blessed dispensation of divorce or annulment. You will have heard of it? If Arran can undo a knot but ten months old, what might not Patrick Gray achieve!'

She shook her head dumbly, Marie Stewart who was not usually dumbfounded.

'Come, you are a young woman who knows her mind,' he declared. 'You have spoken it to me times unnumbered. Now is the time for it – for, see you, it will be necessary to work fast. I . . . we must be furth of Scotland within the month, at the latest.'

The young woman took a deep breath. 'No,' she said.

'No? Think well, woman. It is not every day that Patrick Gray proposes marriage.'

'No,' she repeated. 'I thank you, Patrick – but no.'

Patrick leaned forward, his nonchalance for the moment forgotten. 'See, Marie,' he said. 'For your own sake, for your father's protection, you would do well to come with me, married or other. And your father with you.'

At his changed tone, she searched his face. 'I do not understand you, Patrick. How comes my father and his protection into this?'

The other paused, and then sat back, smiling again, half-shrugging. 'We all walk but delicately at this Court,' he told her. 'There are pitfalls a-many. Your father has his . . . un-friends.'

'Always he had those. But that is not what you meant, I think?'

He leaned over, to pat her hand, himself again. 'I meant that I would constrain you to marry me, anyhow! And you could do worse, you know, my dear. Look around you at Court – and admit that you could do worse!'

'I grant it, Patrick. But . . . you must go to France alone, nevertheless. I am sorry. You must be content with Davy for company.'

'No,' David declared firmly. 'I will not go to France again. I go back where I should never have left.'

'A pox – would you have me go alone, the pair of you? With none to advise and chide me?'

'Does not my lord Duke return with you?'

'Indeed, no. My lord Duke will be otherwise occupied!' Patrick rose to his feet. 'It is not in me to plead with you – with either of you,' he said. 'But perhaps you will change your minds. Women particularly are said to be good at it. And our esteemed Davy has sometimes a likeness to a scolding old dame! Heigho – I hope you do. But it will have to be soon, I warn you – it must needs be soon.' He held out a hand to aid Marie rise. 'Come, I am tired of these cuckoos' mockery. Whom do they mock – your or me? Or just mankind?'

'I am sorry, Patrick,' the young woman said.

Chapter Fifteen

THE hay, though late, was abundant and of good quality, thick with clover. All the Carse smelt of the sweet but vital scent of it, as everywhere men, women and children laboured with scythe and sickle, fork and rake, to cut and dry and stack the precious harvest, so much more important even than the corn and bere of autumn to this predominantly cattle-rearing country, on which the breeding stock would depend throughout the long winter months. My lord of Gray's herds were the greatest in all the Carse, and therefore his servants, and his tenants likewise, must grow and harvest a deal of hay in the reedy water-meadows and rich flood-plain of the Tay beneath and around his towering castle. Always David Gray had loved to work at the hay. This summer of 1582 he could do so again.

And, tossing tirelessly with his two-pronged hay-fork at the endless wind-rows of scythed and drying grass and clover, this was a totally different character from the somewhat morose, guarded, watchful man who walked so warily, uneasily, through the gilded life of court and palace. Here was the real David, who laughed and even sang as he worked – albeit tunelessly – joked with his fellow-harvesters and laboured prodigiously in sweating bare-armed satisfaction. None would have called him dour and humourless, now.

Nearby, Mariota worked almost as effectively under the July sun, her brown arms rhythmically flexing to the steady play of her fork, her deep rounded bosom and strong shoulders all but bursting out of the brief shift that was all she wore above the short skirt kilted to the knee. Red-cheeked, bright-eyed, Mariota clearly throve on motherhood. Her glance swung, almost as regularly as did her fork, between her husband and the coles of hay, flattened and scattered, where the baby Patrick rolled and staggered and clambered, chuckling, whilst around him young Mary danced, hurling clover-heads at him, covering him with grass, trilling her laughter, in her eighth summer of fascinating roguery.

It seemed a far cry from Falkland or Holyrood – or indeed, from the Principal's house at St Andrews.

'You go too hard, Davy,' Mariota protested, as he shook the

sweat off his brow with a toss of the head. 'You will have no strength left for, for . . .' She left that unfinished; it would have been hard to say whether she blushed or no, pink-faced as she was already with exertion.

Without halting in his stroke, David turned to grin at her. 'Try me!' he panted. 'Now, if you care . . . or tonight!'

She glanced down, not to meet his eye. Defensively she threw back at him. 'You work . . . as though this hay, was Patrick . . . and you were tossing the Devil out of him!'

This time his fork did falter and pause. He did not require to be informed to which Patrick she referred. Never a day passed without his brother's name being mentioned – and usually with just the hint of criticism of himself implied somewhere. Poor gallant Patrick! A strange thing, for Mariota made a most loving, happy and uncomplicated wife, and obviously rejoiced to have her husband home with her, even though, like his father, she had held that he really ought to have gone to France with Patrick, to look after him. Patrick – always Patrick! He laid a spell upon them all.

'I would it were so simple!' he said, shortly.

They worked on in silence for a while. Soon however David was at his singing again, and tossing occasional forkfuls of hay at the children.

Again it was Mariota who next interrupted their labours. 'Two riders,' she said suddenly, nodding towards the castle on its rock half-a-mile away across the flats. 'One of them a woman.'

David raised his hand to shield eyes from the sun's glare. 'I see them,' he agreed. 'But how you may tell that one is a woman, at such distance, I do not know.'

She looked at him pityingly.

She was right. As the riders drew closer it could be seen that the better mounted of the pair was dressed in a flowing riding-habit, the hood thrown back from coifed hair. The other looked to be an ordinary man-at-arms. They pulled up beside Tom Guthrie the land-steward, obviously asking a question. Then they came directly towards David and his wife.

It was the Lady Marie Stewart, and an attendant. She rode up to them, and drew rein, to sit looking down at them, un-smiling. 'Davy Gray . . . being Davy Gray at last,' she said, in her grave way. 'And Mariota. And young Mary. And little Patrick, too.'

David, suddenly very much aware of his sweat-soaked shirt and old darned breeches, hastily wiped the back of a hand over dripping brow and tousled hair, thereby smearing the hay-dust the more notably. 'My lady . . .' he began. 'I . . . here is a surprise. How come you here?'

'From Erroll. Where I am staying with the Constable.' She dismounted with a lissome grace before ever David could think of assisting her and shook out the dust from the folds of her habit. 'It is not far. A mere ten miles. But . . . will you not acquaint me with your wife, Davy?'

'Aye. Mariota, this is the Lady Marie Stewart, whom I have told you of. Daughter to my lord of Orkney, the King's uncle.'

'Yes.' Mariota bobbed a brief and stiff courtsey, whilst retaining a firm hold of her hay-fork.

'I hope that he has told you well of me, Mistress Mariota. Even a tithe as well as he told me of you! For I esteem your Davy's regard highly.'

'Yes, m'lady.'

The other smiled then, so faint a smile, yet sweet. 'Call me Marie, surely,' she said. 'Then perhaps we may be able to win Davy round to doing the same! I have been trying, these many months.'

Mariota did not answer that. She was seeking to draw together the gaping front of her shift to hide the deep cleft of her breasts from the admiring scrutiny of the mounted man-at-arms.

'You find us at something of a disadvantage,' David jerked. 'This hay . . .'

'Not so,' Marie corrected him, quickly for her. 'I find you making better use of your time than I have made for many a day. Would that these useless hands of mine could wield a fork as do your Mariota's! I envy her – and in more than that!' She spoke to the mounted man. 'Go back to the castle, Willie, and await me there. Take the horse, too.' Then, turning to the interested Mary, she took a couple of paces forward and sank down on one knee in the cut grass before the child. 'So this is . . . this your firstborn. The charmer that all the Court has heard of – even the King! I can see why, too.'

Woman and child eyed each other steadily, directly. Mary showed no hint of her elders' unease and uncertainty. She never did, of course. Great-eyed, but sparkling, assured, she considered the visitor. 'You have bonny hair,' she said, and reached out a grubby hand to touch the heavy golden tresses that escaped from the coif.

'Mary!' her mother exclaimed, shocked.

But the Lady Marie remained kneeling, and nodded agreement. 'It is the best of me,' she said, seriously. 'We cannot all have . . . what you have got, Mary. See,' she drew a necklace of tiny pink shells from a pocket. 'I have brought you these. Once they were the only gauds I had. And a comfit for your little brother.'

'Thank you,' the child said, and bending down she plucked one of the little heart's-ease flowers which grew everywhere low in the grass, and presented it to the other with the most natural dignity. 'For you.' A royal gesture of bestowal could not have been more gracious.

Marie leaned forward to kiss a sticky cheek, and stood up. 'You are better blessed than I knew, Davy,' she declared, looking from daughter to mother. 'I do not wonder that the Court could not hold you.'

'It has not held you either, it seems, Lady Marie!'

'Me – I have only escaped for a little while. Seeking a breath of fresh air. Patrick was right – it is plaguey dull, and a good place to be furth of. Lennox and Arran and Gowrie all bickering round the King . . . and Arran's wife lying with all three, they say!'

'So – do you wish that you had gone to France, after all?'

She raised her grey eyes to look at him levelly, calmly. 'Do you?' she said.

David frowned. 'By God, I do not!' he asserted, with more vehemence than seemed necessary.

Gravely she nodded. 'Perhaps you speak for me, also. Who knows? We think alike on many things, I would say, Davy.'

Mariota looked from one to the other, and bit her red lip.

The visitor examined her little wild pansy. 'Have you any tidings . . . from Patrick?'

'A letter, a week ago. From Seville, in Spain. What he does there, he did not say – save that the climate and the women were hotter even than in France, and the statecraft colder!'

'Spain . . . !' she said. 'What deep game is he playing, Davy? Is it the old religion? Statecraft cold, he said? That could mean – what?'

'I do not know – save only that he is Patrick. And since he is, his going there will not be out of any whim . . . or mean what may appear on the face of it.'

'No. No – I fear that is true . . .'

'Why must you always be so hard against Patrick?' Mariota exclaimed abruptly. 'Why must he ever be judged so sorely?

Davy is ever at it. My lord, too. And now, you! You are unkind
– all of you! I . . . I . . .' She stopped, undoubtedly flushing
this time.

The other young woman considered her thoughtfully.
'Perhaps you are right,' she said. 'It is too easy to judge, may be.'

David opened his mouth to speak, and then thought better
of it.

'He . . . Patrick is well, at least?' Marie asked, after a moment.
'He did not say . . . anything else?'

'He did not say that he missed my company.'

'Nor mine?'

'Nor yours, no.'

'I see. Why should he?' Without change of expression, Marie
turned to the other young woman. 'A new light is beginning to
burn brighly at Court,' she mentioned. 'A supporting luminary
of my lord Duke's . . . that burns with the sweet odour of
sanctified oil! A notable and godly influence, I am sure.'

Mariota, hurriedly stooping to tend the baby, looked both
surprised and mystified.

'The new Lord Bishop of St Boswells. Better known as the
learned Principal of St Andrews, Master Davidson. A cause for
congratulation?'

'Bishop . . . ?' Mariota faltered.

'Did you not know? Ah, yes, Lennox has had the old lapsed
bishopric of St Boswells, in the Borders, revived for him . . .
with its revenues of Kelso, Dryburgh and the rest. He has
become the Duke's spiritual adviser, in place of the mournful
Master Lindsay. A worthy bridge between Kirk and State,
don't you think?'

David barked a single mirthless laugh. 'So – he has achieved
more through the new religion than the old, after all! Morton
made him Principal . . . and Lennox a bishop! A man of parts,
'fore God!'

'Indeed, yes. A man not only with the cure of souls innumerable and a sure seat in Heaven, but with a seat in the Estates of
Parliament likewise, the income of three abbeys, and through
Lennox the ear of the King! And you are his only child, are you
not, Mariota? We soon will all be curtseying to *you*, my dear!'

Mariota's comely features were working strangely, her bosom
heaving. 'No!' she cried. 'I am no child of his! He told me so, the
last time that we spoke together. He said that I was none of his
hereafter, that he hoped that God would spare him the sight of
me! And I . . . I wish never to hear his name again! I am Mariota

Gray – that, and that only!' She gulped, and bobbed the sketchiest of bows. 'With your permission, m'lady . . .!' Bending, she snatched up the baby, grabbed Mary's hand, and turning, went hurrying at half-a-run across the hay towards the distant castle, without a backward glance.

Marie started as though to hasten after her, but David restrained her with a hand on her shoulder.

'Let her be,' he counselled. 'Let her be. Better so.'

Go you after her, then, Davy. Tell her that I am sorry. I did not mean to hurt her – it is the last thing I would have done! You must tell her so. I did not know that she was thus with her father . . . '

'I should have told you, perhaps. He . . . he did not think highly of me as good-son! He injured Mariota cruelly.'

'And now – and now my talk has upset her. I am a fool! I should not have come, Davy. I thought twice before coming, but . . . I pined for the sight of your honest face . . . '

'And word of Patrick,' he added heavily.

'Yes – that also,' she admitted, quiet-voiced. 'What is it that Patrick does to us all, Davy?'

'I do not know,' he said, and sighed.

In their own room later, with Marie returned to Erroll, Mariota, tense and fretful, turned on David as soon as he came in.

'That woman,' she cried. 'Why did she come here? What does she want of us? What does she want of *you*?'

'I think that she but wanted word of Patrick . . . '

'Aye, that was easily seen! But she wanted more than that, I think. I saw her – the fine lady with her sly looks and hints! I saw the pair of you, and your quick glances . . . '

David jerked a laugh. 'Sly, of all things, I would not call the Lady Marie! She is honest and straight, Mariota – the only one such that I ever found at the Court . . . '

' "We think alike on many things, Davy!" ' the young woman mimicked unkindly. 'Oh, aye – a fine honest loose Court hizzy, with her mocking slow ways and yellow hair! She knows how to twist men round her little finger, yon one – great foolish men, who believe that they turn the world over in their hands!'

Perplexed, he stared at her. This was not like Mariota the gentle, the mild. What had come over her? Surely the mention of her father's advancement was not sufficient for all this? 'You have it all amiss, my dear,' he told her. 'Far from twisting men around her finger, she it was whom Patrick asked to marry him.

And she would not. I told you . . . '

'Aye – and so twisted him the tighter! He thinks to run away to France to escape her, no doubt, to Spain – into dangers and trials without number! Poor foolish Patrick . . . !'

'I' faith – poor Patrick indeed! Lassie, you do not know what you are saying. Patrick uses women as he uses all else – for his own advantage and amusement, and that only. As once he . . . he . . . well, as he always has done. She – the Lady Marie – would not be so used . . . '

'There you are – ever traducing him! You can think no good of him – your own brother! A shame on you, David Gray! And she – she must cozen him to his face, and speak ill of him behind his back! Aye, and when she cannot have *him*, she comes here to lay her soft white hands on you . . . !'

'Lord! Are you out of your mind, girl? I think that she is fond of Patrick, yet sees his faults . . . as only a bemused and gullible ninny would not! And because she knows that I am fond of him likewise, though no more blind than she is, she is drawn to me a little. That is all. We are friends . . . '

'Friends!'

'Aye, friends. Is that so strange? But fear nothing – you will see no more of her! She will not come back, after the tantrums you have shown her, I swear! I do not know what has come over you, and that's a fact!'

'There is a lot that you do not know, I think . . . ' she began, with the first glistening of tears in her eyes. And seeing that gleam, David Gray, as became a man of some discretion, turned and stamped out of the room, and down the winding stone stairway; better causes than his had been lost in the flood of a woman's tears.

David was wrong about Marie Stewart not coming back to Castle Huntly. It was almost five weeks later before she did, but then she came in some urgency, in late August. She arrived, again with a single escort, just as Lord Gray was setting out for Dundee, at noontide on the twenty-fourth of the month. My lord greeted her, in the courtyard, with the somewhat ponderous gallantry and comprehensive leering inspection that was standard with him for attractive ladies. He was a little bit put out that it seemed to be David whom she had come to see, not himself. He delayed his departure, however, while that young man was fetched down from his tower school-room, to entertain the caller.

'Here is the Lady Marie of Orkney speiring for you, Davy,' he announced. 'A right bonny visitor, too, for a damned bookish dominie! A wicked waste, I call it!'

David bowed, unspeaking, and Marie appeared to be in no mood for badinage.

'In this pass, a dominie at his books may have the best of it!' she said coolly.

'Pass? What pass is this?'

'You have not heard, then? It is the King. He has been taken.'

'Taken . . . ? What do you mean – taken?'

'Taken. Captured. Held, my lord,' she answered, though it was at David that she looked. 'Laid violent hands on, and abducted. Whilst hunting, from Falkland. Taken to Ruthven Castle.'

'Fiend sieze me – captured! The King! And taken to Ruthven, you say . . . ?'

'Aye. By your good-brother, sir – my lord of Gowrie, the Treasurer. And others.'

'Christ God!'

'When was this?' David demanded. 'Is the King harmed?'

'I think not. Though he will be frightened. He must be, for, for . . . ' She paused. 'But two days ago, it was. Word reached the Constable at Erroll last night. I came as soon as I might.'

'Gowrie did this,' my lord burst out. 'Is the man mad? Here is high treason!'

'No doubt. But successful treason, may be. And carefully planned, it seems. There are many more to it than Gowrie. All of the Protestant faction. The Earl of Atholl, Arran's own good-brother; the Earls of Angus and Mar and Glencairn. And March, too. My lords Home and Lindsay and Boyd, and the Master of Glamis . . . '

'That black rogue!'

'What of Lennox? And Arran? Where are they?' David asked.

'It was carefully planned, as I say. My lord Duke had gone to his palace of Dalkeith but the day before, to meet the new French ambassador, when he comes to Leith. And Arran was conducting justice-eyres in his new sheriffdom of Linlithgow. He – Arran – has been arrested and held, by Gowrie's command. My father likewise! And . . . the Bishop of St Boswells!'

'Waesucks – here's a pickle!' Gray declared agitatedly, tugging at his greying beard. All this, indeed, touched him much too closely for personal comfort; not only was Gowrie his brother-in-law, but most of the other lords mentioned in the plot were close associates of his own in the Kirk party.

'I am sorry about your father,' David said. 'You have no word of him? His welfare . . . ?'

'No. But I do not fear for him greatly. Most of his life has been spent in custody of a sort, and he has survived well enough.' She smiled faintly. 'He said that this present prosperity was too good to last! He survived Morton's spleen – I do not think that Gowrie's will be so harsh.'

'M'mmm. So Greysteil has become Greysteil again! I wonder . . . ?' David looked at her thoughtfully. 'You said that the King must be frightened. He must be indeed, for he is easily affrighted. But you meant more than that, I think . . . ?'

'Yes. For the Ruthven lords have extorted a royal warrant from him, ordering the Duke of Lennox to leave the country within two days, on pain of death!'

'Lord! He signed that? He was more than frightened, then. Such means terror, no less! His dear Esmé! The apple of his eye! Och, the poor laddie!'

'God be thanked, at the least, that Patrick was safe away in yon Spain,' Lord Gray asserted. 'Or it would have been himself, as well.'

David slowly looked up – to find Marie's eyes on his. Their glances locked. Neither spoke.

'You are sure of the truth of all this?' the older man went on. 'It is no mere talk? Hearsay . . . ?'

'No. The Lord Home himself was sent from Ruthven Castle last night, to Erroll. To order the Constable to keep his house. Under threat. Being a Catholic. He it was who told us. He said much – gave many reasons for the deed. He said that they had proof that the Duke meant to turn Scotland to Catholic again. That he planned to have James sent abroad to be married to a Catholic princess, and meantime he would rule Scotland alone. Lord Home had it that James would never return to Scotland – that he would be assassinated. Then a secret paper would come forth, with the King's signature, naming Lennox as heir to the throne. Then we should have King Esmé!'

'Soul of God!' Gray swore.

'Oh, there was much else. That Lennox had applied for foreign soldiers, Papal or Spanish, to land in Scotland. The Duke of Guise was to land in Sussex, and Elizabeth was to see her nightmare come true, and have to fight north and south. Home said that Bowes, the English ambassador, had told them that Lennox planned to have all the Protestant lords arrested on a charge of treason . . . '

'That does not ring true, at any rate!' David said. 'He could not have dared that. Wild charges.'

'May be. But they are the excuse, whether they believe them or no.'

Lord Gray took a turn or two up and down the flagstones of his courtyard, spurs jingling. 'This needs a deal of considering,' he muttered. 'You say that Angus and Atholl and Mar are in the conspiracy? Powerful men. And what of the Catholic lords – other than Erroll? Huntly, Herries and the others?'

'No doubt they are being attended to, likewise.'

'Aye. I . . . I must see Crawford. And Oliphant. I . . . '

'The Master of Oliphant was another of those whom Lord Home mentioned as in the endeavour.'

'Say you so! God's death – Oliphant too! I' faith – I must be hence. I must talk with, with . . . You must excuse me, ma'am. Davy, see that the Lady Marie receives all attention. That my house does not lack in anything for her comfort. I must be away. I was in fact on my way when you came . . . '

'I understand, my lord. Go you.'

As they watched him ride clattering out under the gatehouse, solid phalanx of men-at-arms at heel, the young woman shook her head. 'There goes a man with much on his mind, I think.'

'Less than his son and heir, I would say!' David amended.

She turned to him. 'Davy – you think the same, do you?'

'I do not know what to think. Save that it all falls into place damnably neat!'

'Yes. I see it thus also. He said . . . that the Court, Scotland, would be a good place to be furth of, this summer.'

'Aye. And that you would be wise to take your father with you!'

'He could not wait. We must be furth of Scotland within the month, he said. He must go to France, then. For what reason he never told us – or me, at any rate.'

'All he said was that, it was on account of Scotland's affairs. But not on the King's business, I gathered.'

'No.'

'And he has been wearying of Lennox for months.'

'You, you think, then, that he could have arranged all this beforehand? Plotted this conspiracy, left his instructions – and then sailed from Scotland in good time, so that none could hold him in anything responsible? All to bring down Lennox? Without seeming to have a hand in it?'

David drew a hand across his brow. 'I do not know. I do not say that he did it. All I say is that it looks as though he knew that it was to happen – and when. Not to a day, perhaps – but when-abouts. Knew – and did nothing to stop it!'

'Remember – when we asked whether the Duke of Lennox would be returning with him to France, he said – how was it? My lord Duke will be . . . will be otherwise occupied! That was it. That was three months ago.' She shook her head. 'And Patrick is not one to know of plots and intrigues and take no part.'

'No. And William Ruthven – Greysteil – my lord of Gowrie – is not the man to have plotted this. Always he has been a fighter, and not a plotter. Patrick thought but little of his wits – his Uncle Steilpate, he called him! Though they have been mighty thick together, since Morton fell.'

Man and woman looked at each other blankly. What more was there to say?

'Your Mariota would berate us sorely for so thinking of Patrick!' Marie said at length.

'Aye, she would.' Involuntarily, David glanced up at the main keep windows. Nobody seemed to be looking down there-from. The young faces of scholars peered out from the corner-tower, however. 'Come – you must need food. Rest. Or will you be staying here, with us? You will not wish to go back to Erroll? A Catholic house . . . ?'

'No. I thank you – but no. I have a sister, natural but dear to me. Married to an Ogilvie laird deep in one of the Angus glens. I will go there until this trouble is past. I can be there in but a few hours.'

Much as he liked her, David hoped that his relief at this announcement did not show too plainly.

'If you have word of Patrick, you will send to me, in Glen Prosen, Davy?'

'Aye. You still . . . would wish to hear of him? After this?'

'Yes,' she said simply.

'Very well. I am sorry . . . for it all.' He said that with difficulty.

'Yes,' she repeated, and looked away and away. 'I wish . . . I wish . . . ' Shaking her yellow head, she left that unsaid.

Esmé Stuart, the Sieur d'Aubiny, Duke of Lennox, was dead. The news reached Castle Huntly quite casually, at the tail-end of a letter to Davy, sent from Rome. Patrick mentioned a dozen other matters first – the interests of foreign travel, kind enquiries for friends, and his amusement over reported events in Scotland. In this connection, he added, he had just had sure word that poor Esmé had died of a broken heart within a few weeks of his return to France. Personally, he was apt to be suspicious of fatalities from this disease – but since Esmé's lady-wife had refused to see him on his somewhat hurried and informal arrival from Scotland, it might be true . . . though they had got on well enough apart for three years. Heigho – women were the devil, were they not? All of them – even the mature Queen of France herself, Catherine de Medici, who pettishly so seldom forgot old scores! How thrice-blest was his good old Davy, with his so reliable and amiable Mariota, whom the gods preserve . . .

For long David conned and considered that letter, and sought to fathom what lay behind it, before sending the gist of it off to the Lady Marie in her Angus glen.

Meanwhile Scotland seethed, but did not boil over. The King remained a prisoner in Ruthven Castle – though, officially of course, he had merely elected to set up his Court there – and many were the rumours as to his treatment that circulated through the land. Arran, too, was held fast, in various strengths, though his wife, who was free to come and go, did so to some tune, working mightily on his affairs, or at least on affairs of some sort, so that she was as much at Ruthven Castle as she was with her husband. A consortium, with Gowrie as its nominal head, ruled Scotland in the King's name. No major effort was made to release the unfortunate James. Relations with Elizabeth, however, were better than almost ever before, and her Mr Bowes' voice spoke loud in the land. The Kirk gave its approval to the godly lords' doings.

So the winter passed. The Earl of Orkney was released, apparently none the worse for his immurement and very ready to co-operate with all concerned. The Bishop of St. Boswells likewise. Marie Stewart stayed on in Glen Prosen.

Patrick's next message, months later when the snows were all but gone from the high blue mountains to the north, did not reach Castle Huntly in the usual fashion, via a Dysart shipmaster, but by the hands of Robert Logan of Restalrig. Patrick's – and for that matter, David's – roystering, fierce, but cheerful cousin arrived in the Carse in person one late Spring day almost a year after Patrick's departure, and after a drinking session with my lord his uncle, slipped a sealed letter quietly into David's hand. It read thus:

'My fine D.,
I think that it is time that our poor J. had a change of company. Do you not agree? It could be arranged with no great difficulty. J's present companions think not highly of his spirit, and overlook him but scantily, I am assured – no doubt with excuse. The lad pines, and would well do with a change. Moreover, his habits are in need of reform, for he still hunts unseasonable deer. I charge you to see to his improvement. Cousin Robert is in a good situation to assist you, because of his mother. But dear Robert is rash and lacks your sober wits. If you see to it, with his aid, all will be well, I have no doubt.

They tell me that Saints Boswell and Andrew are now again in heavenly embrace. Were J. to join them, at the time of the justice-eyres, it would be justice indeed.

Salutations, my good and upright D!
P.'

If David had perused the previous letter long and carefully, this curious epistle set him frowning more fiercely still. Not that its contents and wording mystified him; he perceived the allusions readily enough. Patrick wanted King James rescued from Ruthven Castle, considered that the time was ripe for the attempt, and proposed that it should be done during a hunt – and at the justice-eyres period in late June when so many of the lords, because of their hereditary jurisdictions, must be holding courts in their own baronies and sheriffdoms, just as Arran had been doing a year before when the Ruthven raiders had struck. Apt justice indeed. Cousin Robert's usefulness, because of his mother, must refer to the fact that the Lady Agnes Logan, formerly Gray and my lord's sister, had as a widow married the Lord Home, now so prominent at Ruthven. Through his step-father, no doubt, Logan could learn much that would be necessary for the success of any rescue attempt. Lastly, the picture of Saints Boswell and Andrew in heavenly embrace could only mean that Master Davidson, Bishop of St. Boswells, was back in St. Andrews town, and this, for some reason, would be the place to take the released King. Obviously, however far away, Patrick was kept very well informed.

But none of that was what wrinkled David's brow.

The question was – what was he to do about it? Could he

accept this task, lend himself to this new plot? Patrick, in his lordly way, just assumed that he would do it. But why should he dance to Patrick's tune always? He was no plotter, no schemer. Indeed, he hated it all. Yet Logan assuredly would be in favour of it, whether he himself took part or no – and headstrong as he was, might well end it all in failure. And that could bear hardly on the King. Indeed, he had to consider James in all this – his own loyalty to his King. Was it his plain duty to help to free him, if he could? The boy had been a captive for nine long months. Was it no one's duty to rescue him?

Was the thought that it might well have been Patrick who first arranged that capture, relevant to his own decision about freeing him? It was difficult . . .

David cudgelled his head over it all, and eventually took his problem upstairs to Mariota, who saw it as no problem at all. The King should be freed, she said. Patrick, hundreds of miles away, could see that clearly enough, and had shown how it could be done. It only remained to carry the business out. But carefully. She wanted no trouble, no dangers. And Davy must keep that horrible Logan man in order . . .

So are the major affairs of men settled.

David, doubtful still, went later that night to Robert Logan's room. He wished that he had had time and excuse to visit remote Glen Prosen first.

Chapter Sixteen

ON a heavy sultry morning of late June, leaden and grey, David sat his horse and fretted. Below him, one of Logan's uncouth mosstroopers squatted amongst the young bracken, paring his nails with a naked dirk. Also in the bracken, beside him, a poor unhappy stag lay on its russet side in panting wide-eyed alarm, its long graceful legs bound together at the hocks so that it could only twitch and jerk them. David was sorry for the beast; it had had a bad two days of it. But nobler game than this was to be chased today; moreover, it was to be hoped that the creature would soon regain its freedom, now.

David gazed northwards, over the rolling green Perthshire landscape that sloped down gently towards the River Almond. Down there, a couple of miles away, Ruthven castle's twin towers and grey walls could just be seen against the background of trees. He was waiting to catch the first glimpse of the hunt – the hunt which he hoped would take place, and which had not in fact taken place yesterday. He fretted because there was so much that could go wrong, even though they had taken every precaution that they could think of. A hunt was planned, certainly; Robert Logan had attached himself to his step-father's entourage at Court for the past two weeks, and had sent the word. But then, a hunt had been planned for yesterday too, and had just failed to take place – why, they knew not – after they had made all their difficult arrangements. It might be the same today – and this wretched stag could not be kept thus captive and shackled indefinitely, without dying on them . . . whatever might be the case with the King. And yesterday had been an ideal day for the attempt, whereas today it was threatening rain. Rain now would ruin everything, washing away the vital scent.

Though the morning was still young, David and his assistants had been busy for hours. The captive stag, procured at considerable cost from a forester, and brought to the district secretly and with extreme difficulty by night, they had taken down to within half-a-mile of the castle while it was still dark, and then led back here, hobbled. At least the scent that it left should be strong and evident, for the unfortunate brute had been in a sweating panic all the way, leaping against its bonds, falling time and again, in direst danger of breaking its legs. It was supposed to be a tamed stag, but it looked as though their forester had deceived them with a fairly newly-caught wild one. a broken leg would have confounded their whole attempt. At last, however, they had got the creature here, and Gowrie's deer-hounds should have no difficulty in picking up the scent – if it did not rain.

Ensuring that the hunt came in an exact direction had been no simple problem to solve, and David had spent much time in the district, and dodging the Ruthven foresters, before he chose this spot. Fortunately, with Ruthven Castle sited as it was, hunting must start out in a southerly direction; for eastwards lay the populous lands and Perth town, to the north the Almond curved round in its deep trough, and to the west was Ruthven village itself. South lay the rising open woodlands, mile after mile of them, lifting to the long ridge of Lamberkine. Many were the routes that could be taken approximately southwards, however. Hence the need for this hot scent, fairly close to the castle. It was to be hoped and prayed that no other wandering deer would stray across their track, meantime, to confuse the issue – though that was surely unlikely, with the man-smell so prominent also, inevitably.

Well might David fret. Why had he ever agreed to this crazy enterprise?

They heard the hunting-horns sounding before ever they spied riders, but that only meant that indeed the hunt was on today, and presumably a scent had been picked up – not necessarily that it was the right scent, and coming in the right direction. A smirr of thin rain chilled David's face, and set him cursing.

The horn sounded a few times again, and significantly louder, before at last horsemen became visible – three of them riding hard, and over a mile away, emerging from denser woodland. David gave a sigh of thankfulness. They were on the right line. The huntsmen, they would be. He could not pick out hounds at this range.

A tightly-grouped knot of four or five riders appeared fairly close behind the first trio; Gowrie with the King, no doubt – and, it was to be hoped, Logan of Restalrig. Then, just coming into view, the mass of the hunt, strung out behind. A small company compared with the Falkland hunts.

From his vantage point, David could see most of the ground

between the riders and himself. A spine of wooded ridge ran down almost half-way towards them. It was vital that they took the western side of that. The scent was there to lead them, but he dare not assume that the project would go forward until he saw the leaders past that fork.

He jerked a few words to his seemingly careless companion. 'You are ready, man? They are nearing the parting of the ways – half-a-mile away. When I see them take the right route, I leave you.'

'Aye,' the Borderer said, nonchalantly.

'Be ready, then, in mercy's sake! When they reach yon dead tree – the huntsmen see you – cut the brute's thongs. And quickly. No moment of delay, then – but no moment before either. If the creature seems like to bolt the wrong way, wave your arms, scare it – but do not shout, or the huntsmen will hear you. Then, up after me to the others. You have it?'

'Aye.'

'Do not let yourself be seen – that is . . . Here they come to the parting. I see the hounds now. Aye, Glory – the hounds have taken the right road. Praises be! The huntsmen too. One is holding back, to guide the hunt. I'm off! Play your part aright, and you shall be well rewarded, I promise you!'

The other grinned white teeth in a dark gypsy face, and said nothing. Presumably Logan knew his men.

Forcing his way through the thick tangle of undergrowth and brushwood immediately behind them, David spurred his mount uphill, pushing it urgently up over the littered difficult slope. In a half-circle he climbed, to get well above and ahead of the line of the approaching hunt – and to remain unseen, of course. Timing was everything, now – timing, and the instincts of an ill-used deer.

The immediate wooded slope that he was on ended in a secondary ridge, wooded but fairly sharp. Through this a fast-flowing stream had cut a deep ravine, steep, almost precipitous. It was towards the eastern lip of this that David rode in not too wide an arc. At the summit nick of it, he drew up beside half-a-dozen men who waited there, more of Logan's mosstroopers.

'They are coming. Is all in train?' he panted.

Axe in hand, their leader nodded. 'Gie us the word, Maister, and we'll hae them doon before you can spit!'

David glanced at the three wind-blown Scots pines that over-hung the grassy ride rimming the edge of the ravine. They looked secure enough. As well that there was no wind today to blow them. 'Right – to your places. We shall not have a deal of warning.' He slipped a mask over his face. This, and the rusty breastplate that he wore, was Mariota's idea, that she had made him promise to use, in her preoccupation with being careful.

The green ride that the scent, and therefore the hunt, followed, continued right on up to this point, and beyond, bordering the very rim of the gully. David had selected this spot with infinite care, after days of prospecting. The entire endeavour depended upon the known instinct of a frightened deer to run uphill, always. When their captive stag was released, the chances were ten against one that it would bolt up here. The other slope that it might use would be barred by its late captor. With the hounds in view, it would choose a clear run up the ride rather than any battling with thickets – that was almost equally certain. Strange factors on which the fate of a king should hang.

The men were moving over to the three pine trees, where heaped brushwood would screen them, and David, feeling distinctly foolish behind his mask, was making for a slightly higher spot where he would gain a better over-all view, when the sudden baying of hounds rang out. Without a doubt that meant a sight; the long-legged shaggy-coated grey deer-hounds ran silent on a scent, and only gave tongue on a sight. Immediately afterwards as though to confirm it, a horn wound ululantly, proclaiming to the hunt behind that a deer was seen. The stag had been released, and was running. But running where?

That question was answered only moments later. Into sight round a bend in the lip of the ravine the creature came bounding swiftly, seeming to drift over the ground, no longer the awkward ungainly captive of the past two days but the epitome of grace and speed, long neck outstretched, velvet-clad antlers laid back along rippling shoulders, nostrils distended wide. Up and past the hidden watchers it raced, on over the crest, and down beyond.

The baying sounded close behind, but it was quite a few seconds before half-a-dozen rangy hounds came, in a tight group, noses down, slavering in hot pursuit. If they caught the man-scent, at the crest of the ridge, it did not deflect them for a moment from their quarry. They disappeared down into the dip beyond, clamantly implacable.

The beat of horses' hooves throbbed on the still air now. Round the bend in the green track rode two huntsmen, almost neck-and-neck, horns in hand, leather jerkins already flecked with spume from their galloping mounts. David watched them pass, frowning. It was a pity about the third one; he might possibly complicate matters a little.

There was an interval now, with David beating a tattoo on the pommel of his saddle with his finger-tips; Patrick and others had called him stolid, but he was in fact nothing of the sort. Then the drumming of hooves, many hooves, began to drift uphill towards them again, a jumbled sound that precluded any individual identification.

The third huntsman seemed long in coming. When at last he rounded the bend into view, he came only at a trot, looking back over his shoulder. Worse, at the very summit of the ridge, directly below the group of hidden mosstroopers, he halted his slavering horse, and sat looking back. David shrank in on himself, and felt as obvious as a beacon amongst the bushes.

But after an agonising half-minute or so, the fellow raised his hand and waved – an unnecessary signal surely. Then he turned and rode on.

Now . . .

Into view rode four horsemen, one, two and one – colourful people these, not russet-garbed huntsmen. In front rode the youthful figure of King James, on one of his black Barbaries. Just behind were the Earl of Gowrie – whose justice-eyres of course need not take him from home – side by side with young Johnny, Earl of Mar, who as still a minor could not yet act as magistrate. Then, close on their tails, came Robert Logan. Logan's eyes were busy.

David drew a deep breath. Seventy or eighty yards to go – and no sign of the next group of riders behind. The King, superbly mounted of course, always led at a cracking pace – his one accomplishment.

The mosstroopers' eyes turned on him. David waited.

With the King just below the hidden group of Borderers, David suddenly raised his hand.

Immediately, the half-dozen men were furiously active, pushing and heaving with all their might. The three tall pine trees, their shallow roots already cut through and supported only by props, swayed, almost imperceptibly at first. Then, ponderously, one toppled, its boughs catching in those of its neighbour, expediting its fall. With a great crash it came down, right across the grassy ride below, its dark topmost branches well out over the lip of the ravine – and a bare horse's length behind Logan of Restalrig. The second tree crashed three or four seconds later, and the third, toppling somewhat askew, fell slantwise down the ride in a shower of twigs and cones and snapping wood. The entire ridge seemed to shake and tremble to the fall of them.

Round the bend in the ride, farther down, the first of the next group of horsemen appeared.

David did not wait to see more, but brushing aside his cover, spurred his mount downwards.

At the sound of the crashes behind them, the leaders had sought to rein in their horses in alarm, James gobbling in fear, Gowrie and Mar shouting. Logan whipped out his sword, and rode straight at the two earls. From up the bank his moss-troopers came leaping down, yelling.

David, naked sword in hand likewise, made directly for the King. 'Your Grace,' he cried. 'Fear nothing. It is a rescue. A rescue!'

It is to be doubted whether the youth heard him. He sat his plunging black, petrified with fear, only hanging on by instinct. Cold steel always had that effect on James Stewart.

Gowrie and Mar had little time to spare for reassurance of their monarch. The former, an old soldier, was not long in getting out his own sword, but young Johnny Mar, not very much older than James, was making a fumbling botch of it. Scornfully leaving him to his minions, Logan bore furiously down upon the other, weapon weaving. The clash of their steel rang out above the shouting.

David, eyes busy, ranged his horse right up against the King's Barbary, and grabbed its bridle. 'Come, Sire!' he jerked. 'Nothing will harm you. All is well.' He saw that the Borderers were dragging Mar off his horse, well practised in the art as they were. Through and beyond the barrier of fallen trees, he could just glimpse agitated riders milling around, unable to get their mounts past, veering away from the steep drop into the ravine, and continually glancing up the steep bank to their left as though expecting further attacks from thence. He was wondering whether it was fair to leave Logan, good sworder as he was, to battle it out with the veteran Greysteil, when the sudden appearance of another horseman, halberd couched and levelled, ready to charge, clinched the issue. It was the dark mosstrooper whose task it had been to release the stag. Seeing him directly above him on the bank, and presumably recognising the folly of argument with a seven-foot long halberd, Gowrie sought to back his horse, to disengage. He threw down his sword to the ground, and folded his arms across his broad chest.

David, letting out a sigh of relief, reined his own horse right round, dragging the black with it, and urged them both to a trot southwards along the ride, after the stag, the hounds and the huntsmen. At the same time he whipped off his mask from his face.

'It's ... it's you! Davy! Davy Gray!' James stammered. 'Och, man – it's just yoursel'!'

'Aye, Sire, none other. We had to get you away from the Ruthvens some way. We're Your Grace's friends, never fear.'

'Friends, aye – friends,' tremulous Majesty repeated, pathetically eager to believe it.

'This way, Sire – and quickly. See – down here. It is a steep track, but there's no danger in it. And you are a good horseman . . '

A little way along the ride David swung the horses off sharply to the right, into a tiny track that seemed to plunge right over the edge of the ravine. Daunting it looked, and David heard James's gasp as he eyed it, zig-zagging away down dizzily amongst the bushes and ferns, a deer-track of the woodland stags, no doubt. David led the way into it, but the King was still hesitating on the brink when Restalrig came cantering up, and more or less bustled him over the edge and down. Robert Logan did not know the meaning of either tact or caution.

Sandwiched between the two of them, James was forced down into the ravine, and at no laggard pace. Most of the way his eyes were tight shut, undoubtedly. Fortunately horses do not seem to suffer from vertigo, and have an instinct for the surest road. The foot was reached without mishap.

There was still a lot of shouting from above, but it sounded incoherent, undirected.

'Your men?' David called to Logan. 'Will they get away, well enough?'

Restalrig hooted. 'God's eyes! Think you a wheen Court jackdaws could hold my callants? Never heed for *them*, Davy. It's oorsel's we hae to look after. Yon Greysteil will no' give up that easy.'

At mention of that name, James gulped, his big eyes rolling from one to the other. 'Wh'where are you taking me?' he got out.

'Up the bed of this burn, for a bittie, Your Highness – then an easy way out that I know of. Then across the Earn, and make for St Andrews.'

'St Andrews? Man, Davy – that's a long way . . . '

'It is, yes. But you will want to win a long way from Ruthven Castle, do you not?'

'Aye. Aye – but . . . '

'Come on – there's nae time for idle blethers!' the forthright Logan declared.

They went, splashing up the bed of the stream, screened from above by the overhanging trees. The going was reasonably good, though there were some steps and stairs over which tiny rapids poured. But at a larger waterfall they had to leave the burn to climb the far side of the ravine, by no path but a milder slope. Whether there was yet any pursuit they could not tell, by reason of the intervening woodland.

At the summit they paused for a few seconds, searching the prospect, near and far. Nowhere was there any sign of movement – though the echoes of shouting floated to them across the valley. Away to the east the land began to fall to the wide strath of the River Earn.

'So far, I think, Sire, we are not followed,' David announced. 'But it is a far cry to St Andrews. A long ride before we can consider that we are safe.'

'Safe . . . ?' the King repeated. 'Will I be safe at St Andrews, Davy? Will I ever be safe, man?'

David bit his lip. 'Assuredly, Sire,' he said – and hoped that he was not a forsworn liar.

They were down into the wide trough of Strathearn near Aberdalgie before they perceived that they were in fact being chased. Looking back, they saw coming down off the high ground a long strung-out trail of horsemen, fully a mile away, but riding hard. It was too much to hope that they were unconnected with themselves. Sheer neck-and-collar work was now all that remained for them.

That they did, taxing their beasts to the utmost. With this situation very much in view, David had borrowed the longest-winded horse in his father's stables – a big rangy roan. Logan, who was probably as much interested in horseflesh as he was in anything, was always well-mounted. Even so, the King's Barbary had the heels of them. He at least would take a deal of catching.

They splashed across the shallows of the Earn at a point where it spread wide around a shoaling island of sand and pebbles. Then up and across the rolling northern foothills of the Ochils, with the Tay estuary beginning to open before them to the north and east. High above the woods of Rossie and the tall tower of Balmanno they galloped, and looking back, decided that the leaders of the chase were no nearer, and the majority of it further off.

Keeping to the heights, they drove their steaming foaming horses esatwards. Over the glen of Abernethy and above the shattered Abbey of Lindores, they could only distinguish five horsemen still in pursuit.

'We have them outridden,' Logan panted, grinning. 'Your Grace needs swifter gaolers!'

It was not until they were well crossed into Fife that James accepted that they had indeed shaken off the chase, and the paralysing fear seemed to leave him. Suddenly he was a changed youth. He remembered that he was the King again, and said 'we' instead of 'I'. He laughed and gabbled somewhat, referring to 'our good Davy' and 'our worthy Restalrig', and hinted that superb horsemanship, his own more especially, had won the day. He also pointed out that it was only a few days after his seventeenth birthday, and that hereafter he intended to rule his realm sternly, as Scotland should be ruled.

Nevertheless, as they rode in a more leisurely fashion through North Fife, David came to the conclusion that James had changed fairly radically since last he had seen him – as perhaps was scarcely to be wondered at. He was bitter, suspicious, now childishly and unnaturally cynical, now naturely astute. More than once he startled his rescuers by the penetrating shrewdness of his questions and comments. He asked after Patrick and Arran and his Uncle Robert of Orkney, as well as of March and Bishop Davidson. He cursed Gowrie and the Master of Glamis and Johnny Mar and the other Ruthven lords. The one name, significantly, that he did not mention was that of Esmé Stuart.

David perceived that the boy whom he had rescued was almost a man. A strange man he was going to be. He doubted whether he would like to trust him as a friend; as unfriend, he imagined, he might well prove to be implacable.

Even as the crow flies it is forty long miles from Ruthven to St Andrews – and as the fugitives rode it was half as far again. Accordingly, it was three very weary travellers who eventually spied the towers and pinnacles of the grey university city by the eastern sea, and gave thanks, Logan profanely.

'To where do you take us, Davy?' James asked. 'To the castle? Does not my lord of Moray hold the castle now?'

'That I do not know. My instructions are to bring Your

Grace to Master Davidson, the Bishop of St. Boswells.'

'Eh, so? A godly man – but canny. Is he in this, Davy? Did he plot it?'

'No, Sire.'

'I thought no'. He's ower canny, yon one. Who, then? No' you two? You're bold enough – ooh aye, I'll gie you that. But a longer heid plotted it, I'll swear.' James recollected himself. '*We'll* swear. Who?'

A little ruefully, David rubbed his chin. 'It was the Master of Gray, Sire. From France,' he admitted.

'Man – is that a fact! Waesucks – our good Patrick! Frae France. Aye, but it is like him, like him! He has a long arm, the bonny Master o' Gray, has he no?' Time he was back wi' us. What is he doing away in yon France, man? He should never have gone. All this ill that's come to us might never have been, if he hadna gone. What for did he leave us, Davy?'

'I do not rightly know, Sire.'

Logan snorted a laugh. 'As well ask that o' Auld Horny himsel'!'

They rode into St Andrews town that evening by the same West Port out of which David had taken his new bride eight eventful years before, and which he had never since darkened. In the narrow streets none knew the dusty tired travellers. Though he would, in fact, rather have gone to any other premises in that city, David made for the Principal's house of St. Mary's College, for Master Davidson had managed to retain the office of Principal, and its revenues along with his bishopric, at the trifling cost of appointing an underpaid deputy.

The cattle were gone from the grassy quadrangle, and gardens were being laid out therein, more in keeping with the enhanced status of the establishment's master. David rapped resoundingly on the former chapel door, beside which three horses already stood tethered.

The same supercilious man-servant, now the more so out of his advancing years and much more handsome livery, opened presently, to stare. It was at David that he stared, in undisguised astonishment and hostility, though his glance did show some slight glimmering of respect at the quality of Logan's hunting clothes and general air of authority. The youthful King he ignored completely.

'We would see Master Davidson – the Bishop,' David said. 'Is he at home?'

The other pursed his lips, frowning.

208

'Quickly, fellow!' Logan barked, and the man, blinking, turned and went within. But he closed the door behind him.

'Curst lackey!' Logan cried. 'Sink him – he'll no' keep Restalrig standing at some jumped-up cleric's door, like a packman!' and he thumped loudly on the door-panels with the hilt of his sword.

James was too tired to do more than pluck at his lower lip, and mutter.

The servitor came back in a few moments, his expression a nice mixture of triumph and alarm. 'My lord Bishop canna see you,' he said. 'He is throng wi' important folk. If you have a message frae the Lord Gray, you can leave it.'

'God damn your scullion's soul!' Logan roared. 'Stand aside, fool!' And striding forward, he knocked the fellow reeling backwards with a violent back-handed blow, and stalked within. To the servant's wailing protest, the others followed him.

Logan was marching hugely down the arched lobby, but David heard voices from the same front room in which he had once waited for so long. Without ceremony, he opened the door.

Bishop Davidson was perambulating to and fro on the carpet, his purple cape and cassock flowing behind as once a black Calvinist gown had done. He was holding forth to three men who looked like country gentry or prosperous merchants, and who were listening to him with due respect. At sight of David, he halted in his episcopal steps.

'Sweet Mary-Mother – what insolence is this!' he demanded. 'Get out of my house. I told you – never did I wish to see your face again. Now, go – before I have my men take their whips to you!'

David ignored all that. 'I request word with you, in private, Master Davidson,' he said. 'In the King's name.'

'The King's name! Are you mad, as well as insolent and depraved, fellow?' It was dim out in the lobby, with the evening light, and David stood in front of the King. 'Out with you!'

'These men with you – who are they?' David turned low-voiced to Logan. '*You* had better ask him. We cannot hazard the King's safety.'

'With all the pleasure in the world!' Restalrig cried. 'I will prick this overblown priestly bladder!'

But James asserted himself, for once. He shambled from behind David. 'Good Master Bishop,' he said. 'I . . . we are tired. We have ridden far. And apace. You receive me . . . us but ill. We require comforts . . . food . . .'

'Merciful soul of God – Your Grace! Your Highness! Sire – I . . . I . . .'

'Aye, you quivering bag o' lard, get down on your fat knees?' Logan shouted. 'Or where's your fine bishopric, eh?'

And strange to say, there before them all, the Bishop-Principal did just that. Down on the carpet he sank, in prompt, hearty and urgent supplication, clasping white hands. 'Your Majesty, I crave your most royal clemency! Humbly I seek Your Grace's pardon. I did not know . . . I have been much put about . . . I thought that Your Highness was . . . I meant no discourtesy. All that I have is yours, Sire . . .'

'I ken that fine, aye.' Catching David's eye, James leered a sidelong grin. 'Oh, aye. I'm glad to hear you say it, my lord.'

'But of course, Sire. All, all. If I may have your gracious pardon. I will prove it – prove my enduring devotion and loyal service. By all that is holy, I swear it!'

'I'ph'mmm. Is that so, Master Bishop?' Most evidently young James was enjoying having this august personage grovelling before him. Thanks to Master George Buchanan's tutorship and the Kirk's fiery orators, he had an imbued respect, if no great love, for learned divines. To have one thus before him, was sweet.

It was David who called a halt. 'Sire,' he said bluntly. 'What is important is not Master Davidson's contrition, but your safety. First we wish to know that these three gentlemen are to be trusted? And then to know where in St Andrews you will be safest disposed?'

The three earlier visitors, who had been standing in appalled amaze, forthwith broke into incoherent protestations of loyalty. Davidson, seeing the attention transferred from himself, got to his feet. 'Majesty,' he interrupted earnestly. 'These are sound men – but of no importance. The Provost of this town, just, and his brother and friend. They shall be gone, this instant . . .'

'Wait!' David ordered, briefly. 'We do not wish word of the King's arrival in the town bruited abroad – yet. Who holds the castle?'

'It is part-ruined, since the troubles of . . . of . . . But my Lord of Moray, the Commendator, has a Lieutenant therein . . .'

'Is it still a strong place? His Grace would be safe there?'

'Indeed, yes. My men will guard His Grace to the death . . . !'

'Your men!' Logan jeered. 'Mouthing acolytes and scribbling

clerks! Have we no better warriors than that, in St Andrews?'

'They are good men, and true, my lord,' the Bishop assured, humbly. 'Well founded and lusty. I have two-score of them. And there is my lord Earl of March, his men . . .'

'March!' David and Logan cried in unison. 'How came March to St Andrews? And when?'

'But two weeks agone.' When the Bishop answered David, he did not look at him, but addressed himself as to the King. 'Why he came, I know not. He lodges at the Priory, with full three-score men-at-arms. Did he know, perchance, that Your Grace was to be here?'

David and Logan exchanged glances. This looked like more of Patrick's work, March, the Countess of Arran's deposed husband, and a simple bumbling man, had been used by Patrick before for his own purposes, being rich and gullible.

'Aye,' Logan said, heavily. 'It falls out powerfully convenient.'

David nodded. 'Your Grace, we will send the Provost to request my Lord March to attend you here forthwith. And another of the gentlemen to the Lieutenant of the castle, with orders to have it open to receive Your Highness at once. Will that serve?'

'Aye, Master Davy. But I'm right hungry, mind . . .'

'Master Davidson will surely see to that, while we wait.'

'It is my joy and delight, Your Majesty.'

And so it fell out. The King of Scots, fed, refreshed and to some degree rested, attended by the Earl of March, the Bishop of St. Boswells and the Provost of the town, was installed in the part-demolished but still powerful castle of St. Andrews, seat of former Archbishops, on its sea-girt rock, and the gate locked and barred. And in the safety thereof, he made one of his lightning-like changes of character. Of a sudden he was in command, arrogant, boastful. The admiring courtiers learned a version of the escape from Ruthven in which the King himself was the hero and main protagonist. He damned and cursed the lords Gowrie, Mar, Glencairn, Master of Glamis and the rest, in impressive fashion for a youth of seventeen, and commanded their immediate arrest on a charge of highest treason. He ordered the citizens of St. Andrews to provide for his every need, and to raise an adequate force for his sure defence. James was the King, and no one was to forget it ever again. From now on, he would rule this realm with a strong arm, as a king should. And let the good Captain Jamie, Earl of Arran, be brought to him forthwith.

David decided that it was high time for him to go home to Castle Huntly, whatever Logan might elect to do. He requested permission to retire from Court the very next day, and His Majesty was graciously pleased to grant it.

Chapter Seventeen

PATRICK did not return home just yet. Perhaps that was as well for a peace-loving man like himself, for the Ruthven lords had not quite shot their bolt. Resisting somewhat half-hearted efforts at arrest, they seized the town and castle of Stirling – of which of course Johnny Mar was Hereditary Governor – and manned and munitioned it against the royal forces. This situation at least gave the newly-freed Arran what he wanted – *carte blanche* from the frightened James to take whatever measures he required to restore order, as the only soldier of any experience in the King's present company. Captain Jamie had learned his soldiering in the hard ruthless school of the Swedish wars, and nothing could have pleased him more than to be given the opportunity to demonstrate something of what he had learned – especially against the men who had kept him a prisoner for the best part of a year, wife or no wife. With a force consisting mainly of the followings of the great Catholic nobles, Huntly, Montrose, Herries, Erroll and the rest, he marched on Stirling – and the Ruthven lords, deciding discretion on this occasion to be a distinct improvement on valour, melted away before him, without a siege, into the convenient fastness of the Highlands. The Kirk kept very quiet; James sported a crucifix; Elizabeth thundered from Whitehall; Arran stretched himself in all directions; and the Master of Gray, in response to repeated urgent summons from his monarch, at last arrived back in his homeland at the end of August, a bronzed gallant and carefree figure in the most dashing of the new French modes, a joy and a delight to all who saw him. This was made the more striking in that he brought with him a snub-nosed, freckled and awkward ten-year-old boy, whom he seldom let out of his sight, even for a moment. Whatever malicious tongues might say, however, this boy was with him apparently also at the King's express command. He was Ludovick Stuart, second Duke of Lennox, Esmé's son. How Patrick had convinced Esmé's Duchess, who had refused even to see her husband, to allow him to bring away to hated Protestant Scotland the apple of her eye, is something that he alone could tell.

He rode in, unannounced, under the gatehouse at Castle Huntly, one golden first day of September, with the boy at his side, both mounted significantly on black Barbaries. If anything could indicate high royal favour, that did. The pair did not have even a groom as escort.

In all the wide courtyard only one small figure happened to be there to greet them – the petite and self-possessed person of Mary Gray. She curtseyed prettily, and then stood regarding them with headcocked speculation.

From his saddle, Patrick gazed down at her for appreciable moments, his handsome features unusually thoughtful. It was nearly two years since he had seen her. 'My dear . . . Mary,' he said, and for once forgot to smile. 'You grow . . . you grow more . . . in fact, Mary, you grow marvellously!'

'I do not think that I am very big, sir,' she answered. 'I am nine years old, you know.'

'Aye, 'fore God – so you are! Nine years. But . . . you know me, child?'

'But of course. You are my Uncle Patrick, come from France. Uncle Patrick – who makes my mother look strange, and my father frown. I know you fine. But I do not know this boy. Is he a new son that you have got?'

'H'mmm.' Patrick drew a hand over his mouth. 'No, Mary. Not so. This is Vicky. Ludovick Stuart. He is also my lord Duke of Lennox, but I do not suppose that you will think much of that. He is just near your own age – a few months older. You will be good friends, I am sure. But he speaks very little of our language, as yet . . .'

'I can speak French,' Mary assured. 'My father has taught me. My father went to France, too, long ago. *Bonjour, Monsieur Garçon*,' she said, curtseying again. '*Je parle français. Un peu.*'

The stocky boy on the black horse stared down at her owlishly.

Laughing again, Patrick dismounted, and went to help down the boy from his tall perch. 'Vicky is a littly shy, lass. But you will soon remedy that, eh? Do not be too hard on him, Mary! ! . . .'

'Patrick!' Mariota came running down the timber steps from the main keep, skirts kilted high, a picture of flushed, bright-eyed loveliness. Almost she seemed as though she would throw herself straight into his arms. Then, recollecting herself, she came to a teetering halt in front of him in breathless, attractive confusion. Behind her, David appeared in the iron-grilled doorway, displaying less forthright rapture.

Patrick had no qualms to recollect. He swept up Mariota –

though a little less high than once he had done, for she was a big well-made woman now and no slip of a girl – kissing her comprehensively and enthusiastically.

'My splendid and adorable Mariota!' he cried. 'How beautiful you are! How kind. And generous! What a form! Aye, by God – and what a weight, too!' And he set her down, panting.

'You are home then, Patrick,' David greeted, his voice coming thickly. 'It has been a long time. More than a year. You look . . . as though you throve!'

'Aye, my good stern Davy! He who frowns! It does me good to see you all. You have all grown, I swear – Mary more bewitching, more ravishing; Mariota more beautiful, more desirable, more rounded   and Davy more like Davy than ever!'

'Aye,' David said 'And the laddie?'

'That is Vicky,' Mary announced

'Why yes, so he is. This is Ludovick Stuart, Duke of Lennox . . who resembles his father but little, I think.'

'Lord! You . . . you have brought him here? D'Aubigny's son. *You* . . . !'

'Indeed, yes. On the King's express command. He is, after all, Scotland's only duke!'

'He is the son of the man . . .' David paused.

'The man whom we both knew so well. Surely we can do no less than show him kindly welcome, brother?'

David bit his lip, but Mariota stooped quickly, arms out to the boy, who eyed her but doubtfully.

Mary took him by the hand. 'Come with me,' she commanded. 'I have a hedgepig with babies. In my garden. Come.'

Without enthusiasm, the Duke went with her.

'Patrick!' Mariota exclaimed, rising. 'You are thinner, I think. You are well? Where have you come from? Have you ridden far?'

'I am perfectly well, my dear. We do not all have the facility for growing fat! And have ridden only from St Andrews, of blessed memory! Where James insists in keeping his Court, meantime. A chilly place in autumn mists, as I think you will recollect. We must move him before the winter, I vow! I came thither from Rheims only two days ago.'

'You are not come home to stay, then . . .?'

'I fear not, my dove. Much as I would relish life here with you . . . and with Davy, of course!'

'Have you not done enough? At the Court?' David asked,

pointedly. 'You have a fair heritage here . . .'

'God forbid! Would you have Arran and his . . . lady ruling all Scotland? Save us from that!'

'James himself aspires to rule his realm, I think.'

'One day, no doubt. James will need to rule himself before he rules a kingdom. Meantime, a loyal subject's duty is to aid and guide him, is it not? For the good of that kingdom!'

David began to speak, and then held his tongue, meeting his brother's eye steadily instead. Patrick changed the subject.

'Where is the noble and puissant Lord Gray?' he asked, lightly.

'He is at Fowlis Castle. Has been for some days.'

'Ah! With a new lady, I'll be bound!'

Mariota led the way indoors for refreshment.

Later, with the young woman gone down to the gardens for the children, Patrick manoeuvred his brother out into the courtyard again, where none might overhear. 'The Lady Marie?' he said, abruptly for him. 'She is not at St Andrews. None there know her whereabouts. Do you, Davy?'

David did not answer at once. 'What if I do?' he said, at length. 'Why should I tell you?'

'Why not, brother?'

'It could be that she were better off lacking your company.'

'So-o-o! Are you her keeper, then, Davy?'

'I am not. Only her friend.'

'Ah. And I? What then am I?'

'Aye – well may you ask! It is a question that I ask myself frequently! What are you? Whose friend are you – save your own?'

Looking at his brother, it was Patrick's turn to be silent for a little. 'This is . . . interesting, Davy,' he said presently, 'Aye, interesting. What makes friendship? Judgment? Criticism? Or trust? Understanding? Sympathy?'

'Something of all, it may be. But the trust and the sympathy must be two-sided, I think. Whom do you trust, Patrick? And who may trust you?'

'Heigho – you I hope, Davy! And Marie likewise. Where is she man?'

'If I tell you, will you make me a promise!?'

'I will, of course. Anything that is in reason.'

'It is in reason, certainly. It is just this – that you will not use her in any of your intrigues. That you will use her kindly, and not knowingly hurt her.'

'Lord, Davy – of course I promise it. But . . . this, from you! What does she mean to you man?'

'Just that I will not see her hurt. You understand, Patrick?'

'I hear you, anyway!' Patrick glanced sidelong at his brother, knowing that grim tone from of old. They had walked out beneath the gatehouse into the wide and grassy forecourt. 'You have my promise. Where is she?'

'In Glen Prosen. With her natural sister. who is married to Wat Ogilvie, a lairdling there.'

'Glen Prosen? In the wilderness! I see. Has she been there long? Was she there when . . . when . . . ?'

'No,' the other said briefly. 'She went afterwards. Her father was held, and her brothers scattered.'

'But . . you saw her?'

'Aye. She came here. She it was who first told us of it. Of the King's capture. And what followed.'

'I see.' Patrick kicked a fallen twig out of his way, casually. 'How did the matter appear to her? How did she take it?'

David almost imperceptibly edged his brother over the greensward towards a little path, all but overgrown with long grasses. 'I think that she took it as I did,' he said slowly. 'Took it but ill. Took it that a clever hand was behind it all – a hand that did not appear.'

'Indeed.'

'Yes, a ruthless hand that played with men as though they were but puppets on strings – whilst itself remained safe hidden in a sleeve!'

Patrick laughed. 'A pretty conceit, Davy – but improbable, I think. Was that her invention, or yours? She has a level head on her, that one. I would not think her so fanciful.'

'No?' He took his brother's arm. 'This way, Patrick.'

The other suddenly perceived whither he was being led, guided. He halted, and made as though to turn back. David's pressure on his arm was strong, however. They were on the start of the little track that led down into the birchwood, where once and more than once criticism had taken a physical form.

'I am not dressed for woodland walking,' he said, a little strangely.

'Are you ever? Come you, Patrick.'

'No. This is folly. I have not the time . . .'

'Come, you. We have all the time that there is. I only wish to speak with you, brother.' David said softly. 'Did you think . . . ?'

Patrick mustered a laugh and a one-shouldered shrug. 'We are

217

grown men,' he said. 'Bairns no longer. I am Master of Gray, of His Majesty's Privy Council, Master of the Wardrobe, Gentleman of the Bedchamber, Commendator of St Vigeans – did you know that? – Knight of the White Cross of Castile.'

'Aye. And I am just Davy the Bastard, still! So your lord Councillorship need have no fears. Come, you.'

In silence, nevertheless, and wary-eyed, Patrick paced down the path, through the brushing brackens, beside his brother. 'Well, man?' he said at length, as though it was forced from him. 'Out with it. What is this talk you would have?'

'Wait,' David advised, mildly. 'We are nearly there.'

'But . . .'

They came down to the little green amphitheatre amongst the trees, that Patrick at least had not visited since that day when he had laid the blame for Mariota's pregnancy upon his brother – and had paid some sort of price therefor in battered features and bleeding nose. There David halted.

'Why did you betray Esmé Stuart to his death?' he asked levelly.

Patrick raised finely arching brows in astonishment. 'Betray . . . ? I? Why Davy – what are you thinking of? What foolishness is this . . . ?'

'Why did you betray Esmé Stuart to his death?' the other repeated inexorably. 'You plotted his downfall, encompassed his ruin and banishment, and assured his doom, as surely as though you had stabbed him with your own dagger. Whether you arranged his final death also, is small matter. Why did you do it, Patrick?'

'Christ God, man – are you crazed? Am I responsible for what Gowrie and Lyon and Angus and the others did?'

'I think that you are, yes – since it was you ensured that they did it!'

'You talk of you know not what. Lennox died in France, while I was in Spain.'

'What does that prove? The power of silver – Jesuit silver, perhaps? And a far-seeing eye. How was it that you put it, one time? "Most men are blinded by passion and prejudice. Those who can preserve a nice judgment and a clear head may achieve much." I have never forgotten your creed, Patrick!'

'This is not to be borne!' the other cried, his handsome features flushing. 'So much will I accept from you – but only so much!' And he swung about on his high-heeled shoe.

David's hand shot out to grip his brother's shoulder, and

whirl him round to face him again. 'Not so fast, Patrick,' he remarked evenly. 'This is the place where always truth was spoken, in the end. Let us have the truth, now. That is why I brought you here. Or must I beat it out of you, as I used to do, with my bare hands? We are bairns no longer as you say. Tell me then, why you betrayed your friend. It is important to me, who have been your friend also. For he *was* your friend. You brought him to this land. You helped to make him ruler of all Scotland. If he offended, and went too far, you could have corrected him surely, brought him down a little? But to ruin him entirely, and from a distance . . .'

'That is only your vain imagining, I tell you.'

'Can you deny that you knew that it all would fall out so, before ever you went to France? That is why you went – to let others do your ill work, while you went safe, and retained the confidence of the King? You gave yourself away, to the Lady Marie and myself, yon day by the Eden. You admitted then . . .'

'I admit nothing! You forget yourself, man. I thought that you loved me, Davy?'

'Aye – but does that mean that I must love the evil treacherous ways of you? That I may not try to save you from your own lust of betrayal? And others, too . . . ?'

'Aye – and others too! There we have it! Marie Stewart! It is Marie Stewart you would be the saviour of! *You* talk of lust and betrayal! It is her that you lust for . . .'

Like a whip cracking David's hand shot out and slapped hard across his brother's sun-bronzed features. 'Say that again, and I will make your beautiful face . . . so that you dare not show it . . . to Marie . . . or your maggot-blown Court!' he jerked.

Patrick shivered strangely, fine eyes glittering. 'You whore's-get!' he breathed. 'For that, any other man would die! For you – this!' He spat contemptuously, full in the other's face.

David was stepping forward fists clenched, jawline tense, when a new voice broke in, and turned both their heads.

'Davy! Davy – stop it! Stop it – do you hear?' Mariota came running down to them through the turning bracken, in flushed disarray. 'Oh, how can you! How can you!'

The men stood staring, panting, wordless

'Do not dare to strike him again!' the young woman cried. 'I saw you. You struck him. Oh, that it should come to this, between you!' She halted before them, tears in her eyes. 'Fighting! Fighting like wild brute beasts!'

David said nothing, but Patrick managed to fetch a smile of

sorts. 'Not fighting, my dear,' he protested, fingering his burning face. 'Surely not fighting. Just an argument . . .'

'Fighting,' Mariota insisted. 'And think you I do not know what you were fighting over? It is that woman! The two of you were fighting over that Stewart woman! I know . . .' Her voice broke.

David started towards her, but she plunged away from him. 'Do not touch me!' she cried. 'Do you think that I will come second – to her!?'

'But, Mariota lass – it is not so!'

'Can you deny that it was of her that you talked? When you came to blows. I heard her name . . .'

'Her name, yes. We spoke of her. But . . .'

'My dear, do not distress yourself. It was nothing,' Patrick declared, his assured and smiling self again. 'We but spoke of Marie in relation to the Court. Did you not hear that, also? The Court and its h'm, factions and loyalties. Eh, Davy?'

His brother did not answer.

Patrick took the young woman's arm. 'Surely you know that men may become incensed over statecraft and the like, Mariota my dove? It signifies nothing.'

She twisted away from his clasp. 'Leave me!' she exclaimed. 'Leave me alone. Both of you. She turned, and began to hurry back up the slope, whence she had come. 'You are both nothing but a hurt to me – a hurt and a shame! Both of you!'

Patrick would have hastened after her, but David pulled him back, urgently. 'Let her be,' he said. 'You heard her? She wants neither of us this moment. Not even you!'

The other looked at him, searchingly. 'So-o-o!' he said. 'That is it! Poor Davy!'

Abruptly, his brother swung about and went striding off through the trees, away from the direction of the castle. Patrick looked after him.

'Davy,' he called. 'At the least you saved the King for me . . . after the other matter. Why, if you so mistrusted me?'

David threw no answer back.

'My thanks for that, at any rate,' the Master of Gray said. 'I am sorry, Davy – sorry for both of us!'

He sighed, and then went slow-footed up the hill.

Chapter Eighteen

How strange, frequently, are the things that drive men to a change of course, to active intervention in this cause or that – small unimportant things, it may be, where greater issues have failed to do so. Thus it was with David Gray When the Court of the King of Scots moved to Stirling for the winter of 1583 – where Arran had obtained the Keepership of the Castle, in room of the forfeited Johnny Mar, and even had himself appointed Provost of the town, so that he had all things under his hand – Patrick wrote to his brother apparently anxious to forgive and forget all, requesting that he come thither to be with him again, as secretary, where he would be most useful. He promised that he would find life at Court more amusing than heretofore.

David refused.

Thereafter, the Lady Marie wrote, also from Stirling. She had been weak, she admitted, and had returned to Court. Should she have been strong, rather, and remained to be snowed-up for the winter in Glen Prosen? Was hiding oneself away strength? Anyway, here she was, back with her father and brothers. She was no politician, but even to her it was evident that the course which the new régime was taking boded ill for Scotland, a course in which her father was becoming deep implicated – Arran's course. Arran was acting Chancellor of the Realm now, claiming that Argyll was too sick and old for his duties. He was behaving disgustingly with James, corrupting him blatantly, unashamedly, before all – and accepting bribes, through his wife, from any and every man who had a favour to gain from the Crown. He was attacking the Kirk, selling more bishoprics, and giving the bishops power over the presbyteries, bolstering their authority by getting the Estates to declare James, and therefore himself, supreme in matters spiritual as well as temporal. Refusal to submit to the bishops, appointed in the King's name, was branded as treason. So Arran sought to hold more power in his hands than any man had ever done in Scotland. Free speech was being put down everywhere, the Catholics were being advanced, and there was talk of leagues with France and Spain and the Pope. And all the while, Patrick, whom she was convinced could have greatly affected events for the better, sat back and smiled and played the gallant – and did nothing. It was maddening, she wrote. The man who could, if he would, save the King and the country, scarcely lifted a hand, save to bedeck himself, toss dice, organise a masque, or pen a poem. Would Davy, whom she was assured had more influence with his brother than anyone else alive, not come to be with him again? There had been a quarrel, she believed – and could guess the cause. But Patrick loved him, she was certain, and wanted him at his side. Needed him, she declared. What good might he not achieve there, Patrick being as he was? Would he not come?

Briefly, firmly, if kindly enough, David penned his refusal.

At Yuletide, Patrick, laden with gifts, came again to Castle Huntly, in his sunniest mood. To David he could not have been more kind, more friendly, bringing him a handsome and costly rapier as present. He urged that he return to Court with him, where the King himself, he averred, frequently asked for him, and where undoubtedly, if Davy so desired, some office or position could easily be procured for him. Lord Gray, privately, added his own plea – indeed, it was more like a command – declaring that he would feel a deal happier about Patrick's activities if David was apt to be at his shoulder. David, dourly setting his jaw, declared that he hated the idle artificial life of the Court, with its posturings and intrigues. He preferred to continue as dominie, and assistant to Rob Powrie, the steward.

And then, a mere remark, a casual reference made by a passing visitor to my lord, changed it all. This caller, a minister of the Kirk, on his way from Stirling to his charge at Brechin, mentioned amongst other gloomy forebodings and wrathful indictments, that that Jezebel, Arran's Countess, now went brazenly bedecked in the jewels that belonged to Mary the imprisoned Queen, the King's mother.

Within twenty-four hours thereafter, David's mind was made up and he told Mariota firmly, determinedly, that he must leave her for a while. Mary Queen of Scots reigned yet, in some measure.

It would have been difficult satisfactorily to explain David's intensity of loyalty and regard for the unhappy Queen, to his wife or anyone else. He had never seen her. Most of what he had heard of her had been ill, critical, indeed scurrilous. She had been Elizabeth's prisoner now for fifteen years, all his understanding life, and her legendary beauty could hardly have survived. He was strongly Protestant though not bigoted, where she was insistently Catholic. Yet David, as well as many another in Scotland, still accorded her his unfailing loyalty and deep sympathy. He looked on her infinitely more as his true sovereign than he did her son James. All her hectic life – and ever since, indeed – Mary had that curious faculty of arousing and sustaining devotion in men, a devotion quite unaffected by her own morals, behaviour or follies. She was of the same mould as Helen and Deirdre and Cleopatra. At the word that the Countess of Arran had appropriated her jewels, the sober and level-headed David Gray overturned his oft-reinforced decision, packed his bags, and left wife and home to seek to do he knew not what. Perhaps it was but the last straw? Perhaps it had requ∙red but this? And was it so surprising? In Scotland, men had died for her by the score, the hundred, and even her enemies had been driven to their most virulent spleen for fear of themselves being lost in complete subjection to her allure. John Knox himself was half-crazed with desire for her. And in England a steady stream of devotees had gone to the block for her, some the highest in the land, ever since the fateful day of her immurement. Hence, partly, Elizabeth's cold hatred and fear.

It was a blustery day of March when David rode over the high-arched bridge across the stripling Forth, and into Stirling town. A very different Stirling this from formerly, with every house full with the overflow of the Court, bustle, gaiety and extravagance on all hands, soldiers everywhere – for Arran, as newly-appointed Lieutenant-General of the royal forces, was enlisting manpower determinedly – lordlings, hangers-on, men-at-arms, loose women. It reminded David of the Guises' Rheims.

He made his way up to the great fortress that soared above the town, and had less difficulty in entering therein than he had anticipated. The Master of Gray's name opened all doors.

He found the Court in a state of excitement and stir that surely could not be its normal even under the new régime. Enquiries elicited the startling information that Walsingham was on his way, no further away than Edinburgh, in fact – Sir Francis Walsingham himself, the most feared name in England now that Burleigh was growing old, Elizabeth's cold, ruthless and incorruptible principal Secretary of State. What his visit boded, none knew – but that he had come himself as envoy could only indicate that the matter was of the gravest importance. None could deny that.

Patrick, when David ran him to earth, writing letters in a pleasant tapestry-hung room with a blazing log-fire, and facing out to the snow-clad Highland hills, did not seem in the least perturbed. He jumped up from his desk, and came forward, hands outstretched.

'Davy! My excellent and exemplary Davy!' he cried. 'How fair a sight is your sober face! I am glad to see you – I am so!'

That sounded genuine enough. David nodded dumbly, always at a loss for words on such occasions.

'What brings you, Davy? Love of me?' He did not await an answer. 'Whatever it is, you are welcome. For yourself – and also for this. Look!' He gestured at the littered table. 'Letters, letters. My pen is never idle.'

'Aye. But even so, there are letters that you would never let *me* write for you, I think, Patrick!'

'What of it?' his brother shrugged. 'There are plenty that I would. What brought you here at last, Davy?'

The other did not answer that. 'They say, out there, that the English Secretary. Walsingham, is coming here. Is it so?'

'Aye, true enough. What of it?'

'Elizabeth must have something strong to say, to send that man!'

'No doubt.'

'It does not concern you?'

'Should it, Davy? It is not I who have to answer him.'

David looked at his brother, brows puckered. 'I do not understand you,' he said, shaking his head. 'Even yet – after all these years. To be in so deep, yet to care so little. Ever to move others, and always to remain yourself untouched. What is it that you want, Patrick? What do you seek, from your life?'

'Why, Davy – why so portentous? Should I tear my hair because others do? Because the King bites his nails and pleads not to have to see Walsingham? That is Arran's business, not mine. *He* acts the Chancellor . . . '

'Aye – what *is* your business, then? Once I believed that it was to save our poor Queen. To get her out of Elizabeth's power. That is why I aided you. But what have you done for her? For Mary? In all these years when your hand has been behind so much that goes on in Scotland? Nothing! Nothing, save to write her letters, and spend her money! Aye, and prevent her envoy from having audience with her son! And all the while she rots there, in prison, while you who were to succour her, grow rich, powerful. And now, 'fore God, even this painted woman of Arran's struts and prinks, they say, in the Queen's jewels! It is not to be borne!'

'I' faith, Davy – here is an outcry indeed!' Patrick said softly, staring at the other. It was not often that David gave himself away so quickly, so completely. 'I do believe that is it! That is what has brought you. The Honeypot still draws, attracts – eh? Astonishing! Our staid and sensible Davy . . . !'

'My lord says that you have brought back a further six thousand gold crowns of the Queen's revenues, from France!' David interrupted him harshly. 'That means that she still trusts you – or her servants do.'

'So – our father has heard that, has he? And passed it on. How . . . inadvisable! I wonder whence he got it?'

'Why did they give you it? What do you intend to do with it, Patrick? Apart from lining your own pockets . . . ?'

'Have a care, Davy – have a care! I do not like your questions.'

'Nor I. But that is what I came to ask, nevertheless. Someone, it seems requires to ask them. Someone who is not afraid of you . . . '

'So you are the Queen's champion – self-appointed? Davy Gray is to be accounted to, for the Queen's moneys? De Guise and the Archbishop and Morgan her Treasurer trust me to expend it aright, for Mary's best interests – but not Davy Gray!'

'These others do not know you as I know you, Patrick . . . '

'Do you know me? Have you not just finished saying that you do not! That you do not understand me, do not know what it is I want? Yet you would interfere in what is no concern of yours . . . '

'She is my Queen, as much as yours, brother. If I can do aught for her, here at your shoulder . . . '

David stopped as the door burst open without warning. King James himself came shambling into the room, rich clothes untidily awry, big eyes unsteadily rolling and darting. 'Patrick, man – what are we to do? What . . . ?' At sight of David, he halted, his slack lower jaw falling ludicrously. 'Guidsakes – it's you again, Master Davy! Davy Gray. I didna ken you were in Stirling. What brings you, Davy . . . ? Och – but no' the now. No' the now.' James turned back to Patrick. 'What are we to do with the man, Patrick? With this Walsingham? I'll no' see him. Jamie says I must – but I'll no'. I willna see him, I tell you!' The slurring voice rose high. 'He's a terrible man. They say he's like

225

any blackamoor. Yon woman's sent him to glower at me. I'll no' be glowered at! I'll no' see him . . . '

The tall figure of the Earl of Arran appeared in the open door-way behind the King, frowning. He was somewhat more stout than when David had last seen him, and despite his campaign-ing and lieutenant-generalship, looking less the soldier. He showed no enthusiasm at David's presence, and did not trouble to acknowledge it.

'It is you that he comes to see, Sire, assuredly,' he said, as though in continuation of a discussion. 'Let him glower, I say – glowering will not hurt. It is his message from his Queen that must needs concern us . . . '

'No, I'll no' do it, Jamie!' The King beat a fist on the table. 'Man, Patrick – you will see him for me, will you no'? Yon Walsingham gars me grue! Sir Jamie Melville says he's no' human.'

'Tush, James . . . !'

'I shall be there, of course, Your Grace,' Patrick said easily, soothingly. 'But I would not dream of cheating my lord of Arran out of the honour that is his!' He turned to the other man. 'My lord, I think that His Grace has the rights of it. Better that you should see Walsingham, than His Highness. Undoubtedly Elizabeth has sent him to overawe us, to browbeat the King. It would be suitable and dignified, therefore, that His Grace should not see him, should keep him at arm's length, lower his English pride a little.'

'Aye, Patrick, aye. That is right.'

'He will demand an audience, Gray – it is his right. And stay until he gets it.'

'Not so. Not if His Grace is not here! A prolonged hunting-match, for instance? A tinchel. Into Atholl and the north. Under good and sufficient escort, of course. The deer are not in season – but, heigho, that has happened before, has it not? I think that Walsingham will hardly follow His Grace into the Highlands.'

'God be good – Patrick's right!' the King cried. 'Our Patrick's aye right, Jamie.'

'M'mmm,' that lord said doubtfully.

'When will I go, Patrick? Now?'

'Why not, Sire? The sooner the better. So soon as the escort can be mustered. If you go at once, Your Grace can be at Perth by the time that Walsingham gets here.'

'Aye, Perth. Yon's the place for me this night. Perth.'

'You will not, h'm, be lonely? Overnight, Sire?' Patrick asked solicitously, but with a wicked glance at Arran.

'No, no. I'll bide with Murray o' Tullibardine at yon Scone I gave him – Gowrie's Scone.' At the thought of Gowrie, James blinked. 'Man, Jamie, you'll get me a right strong escort? I'm no' for having more o' yon Ruthven business. Yon Gowrie's running free. Patrick got me to pardon him. I shouldna have done it . . . '

'Do not fear, Sire – I will see to your safety. If you go . . . '

'Oh, aye – I'm going. And you'll see to Walsingham, Jamie. Use him strongly, mind – strongly.'

'Exactly,' Patrick murmured. 'Strongly is the word.'

'But no' too strongly, mind,' James amended, nibbling his lip. 'We dinna want yon woman . . . we dinna want our good cousin Elizabeth ower put out, mind. We are her heir, mind, and . . . and . . . '

'Precisely, Sire – and she must be encouraged publicly to acknowledge you as such.' Patrick stroked his silky dark curls back from his face. 'I think that it should not be difficult for my lord of Arran to put Master Walsingham in his place, and at the same time avoid offending his mistress.'

'How, man?' Arran demanded bluntly.

'Her Majesty of England is greatly fond of jewels, Sire. As fond of jewels as she is of young and handsome men. She uses both alike – to toy with, and adorn herself!'

'Aye, but . . . '

'A superlatively handsome jewel, Sire, as a gift. Hand that to Master Walsingham to give to her, and I swear Elizabeth will overlook his humbling quite! Such a toy as, say, yon great ruby ring in your royal mother's casket.' Patrick glanced quickly at David. 'I do not think that my Lady Arran has it on loan, as yet! Used thus, I vow, it will serve a better purpose than lying in a box.' That undeniably was addressed to his brother, not the King.

'Aye. Fine, fine! Man, Patrick – you think on everything, I swear,' James exclaimed. 'Let it be done so. I . . . we give our royal authority. Now – I had best be off, had I no' . . . ?'

Arran tugged at his beard. 'You think that such will serve, Gray?'

'Assuredly. It is a most notable jewel. A gift of his late Holiness of Rome, if I do not mistake. Which should commend it the more to her Protestant Majesty of England! She will take it to her bed with her, I'll wager!'

'How know you Elizabeth Tudor so well, Gray?' Arran demanded narrow-eyed.

Patrick smiled. 'I have good friends who tell me . . . much, my lord.'

'Aye well – here's no time for blethers ' the King declared agitatedly. 'I must be awa'. Jamie – my escort . . . '

Arran looked at Patrick. 'You will be there, Gray, with me, when I receive Walsingham?'

'But of course, my friend – we shall all be there. Save only His Grace. All the Court. Receive him before all, at the ball tonight. So shall you humble him the more publicly – and therefore the more deeply.'

'Before all . . . ? Not a private audience?' Arran stared and then slapped his thigh. 'Aye my God – you are right! That is the way to treat Walsingham the black snake! A pox on him – I'll do it!'

'Aye, then. Come, Jamie . . . ' the King said, plucking at Arran's sleeve.

Patrick bowed low as the monarch hurried his acting Chancellor out of the room and down the twisting stone stairway.

As he straightened up, he caught his brother's eye, and one eyelid drooped gently.

'What . . . what did you there?' David asked moistening his lips.

'Me? I but preserved one of your poor Queen's jewels from the clutch of Lady Arran . . . for a better purpose. And ensured an amusing and instructive evening!' he replied lightly. 'It all ought to prove an entertainment indeed – and vastly improve upon the ball that I had planned. One ball is so plaguey like another, isn't it? You chose your day to return to Court well, Davy. Now . . . ' He shook his head over his brother's apparel. 'As usual, I must needs find something for you to wear. Where, in the fiend's name, do you get your clothing, man? Let me see . . . ' Patrick paused. 'But, first – I had forgotten.' He rang a silver bell that stood on his table. 'It will not do to neglect the ladies . . . '

In a few moments a youth came running down the turnpike stair from the floor above, a handsomely-clad page, who eyed David superciliously.

'Will, down to the town with you, and request Deacon Graham the goldsmith attend on me forthwith. Forthwith, you understand? Off with you. Oh . . . er . . . request him to bring

228

some of his trinkets with him, Will. Small things. Off.' Patrick turned back to his brother. 'Who would not be a goldsmith? The ladies, bless their hearts, ensure that such folk are ever prosperous!' He sighed gustily. 'Ah, me – they cost me dear, the darlings. But then, I have not your faculty for instilling devotion by merely looking stern, Davy! Come, and we shall see what the royal wardrobe can do for you . . . since I am its Master . . . !'

A distinctly nervous and brittle gaiety filled the great audience-chamber of Stirling Castle – the same vast hall in which the brothers Gray had first clapped eyes upon their King, and which had witnessed the first chapter in Morton's downfall. It was packed, tonight, with a colourful and noisy throng – if the nobility of Scotland could so be described. Few had seen Walsingham, as yet, but all knew that he was in the Castle somewhere, and his name was on every lip, the shadow of the man who was reputed to have the largest spy system in the world at his disposal lay over all the assembly. The fact that the King had left in a hurry, for the north, was also known to all, and two added promptly to two. Arran, dressed at his most extravagantly gorgeous, was very much master of all – just so, it might be said, his wife was mistress of all. Undoubtedly his lordship had fortified himself from the bottle. Patrick, who had arranged this evening's entertainment, like so many another, strolled apparently at aimless ease, greeting all, yet was never very far from Arran.

David watched the scene from a corner, and looked for Marie Stewart.

Whoever else was concerning themselves with the impending arrival of Walsingham, the Countess of Arran was not. Perhaps she believed that she had the wherewithal to tame even him. David eyed her, in astonishment. Once, in France he had been shocked to watch his brother dancing with a woman, whose dress left one nipple exposed. But this woman flaunted both of hers. And deliberately, provocatively, using them to keep all men's eyes turning her way. She was a much less beautiful woman than many who were present there, though magnificently built and shaped, but there was no question as to who caused most distraction – in both sexes, though distraction of a differing sort. It was not only the exposure of her body that counted, but her entire attitude, carriage, expression – blatant indeed yet potent too, and so assured.

David by no means escaped the impact, despite his disapproval. Presently the lady espied him in his corner, and came directly across to him, all smiles.

'Davy Gray!' she cried. 'I did not know that you were back at Court. You are welcome, I vow! All true men are welcome – and you are a true man, I think? Are you not?'

David rubbed his chin, and frowned. Perhaps he should have been grateful for this queenly welcome for a humble secretary whom the lady's husband had already completely ignored? He tried not to look at her, and if that was impossible, to concentrate on the glittering gems in her hair, at her throat and ears and fingers. 'Aye, ma'am,' he muttered.

Directly she eyed him, for she was almost as tall as he was, pink tongue-tip touching her full lower lip. 'You are one of the strong men, Davy, I am told? I like strong men. I am a strong woman, you see.' She came close to him, so close that her thrusting breasts brushed him, and the musky vivid smell of her came to him powerfully.

'I can believe it, ma'am,' he said, glancing around him in embarrassment at all who watched.

'You are very different from your brother, are you not? Of a less ready tongue, assuredly. But otherwise, perhaps, as active?' She laughed loudly, and raised her voice, so that many around must hear her. 'I wonder how you compare with your brother in bed? An interesting question, is it not?'

David looked appalled.

She laughed in his face. 'Patrick has his talents, I admit,' she added. 'But I think, perhaps, you may have the longer . . . wind! Wordless men often have, strangely enough! We must put it to the test, Davy. But not tonight, perhaps. No, no. It is . . . '

'What is not tonight, perhaps?' Patrick's voice asked pleasantly, close at hand. 'Do not say that you are trying to corrupt my good Davy, Bett? Both impossible and unprofitable, surely.'

Thankfully David turned to his brother, for rescue – an unusual state of affairs.

'Think you so, Patrick?' the lady demanded. 'If he is to be your secretary again, then, Lord, I might well win some profitable secrets out of him . . . as well as other satisfactions!'

'Away with you, woman! You should be thanking me, not threatening me. Have I not assured your husband to your bed, this night?'

The Countess made a rude gesture. 'Thank you for nothing!'

She tossed David a smile. 'Remember, Davy!' she said.

As she was moving away, Patrick called, quite openly, loud enough for any around to hear who listened – and undoubtedly there were many who did. 'Bett, you have come apart, down the front. Perhaps you have not noticed?'

She jerked one bare shoulder and breast at him in a gesticulation as flagrant as it was expressive, and strolled on.

'Lord,' David gasped. 'That woman . . . she is more apt to the stews of some sailors' town than a king's court! A common streetwoman is nicer . . . '

'Not so, Davy – that is the daughter of a long line of Stewart earls!' Patrick corrected. 'An extraordinary family, the Stewarts, are they not?'

The glances of both of them slid round the crowded chamber, searching.

'She . . . the Lady Marie . . . will be here?' David asked.

'It is my hope. Her father, you will note, is drunk early tonight.'

'Aye. And Arran like to be joining him!'

'He but ensures a good courage to face Elizabeth's ogre, lad.'

'No doubt. Why are you not doing the facing, I wonder?'

Patrick shrugged. 'Why should I? There is a saw about making a bed and lying therein. Arran is good at beds – like his lady!'

'Yet, have you not had a hand in making this bed, also?'

'You get some strange notions, Davy – God, you do!' The other laughed.

'Perhaps *you* have a notion as to what brings Walsingham here?'

'That is easy. Fear. Fear that the delightfully so-called Reformation is in danger in Scotland – and therefore Elizabeth's Protestant throne is endangered. Fear brings Walsingham, bearing threats.' Patrick's eyes kept turning towards Arran's slightly unsteady figure, where he supported himself against the empty throne. 'Fear is the great spur to action, is it not? Fear sends James scampering off to Perth; fear sends Arran to the bottle . . . and his wife to throw her bed open to all and sundry. Even you! Ah, me, nothing would be done at all without fear, I fear, in this sad world!'

'And you? What do you fear, Patrick?'

'Me? I fear that one, Davy Gray, is about to give me one of his . . . '

He stopped. Marie Stewart was coming swiftly across the

crowded dancing floor towards them, not actually running but hurrying. For so essentially calm a person, her haste was notable.

Patrick took a pace forward.

Coming up, Marie passed him with a significant wave of the hand, which she then reached out to David. 'Davy!' she exclaimed, grey eyes warm. 'How good to see you! It has been so long. When did you come? I had not heard. Have you come to stay awhile? You look . . . just as you always look!'

David smiled, and nodded wordlessly.

'Faith – an Inquisition, no less!' Patrick declared. 'Torquemada could have done no better, I vow!'

'How is your wife – the fair Mariota?' she asked, ignoring Patrick. 'Am I yet forgiven? And the enchanting Mary? And small Patrick?'

'We all fare well enough,' David assured her. 'I thank you.'

'You have not asked *me* how I fare!' Patrick protested. 'I might have the plague, the pox and the palsy, but you would care naught!'

'You look to yourself too well for any such anxiety,' the young woman retorted. 'What brings you, Davy, in the end?'

'Not you, my dear – do not flatter yourself!' his brother answered for him. 'It was another Marie Stewart altogether. The Queen, your aunt. Davy aches for her plight – as do we all, of course – and in especial, interests himself in her jewels. He is . . . '

'Jewels! Davy does?'

'Och, never heed him, Lady Marie. He but cozens you . . . '

'Not so! I swear it is nothing less than the truth. In particular he would, I think, deprive the Lady Arran of her new-won finery.'

'And I with him!' Marie exclaimed. 'That woman is contemptible – beyond all shame. That she should assume the Queen's treasure . . . ! Look at her there – or, i' faith, do *not* look at her! Parading herself like . . . like a bulling heifer! She makes me ashamed of my kind! And to think how nearly she rules the land!'

'At the least, she knows what she wants, my dear – which is more than do some women that I might name! And as to ruling the land, she has her own felicitous methods of choosing the men to do it. First she samples deeply of their purses – which is a very practical test of their ability – and then she tries them in her bed. And if they pass both assizes, they are to be considered well-fitted for bishopric, collectorship or sheriffdom. You must admit that less effective methods of ensuring the continued virility of church and state have been . . . '

'Patrick, how can you talk so? Even you! But to jest of it is a shame – it shames you, and us all. And you – you pander to her!'

'Me? Heaven forbid! Marie, Marie, how can you even suggest it . . . ?'

'Of course you do. Think you I have not seen you at it? Aye – and *you* know her shameful bed as well as any!'

'Tut, lass, in statecraft one must use such tools as come to hand . . . '

'But you no longer play the statesman, you claim! You leave that to Arran and the others, you say – even to my poor silly father, there! You but pen verses and contrive masques and balls, and . . . and chase women!'

'A mercy – this is not Marie Stewart, surely? The serene and imperturbable! What has become of her tonight? Chase women, forsooth! What woman have I been chasing these many months – to no purpose? One woman only – and she a cold grey-eyed virgin whom no plea, no art or artifice will stir. Until tonight . . . '

'What of Eupham Erskine? And Lady Balfour? And Madame de Menainville, wife to the French Ambassador? What of these? Aye, and others! Under what head do you woo all these?'

David had never seen Marie Stewart so patently moved. And seldom his brother so palpably disquieted thereat, though he sought to gloss it over. David indeed found himself to be strangely affected. 'I think that Patrick may be engaged in more of statecraft than he would wish to appear,' he put in, in a jerky attempt to ease the tension. 'These ladies may well have a part in it. The French lady, in especial . . . '

Marie rounded on him with surprising vehemence. 'Do not *you* make excuses for him, Davy Gray!' she exclaimed. 'He is well able for that himself . . . '

She stopped. Indeed she had to stop. The music and dancing and the chatter of the great throng had all along necessitated raised voices. But none such could compete with the sudden ringing fanfare of the heralds' trumpets which sounded from the lower end of the hall, turning all eyes thitherwards. Talk died, dancing faltered and stopped, and the music ebbed to a ragged close.

'His Excellency Sir Francis Walsingham, Ambassador

Extraordinary of Her Grace the Princess Elizabeth, Queen of England!' it was announced into the hush as the flourish died away.

The hush was not complete, however, and resounding as was this announcement it was insufficient entirely to drown a single voice that talked on thickly and laughed loudly. The Earl of Arran, up at the Chair of State, chatting with the Earl of Orkney and others, did not appear to have noticed this development.

Mr Bowes, Elizabeth's resident envoy, stood in the great open doorway behind the heralds, biting his lip, frowning, and tap-tapping his foot. Suddenly he was thrust unceremoniously aside, and a tall, thin, angular man strode past him into the chamber. Stiff as a ramrod, soberly clad, Walsingham paced forward looking neither right nor left, while before him men and women fell back respectfully to give him passage. A man now of late middle-age, grey-haired and grey-bearded, he was of so sallow a complexion as to be almost swarthy, offering one explanation for Elizabeth's nickname for him of 'her Moor'; the other explanation went deeper, and referred to the man's cold, almost Eastern, ruthlessness, his unfailing calm and intense secrecy of nature. A fanatical Protestant, a man of utterly incorruptible morals and piety, and yet one of the greatest experts in espionage and subversion that the world has known, he had been Elizabeth's principal minister for the eleven years since Burleigh's partial retirement to the Lord Treasurership. But not her friend, as had been his predecessor. Faithful, efficient, unflagging, he yet did not love his Queen – nor she him. One look at his lugubrious dark face, hooded eyes and down-turning scimitar of a mouth, might instil doubts as to whether indeed the man was capable of love for any. All eyes now considered him urgently. searchingly, many fearfully, Patrick Gray's not the least closely. Or not quite all eyes those of the Earl of Arran, acting Chancellor of Scotland and deputy for the King, could not do so, for he had his back turned to that end of the apartment, and still joked in loud-voiced good humour with his little group of friends.

David and Marie both looked from Walsingham to Arran and then to Patrick. Other glances made the same circuit. The latter, lounging at ease, made neither move nor gesture.

Almost running behind Walsingham, Mr Bowes called out agitatedly. 'My lord! My lord of Arran! His Excellency is . . .' A guffaw from the head of the room overbore the rest.

234

Walsingham never faltered in his jerky pacing. No sound other than the footsteps of himself and his entourage, and Arran's throaty voice, now broke the silence.

A few paces from Arran's broad back Walsingham halted, and stood stiffly, patiently. When Bowes commenced another outraged summons, his senior flicked a peremptory hand at him.

All waited.

It was Marie's father, the Earl of Orkney, who brought matters to a head. Affecting only just to have noticed the new-comers, he raised his eyebrows and turned to Arran, tapping his padded shoulder.

The latter swung round, a little too quickly. 'Ah! God's Eyes – what's to do?' he demanded. 'What's this? A petition? A deputation? Some favour besought?'

'My lôrd!' Bowes was not to be withheld. 'Here is Sir Francis Walsingham, my royal mistress's principal Secretary and Envoy Extraordinary . . . '

'To see your master, sir.' Walsingham's voice crackled dry, like paper.

'Eh . . . ? Walsingham, is it? Ah, yes. We heard that you were on your way. You travel fast, it seems, Sir Francis.'

'Aye. And with reason. I seek His Grace, your master.' Cold, impersonal, and without being raised, the other's voice carried more clearly than did Arran's.

Beneath his breath, Patrick murmured. 'Here is a cunning game. Do not tell me that Bowes' spies have not informed him that James is gone, long since.'

'The King is not here. He is gône to the Highlands, hunting.'

'In the month of March?'

'S'Death, yes! Our prince will hunt in season and out. There is no containing him. But that need not concern you, sir. *I* govern this realm, for His Grace. What you have to say, you may say to me.'

The corners of Walsingham's mouth turned down still further than heretofore. 'I am accredited to the King of Scots – not to you, or any other!'

'No doubt. That is the usual practice. But His Grace entrusts me to handle all affairs of state, in his name.'

'You are to be congratulated, my lord. But my mission is still with the King.'

'Then, Christ God – you'll bide long enough!' Arran cried coarsely. 'For James will no' be back for weeks, belike. Can you

235

wait weeks, Sir Francis?'

Walsingham shut his mouth tightly.

Patrick Gray seemed to rouse himself. He strolled forward easily across the floor, his high-heeled shoes clicking out the unhurried nature of his progress. He bowed profoundly to both the speakers.

'My lord of Arran – your Excellency of England,' he said. 'My name is Gray – and your very humble servant. If I may be permitted a word . . . ?'

Bowes began to whisper in Walsingham's ear, but that stern man waved him away curtly. He looked directly at Patrick, however.

'It is to be regretted that His Grace should not be here to receive so distinguished a visitor, Your Excellency. But princes, as indubitably you are aware, are not to be constrained. May I propose a compromise? Your despatches, letters, from your royal mistress, are undoubtedly addressed to, and for the eye of, King James alone. They should be sent after him, forthwith – though they may take some while to reach His Highness. But the substance of any representations and proposals, being a matter of government, as between the monarchs' advisers, are surely suitably to be made to my Lord Arran and members of the Council?'

Unblinking, Walsingham eyed him. 'Young man,' he said thinly, 'I do not require lessons in the conduct of affairs. My information is that your prince was in Stirling but this day's noon. I think that he cannot have travelled very far to your Highlands. I have no doubt that either he may be fetched back, or else that I may overtake him tomorrow.'

'Impossible, sir,' Arran asserted. 'Your information will no doubt also have acquainted you with the fact that King James rides fast. It is his invariable custom – and he has the finest horseflesh in three kingdoms. Moreover, the King of Scots is not fetched back, for any man – or woman – soever!'

Seconds passed. 'Can it be that you intend that I do not see the King?' Walsingham said, at length, his voice entirely without emotion, but none the less menacing for that.

'The intention is of no matter, sir. The possibility is all.'

'Sir Francis,' Patrick put in. 'Our prince is young – a mere seventeen years. His rule is entrusted to his Council. Most of that Council is here present. In default of His Grace's presence . . . '

Walsingham ignored him. 'Do I return to my mistress then,

236

my lord, and inform her that her envoy was refused audience of your prince?'

'Not so. That would be false, sir. If you will wait, possibly for a mere sennight or so, His Highness my be back. Who knows?' Arran's sneer was but thinly disguised.

'Beyond this room, sir, is a Council-chamber,' Patrick mentioned. 'Your embassage could there be discussed, in privacy . . . '

'No, Master of Gray,' Walsingham interrupted him. 'The Queen of England does not treat with . . . substitutes! I shall return to her, and inform Her Grace of my reception. And I warn you all, she will take it less than kindly. Moreover she has the means to show her displeasure. Ample means!'

'Would . . . would you threaten us, by God?' Arran cried. 'You are in Scotland now, I would remind you, sir – not England!'

'I do not threaten – I warn. Your prince will, I fear, learn sorely of the folly of his advisers. I bid you goodnight, my lord.'

'As you will. If your message is of so little import. But . . . wait, man – wait.' Arran recollected. 'I have here a gift for your royal mistress. A jewel for the Queen. I understand that she is partial to jewels? You will give her this, sir, with our warm favour and respect.'

Walsingham hesitated. He was placed in a difficult position. Elizabeth's fondness for gems was so well known that any outright rejection of the gift on his part, and in front of all these witnesses, could be construed as a grievous slight to her interests. 'I think that my lady would liefer have your love and worship than your jewels,' he said sourly.

'She shall have both, Sir Francis,' Patrick declared genially.

Arran held out a ring on which an enormous stone redly reflected the light of the candles. 'Take it, sir,' he urged. 'Her Highness would not thank you to leave it!'

Grudgingly, Walsingham took the ring, and hardly so much as glancing at it, thrust it into a pocket.

Arran grinned. 'A good night to you, Sir Francis. And if you change your mind the morn, we'll be happy to treat with you!'

With the stiffest of bows, Walsingham turned about and went stalking back whence he had come. Lady Arran's high-pitched laughter alone sounded from the other end of the room.

Marie Stewart turned to David. 'If I had not seen that with my own eyes, I would scarce have believed it!' she declared.

237

'Has Arran lost his wits, to treat that man so? He must be more drunk than he seems.'

'I think not,' David told her. 'All was planned beforehand, you see.'

'Planned? Arran does not plan what he will say. Patrick . . . ?' He nodded.

Though Walsingham left for the south again the very next morning, by midday all Stirling knew that his mission had been to complain to James about an alliance that he claimed was being negotiated between Scotland, the Guises, and the King of Spain, for a simultaneous invasion of England, to be touched off by the assassination of Elizabeth herself, and a subsequent restoration of the Catholic religion to both countries, with James, in association with his mother Mary, to sit on the thrones of both. Highly circumstantial and markedly unanimous were these dramatic rumours, most obviously representing an inspired 'leak', no doubt from Bowes. With them went sundry threatenings and slaughters and demands, plus the suggestion of an alternative pact, a Protestant alliance, with the removal of the King's present pro-Catholic advisers – the bait to be Elizabeth's long-delayed public recognition of James as her ultimate heir.

From half-a-dozen sources David and Marie heard approximately this story, in while or in part, next day. Patrick, questioned on the subject, laughed and declared that there were surely vivid imaginations about the Court these days. When it was pointed out that he himself had been recently in the neighbourhood both of the King of Spain and the Guise brothers, he protested, but amusedly, that he had gone to the Continent purely as a private citizen, with no authority to discuss pacts, alliances, and such-like. They ought not to take Mr Bowes' considered flights of fancy so seriously. Let them rather be suitably diverted by all this ingenuity, and recognise it as an attempt to stir up the Kirk and the Protestant faction to play Elizabeth's game for her. Was it not all as good as a play?

It took considerably longer than a day, however – weeks in fact – before the news travelled up from London that Elizabeth was very angry. Not so much annoyed at the reception of her envoy and minister, but incensed, outraged, over the fact that Arran had insulted her by sending her a ring with a great piece of red glass in it, instead of a ruby. The stone was a crude fake, it appeared – and the greatest and most impudent discourtesy shown to Gloriana in all her career.

Many were the interpretations put upon this extraordinary development. Needless to say, despite Arran's fervent expostulations that he knew nothing about it, and that it must have been either the former Pope who had sent a sham ruby to Queen Mary in the first place, or else Walsingham himself had done this thing in revenge for his reception – despite this, the most popular theory undoubtedly was that Arran had hit upon the ingenious notion of hitting at Elizabeth and at the same time enriching himself, by substituting the glass in the ring and retaining the great ruby. Most people, indeed, looked to see a large ruby, or a swarm of smaller ones, appearing on Lady Arran's person at any time.

David Gray did not altogether agree with this view.

Chapter Nineteen

THE rumblings of threat and wrath from Whitehall, the rumours of a great Spanish fleet being built to attack England, the reports of the Guise brothers' collection of a large army which was to co-operate with the Duke of Parma's Spanish forces in the Netherlands for the cross-Channel adventure, plus the Pope's comprehensive and violent denunciation of Elizabeth Tudor as an illegitimate usurper, an idolatress and a murderess, worthy of death by any and every means – with a dispensation in advance for any faithful believer who might effect her happy demise, and an absolution for all her subjects of any allegiance to her – all this tended to dominate Scots political life and discussion that summer of 1584. The sense of sitting on a volcano which was liable to erupt at any time was very prevalent. Nevertheless, sundry developments and activities took place at home to counter-balance the weight of foreign affairs, and enliven the Court, if not the nation.

The Earl of Gowrie, ostensibly pardoned by the King on Patrick's advice, when the rest of the Ruthven lords were banished the country, was arrested on a visit to Dundee, presumably on the orders of Arran, removed forthwith to Stirling, and there tried by a hastily assembled but carefully selected panel of his peers on a charge of high treason against the King's person, unanimously found guilty, and beheaded the same night. His servants manged to recover the head from its lofty spike on the Castle battlements, and having sewed it back on to the body, hastily gave the remains a form of burial. So ended the great Greysteil, second only to Morton as James's childhood bogey. Patrick made a speech in his favour, as became an affectionate nephew – but found surprisingly little of good to put forward in his defence. His faithfulness to the end, however, was in due course rewarded handsomely by large royal grants of the deceased's forfeited property, so that the estates did not altogether go out of the family, though Gowrie's widow and sons, of course, were reduced to penury.

Then the Estates of Parliament duly passed Arran's Black Acts, against the violent opposition of the Kirk – the Kirk as opposed to the Church, that is, for of course the new bishops and commendators voted solidly for them. Under their provisions treason became the commonest offence in the land, the King was to rule the Kirk, and its revenues were made readily transferable – far-seeing legislation that even the Pope of Rome could scarcely have improved upon.

In May, Arran had Argyll declared officially unfit owing to ill-health, and became authentically Chancellor. A month or two later he had himself appointed Governor of Edinburgh Castle as well as Stirling, and for good measure, Lord Provost of Edinburgh. There were few more offices that he could usefully aspire to.

David watched all this with alarm, doubt and wonder. Alarm at what misgovernment and personal greed was doing to Scotland, was always doing to Scotland; doubt as to what, if anything, could be done to amend the situation, by such as himself; and wonder that Patrick seemed to be not only so unconcerned but so inactive, so passive, in the face of it all. As Marie had said in her letter, his brother seemed to interest himself in little but amusements, frivolities and gallantries of one sort or another. That this was not, in essence, his nature, David knew well enough. That he was behaving thus, therefore, must mean something. What, fell to be discovered. David, as secretary, spent most of his time transcribing a play that Patrick was writing, making copies of poems, and penning lists for masques and balls and parties. There were letters, indeed, also, to addresses near and far, but none of these, unless they were in a form of code, seemed to deal substantially in statecraft or intrigue.

Marie, of whom David saw much, was equally perplexed. Patrick was assiduous in his pursuit of her favours – but not exclusively so. She kept him at arm's length, yet by no means avoided his company. Indeed it is probable that many at Court presumed that they were lovers, Patrick's reputation being what it was, and their association being so open. David knew better than that.

David and Marie formed a league, purely involuntarily and spontaneously at first, but later deliberately and in collusion, to seek to advance the sadly neglected cause of the unhappy Queen Mary. Not that there was a lot that they might do, that anyone might do, indeed. But they kept on at Patrick about her, assured that somehow, some time, he could do something to aid her if he could be brought to it. Patrick, of course, expressed entire sympathy with their aims, but pointed out the insuperable difficulties in the way, more especially since the worsening of relations between Scotland and Elizabeth. What could he do? What even could James do, short of invading England for the purpose of freeing Mary – the first victim of which undoubtedly would be the imprisoned Queen herself? David insisted that he had sung a different song once, in France – and presumably Mary's own moneys and the Guise subsidies were given him only for this end? Patrick replied that it took more than money to open a Queen's prison-doors – and he was older now, and wiser, than he had been those years ago in France.

In this campaign for Mary the Queen, curiously enough, David and Marie had no ally in the lovely captive's son. James, in fact, had no desire for his mother's release; indeed undoubtedly he dreaded any such thing. Excuses could be made for him, for these unnatural sentiments. First of all, she represented a threat to his kingship, for free, she would assuredly claim the throne at once – indeed she claimed it now, and the idea of an association in the crown between them would quickly become such only in name; for she was all that James was not – charming, fascinating, lovely, vigorous, not such as would play second fiddle to anyone, least of all to her own diffident, awkward and uncouth eighteen-year-old son. Again, James not only had no love for his mother, but only knew her as a source of trouble and intrigue all his life. He would do nothing more than he was forced to do to encourage Elizabeth to cause him further trouble in this respect.

Equally curiously, it was in Arran that the campaigners found an ally, however unconscious of his role. Arran was not interested in Mary, or in anything much save his own aggrandisement. But he know something of Patrick's ostensible link with her cause, and was becoming ever more rapidly jealous and resentful of the said Patrick. He conceived the idea of using one against the other. He obviously found Patrick's presence at Court increasingly irksome, his sway over the King annoying, and his growing influence with the Countess almost more so. Yet he was well aware of his usefulness in council, his intelligence, his undeniable capacity, and he did not wish to make an enemy of him. He therefore thought of the device of getting Patrick out of the way by having James send him as ambassador to London, ostensibly to seek an improvement of relations with Elizabeth, but also to try to gain an interview with Mary. The gesture towards Elizabeth was advisable, for relations had deteriorated alarmingly; there were constant incidents on the Border; moreover, Philip of Spain was blowing hot and cold, proving dilatory in the extreme, and the Guises consequently cautious – possibly as a result of Walsingham's machinations. Scotland was in no position to challenge the might of England alone, and some temporising appeared to be necessary. As for Queen Mary, if she could be induced to sign an undertaking to be only a nominal queen, a sort of junior partner in an association of the throne, then that problem might be fairly easily resolved, and possibly Elizabeth persuaded to release her, as being no longer a threat. This, with an agreement that Scotland should remain Protestant – meantime, at any rate; to Arran, religion was approximately as significant as, say, morality or heraldry.

Arran convinced James of the need for this embassy, but he had more difficulty with Patrick. The latter laboured under no misconceptions as to Arran's motives, and was in no hurry to conform. Moreover, it was highly probable that his own aims and objects in foreign affairs, as in other matters, were quite other than Arran's. Nevertheless he seemed to see certain advantages in a visit to Whitehall also, and clearly was prepared eventually to be convinced – though never forced – to go.

David only realised that he was seriously contemplating the assignment when Patrick asked him if he would accompany him to the South, baiting his suggestion with the lure of actually seeing and talking with the almost legendary Queen of Scots. This, of course, put his brother in a quandary. While he did not want to be away from Mariota and his own life for so long, on the other hand, the pull of Mary the Queen was strong. It might be nothing less than his duty, indeed, to go, to influence Patrick where and when he could in the Queen's interests.

In his doubt, he went to Marie Stewart. Her father, meantime an important figure as useful to Arran, had now a fine house in Stirling and a wing of Holyroodhouse in Edinburgh. The Court being at Holyrood for hunting in the Forest of Pentland that September, it was to the latter that David repaired. He found Marie teaching one of her young sisters to play the virginals, explaining that they had all been sadly neglected in such niceties during their years of poverty.

David came straight to the point. 'This whispered embassage to Elizabeth – it is true,' he told her. 'Patrick is going. He has asked that I go with him.'

'I know, Davy. Already he has asked me the same. But this morning.'

'He has?' Though he would never have admitted it, David was perhaps just a little bit piqued that Patrick should have approached the young woman first.

She nodded. 'He is very persuasive.'

'Offering marriage again?'

'Oh, yes. But that is all but a daily occurrence! This time he has been more cunning. He has arranged that my father shall go with him.'

'Your father! And . . . will he go?'

'Yes. The King is sending him. You know how it is the Scots custom to send two ambassadors – lest one betray his trust! Patrick has asked that my father be the second envoy here. It is an adroit move, for Arran and my father are close, and Arran will esteem him useful for watching Patrick. And, of course, my father would have me accompany him, if you please, like a dutiful daughter – for he would have me married off to Patrick if he could! Master Patrick has excelled himself, this time!'

'And . . . do you go?'

'I am sorely tempted. To see London – the Court of Elizabeth – even perchance to see Mary the Queen, my aunt, herself!'

'And for this you would be wife to Patrick?'

'No, Davy. When I marry, it will not be as part of any bargain. Anyway, how could he marry before he goes, when he has still made no move for a divorcement? That is a matter that I do not understand, Davy. He ever asks that I marry him – and yet, in all these years, he has never moved to end his marriage to Elizabeth Lyon. Is it to be wondered that I doubt his intentions?'

'It is strange, yes, I have asked him, many a time, and always he says that he made one foolish marriage; it is safer and more convenient to be a married man until he can make the true marriage of his life.'

'Aye! How like him – how like Patrick Gray! His own safety and convenience. Caring nothing for others' feelings . . . '

'But he does care for you, I think, Marie. Patrick is . . . Patrick. But I believe that he loves you truly.'

'You do?' Levelly she stared at him for a long moment.

Uncomfortably he looked away over the smoking Edinburgh roof-tops, nodding.

'So you would have me give myself? Overlook all, and . . . and . . . '

'No, no! I did not say that. God forbid that I should seek anything but your weel . . . !'

244

'I know, Davy. I am sorry. I am just a silly vapourish woman Forgive me.' She paused, and ran slender fingers over the keys of the virginal. 'You have not said whether or no you are going to London, yourself?'

'I go, if you go,' David said, simply.

'Very well, my friend – we will both go.'

Chapter Twenty

THEY made an impressive cavalcade as, in clear crisp October weather, they took the long road southwards. Since Scotland's ambassadors must travel in suitable style, there were no fewer than one hundred and twelve riders in the company – mainly men-at-arms, of course. but including also many aides, secretaries, servants and hangers-on, even their own heralds. The Lady Marie was by no means the only woman present, for the Earl of Orkney never went far without just as many high-spirited females as his means would allow; moreover he had brought along a couple of other daughters, doubtfully mothered, whom he hoped to marry off to suitable English lords. Since the object of the expedition was as much to impress as to negotiate – and since Patridk was the leader, and the Treasury had been made available – no expense had been spared in the way of fine clothes, trappings, horseflesh, gifts, and the like. Altogether the entire entourage presented a notable spectacle, which was a source of great admiration and wonder wherever it went, greatly embarrassing the over-modest David – and vastly complicating the problems of overnight accommodation throughout. Arran himself accompanied them for half-a-day's journey southwards, so thankful was he, it was thought, to see the back of the too-talented Master of Gray.

Patrick, whatever his earlier doubts about the necessity for this mission, was in excellent form, the soul of gaiety, hail-fellow with all, gentle and simple alike, apparently without a care in the world. Orkney was always a hearty character and good company within limits; moreover he got on exceedingly well with Robert Logan of Restalrig, whom Patrick had brought along presumably in the interests of the more active aspects of diplomacy. Marie, having decided to come, seemed her serene self again and ready to be amused; while her young sisters obviously looked upon the whole affair as an entertainment. There was a holiday atmosphere throughout, which David did not feel to be entirely suitable, in view of the gravity, for Scotland and its imprisoned Queen, of their mission; but which, recognising that he was too sober a fellow, he sought not to spoil.

Despite all this, Patrick did not dawdle. The first night out they spent at Logan's weirdly-situated Fast Castle, and by mid-day next were in Berwick-on-Tweed, where they gained a reluctant warrant of passage through England from the suspicious Governor, the Lord Hunsdon, Queen Elizabeth's own cousin.

For practically all of the party, save Orkney who had sampled English prisons also, it was the first time that they had set foot on English soil – though admittedly Logan had led many raids across the Border, in the interests of cattle rather than sight-seeing – and great was the interest. Almost as great was the disappointment at finding Northumberland, Durham and even Yorkshire not so vastly different from Lowland Scotland, with most of the people living in even more miserable hovels, when it had always been understood that the soft English all lived in palaces.

The Midlands and the southern shires approximated a little more nearly to the popular conception of England, yet even so it was all much below expectations. The great mansions, certainly, were larger and more splendid and frequent, but there were many fewer good defendable castles, and of ordinary gentle-men's stone towers, none at all. Presumably their lairds lived in these rambling lath-and-clay barn-like dwellings, which any good Scot could cut his way through with his sword. Their churches were more like cathedrals, and their cathedrals enormous – though this was assuredly a sign of decadence. But the common people appeared to be mere serfs, and their villages wretched in the extreme. The Scots came to the con-clusion that they had been considerably deceived by visiting envoys.

It took them twelve days to reach London, twelve carefree autumn days in which Patrick established a personal ascend-ancy over all of them, in which he was the best of company, the most thoughtful of masters. Marie and he had never been closer. David watched and wondered – and doubted his own doubts.

They came to London by Enfield Chase and Islington, and, distinctly affected by the size of it all, the seemingly endless spread of tight-packed houses and winding lanes – not to men-tion the stench, which, lacking the hill and sea breezes of Edinburgh, was worse than anything that they had so far encountered – reached the river in the vicinity of London Bridge. By then, of course, the narrow crowded streets had strung out their cavalcade into a lengthy serpent, the rear of which might be anything up to a mile back.

Enquiries as to the whereabouts of the Queen's palace brought forth stares, jeers and pitying comments upon strangers with outlandish speech who did not know that good Queen Bess had scores of palaces scattered around London. Which did they want – Whitehall, St Mary-le-Bone, Hampton Court, Richmond, Greenwich, Nonsuch, Hatfield, Windsor ... ? Where was the Queen today? God only knew where she might be – Bess, bless her, was seldom still for two days on end. Folk, clearly, who asked such questions, were fools or worse. Catholics, perhaps ... ?'

The problem was solved unexpectedly, and fortunately without the drawing of touchy Scots swords. A major disturbance down at the crowded waterside drew their attention, with considerable shouting and commotion. Inspection proved this to be something like a miniature sea-battle. Up and down the Thames reaches, uniformed guards in skiffs, pinnaces and gigs were clearing all other boats from the wide river – and doing it forcefully, ungently. The waterway obviously was much used for passage and transport – not to be wondered at, considering the congested state of the narrow alleys and wynds which were scarcely to be dignified by the name of streets – and all this traffic, from the wherries of the watermen to merchants' lighters and public ferries, was being protestingly driven in to the shore. Investigation produced the information that these represented new security measures for the Queen's safety. With the recent assassination of the Prince of Orange, the other Protestant stalwart, Parliament had grown exceedingly worried about Elizabeth's preservation, in view of the Pope's *pronunciamento*. The Queen apparently did much of the travelling between her numerous palaces by royal barge. She was now on her way back from Greenwich to Whitehall, and this clearing of the river was a precaution against any surprise attack.

Strangely enough, these tidings seemed to galvanise Patrick Gray into urgent action. Leading the way hurriedly a little further westwards along the waterfront, he pulled up at a cobbled opening from which one of the numerous flights of steps led down to a tethered floating jetty, and dismounted, signing to David to do likewise.

'I want one of those boats, Davy – and quickly,' he said, pointing down, low-voiced. 'Large enough for ... say, six men. Aye, six. Do not question me, man – see to it. Hire one.

Any of these fellows should be glad of the earnings, since they may not use the boats themselves. An hour's hire. Less. Quickly, Davy.'

Mystified, David went down the steps. Half-a-dozen wherries were tied up there, and their owners standing by. The watermen looked at him strangely, began to laugh at his foreign attire and accent, thought better of it on noting the length of his rapier, and then stared in astonishment at his untimely request. However, the silver piece held out talked a language that they understood notably well, and with grins and shrugs a sizeable skiff was pointed out as available. He could have it to sit in, if he cared, to watch the Queen go by – but only that; no waterman was going to risk his skin by rowing out into the river meantime, not for even a gold piece.

Back at street level, David found his brother impatiently holding forth to Lord Orkney and the other principals of his party.

' . . . I tell you, it is a God-sent chance!' he was declaring emphatically. 'You know passing well the fear we have had that Walsingham will not allow us near to the Queen, after what happened at Stirling. Archie Douglas, our envoy, has written as much to the King. Here is opportunity to catch the eye of the Queen herself – and they do say that she loves boldness.' He turned. 'Davy, another boat we need, as well. For decoy. You got one?'

'Aye, easily enough. But they will not row for us. Not until the Queen is by.'

'Who cares? We can row ourselves.'

'Och, this is folly, Patrick!' Orkney objected. 'Yon guards will have us, and we shall end up in the Tower, no' the Palace! I'll no' be party to it.'

'Then wait you here, my lord, and watch.' Patrick turned to Logan. 'Rob, you'll be a bonny rower? You take the second boat. With some of your men. You will row out first – decoy the guards away from us. When I give you sign. You have it? I will see that no ill comes to you afterwards.'

'To be sure, Patrick.' Logan grinned widely. 'I'll lead them a dance. Just watch me . . . '

'No real trouble, now, mind – no broken heads or the like. Just a decoy. Now – where are those heralds? Get the two of them down into my boat. Aye, trumpets and all. Davy and I will row. Get the second boat, Davy . . . '

'Man – this is madness!' Orkney cried. 'You'll have us all undone.'

'Let us come with you, Patrick,' his daughter interrupted. 'A woman in the boat will look the better. I can row, too . . .'

'Lord save us, girl – are you out o' your wits?'

The faint sound of music came drifting up to them, through and above the more clamorous riverside noises.

'That must be the Queen coming,' Patrick exclaimed. 'Haste you, now!'

David ran back down the steps, to acquire another boat. Whether or not Patrick had given permission, he found Marie tripping down after him, riding-habit kilted high to the undisguised admiration of the watermen. There was no difficulty about hiring another wherry; they could have had all the craft there, had they so desired. Logan, who never travelled without some of his Borderers close, came down with three of his fellows. Then Patrick and the two bewildered heralds clutching trumpets and furled banners. Well might the bystanders gape.

They all piled into the two boats, Marie into the bows of the first, the heralds in the stern, and David and Patrick midships on the rowing thwarts. As yet they did not touch the oars.

The music was now much more distinct, punctuated by sporadic and ragged bursts of cheering. From their present position they could not see much to the east of London Bridge. The fleet of small craft bearing the guards had moved on further up river, but three or four heavier barges remained, more or less stationary, held by their oarsmen in the main stream. One lay about two hundred yards downstream of them, the bright liveries of its company making a splash of colour against the dirty water of the river.

Catching Logan's eye, Patrick gestured towards this barge. 'Heavy craft,' he commented. 'Upstream it will be no greyhound.'

Restalrig nodded, and spat over the side, eloquently.

'And you, my dear?' Patrick turned to look behind him, at Marie. 'What do you in this boat?'

'I give you an aspect of the innocent, the harmless. You may be glad of it.'

'H'mmm. At least you have a quicker wit than your sire! But you should not have come. This is no woman's work.'

'It is to impress a woman, is it not . . . ?'

'Here they come,' David jerked.

Into view below the arches of London Bridge swept the royal

procession First came a boatload of soldiers. Then a flat-decked lighter, rowed by hidden oarsmen, on which played a full orchestra of instrumentalists. Close behind was a huge decorated barge, with a thrusting high prow in the form of a great white swan with its wings swelling out to enclose the hull of the craft, ro ved by double banks of white oars, the rowers being garbed in handsome livery with large Tudor roses embroidered on chests and backs. A great striped awning in the red-and-white colours of England covered all the after part of the barge, and u der it, in the well, was a company of gaily-clad men and women. In the stern was a raised dais, and sitting all alone thereon, in a high throne, was a slight figure all in white. Nearby, a tiny negro page stood, bearing a laden tray. Some way behind were another two barges, filled with men on whom metal breastplates glinted and ostrich-plumes tossed – no doubt the celebrated Gentlemen Pensioners, without whom Elizabeth seldom stirred. Another boatload of soldiers brought up the rear.

David glanced at his brother. He did not know just what Patrick intended, but whatever it was, it must now have the appearance of a formidable proposition. He said as much, briefly.

Patrick smiled. 'Wait, you,' he said.

They waited, all save Patrick it seemed, tensely. Timing was evidently going to be all-important, whatever the venture. The watermen on the jetty close by were not the least of the problem.

As the Queen's squadron drew near, Patrick suddenly jumped up, rocking the wherry alarmingly, and leapt lightly back on to the floating timber jetty. 'Look! he cried, pointing away eastwards dramatically. 'Over there!'

As all heads turned, the watermen's as well, he stooped swiftly, and deftly unlooped the mooring ropes which tied both wherries to bollards. Gesturing urgently to Logan to be off, he leapt back into his own boat, the impetus of his jump helping to push it out from the jetty.

Logan and his men had hurriedly reached for the oars, but they had not fitted them into their sockets before some of the watermen, turning back, saw what was afoot and began to shout. Both wherries, however, though only a yard or two from the jetty, were beyond their reach.

After a splashing awkward start, Logan's crew got away in fair style, pulling strongly. Patrick, for his part, ignoring the shouts from the shore, sat still in the rocking boat, smiling

251

easily, imperturbably, not reaching for oars. Up above, the Earl of Orkney sat his horse, tugging at his beard.

Logan was heading his craft straight out into mid-stream. It was not long before the guards in the stationary barge noticed him; the shouts may have warned them, though these could well have been taken as loyal cheers. There was a great stir aboard, and much gesticulation. Then the barge's long sweeps started to churn the muddy water, and it swung heavily round to head off the intruder.

Logan turned a few points to the west, upstream, his four oars biting deep, sending the light craft bounding forward.

From across the river another barge of guards, perceiving the situation, came pulling over to join in the chase.

'What now?' Marie demanded.

'Wait.'

When both pursuing barges were well upstream of them, with others joining in, and Logan's wherry twisting and turning ahead of them as though in panic, Patrick suddenly nodded, twice. 'Now!' he said.

The first of the royal procession, the soldiers' boat, was already past their position, and the musicians' lighter coming almost level. Grabbing up their oars at last, Patrick and David thrust them into the water, and sent their craft scudding outwards. The shouting on shore redoubled.

The brothers had rowed together hundreds of times, in the Tay estuary, in heavier boats than this, in rough weather and smooth. They knew each other's stroke to an ounce. They sent that wherry leaping forward like a live thing.

The Thames here was some two hundred and fifty yards across, and the Queen's array kept approximately in mid-river. The heavy royal barges were being pulled upstream against tide and current. With only a hundred yards or so to cover, in the light fast wherry, Patrick could judge his time and direction to a nicety. Rowing, with head turned most of the time over his right shoulder, he directed his small craft on a line directly astern of the musicians and just in front of the Queen's barge.

'Quickly!' he panted, to the heralds. 'The banners. Up with them. Hold them high. And your trumpets. Sound a fanfare. Aye – and keep on sounding. Hurry! A pox on you – hurry!'

The heralds were but clumsy in their obedience, fumbling between banners and trumpets. One flag was raised, somewhat askew – the red tressured lion on yellow of Scotland's king. A wavering wail issued from one instrument.

'Damn you – together, of a mercy! Together!'

The second standard went up, the red lion on white of the House of Gray. The second trumpet sounded tentatively.

Their presence had not passed unnoticed, obviously. There was reaction apparent in most of the barges. In that in the lead, the soldiers were pointing and shouting, seemingly in some doubt; the flags of course would give the impression of something official, unsuspicious, and probably their officers were more exercised about Logan's errant skiff in front. The musicians played on without any sign of concern, but there was a good deal of gesturing in the royal barge itself and in the boatfuls of gentlemen following on.

Rapidly the gap between the large boats and the small narrowed. The heralds had at long last achieved unanimity, and their high shrilling fanfare sounded challengingly across the water, quite drowning the orchestra's efforts and all but deafening the other occupants of the wherry. Both banners were properly upright now, and streaming, proudly colourful, behind the small boat, by their size making it look the smaller. The brothers' oars flashed and dipped in unison.

The slender white figure on the throne-dais out there, sat unmoving.

'The last boat! At the end. With the soldiers. It is pulling out.' Marie had to lean forward to shout into Patrick's ear, to make her report heard above the noise. 'It is coming up this side. To cut us off, I think. And . . . and on the Queen's boat, Patrick! Harquebusiers! They have harquebuses trained on us.'

'Never fear. They will not shoot. Not yet. Not on Scotland's colours. Nor with you here, Marie. I said not with *you* here. We have yet time . . .'

'Some gigs coming back, too. Down river,' David mentioned.

'Heed them not. We are all but there.' Patrick glanced over his shoulder again. 'Marie – can you hear me? You said that you could row? Will you take this oar when I say? In just moments. Row, with Davy. He will keep the boat steady. Alongside the barge. Can you hear me?'

She nodded, unspeaking.

They were no more than thirty yards from the Queen's craft, now, just slightly ahead of it, and roughly the same distance behind the bewildered orchestra, many of whose members had ceased to try to compete with the stridently continuous blasting of the trumpets' barrage.

Nudging David, Patrick suddenly began to back water,

whilst his brother rowed the more vigorously. The result was to swing the wherry round, prow upstream, on a parallel course with the great barge and less than a dozen yards or so from its rhythmically sweeping white oars.

'Hold it thus,' he shouted. 'Marie!'

She came scrambling to his thwart, almost on all fours, her riding-habit far from helping her. Even so the light boat rocked alarmingly. Patrick, handing his oar to her, squeezed past her, and stepped unsteadily forward to her place in the bows. The exchange was less graceful than he would have wished. Even this brief interval had been enough to bring the steadily-forging barge level and a little more than level, so that the wherry was now opposite the after part of the larger craft. As Marie's oar dug in too eagerly and too deeply, the small boat lurched, and Patrick, who had remained standing in the bows, all but lost his balance. Recovering himself, and grimacing and laughing towards the royal barge, he gestured to his heralds at last to cease their blowing.

The second soldiers' boat, after furious rowing, was now level with the first of the gentlemen's craft, but seemed to have slowed down its rush, doubtfully.

It took a moment or two for the prolonged fanfare decently to die away. In those seconds, Patrick considered the Queen. He saw a thin woman, keen-eyed, pale-faced, pointed-chinned, in a monstrously padded white velvet gown, whose reddish hair though piled high did not yet overtop the enormous ruff which framed her sharp and somewhat aquiline features. Glittering with jewels, she was regarding him directly, her thin lips tight, her arching brows high. Undoubtedly she looked imperious, most dauntingly so.

In the sudden silence, Patrick dofferd his feathered velvet cap with a sweep, and bowed profoundly, smiling. Then, raising his voice, and with a peal of his happiest laughter, he declaimed clearly.

> Fair, gracious, wise and maiden Queen,
> Thy fame in all the world is heard,
> Thy beauty when to eyes first seen
> Bewilders, mutes, this stamm'ring bard,
> Yet peerless lady, withhold not now thy face,
> From stunned admirer of another race,
> Of charity so well renowned,
> Your Grace in grace towards him abound,

Who in far Scotia heard thy virtues hymned
And now beholding them true limned,
Sinks low on knee, dumbfound!

He ended with a most elaborate obeisance, sinking with one silk-clad knee on the wherry's gunwale – no easy performance with the boat rocking to uneven rowing – and thus waited.

Almost immediately a fierce and authoritative voice started to shout from the forepart of the barge, from amongst the group of harquebusiers with menacingly levelled weapons, demanding to know, in the name of the Crown, the Deity and the various powers of darkness, who and what this extraordinary party might be, what they meant by disobeying the express commands of Parliament, thrusting themselves upon the royal presence, and making a fiendish noise fit to deafen the Queen's Grace . . . ? Undoubtedly the Captain of the Guard, recovering from his fright.

Patrick, still in his precarious stance, never for a moment took his eyes off the Queen. He saw her flick a beringed hand towards the shouting officer, and forthwith his shouting died on him as though choked off. Another regally pointing finger beckoned elsewhere, and an elegant and handsome youngish man dressed all in sky-blue satin leap lightly up on to the dais, bowed, and then turned towards Patrick.

'Her Grace would know, sir, who you are and whence you come, who thus address her in passable verse and yet assail her royal ear with execrable bellowings and blowings?' he called. He had a pleasant mellifluous voice and an easily assured manner.

'Why, sir, I am a very humble and distant admirer of Her Grace, Gray by name, who has come far to worship at her shrine.' Patrick smiled ruefully. 'But, good sir, if you have any influence with the fair and royal lady, will you beseech her gracious permission that I rise up off my knees – for I vow that this craft is plaguey hard and I am fast getting the cramps!'

They could hear Elizabeth's tinkle of laughter sound across the water. They saw her say something to her spokesman, who called out,

'My lady would have no man suffer for her in knees as well as heart! Rise, Master Graves, I implore you – for I ache in sympathy!'

'My thanks to your divinity – and mine, I hope!' Patrick declared, rising and balancing. 'I would that she could heal my heart as readily as my knees!' He made as though to strum a lute, and clear-voiced extemporised a lilting tune.

> *How harsh the pangs of suppliant feeling,*
> *Compared with those of suppliant kneeling!*
> *Oh, bones and gristle, more resilient*
> *Than heart smit sore at grace so brilliant!*

The other man, a score of yards off, waved a delightful hand.

> *Sir – almost I envy your Muse,*
> *Combined, 'fore God, with oarsman's thews.*
> *How comes a man who Fate so braves,*
> *With such curst churchyard name as Graves?*

The Queen clapped her hands, the rhymster bowed, and Patrick laughed aloud.

'Not Graves, Sir Poet – but Gray. Commonly called the Master of. But now the mastered! At your service – and at your Princess's every command. She may, I think, have heard it, but no doubt has rightly long forgot my humble name. The Master of Gray.'

Even at that range the change in the Queen's expression was apparent. She leaned forward, staring from under down-drawn brows. Clearly the name was not forgotten. She spoke rapidly to her courtier, and then, with another of those flicks of the finger, summoned a second and more soberly dressed individual up on to the dais. Those in the wherry were at least thankful to see it was not Sir Francis Walsingham. After a short speech with him, the young man in sky-blue called again.

'Master of Gray, your name is known to Her Grace. She asks your errand – other than boating and poesy?'

'Tell Her Grace admiration and worship, as I said,' Patrick answered promptly. 'And also an important compact proposed by my royal master, King James.'

Again a brief conference.

'Her Grace will receive you at the Palace of Whitehall, this night, Master of Gray.'

'I am deeply grateful for her gracious favour.' Patrick bowed. 'And for your courtesy, sir. May I know to whom I am indebted?'

'Surely, sir. My name is Sidney.'

'Not . . . not Sir Philip Sidney?'

'The same, alas. Do not tell me that my small fame has reached even as far as Scotland?'

'Indeed it has, sir. This, Sir Philip, is an honour, a joy . . . '

Like a whip-lash came the sharp rap of one of Elizabeth's great jewelled rings on the arm of her chair. Hastily, at her curt gesture of dismissal, the handsome Sir Philip Sidney stepped back, to efface himself before the suddenly cold draught of Majesty's frown. She jerked a word or two at the other and dark-clad man.

He raised his voice, and much less melodiously than had Sidney. 'Her Highness asks who is the muscular lady, whom you use so strangely, sir?'

For a brief moment Patrick bit his lip, glancing down at Marie. Then he laughed, shrugging one shoulder. 'She is a determined lady who refuses to marry me, sir, tell your mistress. So I bring her here that she may be dazzled and made jealous by my adoration of the Queen's beauty and grace!'

He heard Marie gasp – and something extremely like a snort come across the water from the royal barge. Plain to be heard was the Queens' crisp words. 'Bold!' she snapped. 'Over-bold!' And turning a hugely padded shoulder on the wherry, and her face the other way, Elizabeth Tudor waved an imperious hand for-wards. Clearly the interview was at an end. As Patrick swept a final extravagant bow, the orchestra started up again in front.

'How could you, Patrick?' Marie panted, as he moved over to relieve her of her oar. 'How could you say such a thing – thus, before everyone? It was . . . shameful! Aye, and stupid, too!'

'Not so, my dear. It was salutary, rather.'

'Salutary? To shame me in front of all? And to rally the Queen?'

'Does it shame you that I should offer marriage? That I should have all men know it – and women? I should have thought otherwise.'

'To shout it forth, so! To make use of it for . . . for . . . !' She shook her head. 'Anyway, it was folly. You have but offended the Queen. After all that you had gained . . . '

'Offended, you think?' Patrick matched his oar's swing to David's. 'I wonder? Say rather that I provoked her, challenged her, dared her. And she is the one to take up a dare, I believe. She will be the kinder tonight, I swear!'

Marie stared at his elegant back, bending to the pull of the oar, as they rowed back to the jetty. 'Patrick,' she said, 'have you a heart, at all?'

Turning, he flashed a smile of pure sweetness upon her. 'You ought to know, beloved, for it is all yours!' he declared. 'Now – what has become of our good Rob Logan . . . ?'

Chapter Twenty-one

THE Palace of Whitehall was vast and sprawling – more like a town in itself than a single residence, containing within its precincts avenues of lesser lodgings, churches, barracks, gardens and orchards and ponds, even a bear-pit and a huge tilt-yard for tournaments. It flanked the river for a long frontage, and it was by boat that the Scots embassage approached it that night – and in more orthodox fashion than the afternoon's caper. Lamps and torches blazed everywhere, turning night into a lurid day of wavering, flickering colour and shadow. Never had the visitors seen so much glass, in windows and mirrors and crystal ornament.

The party numbered only six – Patrick, Orkney, the Lady Marie and David, with the two heralds in case they were needed. All were dressed at their finest, the latter colourful in armorial tabards displaying the royal arms of Scotland. Logan and his men had been rescued from the clutches of the Queen's guards, but it was felt that his qualities were not likely to be in demand tonight.

The entire palace area appeared to be alive with a gaily dressed throng that circulated around more than one centre of attraction. Enquiries from their escort, a marshal of the Court, elicited that the famous Robert Dudley, Earl of Leicester, was holding one great ball in his own extensive quarters next the Queen's, Robert Devereux, Earl of Essex, another in his, and Sir Walter Raleigh a third, the Court and multitudinous guests seeming to drift from one to another more or less indiscriminately, the Queen herself honouring them all at some stage during the evening. Elizabeth, it appeared, despite her love of display, had a strong streak of economy, and much preferred her favourites and subjects to pay for such expensive entertainments, rather than herself. King James had better not be told about this.

To the strains of different orchestras, the visitors were conducted through all this magnificence and gaiety, through a series of huge intercommunicating apartments, tapestry-hung, with much marble and lavishly-painted ceilings. The prevalence of silver and gold plate, of fine carpeting, the richness of the clothing worn, and all the aspects of wealth and luxury and prodigality, raised Scots eyebrows – though not Patrick's, who of course had but recently visited the Courts of Spain and France and the Vatican, and moreover himself was seldom outdressed by anysoever; tonight, in white and gold velvet, there was no more eye-catching figure present.

In the fourth of the great salons they were halted. Here the dignified and formal measures of a pavane were being danced – though not in every case too formally. It was disclosed to them that this was my Lord Leicester's assembly, and that was my lord himself dancing with the shepherdess in lilac.

Looking, they saw a tall, extravagantly dressed man, just beginning to incline to puffiness and thickness, with a flushed, dissipated, but still handsome face. He was dancing with a buxom, bouncing young woman, a mere girl, little more than a child, in fact, but a precocious one, holding her very close for such a dance and caressing her openly, expertly, comprehensively the while – yet looking slightly bored at her giggles and wriggles. The Earl of Orkney licked his lips in appreciation.

Patrick turned to their escort – and found Marie looking at him a little strangely. 'You are not shocked, my dear?'. he asked. 'You? After all, he is . . . Leicester!'

She shook her head. 'No. It was not that . . . ' She still eyed him almost searchingly.

Suddenly he understood the searching quality of her scrutiny, reading her mind. 'You wonder whether *I* shall look like Leicester, in a few years of time?' he put to her. And he frowned – but only momentarily. 'I think not.' That was almost curt. He turned back to the marshal. 'The Queen is generous, I think, to her favourites. A broadminded mistress!' He nodded towards Leicester.

'Her Grace has but to snap her fingers and my lord will drop all his pretty chits and come running,' he said. 'None knows it better than the Queen.'

Presently the music stopped, and the marshal went forward to Leicester.

'I do not see Walsingham here,' Patrick murmured to David. 'I do not know how this Leicester will serve us – but Walsingham is the prime danger.'

'Why? Surely this man is of the more importance? The Queen, it is said, has considered marrying him . . . '

His brother shook his head. 'Elizabeth, though a very woman,

259

has a hard man's head on her shoulders in matters of state. Her favourites and her ministers she keeps far separate. To the Dudleys and the Devereux she gives honours, wealth, privileges and her favours – surprisingly close favours! But to the Cecils and the Walsinghams and Hattons she gives the power, great power. Would that our poor Scotland had a prince with so much wisdom!'

'And where would you be then, Patrick?' Marie, listening, asked – and received a grimace for answer.

The Earl of Leicester approached them with a sort of tired swagger, as though he only did it because he knew that it was expected of him. Dressed in purple satin, with a tiny cloak of olive-green lined with ermine, on which was embroidered a great Star of the Bath, his hair and spade-beard dyed a bright orange, he seemed to be covered with orders and decorations, from the Collar of the George down to the blue Garter below his left knee. Marie had never before seen a man with pearls threaded into his beard, nor wearing earrings large enough each to contain a tiny jewelled miniature of the Queen. His jaded glance took in Patrick's superlative good looks and striking costume, without evident pleasure in the sight, skimmed over Orkney, ignored David, and came to rest on Marie. The disillusioned, slightly bloodshot eyes lightened then, somewhat. He bowed to her, disregarding the men.

'The Lady Marie Stewart, my lord,' Patrick mentioned pleasantly. 'Daughter of the Earl of Orkney, here. Who is uncle to our prince, King James. Myself, Gray – at your service.'

'Aye.' Leicester did not take his eyes off the young woman, examining all her fairness frankly, lasciviously. 'Indeed? I congratulate my lord of . . . where did you say? Orkney? Where the devil is that?'

'A larger province than Leicester, I'd think, my lord!' Marie's father chuckled.

The other shrugged, and turned to Patrick. 'And you, sir? I take it you are the play-actor who this afternoon played jester on the river?' He yawned. 'Aye, I can see that you might well arouse Her Grace's passing interest.'

'I am flattered, my lord, to hear it. Especially from you, who once were such your own self!' The slight emphasis on the word 'once' was just perceptible. 'It is Her Grace whom we seek now – at her express command.'

Leicester stroked his pearl-fringed orange beard. 'The Queen, like most women, is unpredictable,' he said. 'My advice, sir, is that you should remember it.'

'I thank you, my lord . . . '

Another brilliant figure came up to them, the sky-blue spokesman of the barge that afternoon, Sir Philip Sidney. Now he was dressed all in crimson, overlaid with silver lace, with long silver gleaming hose below puffed-out trunks. Marie decided that, though his features were not so perfect as Patrick's and his smile a shade less dazzling, he was very good-looking, entirely fulfilling the picture that his reputation had painted of the noblest figure of his day, poet, thinker, soldier, diplomat. She had not thought that he would look so young.

He bowed to her, very differently from Leicester. 'Fairest siren, sweet bargee!' he said. ' 'Tis said that Helen launched a thousand ships – but I swear that she never sculled a one of them! I do not know your name, but I heartily proclaim my admiration of the anonymous gondolieress!'

She curtseyed prettily. 'My anonymity need not trouble you further, sir – though my muscularity, as I think it was named before, is not so easily disposed of! My name is the same as that of *my* Queen – Marie Stewart.'

'M'mmm.' Sir Philip blinked. 'I see that I must needs tread warily!'

'Indeed you must, babbler – for *I* was before you in appreciating the lady's qualities!' Leicester declared. 'Lady Marie, will you step the next measure with me, and reject this windbag nephew of mine?'

Marie had not realised that this disparate pair were indeed uncle and nephew. She glanced uncertainly from one to the other.

Sidney smiled. 'It grieves me to deny you, Sir Uncle, but Her Grace has sent my humble self to bring the Scots party into her presence.'

'Her Grace, I think, is not so desperate anxious for a sight of them that she will fret over one measure of a dance,' Leicester said easily.

The young woman looked at Patrick for aid, but he only smiled, and nodded airily. 'To be sure, Marie, you must not disappoint his lordship. We shall await you.'

Surprised, David considered his brother. He had not expected this. Marie likewise seemed somewhat put-out. Even Sidney raised his eyebrows. But Orkney laughed, and pushed his daughter forward, with what was practically a slap on her bottom.

Leicester turned and waved to the leader of the orchestra, who, it seemed, seldom took his eyes off his patron. The music recommenced at once, and the Earl led Marie out on to the floor.

'Sir Philip, I esteem myself fortunate indeed in this meeting,' Patrick announced. 'It has long been my ambition to meet the author of *Arcadia,* and to pay my tribute to

> . . . *the ornament of great Liza's Court,*
> *The jewel of her times.*

I trust, sir, that this day's cantrip on the river did not cause you aught of embarrassment with Her Grace?'

'Lord, no, my friend! The Queen was smiling again in two minutes. You gave her more to smile at, than to frown at. Indeed it was an entertaining introduction to one whose name is not unknown here in London . . . as well as in the wider realms of Paris, Madrid and Rome!'

Patrick bowed, but he eyed the other keenly. 'You do me too much honour,' he returned. 'I fear that my poor repute cannot serve me so kindly as does *your* fair renown?' That was really a question.

'Your repute has its own . . . efficacy, I assure you, Master of Gray,' the other told him. 'The Queen will be much intrigued to speak with you. After your exploit with the boat, she is prepared to find that your speech will fully measure up to your letters. I feel convinced that she will be noways disappointed.'

David darted another glance at his brother. Letters . . . ? To Elizabeth?

Patrick cleared his throat. 'You are very kind, Sir Philip. Your guidance is appreciated. Tell me, if you will – is Walsingham with Her Grace?'

'No, sir. He is not yet returned from Theobalds Park, where he confers with my Lord Burleigh.'

'Thank the Lord for that, at any rate!' Patrick said, with one of his frank smiles. 'Your Lady's Chief Secretary is scarcely to my taste as sponsor!'

'I dare say not, sir – though mark you, he makes a surprisingly useful father-in-law!'

Patrick started. 'Dear God – yours?'

'Why, yes. I have the honour to be married to the daughter of Sir Francis.' Sidney laughed understandingly, and patted the other's padded shoulder. 'I have some devilishly awkward connections, have I not?' And he gestured to where Leicester danced.

'H'mmmm. I am . . . overwhelmed by your good fortune, Sir Philip!' It was not often that Patrick Gray was silenced.

They stood looking at Leicester and Marie. The Earl was holding her much more closely than was usual, yet not nearly so blatantly as he had done with his previous partner. She held herself, not stiffly, but with a cool and most evidently amused detachment that undoubtedly had its effect upon Leicester. Many eyes were watching their progress. David, who found himself as hotly indignant against Patrick as against Leicester over this, recognised now that his brother had deliberately used both Marie and the Earl's lecherous demand to give himself time for a feeling of his way with Sidney preparatory to the forthcoming interview with the Queen. As though he read David's mind, Patrick nodded easily, though he addressed himself to Sir Philip.

'Marie Stewart is well able to look to herself, is she not? A plague on it, I ought to know, whom she has held just slightly further off than she does now my lord, for years!'

The Englishman looked from the speaker to the dancers and back, thoughtfully, and said nothing.

When the dance was over, Marie came back to them alone, Leicester finding other matters to occupy his attention. His nephew, declaring still more profound respect, pointed out that it was not every day that a woman could put his Uncle Robert in his place. He asked them to follow him now, and he would conduct them to the Queen.

Since no one indicated that he should stay behind, David went with the other three.

Sidney led them down a corridor, through a handsome ante-room where gentlemen waited and paced, past gorgeously liveried guards flanking a door, into a boudoir wholly lined with padded and quilted pale blue silk, where four or five of the Queen's ladies sat at tambour-frame or tapestry whilst a soulful-eyed gallant plucked a lute for their diversion. Three doors opened off this boudoir, and at one of them Sir Philip knocked, waited, and then entered, closing it behind him. The lute-players twanged on with his slow liquid notes.

After a few moments, Sidney came backing out again, and signed to the Scots party to enter. Patrick went first, bowing the requisite three times just within the doorway, followed by

Orkney, Marie, and, since Sidney seemed to be waiting for him, David also.

They found themselves in a strange apartment that at first quite confounded them as to shape, size and occupants, for it was panelled almost wholly with mirrors, reflecting each other and the room's contents times without number. It was only after a moment or two that it became clear that there was, in fact, only the one occupant other than themselves.

The Queen sat on a centrally-placed couch of red velvet, a stiff, brittle-seeming figure, positively coruscating with such a weight of gems as to seem almost entirely to encrust her. In a padded, boned and rucked gown, so sewn and ribbed with pearls that it would have sat there by itself without body inside, she glittered and glistened, her now Titian hair, obviously a wig, wired with droplets and clusters and pendants, such of her somewhat stringy neck as was not covered by the enormous starched and spangled ruff being all but encased with collars and chains and ropes of jewels, her wrists weighted with gold, her fingers so comprehensively ringed as to be barely movable. So she sat, upright, motionless, alone, and the mirrors all around her and the crystal candelabra projected and multiplied her scintillating image to all infinity.

Whatever the first arresting and confusing impression of all this, however, it took only seconds for a very different impression to dominate the minds of the newcomers, produced by another sort of gleam and glitter altogether. Elizabeth Tudor was fifty-one, but her dark brown eyes, ever her finest feature, were as large, brilliant, searching and shrewd as ever they had been, seeming almost unnaturally alive and vital in the midst of that curiously inflexible and inanimate display. Thus close, she could be seen to have no other claims to beauty save those eyes. Long-headed, long-nosed, long-chinned, heavy-lidded, thin-lipped, her skin was so pale as to be almost entirely colourless, the patches of rouge on her high cheek-bones but emphasising the fact, her brows and eyelashes almost white and barely visible. But no one there, under the blaze of her eyes, might dwell upon her lack.

Almost imperceptibly she inclined her head to the obeisances of her visitors but there was nothing rigidly formal about her voice. 'The bold young man who looks too beautiful to be honest,' she said quickly, crisply. 'The young female who would like to play the hoyden but cannot. The second young man who is not so humble as he would seem. Who is the fourth?'

Patrick, glancing quickly over to Sidney, cleared his throat. 'He is the Lord Robert Stewart, Earl of Orkney, uncle to our prince, and ambassador to Your Grace with my humble self,' he said. Orkney bowed again.

'Ah – one of the previous James's brood of bastards!' the Queen said. 'Less of a fox, I hope, than his brother Moray, who cost me dear! Sent, no doubt, to seek keep *you* in order, Master of Gray – a task beyond him quite, I fear!'

As Orkney's mouth opened and shut, Patrick blinked and then smiled. 'The lady is his eldest daughter, Marie, Your Grace.'

'I believe he has a-many,' Elizabeth said baldly. 'Most of them natural.'

'*My* royal father married but one of his ladies, Highness,' Orkney got out, red-faced. 'Myself also. 'Tis a habit we have in Scotland!'

Patrick held his breath at this undiplomatic rejoinder, reflecting upon the matrimonial habits of Elizabeth's own father, Henry the Eighth. But the Queen only smiled thinly, briefly. 'Other habits you have in Scotland, less respectable,' she observed. 'And the young man with the obstinate chin, who scorns clothes and queens alike? Who is he?'

David caught himself frowning, bobbed a travesty of a bow, and stood hands on hips, wishing that he had not come, but more bull-like than ever.

'He is my half-brother and secretary, David Gray, Your Grace. He, ah, is that way always. But sound . . . and very discreet.'

'I would trust him before you, rogue, anyway,' Elizabeth announced. 'Stand up straight, man, and let me look at the renowned Master of Gray. So-o-o! And you call yourself the handsomest man in Christendom?'

'Lord, Madam – absolve me from that! You are well informed as you are well-endowed, I swear – but I would never say such a thing . . . '

'But you would believe it, natheless! Handsome men, I have found, are even vainer than handsome women – save only our good Philip here, whose vanity takes other forms! Think not that I shall price you at your own value, Master Patrick – any more than I believe your flattery of my own person.'

'Then you value me low indeed, Your Grace. Fortunately, however, our own poor worth is not the measure of our mission.

265

It is our privilege to represent the goodly Realm and Crown of Scotland.'

'Aye – if you can call that privilege! For me, I beg leave to doubt it! A Realm and Crown that can treat with my enemies, harry my subjects, mistreat my ministers and grossly insult my person . . .'

'Madam, you have been misled. I swear. You are mistaken . . .'

'I do not mistake glass for ruby, sir!' the Queen told him shortly, tartly. 'Does James, or the man Arran, take me for a fool, 'fore God?'

Patrick dropped his glance. 'Your Highness, that would be the primest folly of all time. Worse than the folly that played yon scurvy trick – but of which I pray you will absolve my prince, who knew naught of it. Let blame lie where blame is due.' And putting a hand within his white-and-gold doublet, he brought out a great red stone, which even amongst the competing brilliance there present, blazed and glowed with a rich and vivid fire.

Almost involuntarily the Queen's beringed hand came out for it. She took it from Patrick, and held it up before her, for the moment speechless.

David felt a jolt like a kick somewhere within him. In that moment, much moved into its due and proper place in his mind; he knew, suddenly, so much more than what he merely saw. He knew that here was infamy. He knew, as though Patrick had personally confessed as much, that it was not Arran who had exchanged the glass for the ruby in the Queen's ring; that it was for this that the Stirling goldsmith had been summoned to his brother's quarters that day when James had scuttled off to Perth to avoid Walsingham – and on Patrick's advice; knew now why Patrick had so advised; knew why he had urged Arran publicly to offend Walsingham. All was clear, Patrick was using them all, Arran, Walsingham, James, even Elizabeth here – aye, and Marie and himself also, undoubtedly – as a chess-player uses his pieces. To what end? That David could not yet perceive – save that the downfall of Arran almost certainly was involved. Did Patrick himself wish to rule Scotland? It did not seem as though he did. When he had brought Esmé Stuart low, he had not stepped into his place as he might well have done. Indeed, to some extent he had built up Arran, as indubitably he had built Lennox. To destroy him? Was it the destruction, then, that was Patrick's ultimate aim and object? Not position, power as such, statecraft, government – but just destruction? Was his winsome, talented, handsome splendid brother just a destroyer, a force for wreck and annihilation and nothing more? Could it be anything so horrible ... ? In that extraordinary room of mirrors, before the great Queen whose word was life and death to so many, David abruptly knew fear, real fear. And it was not fear of Elizabeth.

The Queen was speaking now. 'Whence came this, Master Patrick?' she asked softly. 'And how?'

'I pray that you do not ask me that, fairest lady. So much would fall to be told, of others, in high places, where my lips must be sealed. Suffice it, Your Grace, I beseech you, that it is yours now as it should have been yours from the start, as my prince intended it to be. And who, in all the world, could adorn it, and it adorn, so well?'

'I see.' Thoughtfully Elizabeth looked from Patrick to the great red gem – which in fact belonged to her prisoner Mary – and back again. 'I see.'

'I knew naught of this stone, Madam,' Orkney put in, doubtfully, looking sidelong at Patrick. 'But we have brought other gifts ... '

'No doubt, my lord – and no doubt a host of petitions and requests likewise! The morrow will serve very well for all such exchange. This is but a private audience.'

'For which we are deeply grateful, Highness,' Patrick assured. 'Perhaps, however, Your Grace would now accept the credentials of our embassage from our prince, and so save time ... ?'

'No, sir – My Grace would not! In such matters of state, I prefer that my ministers be present. You would not wish it otherwise, surely?' Thinly the Queen smiled. 'You have met my good Secretary Walsingham, I believe? My Treasurer Hatton – no?'

Patrick schooled his features to entire equanimity. 'As Your Grace wills. The vital subjects which we have to discuss no doubt will interest these also – the possibility of a defensive Protestant league; the machinations of Jesuit plotters; the matter of our prince's eventual marriage; the question of a limited Association in the throne of King James and his lady-mother; the ... '

'Never!' Elizabeth snapped – and then, frowning, held up a glittering hand. 'Not another word, sir! No matters of state tonight, I said. You shall not cozen and constrain me! Keep your tricks, Master Patrick, for innocents!' She rose briskly to her feet, no longer stiff. 'Now – my lord of Leicester, I understand, has a most fair spectacle for our delight tonight – apes that make a play, purchased from the Prince of the Ethiops. He but awaits my presence. I shall see you tomorrow, Master of Gray, and you, my lord, when, never fear, you shall have your say – and I mine! Come! Philip – the apes!'

Stepping aside right and left for her, the men bowed low. Passing David, the Queen raised a hand and poked him quite sharply in the ribs.

'Can you smile, man – *can* you?' she demanded abruptly.

David swallowed. 'When . . . when there is aught to smile at – yes, Ma'am.'

'I see. The honest one of the pair! Aye – then come you to-morrow with your brother, Master . . . David, it was? Tomorrow, to our audience. Then I shall be able to watch your face and know when Master Patrick is for cheating me! That is my command, and I call you all to witness.'

Elizabeth swept out, with Sidney holding the door for her.

And so when, the following mid-day, a Court marshal came to the Scots' lodging to conduct the two envoys to their official audience, David once again accompanied them. Embarrassed, he did not go with any eagerness; but though he would have expected Patrick to be still less enthusiastic, his brother in fact appeared to be perfectly pleased with his company. Davy had evidently taken the Queen's fancy, he declared, with his notably individual sort of Court manners – and with a woman, even Elizabeth Tudor, that was half the battle.

This time they were escorted to a different part of the palace altogether, with a minimum of fuss and display. They were shown into a smallish wood-panelled chamber overlooking the river, where, before a bright log-fire, the Queen sat at the head of a long paper-littered table, no scintillating bejewelled figure now, but simply though richly clad in dark purple grosgrain, with a moderately sized ruff, her greying reddish hair drawn back beneath a coif. David at least thought that she looked a deal better than on the night before. Soberly dressed men sat two on either side of her, first on her left being the grim-faced Walsingham. The entire atmosphere was businesslike, more like a merchant's countinghouse than a royal Court. Patrick and Orkney looked shockingly overdressed, like peacocks in a rookery. Here was no occasion, obviously, for heralds' trumpetings or flamboyant declarations. The contrast to the previous night was extraordinary.

Only a clerk at the foot of the table rose to his feet at their entrance. 'Your credentials, gentlemen?' he said.

Patrick, straightening up, and with a swift glance all round, handed over the impressively sealed and beribboned parchment. The clerk took it without ceremony, unrolled it, and read out its contents in a flat monotonous gabble, like a weary priest at his fifth celebration of Mass, thereby robbing the carefully chosen and resounding phrases of almost all significance. Not that any of the hearers appeared even to be listening.

Whilst this was proceeding, the newcomers eyed the sitters – and were not themselves offered seats. The Queen's expression was sternly impassive, revealing nothing; she might never have seen her callers before, nor be in the least interested in what they had come to say. Walsingham sat immobile, as though frozen, eyes almost glazed – though that was not unusual. On the Queen's right was a stooping, white-haired, elderly man, with a sensitive weary face, toying with a pen-feather; sitting in that position, he could be none other than William Cecil, Lord Burleigh, himself. Next to him sat a handsome, keen-eyed, stocky man of middle-years, who wore a great key embroidered on his dark doublet – one of the few decorations to be seen in the company; almost certainly he would be Sir Christopher Hatton, Keeper of the Privy Purse under Lord Treasurer Burleigh. The fourth man, sitting next to him, was younger, dark, wiry, with a quick intelligent face and darting lively eyes. He was different from the others in more than years – a man perhaps somewhat after Patrick's own mould.

When the clerk had finished, and rolled up the parchment, it was Walsingham who spoke, coldly, unemotionally.

'Master of Gray and my lord of Orkney,' he said, 'my princess treats your prince's envoys a deal more kindly than yours did hers. Can you name any reason why she should not turn you away unheard, or worse?'

'Only Her Grace's well-renowned clemency and womanly forbearance,' Patrick declared easily.

'You can stretch Her Grace's clemency too far, sir.'

'Not, surely, towards her youthful and fond cousin, who must learn kingcraft only by her guidance and favour? The fault lay not with my prince but with his advisers.'

'Of whom yourself, sir, and Lord Orkney are principals – by these credentials.'

'Alas, you do us too much honour, sir. King James has other advisers, and closer.'

'Aye,' Orkney agreed. 'A deal closer.'

'So that you accept nothing of responsibility of what occurred. Yet you both were present, and in close association with the Earl of Arran . . . '

The Queen coughed slightly, and Burleigh intervened, quite gently.

'Master of Gray' he said. 'Your present mission treats of great matters. Are these matters according to the mind of your young prince, of the Earl of Arran, or of your own?'

Patrick's sigh of relief was almost audible. 'They represent the mind of the King in Council, my lord. As such they are authentic, the voice of Scotland. In their name we have full power to discuss and treat.'

Burleigh nodded his white head. The old eyes were washed-out and colourless, but shrewd still. 'Treat is a large word, sir. How far may you treat, for instance, under your first matter of a defensive Protestant pact? Are you not a Roman yourself?'

'On the contrary, I am a member of the Kirk of Scotland, born into it, baptised and communicate.'

'And wed,' the dark younger man mentioned, from down the table.

'Yet in every country of Europe you have acted the Catholic, sir,' Walsingham intervened harshly. 'At all times you have associated with Catholics. I am not utterly uninformed.'

'And you, Sir Francis, associate with Jesuit priests – Father Giffard, for instance. But I do not hold that such makes you a Catholic, or unfit to transact your Protestant lady's business! I, too, am not utterly uninformed, you see!' Patrick essayed a laugh.

David saw a mere flicker of smile cross the Queen's sharp features, and then she was stern again. Walsingham never changed his expression, but he sat very still, silent. Father Charles Giffard, a Jesuit missionary and agent of the Guises, had recently been serving as a counter-spy for Walsingham also. That this should be known to the Master of Gray, and therefore presumably to Giffard's Catholic employers also, must have been a telling blow to the Chief Secretary of State.

Again it was Burleigh who took matters forward. 'And your proposals anent this Protestant alliance are, sirs?'

'We propose that an alliance of our Protestant realms and Crowns of Scotland and England shall ensure and cherish Her

Grace's northern borders from all assault, shall act together against the attacks of all Catholic states and princes. We shall also send ships and soldiers to aid in your landward defence.'

Five pairs of eyes searched Patrick's face intently, wondering. David's also. Such proposals, indeed, seemed barely credible, in view of Scotland's traditional need and policy to play off her powerful southern neighbour against France and Spain; it was, moreover, the reversal of all the trend of Arran's, and indeed Patrick's, previous outlook. Well might they stare.

Patrick went on, easily. 'In addition, it is proposed that our prince shall agree not to marry for three years, during which time it is hoped that Your Grace will find a suitable English lady worthy to be his queen.'

Even Walsingham could scarcely forbear to look surprised at this extraordinary piece of conciliation. Elizabeth's known dread of James producing a son and heir was not merely the pathological jealousy of a barren woman who could not herself do the same; a son would make him more desirable as heir to her own throne, for nothing was more necessary to the stability and internal peace of England than the assurance and continuity of the succession. It was the Queen's fear that if James had a son, some might prefer to see this desired stability established sooner rather than later; it was not as though the threat of assassination was unheard of. This proposed concession, therefore, could mean a lot in security – and the selecting of a bride for the Scots king an opportunity to sway him and his country greatly.

'And the price?' That was Elizabeth herself, the first words that she had spoken in this audience. They were all but jerked out of her.

Patrick gestured magnanimously, as though any sort of bargaining was hardly to be considered. 'Only Your Grace's goodwill,' he said. 'Your continuing affection for our prince and people.'

'I would not wish to name you liar, Master of Gray! The price?'

'It is nothing, Madam – or little. Agreement to a limited Association in the Scottish Crown of our prince and his mother; your declared acceptance of King James as your eventual heir – which may Almighty God delay for a lifetime yet – and meantime a suitable annual pension, so that His Grace may worthily maintain a style apt for your successor. That, and the return to Scotland and their due trial, of the intransigent Ruthven lords,

271

who now harass my prince's borders from your kingdom – the lords Mar, Lindsay, Bothwell, Master of Glamis, and the rest.'

Elizabeth's snort was undisguised and eloquent.

Burleigh spoke. 'A pension, young man? Is your prince a beggar, then?'

'Not so, my lord – but I think that you will agree that he has much to offer that you need.'

'Need, sir?' Walsingham said flatly. 'You mistake your word, I think.'

'Perhaps I do. You undoubtedly will know better whether or no you *need* a secure northern border. Or an ally against Spain, France, the Empire and the Pope.'

'How large a pension does King James look for, sir?' Sir Christopher Hatton asked.

'That, of course, he leaves to the generosity of Her Grace – who, to be sure, knows well what a crowned monarch may suitably give or receive.'

The Queen grimaced.

'Any Association in the Crown would require the return of the former princess, Mary Stuart, to Scotland,' Burleigh observed.

'Which is not to be considered,' Elizabeth added incisively.

'Queen Mary in Scotland would mean fewer plots and intrigues in England, Highness.'

'Think you that Mary, once in Scotland, would lose a day in snatching back her throne from under her son? Or another day in plotting to have mine from under me! God's death, man – do you take me for a fool?'

'I take you, Madam, for a great princess who knows wherein lies her own strength and others' weakness. It has been sixteen long years since Queen Mary became your . . . guest. In such time, undoubtedly, she will have changed much, learned much. But, alas, in that time also she has had little to occupy her save to plot and intrigue. Give her back work to do, her kingdom to part-rule, and she will have but little time for plotting.'

'You admit, then, that she plots and schemes against me, sir?'

'To be sure. Though not against Your Grace, but for her own freedom. It is inconceivable that a woman of spirit would not do so. I dare to suggest that Your Highness, in a like plight, would do no less.'

'You are very persuasive, Master of Gray, but I am not yet persuaded! This will all require much consideration.'

'In a defensive Protestant alliance, sir, how could a Catholic princess concur?' Burleigh demanded. 'Will Mary Stuart reform her religion?'

'Three years, I think you suggested, sir, that your prince would remain unmarried?' the dark younger man put in. 'Is this King James's own desire, or only his advisers'?'

'The banished lords of the Ruthven venture are all good Protestants,' Walsingham declared. 'In the event of a Protestant league, will they be pardoned and their estates restored?'

For a while Patrick answered a bombardment of questions as to details in his own skilful, quick-witted fashion, elaborating, explaining, reassuring, good-humoured and unflurried throughout despite the atmosphere almost of a trial that prevailed, with three prisoners at the bar, rather than the audience of envoys of an independent monarch. Orkney ventured one or two insertions, had them savaged by the trained and fiercely keen minds of the Queen's ministers, and was thereafter glad to leave all to his colleague. David, wondering at his brother's ability, wondering at what lay behind his proposals, wondering at the unfailing arrogance of these Englishmen's attitude, noticed the Queen's eyes often upon him, and sought to school his countenance to a determined impassivity in consequence – achieving in fact only an implacable glower.

At length, it was at David rather than to him that Elizabeth spoke. 'I have been watching your secretary, Master of Gray – and seldom have I seen a man less sure of his cause. You have been mightily eloquent, but I think that you have not convinced Master David any more than you have convinced me! You may retire now. I shall consider all that you have said, in council with my ministers, and shall inform you in due course. Meanwhile,' her eyes glinted, 'tomorrow being our Lord's Day, I shall expect to see you at good Protestant worship. At our Chapel of Saint John the Divine. Ten of the clock. You have my leave to retire, sirs.'

They backed out of a distinctly hostile and unbelieving presence.

Patrick spent the afternoon with Sir Philip Sidney, with whom he seemed to have struck up a spontaneous friendship, and it was evening before David saw him alone.

'You look even more gloomy that your usual, Davy,' Patrick declared gaily. 'Does the English food lie heavy on your stomach?'

'I cannot see that you have much cause for cheer, yourself,' David gave back. 'Your mission scarcely prospers, I think. The Queen and those others will have none of it. Nor do I blame them if they scarce believe what you now propose.'

'Do not tell me that *you* have become a doubter!' his brother mocked.

'Who would not doubt your Protestant alliance, man? Or King James's sudden desire for an English wife? It is only a game that you play. But a dangerous game, I think.'

'Heigho – but is not life itself a dangerous game also, Davy?'

'Is it a woman's life that you are playing for? Mary the Queen's?'

'I suppose that you might say so, yes.'

'Yet you admitted to Elizabeth that our princess was plotting against her.'

'Why not? Walsingham has spies in Mary's very household, amongst her own attendants. Think you that they do not know well all that goes on?'

'Yet you still hope to effect her release?'

'Hope, yes. That today was but a beginning, a formality. I shall be seeing the Queen again, later. In private. Philip Sidney is to arrange it. Then, it may be, I shall get her to sing a different tune.'

'By singing first another tune yourself?'

'Why, as to that, who knows? You would not have me to go beyond my mission, Davy?' He smiled. 'Have you seen Marie?'

'Aye – she is over in the Earl of Essex's precincts, with a host of English lordlings round her and her sisters.'

'That may please her father – but I think that I must go rescue her, nevertheless. It would be a pity if she was to become entangled, would it not?'

David did not answer.

Chapter Twenty-two

NONE sang the hymns more joyfully and tunefully, none made their responses or said their Amens more fervently than did Patrick Gray next morning in the Church of Saint John the Divine attached to the Palace of Whitehall. The Queen watched him shrewdly from her throne-like seat just within the Chancel; she had had the Scots party placed in the very front seat, a bare half-dozen yards from herself, where she could observe their every expression. David found her imperious yet inquisitive gaze frequently upon himself, and though he was a good enough Protestant, grew the more uncomfortable. Not so his brother, most obviously.

After the service, Sir Philip Sidney came up to Patrick, and David heard him say, low-voiced, that the Queen would see him privately that night. Marie Stewart, walking beside him, looked at David.

'You heard that?' she said. 'Tonight. Perhaps you will learn now the answers to some of the questions that we ask ourselves.'

But when Sidney came to conduct him to Elizabeth late that evening, Patrick did not ask his brother to accompany him.

This time Patrick was taken to a small library in the Queen's own wing of the palace, where Elizabeth sat alone before a fire. She eyed him coolly.

'Well, Master Patrick,' she said, unsmiling. 'It is not every envoy who requires three audiences! My good Philip here has persuaded me to see you once more. I hope that it is to good purpose!'

'I am grateful to Your Grace – and also to Sir Philip. I do not think that you will regret this condescension, Madam.'

'No? What is it to be this time, sir? Poetry, or child's stories?'

'Neither, Highness. Now you hear what was not to be said formerly.'

'But by you only, eh, my friend? Not my Lord Orkney, nor even in your brother's hearing?'

'That is so, Your Grace.'

'I see. Philip, leave us. I am not to be disturbed until I ring this bell.'

'Of course, Majesty.'

When Sidney had gone, the Queen made room for Patrick on the couch on which she was sitting. 'Come, sit here, my handsome liar,' she commanded. 'As well that you are so well-favoured, or even for Philip Sidney I would not have allowed this. But do not think that you can cozen me with your pretty face any more than with your pretty words, sir.'

'I would that I might, fairest lady – for other advantage than matters of state!' Patrick asserted boldly. 'It would be a joy – reserved alas for a prince or an angel!'

'But not a devil, sir, not a devil – in especial a Scots devil.' She leaned over closer, so that the white but no longer youthful bosom divided for him, and tapped him with her fan. 'Am I safe with you, Master Patrick – a helpless woman?'

'That is a difficult question, Madam,' he said cunningly. 'To which it would be difficult to answer yes or no. Shall we say that you are no safer than you would wish to be?'

'Clever,' she gave back. 'Too clever. Do not presume on your cleverness, Patrick. For I am clever, too!' Reaching out, she first caressed his ear – and then suddenly tweaked it, hard. 'You will remember that, will you not, Patrick?'

'Assuredly, my lady,' he told her, and smiled. 'It is not a matter which I could forget.'

'Good. Then we may get on very well.' The Queen took his hand in hers, and stroked it. 'And so, my friend – what have you to tell me?'

'First, lovely one, this.' Patrick drew from his doublet a fine gold chain on which hung a handsomely-wrought heart-shaped locket set with diamonds and amethysts. Carefully withdrawing his other hand, he leaned over to clasp this round the royal neck. The locket itself he guided gently into the hollow between the Queen's small breasts. When she did not stir, he allowed his hand to linger there.

Happy the gift to be enbowered there,
The giver sighs; such bliss he may not share!

he murmured.

'Very commendable, Sir Gallant,' Elizabeth acceded, brows raised. She rapped his hand sharply with her fan. 'But not all for love of me, I fear! What do you seek now?'

'Your kindness. Your esteem. And your belief that I speak true.'

'That I shall decide when I hear you, sirrah. What do you wish me to credit . . . for this bounty?'

'First, Madam, that you should know that your realm is in greater peril than even your Sir Francis Walsingham can tell you.' Patrick was all serious now. 'He no doubt informs you that ships are building in every harbour in Spain and the Netherlands for the invasion of your land. But he cannot know that there are plans to welcome the ships in Scottish ports; that Spanish soldiers are to land there, so as to attack at the same time as the others, over the Border. Also, French and Spanish forces are to land in Ireland, and to assail you from there. These plans are well advanced.'

'Christ God, man – and you come to me with a Protestant league! Is this true? Is this your James's true dealing? Is this the worth of your Scots Council?'

'Not the King, no. The King knows naught of it. Nor even the Council – or much of it. It is his . . . advisers.'

'The man Arran, you mean?'

'Alas, yes. My lord is misguided enough to see Scotland's place as with the Catholics.'

'But your Kirk . . . ?'

'The Kirk, my lady, is being ever weakened and brought low. Arran's new Black Acts make the King supreme in matters spiritual also, and all resistance treason. He has the power to silence the Kirk.'

'And James?'

'The King is young, inexperienced, and Arran holds him in the palm of his hand . . .'

'And in his bed, the catamite – so I am told!' Elizabeth interposed bluntly.

Patrick shrugged. 'That is as may be. But Arran will turn Scotland Catholic, if need be. And if James proves difficult, this Association in the Crown with his mother will solve all. Queen Mary will not prove backward in such an enterprise.'

'God's passion, she will not! And you ask me to free her – for this?'

'No, Madam. I do not ask it.'

'Eh? See you, Master of Gray – with what voice do you speak? Whose envoy are you? Where lies your loyalty?'

'To my prince and his realm of Scotland, lady. For that I work. I spoke yesterday as I was instructed, for the King and his Council. Today I speak in your secret ear, as Patrick Gray.'

'Then your embassage is folly, and worse – false!'

'Not so, Your Grace. It represents the expressed desire of my prince, and is true and wise in all respects save in this proposed

277

Association of the Queen and her son.'

'The *former* Queen!' Elizabeth corrected. 'You, then – *you* advise me not to release Mary Stuart?'

'Who am I to advise as between two crowned princesses, Your Highness? All I say is that if Queen Mary returns to Scotland, Arran will use her to further the Catholic encirclement of England.'

'Arran than does not agree to this Protestant league? Yet he is Chancellor.'

'Arran is cunning, Madam. He does not oppose it openly. But he works against it. Once he has Mary back in Scotland . . . '

'I see.' The Queen was looking thoughtful. 'There were two other proposals in your mission – James's marriage, and the return of the Protestant lords. Is Arran against these also?'

'No, not against them. They were, indeed, his own proposals. He would not have the King to marry, in especial with a Protestant princess, since that would strengthen James's position and weaken his own. So he proposes this stratagem – and for three years he is safe. And he would have the Ruthven lords back, that he may have them executed for treason, and so dispose of his rivals and gain their forfeited estates.'

'Aye, that is ever the way of it. A nice rogue, this Arran, of a truth. A fool also, if he thinks that *I* know not glass from ruby! It is time that he had a fall, 'fore God!'

Her visitor said nothing.

'Well, what do you propose, sir? Do not tell me that you have revealed all this to me for no purpose!'

Patrick shrugged one elegant shoulder. 'With the full weight of Your Grace's support, *I* could supplant the Earl of Arran. Already I have much sway with King James. I could have more. I could unite Scotland and your realm in an indissoluble league, and overturn all the secret plots of the Catholics.'

'I thought as much! You shoot a high shaft, Patrick. And so you would wish me to leave the banished lords in England?'

'Not so, Highness. Send them home, as King James requests – after I am back. Separately, one by one, in secret, I could use them to ensure the triumph of our Protestant cause – and Your Grace's.'

'You are a fervent convert, sir! And the princess, Mary Stuart?'

'The peace of Europe and the survival of the Reformed Church demand that she be kept separate from her son, Madam. Do you not think so?'

'I think that *you* have done a deal of thinking, Master of Gray! Who would have looked for it in that beautiful head! But . . . my good Walsingham assures me that you are one of Mary's men, trained in France to her service, and the recipient of her moneys. I cannot believe that he is entirely mistaken!'

'Your good Walsingham is not. But the fair unfortunate Mary's weal and good do not necessarily demand that she should rule in Scotland, and there cause bloodshed, religious persecution and war. I would help my princess otherwise.'

'God – you are frank, man!' the Queen declared.

'Such was my intention, in seeing you alone, Madam.'

'And how would you help her, if you could, I would ask?'

'I would have her, with Your Grace's permission, return to France. There, with England and Scotland united in a Protestant alliance, she could work no harm. And . . . the Queen-Mother, Catherine, who hates and fears the Guises, would see that she never set sail for Scotland again.'

Elizabeth's sharp eyes blinked. 'God's wounds, man, where did you learn your business?' she almost whispered. Then, in a different voice, 'And think you that she would go – Mary?'

'I believe that I might persuade her to it.'

'You? And you think that I would permit you to see her? You, of all men?'

'Why yes, lady, I do. Both as a wise ruler and a wise woman, I believe that you will.'

For moments on end Elizabeth stared at him, almost through him. 'One day, Master Patrick, you are going to take one step too far!' she said at length. 'And then that so fascinating smile will be gone – for ever!'

He smiled still, and said nothing.

Abruptly the Queen lifted to her feet. 'Leave me now, Patrick . . . before I . . . I forget myself,' she said, a little breathlessly for so great a monarch.

'Would that such were possible – even for a moment, sweet princess.'

'Enough! Enough, sir. Go!'

He rose, as she reached over to ring a little silver bell. 'I go . . . desolate,' he told her.

'So long as you go . . .'

The door opened, and Sidney stood there. 'Fair lady?' he said.

She looked from one to the other, frowning. 'Demons!' she declared. 'Limbs of Satan! Sent to tempt and try and mock me!

Both of you. Begone, begone – before I deal with you as you deserve.'

Sir Philip glanced quickly at Patrick.

That young man sighed, and bowed.

Elizabeth held out her hand to him. He stooped low over it, and then raised it to his lips. Slowly the hand turned over in his. He kissed the palm, the wrist, and was part-way up the forearm, before the Queen flicked him away.

'Off to your grey-eyed Lady Marie,' she ordered, hoarsely. 'I do not wonder that she will not marry you.'

'And the princess, her namesake, Your Grace? Have I permission to go speak with her?'

'We shall consider it, man. We shall see. But do not think it assured. Do not think anything assured.' She turned her slender back on them.

They bowed themselves out.

David waited for his brother in their lodging. 'Did you see the Queen?' he demanded. 'Did you find her more to our favour? Did you speak of the Queen – *our* Queen?'

'I did, Davy.'

'And what does she say? Will she release Mary?'

'Not so fast, man – not so fast! That will not be achieved in a day. But I think, yes, I think that I will convince her.'

'And the Association in the Crown? Will she agree to that?'

Patrick shrugged. 'That is less certain. Perhaps.'

'The banished lords?'

'I think, that she will send them back. Time, Davy – just a little time.'

'Time for Queen Mary has been long, long.'

'I tell you, I do not think that it will be long now.'

'Why are you doing this, Patrick? Urging the Protestant alliance, working for the English advantage? It is not like you, like all that you have done hitherto. Are you doing it all on behalf of Mary, of the Queen? At last?'

'I suppose that you might say so.'

David rubbed his chin. 'Then, Patrick,' he said stiffly, awkwardly, 'I would say that I love you for it. I have said many things ill of what you have done, spoken against your seeming forgetfulness of our poor Queen. But this – this is a great thing that you are doing now. To go so far, to harry Elizabeth herself, to change even the King's policy and risk all . . .'

His brother eyed him sidelong. 'I am overwhelmed, Davy!' he murmured.

'Marie . . .she will love you the better for this, also.'

'Indeed! That is, h'm, a consolation.' For once Patrick did not smile.

'When shall we know? Know whether Mary goes free? Know what is decided?'

'We can only await Elizabeth's pleasure.' Abruptly Patrick turned away. 'I am tired. I am going to bed . . . '

Chapter Twenty-three

WAITING on Queen Elizabeth's pleasure was not apt to be a static business, however protracted and uncertain. The waterman had been right when he said that the Queen changed palaces day by day. She was possessed of a great restlessness and nervous energy, which seemed to drive her on to incessant movement, constant change. And all her Court and those who circled in her orbit must move likewise.

On the Tuesday, apparently without warning or prior arrangement, she decided to go on one of her frequent progresses. These peregrinations around the houses of her lords and powerful subjects served the purpose not only of satisfying her restlessness but of seeing and being seen by her people, and incidentally helping to reduce any unseemly surplus wealth which the said lords might have accumulated, and at the same time conserving her own resources; indeed, she deliberately planned her itineraries so as to include those whom she considered most in need of such blood-letting. Since she travelled with anything up to three hundred of a retinue, and expected entertainment suitable for a queen, her descent upon an establishment for even a day or two could have a salutary effect.

They left Whitehall in fine style, the Queen driving in a white-painted glass coach drawn by six plumed white horses, their manes and tails dyed orange. Around her rode her gorgeously attired corps of Gentlemen Pensioners, splendidly mounted, led by Sir Walter Raleigh and Sir Francis Bacon. Then came her ladies-in-waiting, a blaze of colour, followed by her favourite courtiers – Leicester, Essex, Oxford, and the others, each surrounded by his own little court of admirers and hangers-on.

The Scots party rode with Sir Philip Sidney, who was rapidly becoming the inseparable companion of the Master of Gray, and quite soon they were joined by the dark, wiry, youngish man who had been one of the councillors at the official audience and whom Sidney introduced as Sir Edward Wotton, one of Walsingham's foremost deputies in the realm of foreign affairs. He was affable, charming, paying particular attention to Marie, and strangely enough, to David. Patrick was genially wary with him, as well he might be; anyone high in Walsingham's service was not a man to be underestimated, however delightful.

Progress was slow, for the narrow London streets were crowded with cheering people and the Queen's coach could only proceed at a snail's pace. The Scots were interested at the crowd's obvious affection for Elizabeth. This was something new to them. In Scotland the common people were not great cheerers, and seldom saw much to cheer about in their rulers. The visitors knew of the Queen's boast that her greatest strength lay in the love of her ordinary folk, but it had never meant more than a saying to them, a mere theory.

'Why should your Queen be so well-loved by these people?' Marie asked Wotton. 'What has she done for *them*?'

'She has given them much that they never had before, my lady,' he told her. 'She thinks for them, protects them from the fire and the gibbet of Rome, has paid back her royal father's debts to the city of London, gives them plays and spectacles, and lets them see her. No monarch before her has thought to do all this for the commonality. They love her because she loves them also.' He smiled. 'Your prince, I take it, is not so?'

She shook her head. 'No, I fear not. How could he be? He has never known the people, or they him – kept apart all his life. We had a king like that in Scotland once, who went about amongst the common folk – James Third. They called him the Gudeman of Ballengeich. But his lords resented it, and made constant trouble. Do your nobles here not do likewise?'

'Why should they? If the Crown is strong, the realm is strong, and they are secure therefore. It was not so under the late Queen Mary, Her Grace's sister, nor under previous monarchs. Only fools would change it now.'

Marie sighed. 'I wonder when it may be thus in Scotland?' she said. 'Our lords look for more than peace and the strength of the realm, I fear.'

'If a Scots king could live and reign long enough to gain his full strength, it might be so,' David put in. 'For generations we have not had a prince who did not die young and leave a child as heir.'

Patrick, a vision of elegance, riding just a little in front, with Sidney, looked back over his shoulder, and smiled at them mockingly, saying nothing.

Once free of the congested streets they made but little faster progress with the heavy coach slow on the atrocious roads. A succession of lords and gallants were summoned up to ride for awhile in the royal presence, but no invitation came for Patrick

Gray. When Orkney and Marie were sent for to go forward, David drew the obvious conclusions.

'You have offended the Queen, Patrick,' he declared. 'I fear that you have gone too far with her. And on our Mary Queen's behalf. I am sorry.'

'Never think it, Davy. Give her time. She is a woman, and will act the woman. But she will act the princess also, never fear. I believe that I have convinced her what is the best policy where our Queen is concerned. Wait, you.'

When Marie came back, she spoke in the same fashion, lowering her voice so that none others should hear. 'She must be displeased with you, Patrick. I tried to bring her to speak of you, but she would not. I wanted to ask her about Queen Mary, but could not. I fear, Patrick – I fear the hopes for our lady are in vain, despite all your efforts.'

'Have patience, my dear. There is no reason for despair. It is a great matter, and Elizabeth must have time fully to consider it. That she may wish not to discuss it with me until she has done so, is but natural. I have just been saying the same to Davy – give her time.'

'You are wonderfully patient, Patrick. In all this you have . . . surprised me. All who love my aunt will thank you for it.'

'Do you think that I do not love Mary also?'

'I do not know whom you love, Patrick. I have sometimes thought, only yourself. But now . . .'

'Have I not told you a thousand times that I love *you*?'

'Told me, yes. But deeds speak louder than words.'

'What would you have me do, then? Must I force myself upon you, seduce you, to prove my love?'

'Even that might be preferable to merely using me for your *other* purposes, Patrick,' she said quietly.

He looked at her thoughtfully, and said nothing.

'At any rate, in what you are seeking to do now, Patrick, even though Elizabeth loves you the less, others do not.'

'That thought will sustain me in all my disappointments!' he declared. And at the cynical note in his voice, she bit her lip.

With the early October evening almost upon them, they came to Theobalds Park, Lord Burleigh's great red-brick house in Hertfordshire, down a mile-long avenue of cedar trees. They found it all lit up for them with coloured lanterns, fountains playing, and hosts of servants. Though a man of simple habits himself, Burleigh knew his mistress's tastes very well, and created this vast establishment largely for her entertainment.

It was a convenient day's journey by the coach from London, and most of her northern progresses started from here. Beside it, even Morton's fine palace at Dalkeith paled to insignificance.

Presumably Burleigh had had a few days' warning of this excursion, for he had an evening of ambitious feasting and amusement arranged. It was to be a 'ladies' night'; while the spectacle of musicians, dancers, tumblers and masquers went on, the Queen dined alone at a table at the top of the huge hall, waited on by her host and four earls – Leicester, Oxford, Essex and Warwick. Tonight she was ablaze with jewels again. Patrick did not get near enough to see whether she wore his locket. At a lower table were six countesses, served by lesser lords; at another the Queen's ladies-in-waiting with Raleigh, Sidney, Bacon, Wotton and others in attendance; this table Marie was invited to join. Following the Queen's example, the ladies fed tit-bits and sips from their glasses to the gallant and noble waiters, who made extravagant gestures of gratitude and adoration. Frequently Elizabeth summoned up one or other of the gentlemen to be presented with a sweetmeat or a glass of wine. Orkney was so favoured, and almost all of her intimate courtiers. But not Patrick Gray. Anxiously the Scots party noted, and waited.

Later, when Marie went out through the gardens to the dower-house where their party were quartered with many others, and David would have accompanied her, leaving Patrick to the continuing festivities, his brother shook his head and insisted in going with her himself. England's Queen could well do without him tonight, he observed, apparently entirely care-free. David could squire Marie's sisters back, in the unlikely possibility of their requiring such – their father being already much too drunk.

For a while Patrick and Marie walked wordless between the shadowy clipped yew hedges and the pale-gleaming statuary, the man's hand at the young woman's elbow. At length, it was Marie who spoke.

'You are silent tonight, Patrick. It is a strange experience for you to be the outcast, rejected. Poor Patrick!'

'I am not rejected yet, my dear – save by you this many-a-day! Even so, and if I was, I would be blithe and happy if I could reverse your rejection with the Queen's.'

'I do not think that is the truth. But assuredly, Patrick, I do not reject you.'

'No? Here is joyful news, then.' He held her a little closer.

'Do not tell me that this cool, sober heart of yours is warming to me, at last?'

'My heart has never been cool to you. You are a difficult man to be cool to.'

'Do not say that you have been deceiving me, all this time?'

'There are more sorts of heat than one, to be aroused in a woman's heart.'

'Aye. I pray that it may be the right sort that I have aroused at last, then. Let me feel, and see.' Sliding his arm around her, he brought his hand to rest on her firm left breast.

They were walking very slowly now. She neither paused nor shook him off.

'It beats,' he murmured. 'It beats, undeniably. But what does it say?'

> *Beat, beat, cool heart, and speak me clear,*
> *Your beauty warms my hand so near,*
> *But truer glow than that I crave,*
> *The flame of love my heart to save!*

'Save your poetry and, and posing for Queen Elizabeth!' Marie told him, but with a faint tremor in that level voice. 'Myself, I prefer plain honest words that mean what they say.'

'You do not believe that I love you, Marie? Despite all the times I tell you?'

'I do not know – I do not know at all, Patrick.'

'Then let me prove it, my sweet.' Gently but firmly, he turned her round, to face him, and bent his head to hers.

She did not turn away as their lips met. Lingeringly, expertly, he kissed her, and, as her mouth stirred a little under his, strongly, ever more fiercely he bore down upon her. But she parted her lips no further, though he felt her bosom heaving against his own chest. At length he loosed her and drew back a little, to peer into her eyes in the gloom.

'That . . . proves . . . nothing,' she said, as even-voiced as she might. 'You do as much, and more, for any woman who takes your fancy – or who can serve some purpose of your own.'

Patrick sighed. 'You are hard, Marie – like flint. I had hoped . . . ' He stopped.

'I am not like flint, Patrick – I would that I were, I think.'

'So calm, so sober, so sure of yourself.'

'Not inside of me.'

'No? How may I reach that inside, then? My avowals of love do not reach there. Nor my offers of marriage. Nor my poetry,

nor yet my kisses. What may I do other than I have done?'
Abruptly he laughed in the darkness. 'You said that I would do
as much and more, for other women. Come you into this arbour
here, my dear, and we shall see how much more I shall do for
you – and you alone! And, it may be, I shall gain that inside of
you at last!'

She shook her head, but not angrily. 'That is not the way
either, Patrick. Not . . . yet.'

'Not yet! Then in God's good name – when, girl? And how?
I have been wooing you for years. How can I make you love me,
woman? Or must I ask Davy that?' In anyone else but Patrick
Gray his voice would have seemed to grate, there.

'No, Patrick, that is not your task. Not to make me love you.'

'You mean . . . ?'

'I mean that I love you already,' she stated simply.

For once the man was silenced. He gazed at her, gripped her
arms, and said nothing.

'Are you so surprised, then?'

'You . . . this is . . . for how long, Marie?' he got out.

'For all the same long years that you have said you wooed
me.'

'For years? Can that be true? Me – not Davy? Never Davy?'

'I love Davy, yes – but quite otherwise.'

'You love him? Then . . . then how do you love *me*? Otherwise from him?'

'I have never dreamed that I might marry Davy,' she said
quietly.

'So-o-o! Then, why? Christ God, Marie, why have you held
me thus away? Why injure me, and yourself as well, all this
time? If you did not doubt your love . . . ?'

'It was not my love that I doubted, Patrick – but yours.'

'Mine! But I have told you, assured you . . . '

'Telling is not enough, for me. Nor kissing. Nor that other you
propose. Before I marry a man, he must put our love before all
else. Before his ambition, his freedom, his convenience. He must
act as though to be my husband was the greatest project of his
life. Perhaps I am foolish and ask too much – but that is the
fashion of me. He must earn the right to marry me, Patrick.'

'And have I not earned that right, in all these years? I have
known other women, yes – but they meant nothing. Would you
have me a celibate, a recluse?'

'No – since it is Patrick Gray that I love, to my cost!' She even
smiled faintly there. 'These others – they may mean nothing.

I am prepared to believe that. But it is not of them that I speak. The truth is that you have no *right* to marry anyone, Patrick. You yet have a wife, already. In that fact lies the answer to your questions and my doubts. You still *have* a wife. In all these years you have taken no step to end your marriage . . . '

'But that was no marriage – never was, from the first. I am as much wed to any women that I have ever held in my arms, as to Elizabeth Lyon.'

'Yet she is still your wife. And her property is still in your grasp! And should her young and weakly brother die, she is the greatest heiress in Scotland! So she is still your wife – and I doubt, Patrick. I doubt.'

He stroked his small pointed beard. 'So – that is it! Elizabeth Lyon. For that you have repulsed me, always.'

'For that – and what it signifies of your mind, my dear.'

'Lord, if that is all, then I shall seek an annulment of that piece of folly – my noble father's folly more than my own indeed – forthwith, Marie. I do not require Elizabeth Lyon's wealth, now.'

Again that faint smile. 'Not now? Oh, Patrick – for so clever a man, you are a child yet.'

'If I do this, if I end this marriage that is no marriage, will you wed me, Marie? Have I your promise?'

'No, my dear, you have not. But come to me a free man, and I shall give you an answer, an honest answer. I hope that it may content both of us.'

He frowned, took a pace away from her, and turning, came back to hold her arm. 'And meantime, my love . . . ?' His voice had become a caress.

'Meantime you may take me to my chamber, Patrick. To the door of it, only. But I hope that one day that door will stand wide open for you. It lies in your hands to make it so.'

'Dear God!' Patrick Gray said. 'Come you, then.'

The next night and two days following, the great cavalcade stayed at the Lord Howard of Effingham's magnificent new house of Long Barnton. He had accumulated a vast amount of treasure through the naval activities of the privateers and sea-rovers under his command, against the Spanish plate fleets from the Indies, and no doubt his Queen felt that some attention might not come amiss. Certainly he showed no grudging spirit in her entertainment, far outdoing Burleigh's efforts. The first night there was a notable fireworks display, the next day a pageant in which most of the adjoining town seemed to take part, that night a mock naval battle on the large artificial lake, with Spanish galleons going up in flames; and the second day a tournament of jousting in which most of the gentlemen took part and in which the Master of Gray particularly distinguished himself. The Queen presented the prizes, and so Patrick must go up to her, with the others, to receive his awards; but it was noticeable that she said but little to him on these occasions and was distinctly cool about it.

David grew more and more depressed, even if his brother did not. Sidney, watching it all shrewdly, wondered.

By the end of the week, at Kirby, Sir Christopher Hatton's seat in Northamptonshire, with still no sign of favour from the Queen, David, with Marie, came to his brother just before retiring to bed.

'It will not serve, Patrick,' he declared. 'We shall never have our Queen Mary released thus. Elizabeth will have none of you, or of our mission. Do not say again to give her time. She shows her disfavour of you over-plainly. She will be sending us back to Scotland, with naught accomplished.'

'You are too impatient, Davy. Besides, much is accomplished already, I am sure.'

'But not the great thing – not the release of our princess. If we are to free the poor lady, we must use other methods.'

'You think so? What do you suggest?'

'I suggest that we stop profitless asking, and take.'

Patrick turned to stare at his brother. 'Lord, Davy – what is this? What do you mean?'

'I mean that our Queen deserves better of us than that we should only beg proud Elizabeth for her, patiently wait her pleasure, and humbly accept her decision.'

'Instead of which, brother, you would do – what?'

'Lift Mary out of her prison . . . by either guile or force. Or both.'

'But how, man – how? There have been a hundred plots to that end since she was imprisoned sixteen years ago. Think you that you can succeed where all others failed miserably?'

'Me? Should you not say *we*, Patrick?'

'You or we, it makes no difference. Mary is straitly guarded, held fast.'

'So was her son, at Ruthven Castle. Yet you planned his escape, from France – and I achieved it, with but a handful of Logan's Borderers.'

'That was quite otherwise, Davy. That was in our own country, where all might be arranged. Mary is held fast deep in the centre of this England.'

'We outwitted Catherine's soldiers deep in the centre of France.'

'He is right, Patrick,' Marie put in. 'We must do something.'

'I came to England only to aid our Queen. To see her if I might.' David spoke doggedly. 'I'll no' go home without attempting something.'

Patrick looked from one to the other thoughtfully. 'You have talked of it together, I see, the two of you. Have you any plan?'

'Of a sort, aye. Our Queen, since August, is held at Wingfield Manor, in Derbyshire. On our return journey to Scotland, we can travel that way. Mary goes riding and hawking and hunting under guard of Sir Ralph Sadler and Sir Henry Nevil and their men. I cannot believe that they attend her, on such occasions, with so many men-at-arms as have we as escort.'

'But, man, Derby is not on our true road to Scotland. Think you, that if we went that way, towards this Wingfield and not by the direct road, Walsingham and Elizabeth would not know of it within a few hours? Little indeed escapes Walsingham's spies. I have no least doubt that we are watched all the time. A large force would be sent after us, forthwith, and Mary confined to her rooms that same night.'

'There are gentlemen of Derby in this Court – Lord Fenby, Sir William Soames, and others. It should not be beyond your ability, Patrick, to make friends with one of them – to make excuse to ride north with him, to see his house, or his hawks or his cattle. Or his wife, indeed! Even your fine Sir Philip Sidney has a property near to Chesterfield, I have discovered. He is Walsingham's gudeson – none would suspect if he came with us. Thereafter, we can see that he does not inconvenience our project.'

'I would not wish to use a friend so, Davy.'

Brother eyed brother levelly. 'It is a deal better than you used your friend Esmé Stuart!' David declared bluntly. 'Is not your first loyalty to your Queen, rather than to your new English friends, man?'

Patrick seemed about to answer, frowning, but Marie intervened calmly.

'Better if it was not Sir Philip, perhaps. He has been very kind. But whoever we go with, need not be so hardly used, surely? Only allowed to know nothing of our plans.'

'Plans!' Patrick took her up. 'What plans can you have?'

'Few, as yet,' David answered. 'Until we see this Wingfield, and how it lies. But it will be a strange thing if our wits cannot devise a way to see our Queen once we are near her. You, Patrick, have solved greater problems than this, I swear.'

'H'mmm. And after?'

'Send the women and the baggage on before us, with a small escort. We are well mounted – as well as any that Walsingham can find to send after us, quickly. With our escort of nearly five score, we can ride for Scotland with Mary – and who shall stop us?'

'I think that you are too sanguine, Davy. It would not be so simple and easy as that.'

'Who would expect it to be simple or easy? But it is our plain duty.'

'I cannot see that it is mine – as King James's and Scotland's ambassador.'

'To save Scotland's monarch and James's mother?'

'But not this way, Davy.'

'We have tried your way. You did as much as any man could. But Elizabeth will have none of it. We have waited her pleasure for long enough. We have tried talk. Now we must use deeds, Patrick.'

'What Davy says is true, Patrick,' the girl asserted again. 'We have an opportunity, a great opportunity, with our strong armed escort. Never have plotters for my aunt's release had this – armed men who need not go secretly. I believe that it would be wrong not to take this opportunity.'

Patrick looked away, sighed, and shrugged. 'When do you propose that we attempt this . . . adventure?'

'Before long,' David declared. 'It is time that we went home. It lacks dignity thus to wait on Elizabeth's whim. Besides, the sooner we attempt it, the less the opportunity for Walsingham.'

'Aye. Very well, we shall see.'

'Restalrig had best not be told, as yet. He talks . . . '

In Sidney's room in the main house, the following evening, Patrick smiled. 'I think that you will find that she will see me, Philip. Tell her that I believe that it is necessary, and urgent. She will not say no.'

'My dear Patrick, perhaps, you are right. But no other man that I know would demand an audience thus. Do you have an understanding with her? In spite of how she is treating you this week? I think that perhaps you have, my friend.'

'I would not presume to name it that.'

'No? Very well. I will do what I can, Patrick.'

To the surprise of the attendant courtiers, in half-an-hour Patrick was shown into the Queen's private apartments – indeed into her bedroom. Elizabeth sat up in bed, in a state of highly elaborate undress, her head bound in a jewelled turban.

'Leave us, Philip,' she commanded, very much the queen despite her décolletage. 'The Master of Gray is showing more marked attention to his Lady Grey-eyes, so I think my maidenly virtue may be safe from him for a space!'

Patrick grimaced, as Sir Philip retired. Walsingham did not miss much, clearly.

'Well, sir?' the Queen said, suddenly business-like. 'What is it? What is this important matter which you must tell me?' She made no comment on her arm's-length attitude of the past days.

'It concerns our princess, Your Grace,' he told her.

'What of her?'

'May I be so bold as to ask, has Your Grace decided whether or no I may see her, and whether you will release her should she agree to renounce the Crown and retire to France?'

'Impertinent, sir! What the Queen of England has decided, and when, is not a matter for *your* enquiry.'

'Yet, dearest Madam, without knowing your mind on this matter, I cannot know what action to take in a new situation. A situation that affects Your Grace's interests as nearly as it does mine.'

'A new situation, Master Patrick? With regard to Mary Stuart? What is this? How can this be? Is it a new plot? My good Moor has reported none such.'

'I fear that even your well-informed Sir Francis cannot be apprised of this, Lady.'

'Cannot? Cannot is a large word, sirrah. What is this situation?'

Patrick offered a convincing display of hesitation. 'May I say, Majesty, that it makes the need for a decision on the matter of our princess urgently necessary. Else events may move beyond even Your Grace's grasp.'

'My God, sir, will you play cat-and-mouse with me? Out with it, man – or I shall find means to make you talk plain!'

Gustily the young man sighed, and spoke with every appearance of reluctance. 'There is a project to rescue our princess from your . . . hospitality, Madam. One that, for once, may well succeed. One that for once, also, is simplicity itself.'

'I do not believe in this marvel of a plot, sir.'

'If you know my brother Davy as well as I do, Highness, you would be the more ready to believe.'

'Your brother . . . ? The honest, unsmiling Master David? *He* plots against me?'

'Not against you, Your Grace, but *for* our Mary Stuart. He is her man, heart and soul. There are many in Scotland still, like Davy Gray.'

'Indeed. But not you, Master of Gray?'

Patrick shrugged. 'While I am devoted to the well-being of the unfortunate but headstrong lady, as has been my father, to his cost, I can take the wider view.'

'I see.' Through narrowed eyes the Queen inspected him. 'And this plot of your brother's, sir?'

'It is not so much a plot, as a simple plan of action. On our way home to Scotland, we make shift to go to Derby, to visit the seat of some lord. Near enough to Wingfield Manor to make a descent upon it, by surprise. With our escort of five score armed men. Mary goes hunting, hawking, riding – guarded indeed, but by sufficient to withstand our many Scots mosstroopers? I doubt it. Your people would pursue us, naturally, but we are well-mounted, vigorous . . . and the North of England is traditionally of Catholic sympathies.'

'Christ's wounds – they would attempt treachery! Such base ingratitude for my fond hospitality! Your graceless Scots would so outrage my trust? I shall know how to deal with such, 'fore God!'

'That is what I believed, Highness, and why I told you. That, and my love for you.' He essayed to touch her jewelled wrist, lightly.

Elizabeth snatched her hand away. 'You tell me, you betray your brother to me – if so be it this is true – only for some very good purpose, Sir. Good, for you! But do not think that you may bargain and chaffer with Elizabeth Tudor.'

'That would be unpardonable – and foolish, Your Grace. Also unnecessary. The sure and wise course is so evident.'

'The sure and wise course, with treason, is to the Tower and the block, sir! That is where your precious Davy and the rest should go, forthwith.'

Patrick actually laughed, though not disrespectfully. 'But that is not where the astute Gloriana will send them, I swear!' he said.

'No? Where then, sirrah?'

'Where but to Mary herself, Lady? To Wingfield. To speak with her – under due restraint, to be sure. To take strong measures against our company would set back Your Grace's relations with Scotland grievously, offend King James, and greatly rejoice France, Spain and the Pope. Yet this project was devised only because Davy and the others believe that you will not permit us to see Mary. Allow that, under what safeguards you desire, and there is no need for this desperate venture – no rift in Your Highness's relations with Scotland.'

Elizabeth drew a long breath, and then exploded into urgent speech. 'God's passion – I believe that you have devised it all your own self, Patrick Gray, in order to constrain me! It fits all too close, too snug by far. It is *your* work, you devil . . . !'

'Not so, dear Madam. For I have patience, and entire faith in your wisdom. My brother and his friends it is who are thus headstrong, not me.'

'Either way, you are a devil, Patrick. Why I permit you even to speak with me, I know not . . . ' she paused, and from the littered table at her bedside picked up the locket which Patrick had given her some days before, weighing it in her hand. Though he smiled gently, the young man watched that beringed hand keenly. 'I should return this bauble to its shameless giver,' the Queen went on. She dangled it back and forth. 'Should I not, Patrick . . . ?'

He leant over. 'If Your Grace wishes to break my heart,' he told her.

'Have you a heart, Patrick – or but a busy, black, scheming mind? And a honeyed tongue?'

'Feel you whether or no I have a heart, Lady. Feel whether it throbs,' he advised, and reaching out, took her hand and placed it against his chest.

'Lord – you are so padded, man, I feel naught but stuffing . . . !'

Smiling, he opened his white velvet doublet, and guided her hand therein.

'I think . . . yes, I think that you have a heart, Patrick,' Elizabeth murmured. 'I feel something. But . . . it beats but slowly, sluggishly, it seems. What dull cold message does it spell out, I wonder? Come nearer, lad, that I may listen.' She patted the bed at her side.

'If mine is cold and slow, yours must be hot and fast indeed fairest one,' he asserted softly, sitting down. He took the locket and chain from her other hand, and proceeded to settle it, as before, between her breasts.

'Rogue liar!' she said, but leaned the closer. 'Mary Stuart, they say, is growing fat. You must tell me, Patrick, when you return, the truth of it. Will you, boy – the truth?'

'Assuredly, dear lady – always the truth. As now . . .'

Chapter Twenty-four

WINGFIELD Manor belonged to the Earl of Shrewsbury, who had long been burdened with the expense of acting gaoler to Queen Mary in his various strongholds – for in her usual fashion, Elizabeth expected her faithful subjects themselves to pay for the privilege of entertaining her guests, voluntary or otherwise. In this instance, however, Walsingham had found a deputy for Shrewsbury – no doubt because he feared that the Earl might be growing soft where Mary was concerned – in the person of Sir Ralph Sadler, a stocky, square, impassive man in his early sixties, a soldier, stiff, unsmiling and a little deaf. The Manor of Wingfield was a large and compact house, standing in a strong position on a steep promontory, in foothill country about ten miles north of Derby, its only accessible side guarded by a moat.

As Sir Edward Wotton, Walsingham's deputy, introduced the four visitors to Sadler, under the fortified gatehouse, the drawbridge lined by his men-at-arms, he greeted them without betraying emotion of any sort, nodded to Marie rather than bowed, and turned away forthwith to lead them within. The choice of the unhappy Queen's gaolers-in-chief was always something of a mystery. Presumably Walsingham selected them for qualities which were no doubt of vital importance. Whatever their differing types, it was essential that they should be staunch Protestants, past the age of probable susceptibility to women's wiles, stern of heart.

'A single-minded gentleman, undoubtedly,' Patrick murmured.

'Necessarily so.' Wotton smiled. 'I would not play host to your princess for a dukedom! I would end in the Tower, I have no doubt – and very quickly.'

'I wonder!'

The house formed two squares, one within another, around a central grassy court where fantail pigeons strutted, ducks from the moat quacked, and women washed clothing at a trough beside a well. Wotton informed them that one of the internal wings was allotted to Mary and her small entourage, and another to her guards and Queen Elizabeth's respresentatives.

David's eyes were busy on strategic details as he followed Patrick, Orkney and the Lady Marie.

At the entrance to Mary's apartments, a thin saturnine stooping man, like a moulting crow, met them, and was introduced as Mr. Secretary Beal, a Clerk to the Privy Council and Elizabeth's 'envoy' to her royal cousin – in fact, her principal and very efficient spy. Behind stood Monsieur Nau, Mary's own secretary – he who had once been refused audience of James at Falkland – and also Sir Andrew Melville of Garvock, her most faithful attendant, styled Master of her Household, who had elected to stay with his mistress throughout the long years of her captivity, brother to the better known Sir James of Halhill and Sir Robert the soldier.

Beal spoke coldly, nasally. 'I understand, Sir Edward, that these gentlemen are to be permitted a short exchange with the former princess, Mary Stuart?'

'That is so, Mr. Secretary – in your presence and mine, naturally.'

'If Her Grace permits an audience,' Melville put in, valiant yet.

Beal sniffed, Wotton smiled, Sadler stared straight ahead of him, but Patrick bowed. 'Indeed yes, sir,' he declared. 'It is our humble desire and request that such audience may be granted to us, her loyal subjects.'

Orkney chuckled. 'Mary will see me, never fear. I am her brother – God help her!'

Melville, and Nau also, bowed and withdrew.

'The lady maintains this ... comedy,' Wotton observed, shrugging. 'She never wearies of it. Extraordinary.'

'Is comedy the word, sir?' That was Marie, eyeing him levelly. 'She is anointed Queen of Scots, and Queen-Dowager of France. Where is the comedy?'

'Your pardon, lady.'

They waited, in silence.

Presently Melville returned. 'Her Highness is graciously pleased to receive you,' he announced.

He led the way indoors, into and through a chamber where two ladies mended garments. At an inner door he glanced back at Wotton and Beal, who had come long behind the Scots party. 'Her Grace prefers to receive her Scottish subjects in private audience, sirs,' he asserted evenly.

'No doubt,' Wotton answered. 'But the Queen's command is definite, sir.' Never did Elizabeth or any of her servants accord

Mary her title of queen. 'Your lady may not see these, or any visitors, save in the presence of myself and Mr. Beal.'

Tight-lipped, Sir Andrew turned and resumed his walking.

They passed through a kitchen, and then up a narrow twisting staircase. Undoubtedly these had been the servants' quarters of Wingfield Manor. In the little corridor above, Monsieur Nau stood on guard outside a closed door. As the party came up, he turned solemnly to rap on its panels with his little staff, slow dignified knocks.

In marked contrast to this somewhat laboured and pathetic striving after royal style and ceremony, the door was flung open swiftly, and a woman stood framed therein, smiling. A rivulet of laughter, spontaneous, unaffected, silvery, seemed to cascade around the company.

'*Alors, mes amis* – visitors! True visitors, from Scotland!' a clear musical voice rang out. 'Happy this day! Ah, I am glad, glad!'

In front of her all were dumb – even Patrick, even indeed the insensitive and hearty Orkney, her unlikely brother. David, looking, found himself to be incapable of any coherent thought, only of powerful and conflicting emotions. He was aware of a quite shattered admiration, an eager and overwhelming sense of devotion, and a great pity.

He perceived, after some fashion, that though Mary Stuart was indeed lovely, beautiful, that was not the heart of the matter. Nor was her attractiveness, her fascination. These affected him, undoubtedly – or he would have been no man. But it was something other than all this, something of such extraordinary quality and radiant personality that held him transfixed, transported, so that he could neither have moved nor spoken had he been called upon to do so. It was was not he was blinded by emotion. He perceived well enough that she was not the ravishing girl who, sixteen long years before, had crossed the Border and thrown herself upon her cousin Elizabeth's mercy – saw even, with a pang at his heart, that the knuckles of the slim white hand that she held out to her brother were swollen with rheumatism. It was that he perceived that she had no need of the chiselled perfection of her small and delicate features; of the alabaster transparency of her skin; of the flaming glory of her red-gold hair, as yet barely touched with silver; of the amber-and-green translucence of her eyes; of all the vital grace of a slender and almost boyish yet supremely feminine figure that the years were only just beginning to thicken. Without all these she would still have been, for David Gray, the same glowing magnetic being that was Mary Stuart and Mary Stuart only.

Well might Elizabeth Tudor insist that she should never set eyes on her.

'*Robert*,' she cried, pronouncing the name in French fashion, 'You are an old man! What have they done to you, *mon cher Robert*? Your belly is enormous!'

Orkney guffawed, but even he was not unaffected. He could find no words. He looked at her – but later had to ask Patrick how she had been dressed. She was indeed all in black, save for white lace at neck and wrists, and wore no jewellery, the black velvet threadbare and mended. But how she was clad was quite unimportant, irrelevant, with Mary Stuart's beholders – however fond she was of clothes. What she wore was seldom noticed at the time.

Laughing warmly, the Queen turned to her niece. 'And this – this can be none other than *ma petite Marie*, my namesake? So fair, so true, so douce! My dear, let me kiss you. I swear that you are the prettiest thing that these eyes have seen for long years. Ah me, once I was like you. And behold me now!'

'You . . . Your Grace.' In face of that unlooked for sparkle and lively humour, the younger woman could only stammer. She curtsied, for her, clumsily. It seemed incredible that Mary should still laugh, after all the years of sorrow and prison.

The Queen's extraordinary eyes rested on Patrick, and changed expression. 'So-o-o! For once rumour has not lied,' she murmured. 'The Master of Gray is even more beautiful than has been told me. Is all else likewise true, I wonder?'

He sank down on one satin knee, to kiss her hand. 'Madam,' he said thickly. And again, 'Madam.' He bowed his head. 'Accept my . . . my devotion.' That was not like Patrick Gray.

'I do accept it, sir – for I need all such, direly. But that you know as well as I do.' She raised him up. 'I thank you for coming. For achieving what few others have done these endless years – this meeting with friends from Scotland.'

She turned to David. 'Who is this brave one who stands so surely on his two feet?'

'He is David Gray, Highness. Secretary to this embassage. Brother to myself as the Lord Robert is to you.'

'Ah. Another son of my good friend, your father. And a very different son, I vow! But, *pardieu*, I would not have thought him a secretary! Eh, Master Beal?' There was flashing scorn in that last – but not for David.

As in a dream he took her proffered hand. He did not sink down on his knee. He did not even bow. Nor did he speak, nor raise that hand to his lips. He merely stood and looked his adoration, his worship, lips parted.

Brilliantly the Queen smiled on him, and the hand which he clutched stirred and slid up to touch his face, briefly, lightly. 'Yes, very different, *mon cher*,' she repeated softly. And then, in another voice, 'Come,' she commanded.

They followed her into a sitting-room of modest dimensions and scant furnishing, where another lady sat stitching in the autumn sunshine at a window. The company all but filled the apartment. As though noting it, the Queen turned.

'Mr. Beal, and you, Sir Edward – you may retire,' she said, all regal suddenly.

'That is not possible, Madam,' Beal declared, in his rasping voice. 'We must stay.'

'Unbidden, sir? In a lady's chamber? *Any* lady's chamber?'

'It is the Queen's command.'

'The Queen? Ah yes, of course – the Queen. My sister is ever ... thoughtful.' She shrugged, Gallic fashion. 'The Lady Melville will entertain you, then, gentlemen.'

The woman at the window, Sir Andrew's wife, rose and came over to the Englishmen. Beal brushed her aside with a wave of his hand, however, and continued to eye the Queen.

'You have not long, Madam,' he warned. 'These gentlemen needs must return to Derby forthwith.'

Wotton had the grace to look uncomfortable, and to mutter apologies.

Mary ignored them both thereafter, as though they were not present. She turned to Orkney. 'How is my son, Robert?' she asked. 'How fares James – my poor James?'

'Och, the laddie does well enough,' her half-brother told her, grinning. 'He warstles his way towards manhood ... o' a sort!'

'He grows the man? He is tall? Fair? Of a noble countenance? *Mortdieu*, to think that I must ask the aspect of my own son! Whom does he favour? Does he favour Henry, or rather myself?'

Orkney guffawed. 'God kens whom he favours, Ma'am. No' your own self, and that's a fact. Maybe he has something o' auld Lennox to him – yon slippit mouth and gangling gait ... '

'His Grace is not tall, Madam, but his proportions are adequate,' Marie put in hurriedly, 'and his eyes are very fine – Stewart's eyes. He is the most learned youth in the land, and of great talents.' She knew that she gabbled, but could not help herself. Indeed, it seemed utterly impossible that this superlative, radiant creature should be mother to the shambling, sly and frightened James. 'He reads the Latin, Greek and Hebrew. He writes poetry . . .'

'But not to me, alas,' the Queen interposed sadly.

'His Highness sent his most devoted filial greetings, Your Grace,' Patrick announced. 'He assures you of his duty and affection. And he would have you to know that he does all in his power for the easement of your situation and the improvement of your state.'

'I am happy to hear it, sir,' Mary mentioned, a little dryly. 'It would seem to be a prolonged process!'

'It is, yes, unfortunately, Madam – with the fate of realms in the scales. But, at last, the clouds open and the way becomes clear. Your Highness may take heart. Your long and weary vigil is like to be nearly over.'

'Do you say so, Master of Gray? Ah, how often have I heard that before! *Ma foi* – soon now, this one assures me. Wait but a little longer, another says. And I have waited – aye, *le bon Dieu* knows how I have waited . . . !'

'I also know it, Highness – we all do. But this time, it is different. I . . . we come direct from Her Grace of England. The King, your son, gave us full power to treat and negotiate. And at last we have something that Queen Elizabeth desires, something that Scotland may treat with.' Patrick's glance flickered over to where Wotton and Beal stood.

Mary looked in that direction also. 'But does Elizabeth desire that I ever return to Scotland? Indeed, does my son, sir?'

Patrick coughed. 'It may be that Scotland is not the next step for you, Madam. It may be that meantime you should look southwards rather than north, for your freedom. I believe that Your Grace loves France second only a little to Scotland?'

The Queen's lovely glowing eyes looked deep into Patrick's own. 'I think that you should speak me plain, Master of Gray – in especial if, as these gentlemen of England say, we have but little time. What is this of France? And what that my sister of England desires, which Scotland may give?' Though that was said calmly, there was no doubting the tension behind the words.

Patrick took a long breath. Seldom had Marie seen him less master of a situation, less at ease. He picked his words with obvious care. 'The King, Madam, proposes a, h'm, limited

Association in the Scottish Crown.'

'Limited? *I* first proposed such Association. Limited in what, sir?'

'A sharing of the style and address, Your Grace. Also of certain revenues – in a due proportion, of course. With mutual powers in the granting of titles of honour, appointments of patronage . . .'

'These are fripperies, sir – *pouf*, mere nothings!' The Queen interrupted, with an expressive gesture. 'What of the rule and governance of my kingdom?'

Patrick moistened his lips. 'That, His Grace and Council have decided, must meantime be left to himself. Neither the Kirk, nor Her Grace of England, will consider it otherwise. It is . . .'

'*Sacrebleu* – you come to me with this! This insult! I am to yield all my rights and powers as ordained monarch to my son, a youth not yet of age, at the behest of the ministers of the Kirk and the Queen of England? How think you of me, Master of Gray? How thinks my son of me? Do I seem a shadow, a ghost? Look at me, sir. What do you see? A cipher? Or a fool?'

'I see a very fair lady long held captive, Madam, for whom freedom of a surety must speak louder than any other word.'

'But not freedom at any price, Monsieur. One may pay too dear for even such bliss. I have taken solemn vows before God, at anointing and coronation. I cannot divest myself of them as of a worn-out dress. I am Queen, not of Scotland but of the Scots, I would remind you. I cannot un-queen myself, at the behest of others. Sometimes, but yes, in weak moments, I have wished that I could, *pardieu*. But it is not possible.'

'But . . . for sixteen years, Madam, you have exercised none of the powers and rights of monarch. You have been in all matters a prisoner. Surely, what now is offered is infinitely to be preferred? A release from this bondage. Your freedom. To live your own life again . . .'

'My life is not my own – it is my people's. If I forgot that once, I have paid sufficiently, have I not? I shall not forget it again. How shall I live amongst my people in Scotland, and take no hand in their affairs, do naught for their needs, leave their care, for which I am responsible before God Almighty, to other hands? How shall I, sir?' Mary spoke warmly, passionately.

Patrick cleared his throat. 'That trial would not arise, Your Grace, were you to dwell in France – in your beloved France. There you would be free in truth – free of this bondage, and of the affairs of state also.'

'To the satisfaction of my sister Elizabeth!'

He shrugged. 'To your own also, surely. The two are not irreconcilable, I do believe.'

Mary looked from Patrick to Orkney and the others. 'Whose device is this?' she demanded. 'Elizabeth's? Or the man's who calls himself Arran? Or your own, Master of Gray? For I swear it is not that of the son of my loins, to torment me with a freedom that I may not grasp.'

'The Association in the Crown is the policy o' the Council, Mary,' her brother averred. 'Adopted out o' your own proposal. This o' France I ken naught of.'

'The Association that I agreed to was to share the duties and responsibilities of the Crown equally, in partnership, Robert. This is quite otherwise – a travesty, a mockery!'

'Yet even this, Your Grace, has been hard won. Agreement to it by Queen Elizabeth has been achieved only after much entreaty and difficult negotiation,' Patrick declared. 'I beg you to consider it well.'

'And what choice favours did you promise Elizabeth, that she agreed to this so noble and generous gesture, sir?'

Orkney laughed coarsely. 'Waesucks – it cost us a-plenty! Spit on it not, Mary, for it cost the reversal o' all auld Scotland's policy. It cost a Protestant league, nae less.'

Patrick bit his lip as Mary's eyes widened.

'Mother of God – a Protestant league, you said? Scotland and England?' she cried. 'Against France? Against Holy Church? No – never! I'll not believe it. Never could I agree to such a betrayal!'..

'I'm thinking you're no' asked to agree it, Ma'am,' her brother pointed out baldly. 'It's been agreed. By King Jamie and the Council.'

'But they cannot do such a thing. It is against all Scotland's interests, her safety. Her ancient alliance with France, that is her shield and buckler. James is a mere boy, led astray by evil self-seekers. He cannot do this . . . '

'He is King of Scots, and head of Scotland's Kirk, Madam – a Protestant Kirk. He can do it, and has done,' Patrick assured.

'And you? *You* tell me this, sir! You who were trained to my service, have dipped deep of my revenues! The Master of Gray, son of my old friend, bears me these tidings!'

Patrick did not answer. Nobody spoke. Even Beal and Wotton looked away, embarrassed.

The Queen gazed round them all, and though anguished, mortally disappointed, helpless, never could she have seemed more a queen. 'If this is your mission, gentlemen, then you have my answer,' she said, quietly now. 'The Queen of Scots does not purchase freedom so.'

David heard Marie sob in her throat. Then, almost surprised, he heard his own voice speaking.

'Your Grace – think for yourself,' he urged, the words coming thickly, unevenly. 'I . . . I have no right to speak. But think for yourself in this – not for Scotland, Scotland has thought but little for you. Go free, even on these terms. It is your right, your life. Forgive me . . . but you have suffered enough for state-craft, Ma'am. I . . . I . . . forgive me . . .'

Those glorious eyes considered him, closely, thoughtfully. She even mustered a wan smile. 'Thank you, Master David. There speaks a true heart. But think you, even if I forgot my kingdom and my people's weal, that in Catherine's France I should remain free? Think you that the Queen-Mother would tolerate another queen in her son's realm? *Parbleu* – I should fare not better with her than with Elizabeth! The Queen of Scots may only *be* Queen of Scots – or she is nothing, and less than nothing. Under God Almighty, it is my destiny.' Mary waved a sorrowful graceful hand. 'We shall speak no more of it. The issue is closed, finished.' She turned to the younger woman. 'Marie, my dear, tell me of Scotland. Do the folk still speak of me? Have they forgot me? Is the Kirk still as hot against the Harlot of Rome? Against the Scarlet Woman who would seduce poor Scotia to the Devil? And how fare my friends – my Maries, such as remain? Huntly? Seton? Herries? My lord of Gray, himself? Do the buck still run sweetly in my forest of Ettrick? And the wildfowl flight at dawn and dusk from the sea to Falkland marshes? Has the heather faded yet on the Lomonds, and the snow come to the Highland hills? Tell me, *ma chérie?*'

Marie Stewart could answer her never a word from between her quivering lips.

Mr. Secretary Beal spoke for her. Time was running out, he said. His orders were definite. If the Scottish envoys were nearly finished . . . ?

Mary ignored him. 'You bring me word of more than grudging policy and the like, surely, my friends?' she chided, but gently. 'Is that all that you will leave with me? I danced once in the halls of Holyrood; do any dance there now? Linlithgow, where I was born – I was building a water-garden at the loch, and a new fountain in the courtyard; did they ever come to completion? In St Andrews by the sea, the grey northern sea, I planned a fair new college . . .'

'The new college is near finished, Your Grace. King James is very hot for learning . . .'

'But no' for Linlithgow. Jamie cares naught for the place, Mary. But Arran's lady finds it to her taste, so it's no' just deserted! Lord, she has . . .'

Marie again hastily interrupted her father. 'The Court is not a great deal at Holyroodhouse. The King prefers Stirling and Falkland, and even St Andrews. He does not dance, but is a great huntsman. He plays at the golf, also . . .'

'Enough!' Beal exclaimed, testily. 'Her Grace the Queen did not authorise this meeting for the exchange of tittle-tattle! Come, gentlemen.'

'I fear that we must insist,' Wotton agreed, if more civilly. 'It will be dark in no more than a couple of hours, and our strict instructions are that we must be back in Derby before nightfall.'

David looked over at the Englishmen thoughtfully. Could they possibly suspect some attempt at rescue, by night?

'We must go, then, Highness,' Patrick acceded. 'You will consider our proposals, I hope, with much thought, much care, since so much depends upon them. Has Your Grace no message, no word of hope which we may convey to the King your son?'

'Aye, *mon Dieu* – I have! I send him all a mother's love and devotion. Tell him that I remember him daily in my prayers, and beseech Our Lady and Her Son to look in mercy upon this unfortunate woman and *her* son, riven cruelly apart. I pray that my son may not be led astray by false councillors, of which I fear Scotland breeds a many, Master of Gray! Above all, tell him that I pray that he may remain true to his trust, to the people of Scotland whom God has given into our hands. To look not only to the immediate advantage, but to the continuing weal of our realm. An alliance with England, be it Protestant or other, for Scotland is but a marriage of lamb and wolf, of fly and spider. England is too close, and too powerful, too sure of her mission to lesser men. Such a compact must end in Scotland being swallowed up. Always it has been thus, always the cat has wanted to swallow the mouse. Always the first and surest foundation of our country's policy, if she would preserve her precious independence, is to keep England at arm's length, by cleaving to France and even Spain. Without that our small land is lost, I tell you. I am a Catholic, yes – but I do not speak as one, now. Only as Queen of Scots. Surely you know it – you all know it? Tell James that he must not proceed with this alliance, sir. You, Robert – tell him well. Promise me that you will assure him of it. Promise, sirs.' That was a command, passionately, fervently, but royally given.

Orkney mumbled, eyes on the floor.

'He shall be told, Madam,' Patrick said levelly, tonelessly.

'Then adieu, my friends. I thank all the saints for the sight of you. I thank even my good sister Elizabeth! If you see her, convey my gratitude for this at least, and my warm well-wishes. But view her not as the friend and ally of Scotland, at your peril and mine – for that she was not born to be. And . . . the good God go with you all.' The Queen's voice broke as she said that last, and swiftly she turned her graceful back on her visitors and walked unsteadily towards the window.

Bowing and backing, the Scots withdrew, Marie at least stumbling, unable to see where she went.

The two Englishmen were last out, face foremost, and Sir Andrew Melville closed the door on them.

'God damn you!' he said savagely. 'God damn and flay you! God's curse upon you all!' To whom he was speaking was not apparent; he did not seem to be looking at anyone. But his face was twisted as with pain.

It was a silent company that rode across the reedy pastures and rolling slopes towards Derby. David, like Marie, was profoundly depressed. This surely should not, could not, be the end? But what to do, what to hope for, now – since all too clearly Mary Stuart would not change her mind? His thoughts had turned at once, of course, even whilst they were in the Queen's chamber, to his earlier idea of a rescue by force; but on riding out from Wingfield Manor again, he had glimpsed an encampment behind some woodland, an armed encampment of scores of men and horses, where tents were being erected. And later, on the road, they had passed another column of men-at-arms riding towards Wingfield. Most evidently, Mary's guard was being massively reinforced. Why, he wondered? A mere unfortunate coincidence? At all events, it would seem to rule out any attempt at a rescue, meantime.

Patrick, strangely enough, though silent also, did not seem to share the others' depression. Indeed, he hummed snatches of song to himself as they rode, and occasionally made cordial, even jocular, remarks to Wotton who still escorted them.

Patrick seldom acted obviously, of course. David, low-voiced, assailed his brother, at length.

'Could you not have done more, Patrick?' he demanded. 'Could you not have made it easier for her? Is this *all* that we can do? Are we so quickly defeated in our endeavour?'

'Who is defeated, Davy? What gloomy talk is this? Today has been one small episode, a mere chapter – not the end of the story. Indeed, I expected little else. We have but sown the seed. The fruiting will come later.'

'The Queen seemed certain enough in her decision. She will not change her mind, I think.'

'Minds are made to change, Davy – especially women's minds. She knows now that she *can* go free. That is a hard thought to live with, in prison. In her solitary days that will work as leaven in a dough. The fair Mary will come to it never fear.'

'And you think that is right, seemly? When it is against her conscience . . . ?'

'Lord, you cannot have it both ways, man! And what is conscience . . . but the flagellant courtesan we hire when we tire of the good wife of sound common sense?'

David stared ahead of him, and said nothing.

At Hampton Court Palace, where they eventually found Elizabeth and her Court the following night, Patrick had no need to seek to arrange a private audience. The Queen sent for him forthwith. He found her pacing alone with almost masculine strides up and down a long gallery. Courtiers watched her covertly from alcoves and doorways, but none shared her stern promenade.

'Well, sir?' she snapped, as he fell into step beside her. 'So you talked nonsense! You made me took the fool! Mary Stuart would have none of your proposals – or *my* generosity. You have wasted your time and my patience. I do not love bunglers, Master of Gray!'

Patrick affected to look at her with astonishment. 'What misconception is this, Your Grace?' he wondered. 'What distorted mirror of events has been held up to you? I had esteemed Sir Edward Wotton – since he it must be – to have more wit than this!'

'Do not wriggle and twist, sirrah! Do not blame others for your own failure. Mary refused what you proposed – no clever talk will alter that.'

'Of course she refused, Madam. I expected naught else. She could do none other, without renouncing her Crown for the

307

second and final time. Nor could she swallow our Protestant alliance. That was clear. The one tied to the other made the issue certain.'

'But, man, this is not what you told me before! Have you been mocking me – *me*?'

'Far from it, Highness. But the questions had to be asked, put to her. That was essential.'

'But why? Why go to this trouble, 'fore God? Why make the offer, if you knew that it must be refused?'

'Because the offer is everything, Your Grace – the refusal nothing. The offer blesses you, honours you. And King James. And the refusal condemns Mary only. I have changed Mary Stuart for you, dear lady, from a millstone to a jewel. Do you not see it? Before – you will forgive me saying it – men criticised you for holding Mary fast all these years. They may do so no longer. You have offered her her freedom, and she has rejected it. James has offered her an Association in his Crown – and she has rejected that also. He is now free to do as he will – under your guidance, and I hope, mine. And you are justified before all men. Heigho – and you talk of my failure, Madam!'

Elizabeth had halted in her pacing, to stare at him. Smiling confidently if respectfully he returned her scrutiny. Never was a man more assured of himself. Tight-lipped she shook her bewigged head. It almost looked as though Elizabeth, Elizabeth Tudor, did not trust herself to speak.

'I will make so bold as to suggest that you will not deny the truth of what I say, Majesty,' he went on. 'In all modesty, I would claim to have earned some small thanks. King James's, also. Now, as regards Mary, your position is assured. No longer can you be blamed for holding her. And if she changes her mind, and agrees to the terms offered, Catherine de Medici will take over your burden, and she cannot upset your relations with James and Scotland. Is it not so?'

The Queen did not controvert him. Instead, she spoke wonderingly, obliquely. 'Whence comes a man like you, Patrick Gray? Under what strange star were you born? How came such a man of your father and yon long daughter of old Ruthven? God's death, but I think that I am frightened of you, Master of Gray!'

'You jest, Madam,' Patrick said shortly, almost abruptly, and despite himself he frowned.

Elizabeth eyed him sidelong. 'If I was James Stewart, sir, I think . . . yes, I think that I would shut you up in the dread bottle-dungeon of Edinburgh Castle.'

Recovering himself, he smiled. 'King James, Madam, I am sure has more wit than that! As indeed have you. Send me back to Scotland with Your Grace's sure support, as I have besought you before, and I promise you that Scotland will no longer be a thorn in your flesh.'

'No?'

'You do not doubt my ability?'

'I do not doubt your ability, Patrick.' Sombrely she said it. 'If I have doubts, they are . . . otherwise.'

'I shall prove them baseless.'

'Perhaps. I hope so. So be it. Go back, then, Master Patrick, and fail me not. For I have a long arm!'

'And a divinely fair hand at the end of it, Gloriana!' he whispered triumphantly, and raised her unresisting fingers to his lips.

Chapter Twenty-five

MARIOTA GRAY nibbled her lip and shook her head in indecision, her deep soft eyes troubled. 'What should we do in Edinburgh, Davy – in a great city? The children and I? We should be lost in the streets and wynds, choked amongst all those houses, in the stench. It would be worse than St Andrews, much . . .'

'It is not so ill as that, my dear,' David protested. 'Edinburgh is a fair town. We should have a house high in one of the tall lands, where we can look out far and wide. Patrick is generous with his money – wherever he gets it. We can pay well for a house such as we want.'

'What would my lord do without us?' Mariota shifted her ground. 'You know how he dotes on Mary. He requires me to look to his needs . . .'

'And do not I – your husband? My lord managed very well before you came to Castle Huntly, girl. He will again. You are *my* wife, not my lord's. We have been apart too much, I tell you. Do you not wish to be with me, Mariota?'

'Aye, to be sure, Davy – you know that I do. You know well how I have hated all this parting. But . . . *need* you go? Must you be off to Edinburgh, at Patrick's whistle? You are but newly back from England. Has he not used you sufficiently? Can you not stay at home, now? Is Castle Huntly no longer good enough for you?'

David ran a hand through his unruly hair. 'It is not that. I would that I could return now to my old life here. It is what I intended, and looked to do.' Even as he said that, he knew that it was both truth and a lie. While one part of his mind longed for the simple country life and the verities and satisfactions of home and family, another was appalled at the thought of spending the rest of his days teaching unwilling and uncaring scholars in this quiet backwater, after the excitements of life with his brother at the centre of events. 'But Patrick needs me. He insists that I stay with him, in his present need.'

'And is Patrick your keeper, your master, now? Must he rule our lives?' Mariota's voice quivered a little, strangely, as she said that.

'No. No – but . . . he is next to ruling Scotland, now.' David took a pace or two back and forth, in the room that was now theirs in the main keep of Castle Huntly. He had been back less than a month from the London embassage, and there was no hiding his restlessness. 'You know how it is, lass – how I am placed. I believe that Patrick *does* need me. Och, I know that it is little enough I can do, and that there is nothing so notable about Davy Gray. But the truth is that in some things I can affect Patrick, sway him. Not much, but a little. And, 'fore God, I need not tell you that often he needs the swaying! There's nights I canna sleep for thinking of what is in him, what devilish force, what power for ill. And good, too, I suppose – for he is the ablest man that I have ever known. But it is the ill that I ever fear will prove the stronger . . . '

'But is much of it not in your own mind, just, Davy? Always you have seen Patrick so, as though he was some sort of a monster. About him you are a little crazed in your mind, I think. Long I have felt that . . . '

He frowned, shaking his head impatiently. 'That is nonsense. I know Patrick – know him better than does anyone else. I tell you, I have *felt* the evil in him, again and again. It has done much harm, already. One day, I fear, it may destroy him – and God knows what else with him! If I can save him from that, even a little . . . '

'And so you must follow him, always, like a cow's calf? Oh, Davy – must you go?'

Stubbornly he jutted his jaw. 'Aye, I must. He is doing, now, what he has never done before – taking more and more of the rule of the realm into his own hands. Why, I know not – but he is. The King and the Privy Council are not stopping him. He needs a helper, a secretary, as never before. And there is still Mary the Queen to think of. If there is anything that I may do for her, it is with Patrick that I shall do it. That is certain. The Lady Marie says . . . '

'Aye – the Lady Marie says! She says aplenty, no doubt. And you heed her well, both of you! She . . . she is to be in Edinburgh also? Then – then perhaps I had best come with you, indeed!'

David smiled then. 'Och, do not say that you are jealous, lass? Of the Lady Marie! Save us – what next?'

'What next, indeed! You are ever speaking of her – and uncommon highly! I know her kind. Men are easily led astray by a pretty face . . . '

'Lord – then what about *your* pretty face, my dear? You are more beautiful than Marie Stewart, by far. Who are you leading astray? Only your poor husband, I hope?'

She still flushed like a girl when he spoke that way, and was the more lovely for her blushing. 'Do not think that you can cozen me, Davy Gray! Nor wheedle me into going to Edinburgh . . . '

'I neither cozen nor wheedle, woman – I command!' he declared, straight-faced, loudly. 'It is high time that I asserted myself, I see. You are my wife, and you will do as I say. You come to Edinburgh, and look after me, and warm my bed for me these winter nights, as is your plain duty . . . and keep me out of the clutches of the Lady Marie Stewart!'

She swallowed. 'Very well, sir,' she said.

And so, that winter, the David Grays were installed in three rooms high in a tall tenement in Edinburgh's Lawnmarket, near to the great house, former town mansion of the Earl of Gowrie, which his nephew Patrick had taken over. From their north-facing windows they could look out over lesser roof-tops and smoking chimneys, over an almost illimitable prospect, over the Nor' Loch and fields beyond, across the silver Forth to the green uplands of Fife, to the soaring Ochils and the blue bastions of the Highland Line. Directly between, if far behind, the thrusting breasts of the twin Lomonds, David pointed out, lay Castle Huntly beyond the Tay, and often Mariota gazed thitherwards and could feel that she was not so very far from her own place, after all. She did not love the city life, as she had feared, nor indeed did her husband, but she made the best of it; and the children revelled in it. They were all quite proud, moreover, of this, the first house that they had really been able to call their own.

David, at least, did not find time to hang heavily. Never had he been so busy. Patrick was responsible, of course. Indeed, ever since the day of his return to Scotland from London, Patrick had been a changed man. Gone, apparently, was the idling gallant, the trifler with poetry and play and women, the dallier with only the graces of life. Instead he had swiftly and deliberately become the active man of affairs, the vigorous and tireless statesman, drawing the reins of government ever more tightly into his own hands. Circumstances aided him in this. The King was delighted with him and the results of his mission – particularly the pension, provisionally set at £2,000 a year, which Elizabeth had reluctantly agreed to produce. Also, privately, the fact that he need no longer worry about his mother coming back to take part of his kingship away from him. The Privy Council, as it was now composed, welcomed the improved relations with England and the Protestant alliance which Patrick had negotiated. They were more than ready to allow him to take on further responsibilities, for Arran's régime was lax, ineffective, appallingly corrupt, and growing ever more unpopular. His notorious Black Acts had turned the Kirk solidly against him, and much of the people with it; his boundless appropriations of lands and wealth, and his open contempt of the laws, were too blatant even for Scotland, while his wife's rapacious bribe-taking, office-granting, and wild orgies offended all save the utterly depraved. Arran was essentially a lazy man, however ambitious, and it seemed that he was well enough content for Patrick to pick his chestnuts out of the fire for him, to put right much that was going wrong, and to accumulate numerous offices of state. He himself remained secure in the key position of Chancellor and President of the Council – and in James's affections, and, as was generally assumed, his bed. Certainly no open rupture occurred between the two men during this quiet but steady transfer of power.

It was largely through Patrick that the Court became centred in Edinburgh, for he saw that efficient government could not be maintained from ever-changing localities. James and Arran still spent much of their time elsewhere, hunting, hawking and riding the kingdom, but more and more the capital city reverted to being the seat of government. In this, strangely enough, Patrick was aided by the Lady Arran, who disliked traipsing about where she could not surround herself with non-transportable luxuries. She quickly perceived that Patrick was infinitely more efficient in most respects than was her husband, and acted accordingly. There were not a few who suggested that she might well be preparing to switch husbands once more.

David watched all this extraordinary change in his brother with wonderment, for he could not believe that Patrick's ambitions really lay in garnering a multiplicity of offices, in the wielding of executive authority, in the daily management of affairs. If he was doing all this, he was doing it for some specific purpose, David felt sure. The fact that Patrick's closest companion, these days, tended to be Sir Edward Wotton, whom Elizabeth had sent north to replace Mr Bowes as English ambassador, worried his brother. Also the great sums of money which Patrick undoubtedly now had at his command, and which did not seem to come from the chronically threadbare Scottish Treasury.

Not that David had much time for worrying. Being Patrick's secretary, under this new dispensation, ceased to be a sinecure, a mere nominal position, and became an office of much responsibility in itself, demanding all his time and attention. He did not particularly relish the work, nor the mass of detail in which he became involved. Had he wished, undoubtedly he could have had a choice of lucrative and more or less permanent positions for himself, in some sphere of government with which he was in daily contact; but he preferred to remain free, his brother's secretary and left hand. That he was not his *right* hand, he knew very well; clearly there was a great deal that Patrick kept from him, particularly in his relations with Wotton and the English.

One of the English items with which David was not fully conversant, was the matter of the exiled Ruthven lords. One of the points of Patrick's embassage had been James's, or rather Arran's, request to Elizabeth to take steps against these nobles, who had settled just over the Border in Northumberland and constituted a constant threat; a plea that she would send them back to Scotland for trial. Elizabeth did indeed remove them, ostensibly out of danger's way, but only deeper into England. With this the King had to be content. And secretly, David knew, one of them, the Earl of Angus, Morton's nephew and head of the Douglases, had already returned home and was in hiding somewhere in his own Douglasdale. Patrick seemed to suspect that the others might follow at short intervals. As to the purpose of his manoeuvre, Patrick did not commit himself.

The Master of Gray did not allow his preoccupation with English affairs to prejudice other matters, of course; for instance, his good relations with the Guises. He kept up a regular correspondence with them, through the Archbishop of Glasgow and the Jesuit couriers – with not all of which was David conversant either. One letter which he did see, however, contained an extraordinary document – a Papal *pronunciamento*, no less, declaring Patrick Gray's marriage to the Lady Elizabeth Lyon to be null and invalid, on account of the ceremony being heretically and improperly performed. Patrick laughed at David's expression when he saw this. A precaution, he asserted – a mere question of providing for all contingencies. One could not be too careful where these divines were concerned, could one?

Arrangements for the annulment of Patrick's unfortunate

marriage were in fact going on through certain channels in the Kirk, Bishop Davidson indeed having the matter in hand, most suitably. Divorce being more difficult and apt to be prolonged – moreover requiring some small co-operation from the lady in the case – annulment seemed the preferable course. That the parties to the marriage had both been minors at the time was a great convenience. Patrick also claimed duress on the part of his father and Lord Glamis. If this failed, he could always assert that he had, in fact, been secretly married prior to the wedding, to an unnamed woman now fortunately dead. But he did not think that it would be necessary to go to such lengths. Elizabeth Lyon or Gray, it seemed, was now showing a certain interest in young William Kirkcaldy of Grange.

David did not have to wait long to hear further word of Mary Stuart. She had been moved to Tutbury Castle soon after the Scots visit to Wingfield, presumably as an added precaution. Then, one January afternoon, Sir Edward Wotton came strolling into the room in Gowrie House where Patrick worked amidst parchments and papers innumerable, and David with him. Sir John Maitland, the Secretary of State, was there also, brother to Mary's late Maitland of Lethington.

'Ah, you are busy, Patrick – always busy!' he said. 'You have become a very glutton for papers, I do declare. I had hopes of better, from you! I will see you anon.'

'I am just finishing,' Patrick assured. 'Davy, the blessed Davy, will do the rest for me. I believe that he actually *likes* handling pen and paper! And Sir John is just going – are you not, Mr. Secretary?'

Maitland, a thin, ascetic, unsmiling man, able but friendless, looked sourly at the English ambassador. He did not like him, nor anything to do with England. Yet he was accepting Patrick's money, David knew, as were many others – and not enquiring whence it came. He bowed stiffly, and stalked out.

Wotton came and sat on the edge of Patrick's littered table. 'I have despatches,' he said. 'Some of which will interest you, my friend. Your Mary Stuart is a great letter-writer – which is a great convenience.'

Patrick sat back. 'You mean that Walsingham has been reading her correspondence – and has intercepted something else of interest to England?'

'Exactly. She is remarkably explicit in her writings, the good lady.'

'I wonder that she does not realise that her letters will be

tampered with. If not herself, Nau or Melville at least. It seems
. . . elementary.'

'Ah, but she does, Patrick. We have allowed for her unkind
suspicions, however. Walsingham arranged for the brewer who
supplies the beer to her household to claim to be a fervent
Catholic and supporter of Mary, and to offer her the use of a
specially-contrived beer-barrel which should go in and out of
her quarters with a secret container within for letters. And so the
fair lady may now write to whom she will, with an easy mind –
and Sir Francis has a convenient inspection of the letters and
their answers. A truly useful barrel!'

David, head down over his papers, had to choke back his fury
and indignation. Patrick laughed, however.

'Very neat,' he admitted. 'And I take it that something of note
has now come out of your barrel?'

'Indeed it has. Many things. But in especial one in which you
will be interested. A letter written to Mendoza, former Spanish
ambassador to Elizabeth, and a friend of your Mary, as you
know. In it she tells of your interview with her and declares that,
to bring her son to his senses and to halt this Protestant alliance,
she proposes to name Mendoza's master, Philip of Spain, her
heir instead of James – heir to the throne of Scotland, and her
reversion to the throne of England likewise! How think you of
that, Master Patrick?'

'Lord!' Patrick was sitting up straight, now. 'This is . . .
fantastic! She would do this? The proud Mary would go so far?
To disinherit her own son – for the Spaniard!'

'To *say* that she would do so, at all events.'

'Aye. It is likely but a gesture, a ruse.'

'But a potent one, i' faith. For you will see where it leads. It
would give Philip what he greatly needs – the sure support of the
English Catholics. We know that he plans invasion. If he can
rely on our dissident Catholics to rise in his support . . . ! The
Pope has declared Elizabeth to be illegitimate and a usurper,
and Mary the true Queen of England – St. Peter roast him! If
Philip is her heir, and she a prisoner, then he will have all good
Catholics seeing his coming as a rescue, not an invasion. Our
good Queen's life becomes the more threatened. Ah, a subtle
and dangerous gesture, indeed. Who would have thought the
woman capable of it!'

'M'mmm,' Patrick examined his finger-tips. 'Extraordinary!
She is a fighter yet.' There was admiration in his voice, un-

doubtedly. 'And has Walsingham passed on the letter to Mendoza?'

'Dear God – no! Why scourge our own backs? The question is – to tell your King James, or no? It is left to my own decision, meantime. A little difficult, as you will concede I think. How would he take it? Would it move him for the alliance, or against, think you?'

Patrick toyed with his goose quill for a moment or two. 'I would advise that you do not tell him, Edward,' he said at length. 'James is easily frightened. He is firm enough for the alliance now. But this might scare him away from it – as is his mother's intention. The succession to Elizabeth's throne is his dearest ambition – to rule both realms. Any shadow that might come between him and that vision could terrify him into a folly. Better that he does not know. If Mary writes to him, therefore, to the same effect, I'd take it kindly if the letter comes to me.'

Wotton nodded, and glanced over at David, eyebrows raised.

Patrick answered his unspoken question. 'Davy is discretion itself,' he assured. 'All secrets are safe with him.'

Looking up, David opened his mouth to speak – and then shut it again, almost with a click.

'Very well – James shall not know.' Wotton lifted himself off the table, and moved over to the door. Then he paused. 'It may interest you to know, Patrick my friend, that Mary Stuart added an amusing footnote to this dramatic letter. She said that she believed now the Master of Gray to be a traitor to her cause, and that she would not trust him hereafter!' He laughed lightly. 'How misguided are women!' And nodding, he opened the door and passed out.

For a long moment there was silence in that room. David stared at his brother. Presently Patrick met his gaze, and sighed.

'Ah, me – you see how I am misjudged, Davy!'

'Are you, Patrick?' That was but a husky whisper.

'Need you ask?' There was sorrowful reproach in the other's melodious voice. 'You know the risks that I took for her. All that I have done, as you know also, I have done in her best interests. But . . can she see it, poor lady? I do not blame her, mark you, shut up there, cut off from her friends, from guidance and advice. But it is . . . hard.'

'Are you so sure, Patrick? So sure of your judgment? Her best interests, you say. Can you be so certain? So much surer than Mary herself? Do you never doubt yourself, man?'

'I leave the doubting to you, Davy – who have a talent for it! Myself, I use the wits the good God has given me.'

'Aye. But once you told me that, since most men are blinded by prejudice, and fettered by beliefs and misconceptions of religion and honour, a man who keeps his wits unfettered may go far, rise high on the weakness of others. You have gone far, brother, risen high by those wits God gave you. But . . . does the cost to others count with you? What of the cost to Mary, of your best interests for her? I have doubted often, yes – but have not turned my doubts into action. It may be that I have been weak. I have stood by and seen you undermine and betray much and many, in the name of clear wits and . . .'

'Have a watch what you say brother!' Patrick interposed, half-rising.

'That is what I am doing, yes,' David went on levelly, holding the other's eyes. 'I am warning you, Patrick. If ever I come to believe that you have betrayed Mary of Scotland, I will stand by no longer. I will act, Patrick – act! Forget you *are* my brother. Believe me, brother, you would never betray another! You have it?'

The other moistened his lips. 'Are you crazed, man?' he got out. 'What . . . what fool's talk is this, of betrayal? You know not what you say.'

'I may be a fool, Patrick – as well as weak. Indeed, I often judge that I am. But I mean what I say.' Heavily David spoke. 'See that you do not forget it.'

Patrick's glance fell before his brother's burning regard. He began to write.

That same night a courier rode into Edinburgh with other news for Patrick Gray – news which affected the man more notably than his brother had ever seen before. Sir Philip Sidney was dead. He had died heroically, of wounds, on the battlefield of Zutphen, on an expedition to aid the Protestant Netherlands. Dying, he had sent a message to Patrick, with certain of his unpublished poems.

Patrick wept. 'War!' he cried. 'War and bloody strife! The folly of it – oh, the damnable folly! It plucks the flowers and leaves the nettles to flourish! There lies the finest flower of this age, rotting on a foreign field . . .'

David had never known Patrick so moved, so hurt, so affected by anything. He had not realised how deeply he had felt for Sidney, that their friendship had been more than the mutual appreciation of two able minds. Himself he sorrowed now for his brother's pain and sorrow. But something in him was glad also – glad. For he had begun to fear that Patrick was perhaps incapable of such love towards any. He knew a great relief in this proof that he was wrong. Perhaps he was wrong in other matters also?

Chapter Twenty-six

DAVID rode hard and alone down the winding valley of the Gala Water, with the green rounded hills of the Borderland crowding in on every side. His body and his senses rejoiced in the freedom and exercise of it all, the scents of broom and pine and raw red earth, the colours of golden gorse, emerald bog and sparkling water under a cloud-flecked sky, the sounds of the trilling curlews, the screaming peewits and the baaing sheep. After the long months cooped up in Edinburgh, buried amongst parchments and books, this headlong riding represented a welcome release.

His mind was preoccupied with anxiety, however, and on a subject very close to his heart – Mary the Queen. The day before, a message brought by urgent courier from one of Patrick's trusted informants in London, had revealed that Walsingham had uncovered a new Catholic plot which was to involve the assassination of Elizabeth and the placing of Mary upon her throne – a plot for which plans were well advanced, the details revealed by the torture of a suspect. The English Parliament, informed, had exploded into great wrath, and amongst other measures, had demanded the immediate bringing to trial of Mary herself on a charge of treason. How one monarch could be charged with treason against another monarch was not explained – but the situation was fraught with danger for Mary, obviously. She had been moved once more, from Tutbury to Chartley, and was now little better than a felon in a cell. Representation on her behalf, action of some sort, was urgently necessary.

Unfortunately, the King and Arran, with much of the Court, had a few days before gone to hunt in Ettrick Forest, deep in the Borders, lodging at the Castle of Newark. For some unexplained reason, two days later, Patrick had followed them thither, which was not his usual practice, leaving David behind to deal with many unresolved matters. Hence the latter's hurried dash after his brother. At an hour's notice he had set out, and got as far as Borthwick that same night.

What Patrick might do, what the King might be able to do, in the circumstances, David did not know. But assuredly something must be attempted, some forceful representations made to Elizabeth. She wanted this Protestant alliance; pressure could be exerted over that, surely?

It was early evening before David reached Newark, in the fair valley of Yarrow – only to find that Patrick was elsewhere. The King was there, and most of his following, though Arran was absent too. He had gone to Ferniehirst Castle, near Jedburgh, where the laird was his close friend Andrew Kerr, Scots Warden of the Middle March. The seasonal formal meeting of the English and Scots Wardens of the Border Marches was to take place in two days' time, when all current Border disputes were discussed and if possible resolved, and it was presumed that Arran had gone to talk over certain outstanding issues beforehand. It was also presumed that the Master of Gray had followed him to Ferniehirst.

Though tired, after borrowing a fresh horse David set off again forthwith, cursing these delays which might mean much to his trapped and threatened Queen. He headed southeastwards now, over into the vale of Ettrick and on beyond, climbing into high ground, till the late summer darkness enfolded him and he slept briefly at the remote upland village of Ashkirk. Off early in the morning, once more, he rode through empty hills of grass and gorse, down to the great trough of Teviotdale at Denholm-on-the-Green, to turn eastwards, under the graceful peak of Ruberslaw, through the Turnbull country. He reached Ferniehirst's grey strength soon after mid-day.

Once again he was disappointed. Patrick was not here either, had never been here. Arran he saw, with Kerr and some of his cronies, and a new light-o'-love, the Lady Hester Murray. But the Master of Gray was neither present nor expected.

At a loss, David racked his brains. Where could his brother have gone? What errand had he been on? Where might he look for him now amidst these green hills, with his fateful tidings? He had no pointer to guide him, save for the fact that his brother had indeed called at Newark and on leaving there had been assumed to be coming here to Ferniehirst. Which meant that at least he must have started by turning in a south-easterly direction. So Patrick must have intended to turn up the Ettrick valley, or else cross over into Teviotdale as he himself had done. The Ettrick led nowhere, save by a high and difficult pass into Eskdale and the west; if Patrick had wanted to go in that direction, surely he would have taken the shorter and easier route up Yarrow? So the chances were that it was Tevoit. Back

321

whence he had come David turned his horse.

It was late afternoon when, at Denholm again, after asking fruitlessly at tower and cot-house all the way up, the village blacksmith gave him what might be the clue that he sought. The man knew nothing about the Master of Gray, but Logan of Restalrig and a small troop had stopped at his smiddy the previous afternoon, with a horse that had cast its shoe. To David's eager description of his brother, the man had nodded and agreed that there had been a Frenchified gentleman with Logan – who was of course well-known in the Borders. They had left Denholm for the south, by the drove road which led through Rule Water.

And now David drove his jaded mount fast and free. The road before him plunged deep into the wild Cheviots, which constituted the Border between Scotland and England. Only two routes led out of Rule Water – both to high passes into England. One, to the east, was the well-known passage of the Redeswire, on Carter Fell; the other, to the west, was the lonely pass of the Deadwater, at the head of Tyne.

At a tumbledown herd's cabin where the drove-roads forked, many miles on, the savage-looking occupant admitted to David that a party of riders had taken the route to Deadwater early that morning.

What in Heaven's name brought Patrick to these lonely fastnesses? And in Robert Logan's company. When Restalrig came on the scene, violent action of some kind usually followed.

His route, the only route, now lay along an ancient Roman road, ever climbing across the desolate uplands which heaped themselves in heathery billows around the mass of mighty Peel Fell. This was the Debatable Land, where no king ruled, unless he be an Armstrong or a Turnbull chief, and the only law was that of cold steel and hot blood. Men seldom rode this country alone, and David loosened his sword in its scabbard uneasily.

Darkness overtook him high on the swelling flank of Peel Fell, but he still pressed on, the Roman road a clear straight gash in the shadowy hillside before him. And halfway down the long slope beyond, into the valley of the infant Tyne, he saw the red gleam of camp-fires. Weary horse and rider made for them, thankful, but wary also.

David was challenged fiercely by a heavily-armed sentinel while still some distance from the fires, and relievedly discovered the man to be none other than the dark mosstrooper who had once helped release a bound stag on the heights of

Ruthven in far Perthshire. Companionably he clapped the visitor's drooping shoulder, and brought him stumbling to the circle of the firelight.

Perhaps a score of men lay asleep, wrapped in cloaks and plaids. But around the fire a group still sat, in talk. His brother was there, and Logan. It was not at them, however, that David stared, but at the Lord Home, the Earl of Mar, the Earl of Bothwell, and – yes, the Master of Glamis.

The mosstrooper had not been the only link with Ruthven.

'Lord – Davy! What . . . what in the fiend's name is the meaning of this?' Patrick cried, starting up, and less than welcoming.

David felt like asking the same question. 'I have a message,' he said. 'An important message. On a private matter.' He said no more, for these men were the Queen's enemies. They looked at him suspiciously, inimically.

Patrick frowned, shrugged, and then bowed to his companions round the fire. 'Gentlemen – if you will excuse me . . . ?'

Patrick listened to his brother's tidings almost impatiently. As David stressed the seriousness of the Queen's case, the other interrupted.

'Yes, yes, man – but there is no need to come running after me with it, thus. She has brought it on herself. It can wait . . . '

'It cannot wait, Patrick, I tell you, the English Parliament is demanding her trial, for treason. Allow them to start that, and no protests will avail anything – for they must finish the business or be made to look fools. This folly must be stopped before it starts.'

'How think you that *I* am to stop it? Is their Parliament to listen to me? Halt their courses because I forbid it? What can I do? Or even the King?'

'You can do much – you *and* the King. I think. You have the means, in this alliance. You yourself negotiated its terms. Elizabeth wants it, and so no doubt does her Parliament. Send swift word that Scotland cannot proceed with it whilst her Queen is unlawfully charged with a treason which she could not commit . . . '

'But, Lord – she probably *was* deep in this plot! She has been in many another.'

'Mary would never countenance the assassination of Elizabeth. But even so – !'

'She countenanced the assassination of her own husband, Darnley!' Patrick asserted grimly.

'That was never proved. Do you credit the words of dastards like Morton and Archie Douglas? But that is not the issue, Patrick. Can the crowned monarch of one realm be accused of treason against that of another? It is impossible. Indeed, how can a king or a queen commit treason, at all? Treason is for subjects. This trial would be no trial, but a savagery. A savagery against a poor, defenceless lady. And an insult to Scotland, also.'

'Ah well, Davy – I will think of it. Consider the matter . . . '

David gripped the other's arm. 'Brother, you will do more than that!' he said, low-voiced, tense. 'And swiftly. You can and you will! You recollect what I said yon time . . . ?'

'Mary Stuart has smitten you crazy, man!'

'Call it that, if you will. But act, Patrick. For Mary. Or, in my own way *I* will act for her! And forthwith.'

His brother sighed, and shrugged that one shoulder. 'Very well. I should have done what I could anyway, of course . . . but without these dramatics! Now – these lords are becoming restive. I must go back to them. Tell them something to keep them quiet. But not this, of Mary . . . '

'No – for these are no friends of the Queen's! These indeed are her enemies. The King's enemies, too – the men who held him fast at Ruthven. You keep strange company, I think, Patrick, for one of the King's ministers? And a strange meeting-place!'

'Your comments on the matter must await another occasion, Davy,' his brother declared coolly. 'Meantime, I would prefer that you hold your tongue before them.'

'You need not fear – I wish no dealings with them. My wonder is that *you* do. The last time I saw the Master of Glamis, both of you had swords in your hands!'

'That was long ago – and some of us at least have learned some wisdom since then! These men are not the King's enemies. Indeed, they may be more than useful in the King's service. We want our Scotland united, do we not? How else shall the realm flourish? I could not speak with them, save thus in secret and just over the English march, for Arran would have the heads off each of them if he could.'

'Did not Elizabeth agree to remove these lords deep into her own country? It would seem that she failed in her under-taking . . . '

'Enough, man! I tell you, another time.' Patrick took a pace away, and then paused. 'How did you find me here?' he asked, of a sudden thought. 'None could have told you . . . ?'

'Say that I smelt you out. I have a good nose for some things, brother! But do not let me keep you from . . . your friends!'

David, with arrears of sleep to make up, did not awake next morning until Patrick roused him with the word that they would be off shortly. By which time the exiled lords had disappeared. The mist-shrouded desolate hills of the watershed where Tynedale and Liddesdale were born effectually kept their secret.

Patrick was almost his usual unruffled sunny self this morning. Indeed he was never the man to bear a grudge or to sulk, and David, less admirable in this respect, as usual grew to feel himself to be in the wrong, somehow. Riding north again, between the boisterously hearty Logan and his smiling brother, he contributed little to the good company.

Where the drove roads joined, near the headwaters of Rule and Jed, the company turned to the right, eastwards. To David's prompt query, it was pointed out that this was the way to Ferniehirst. Patrick required a word with Arran, and the Chancellor was reliably reported to be at present keeping company with Dand Kerr of Ferniehirst. To David's remonstrance that it was the King whom they should be hastening to see, on Mary's behalf, Patrick countered that James could be persuaded to any suitable course of action much more readily than could his Chancellor; and since any effective move would require the Council's backing, it was only elementary common sense to convince its President first.

When, at the lonely upland peel-tower and church of Southdean, they turned still further back into the south, to face the great hills again, David fretted. His brother explained patiently that, since this was the day of the half-yearly meeting between the Scots and English Wardens of the Marches, and Arran was almost certain to accompany Kerr the Scots Warden to the assembly place at the Redeswire, they would save time by seeking him there rather than awaiting him at Ferniehirst Castle. This, of course, sounded true enough. Perhaps David Gray was hopelessly suspicious by nature.

It was nearly noon before, climbing the long, long flank of Carter Fell, their track brought them out on to the level tract of tussocky grassland, high on the very roof of the Debatable Land where the River Rede grew out of a bog, and where tradition ordained the meeting of the two countries' representatives. Already the greensward was astir with men, and while from a distance it seemed no more than a milling crowd of men, horses and banners, closer inspection revealed that, though there was some small fraternisation, on the whole a long narrow gap split the two companies, so that one faced south and the other north.

The Earl of Arran was easily found, his banner fluttering near that of Kerr and indeed just opposite that of Sir John Foster the English Warden. As the newcomers rode up, the two Wardens were sitting their horses a few yards apart, and hearing the case of one Heron, an Englishman, who was claiming the return of certain cattle lifted from his land by a Turnbull of Rulehead; he was not objecting to the principle of cattle-reiving, since this was normal Border usage, but asserting that although he had paid an appropriate mail for his beasts' return, Turnbull had in fact retained the cattle. Turnbull, for his part, vowed that he had never received the mail and Heron's emissary must have stolen it. This hundrum case, of which no doubt there would be a score of others similar, was exciting very little attention from the throng of lairds, squires, farmers, mosstroopers and men-at-arms, though there was nevertheless a general watchful tension on all hands, for these brief truces on the Border by no means always passed off without violence, and only ten years before, on this same venue, a full-scale battle had developed, with numerous slain on both sides, known as the Raid of the Redeswire.

Patrick went to talk to Arran, Logan found numerous cronies of his own, and David, still starved of sleep, lay down amongst the tussocks a little clear of the crowd – and did not remain awake for more than a few seconds.

For how long he slept he did not know. He was awakened by a great hullabaloo – bawling, cursing, the clash of steel and the neighing of horses. Everywhere around him men were running, drawing swords and whingers as they ran, some already mounted, some afoot.

Rubbing his eyes, David stared. It seemed to be a general mêlée. The two Wardens were in the middle of it, the English one at least shouting, gesticulating, seeking to order his men back, but with little apparent success. Any spark was enough to cause a conflagration on such an occasion. The whistle of an arrow winging past his head and plunging into the soft ground behind with a phut, jerked David out of his dazed preoccupation. He ran for his horse nearby, and vaulted into the saddle.

Mounted, he could see better. Though a lot of swords were drawn, the actual fighting seemed to be confined mainly to a comparatively small group. In towards the centre of this Sir

John Foster, his standard-bearer at his side, was fighting his way, beating right and left with the flat of his own sword, ordering men apart. Kerr of Ferniehirst, however, his Scots counterpart, appeared less anxious to intervene, sitting his horse further back, grim-faced. Blood was already flowing. David counted three men squirming on the grass, transfixed by long-shafted arrows – all on the Scots side.

He looked about for Patrick, but could not see him amongst the tossing plumes, rearing horses and brandished swords and lances. Logan, he thought – Logan was the man to stop this, if he would, with his tough mosstroopers and strong Border reputation. Where was Logan . . . ?

Anxiously he searched for his brother and their cousin. He saw Arran, looking alarmed, shouting something to Kerr, and that man at length plunging forward with his bodyguard of men-at-arms to the aid of the English Warden. He saw Scott of Harden in the thick of it, striving to drive back his own folk. And suddenly, in the press of the English, he glimpsed another face that he knew and that gave him pause – that of Home of Bonkyldean. He had seen this man only the night before, at Patrick's camp, one of the exiled Lord Home's lairds and companions. What was he doing on the wrong side of this scuffle – and with blood on his upraised sword?

Then David perceived Patrick and Logan, with the latter's men in a solid phalanx, boring their way into the mêlée, shouting 'A Logan! A Logan!' and scattering men like chaff on every side. David spurred to join them, his sheathed sword drawn. Scot and Englishman alike they beat aside lustily, and none might penetrate their tight spearhead formation. These were the experts.

This vigorous if belated intervention, added to the efforts of Foster and Kerr and Harden, turned the tide. Indeed, in a few hectic minutes it was all over. Angry men were pressed back to their own sides of the score in the turf that marked the actual Border-line, nursing their wounds, shaking their fists, and hurling bloody threats. But these were mere echoes; the storm was past.

What had provoked it, nobody seemed to know for sure. There were half-a-dozen wrathful assertions. The Scots were unanimous that it was amongst their ranks that men had fallen first – shot by unheralded English arrows. Sir John Foster denied this, swearing that his friend, the Lord Russell, had been the first to fall, quite close to his side. And, sure enough, amongst the actually few slain lay the handsome son of the Earl of Bedford, with an arrow projecting from between his shoulder-blades. David, had his opinion been asked, would have said that he had been shot from behind, whilst facing the north.

By mutual consent the meeting broke up without more ado, even though its business was by no means finished; the atmosphere was no longer conducive to negotiation and sweet reasonableness. Not that anyone took the disturbance seriously, for on the Borders violence was the rule rather than the exception. It was just unfortunate that amongst the casualities should have been an earl's son, all agreed.

Just how unfortunate that fact was, few however could have guessed.

David himself, two days later, copied out the letter to be sent to Elizabeth, signed by James, protesting in dignified terms at the proposed trial of the Queen of Scots, insisting upon the impossibility of a charge of treason being levelled against a crowned monarch, and indicating that unfortunately, whilst any suggestion of such a trial remained, the Scots Privy Council would most assuredly refuse to consider the ratification of the proposed Protestant alliance. David indeed actually adjusted some of the wording himself, to his brother's mild amusement, for the King's signature, and helped impressively to seal and despatch by urgent courier the precious document. He did not see, however, the private letter which Patrick sent by the same courier.

It was while they awaited an answer from Elizabeth, David at least with much anxiety, that a quite different storm burst upon the Scottish Court from the south, all unexpectedly – at all events, once again, to David Gray, as to others much more loftily-placed. It came in the form of a furious letter from Elizabeth, a second from the Lord Burleigh, and vehement supporting representations from the English ambassador on the instructions of Walsingham. Like an explosion it rocked Edinburgh.

The Queen of England was enraged. One of her most gallant and favoured subjects, the excellent Lord Russell, had been savagely and barbarously done to death, whilst on an official mission and on English soil, by the minions of the Earl of Arran. Arran had indeed been present at the dastardly outrage. Assuredly nothing of the sort could have occurred in the presence of the Scottish Chancellor without his approval and instigation. Arran was therefore the murderer of one of the Queen's most beloved friends. She demanded forthwith that he be handed over to her Governor of Berwick, to stand immediate trial for his crime.

To say that James was appalled by this extraordinary communication, is to put it mildly. The young King indeed took to his bed, and at first refused to see anyone, Arran included. For Burleigh's supporting letter left no doubts as to the seriousness with which the matter was viewed in London, though nobody in Scotland had ever heard of Lord Russell being prominent at the English Court. Burleigh, repeating the Queen's charges, announced that should her demands anent the Earl of Arran not be met immediately, James's pension would cease, all diplomatic relations would be broken off, a punitive expedition would be despatched to the Border, and a Bill would be rushed through Parliament debarring James from any possibility of the succession to the English throne.

The King turned his face to the wall, and wept.

Well might Arran fume and curse and plead, mystified as he was wrathful. James would not hear him. The younger man was struck in his most vulnerable spot – his overmastering ambition for the dual throne of England and Scotland. He would hear nobody indeed, shutting himself away, while his Court wondered and questioned and debated. Never had a storm arisen out of so small a cloud. Border incidents were an everyday occurrence, and many more prominent men than this Bedford heir had died in them. What did this mean? And what would be the outcome? It was inconceivable that the King could hand over his Lord Chancellor and favourite to an English trial . . .

Yet, when at last a puffy-eyed, nervous and stammering James was brought to the point of granting the audience that the English ambassador demanded, it was on this impossible condition that Wotton insisted. Arran and Kerr of Ferniehirst must be delivered up, he declared. His instructions were adamant. James gabbled and shrilled and choked. Wotton would not budge – and reiterated the consequences. The English Parliament had never been so anti-Scots, he pointed out, especially with the other matter of Mary Stuart's plot and the threat of assassination against Elizabeth. They would debar the Scots succession without any urging from the Queen; indeed, it would undoubtedly require Elizabeth's active intervention on his behalf to save his claim now.

James's tears overflowed again. He wailed that he would that all the lords of his Borders were dead and the fine Lord Russell alive again.

It was the Master of Gray who, presently, suggested a compromise. While it was unthinkable that my Lord of Arran should be handed over to the Governor of Berwick like some English renegade, it might be advisable and acceptable that His Grace should confine him in some assured stronghold where he could be held secure until this unfortunate business was suitably adjusted and resolved to the satisfaction of all parties . . .

'Yes, yes,' James cried, clutching at a straw. Assuredly, that was the solution. His good sister Elizabeth would surely be satisfied with that! Captain Jamie should be shut up, at once. Let it be seen to. In St. Andrews Castle, for sure. It was the strongest. Aye, right away. He would send a letter to Her Grace of England – a special envoy – explaining the matter. Ferniehirst should be punished, of course – hanged.

Wotton, professing serious doubts, withdrew on Patrick's pressing his arm.

And so, ridiculously, fantastically, for one of the few crimes that he had not committed, fell Captain James Stewart, Earl of Arran. Or commenced his fall, for his was a somewhat prolonged descent. He was immured in St. Andrews Castle, deprived of his high offices, and James mourned for him as though dead – but not quite as he had mourned for Esmé Stuart. And the Master of Gray ruled in his stead – though modestly he refused the style and title of Lord High Chancellor. He did however preside over the meetings of the Privy Council, even though in a determinedly unofficial and temporary capacity. No jealous earls or lords might say that Patrick Gray thrust himself into the highest office under the Crown.

Elizabeth Tudor informed her Parliament that she could not countenance the public trial of her erring sister Mary Stuart – meantime. But an Act passed, naming as liable to summary execution not only all who plotted against her life but those in favour of whom the plots were made, would be a sensible and just precaution. The Act was passed with acclamation.

Bishop Davidson announced to Patrick that he was now a free man. The Kirk, after due and devout consideration, had decided that he had in fact never been married at all to Elizabeth Lyon.

Chapter Twenty-seven

IT was always difficult to know whether there was some sort of large-scale entertainment going on in the Earl of Orkney's apartments at Holyroodhouse, or whether it was a mere domestic evening. Orkney was so prolific of progeny and so fond of a multiplicity of female company – as indeed were his sons – that he had always sufficient members of his own establishment respectably to fill a ballroom; moreover, apart from Marie, who was so out-of-type as scarcely to seem to belong to the same family, they were all of such hearty, lusty and extrovert nature that it was seldom indeed that their quarters did not sound as though either a rout or a rape was in full progress. More dull and sober members of the royal household had long given up complaining; only solitary confinement, it had been ascertained, would change the King's uncle.

Patrick was faced with the usual problem as he strolled round Orkney's eastern wing of the palace in the September dusk. Laughter, shouting and skirling, it seemed, issued from every window. Yet it was unlikely, surely, that here was an invited company, for would anybody at Court hold such a function without seeking the exalted company of the acting Chancellor, especially Orkney who had never made any secret of his designs upon the Master of Gray as a prospective son-in-law?

Patrick slipped in through a side door, looking for a servant to ask the Lady Marie's whereabouts. He could find none; Orkney's servants tended to take after their master. One room from which he heard voices, on his opening the door, was revealed to contain two persons grovelling on the floor in extraordinary and vigorous embrace. Another he did not trouble to look into, the sound of a woman's giggles and screeches being sufficiently informative. These were the servants' quarters. He mounted the first stairway that he came to, and was promptly all but knocked over by a laughing, uproarious, stumbling trio, a young girl in front, dishevelled and all but naked to the waist, one young man behind grasping her flowing red hair and another her torn chemise. One of the gallants, Patrick recognised as a son of Orkney's; probably the other was, also. Presumably they would not be disposed, meantime, to guide him to their sister.

Not for the first time, Patrick asked himself how in the name of all that was wonderful, Marie Stewart had managed to grow up such as she was in this atmosphere.

By following the music to its source in a long picture-hung gallery, he ran Orkney himself to earth – but not just as he expected. It was the Earl indeed who was doing the fiddling, sitting at a lengthy and almost empty table of broken meats and spilt wine, over which one or two figures still sprawled. Patrick had not realised that the man had this attribute. Though obviously drunk, he was leaning back, glazed eyes fixed on a frowning painting of King Alexander the Second, and playing the instrument with great pathos and sweetness. One of his current young women leaned against his shoulder, despite her clothing managing to look extraordinarily innocent because she was asleep, and further down the table an older woman beat solemn time to the music with a slopping goblet of wine. Marie was not there. Indeed, the only other sign of life was a large wolfhound which methodically moved up the table, forepaws on the board, selectively clearing the various platters of their débris.

It was in the garden that Patrick eventually found Marie, in an arbour – and with a companion. Though the pair were only sitting on a seat together, he was profoundly shocked – infinitely more so than by any of the scenes that had presented themselves within the house. He knew the fellow – a George Ogilvie, brother to the sister's husband in Glen Prosen in Angus. He had been hanging around the Court for a while . . . with this as attraction?

'I beg your pardon,' Patrick announced, coldly. 'I had not realised that you were thus engaged. I will retire.'

'Why, Patrick, there is no need,' Marie assured. 'It is good to see you. We are but seldom so honoured, these days. You are so important a figure . . .'

'Nevertheless, I will await another occasion, I think. With your ladyship's permission!'

At his tone, she raised her fine brows, and then smiled. 'Was it myself, then, that you came to see? Or Mr. Ogilvie?'

'I can conceive of no subject which I would wish to discuss with . . . this gentleman,' he answered. Ogilvie, on perceiving the newcomer's identity, had started up.

'I . . . I shall be off, Marie,' he faltered. 'A good night to you. And to you, sir.'

'No, no, George. Do not go . . .'

Ogilvie went, nevertheless.

For a while there was silence. Patrick paced to and fro in front of Marie's seat.

'If it is exercise that you came here for, Patrick, let us walk, for sweet mercy's sake!' the young woman said, a little tartly for her, rising.

He frowned, and halted. 'Not so,' he said. 'Unless you are tired of sitting? Perhaps you have been at it overlong? Perhaps you are chilled, now that he is gone?'

Unspeaking, she looked at him in the gloom.

'It may be that I should be grateful that at least you are but sitting, and not lying, as are most of your peculiar family, it seems! This Ogilvie – he is not lacking in the necessary virility, I hope?'

'Patrick – George Ogilvie is my sister's good-brother – and my good friend,' Marie said evenly. 'I would ask that you speak honestly of him in my company . . . if not of myself!'

'Of course, of course, my dear – I am all respect! My only hope is that I have not ruined your evening!'

'You are in a fair way to doing so, sir, I think,' she gave back. 'May I ask, had you any other purpose in your visit?'

'Nothing that need give you a moment's concern, no! Nothing that in the circumstances could do other than amuse you, Marie. I did but come once more to ask if you would marry me. So wearisome an errand, I must admit.'

She turned her head away, biting her lip.

'Undoubtedly I should have sent you warning. It is thought-less to descend upon a lady unawares! Another time, I shall remember.'

'Do,' she said swiftly. 'As no doubt you do for any of your other women – the Lady Hartrigge . . . Eupham Erskine . . . Madame de Courcelles . . . or even Elizabeth Arran – though perhaps *she* does not require warning! We all deserve a like courtesy, surely?' She took a deep breath. 'Or is it too much to ask, now that you have become so great a man, so busy? Master of all Scotland, indeed – and therefore, of course, of all its women!'

Quite suddenly Patrick laughed – and amusedly, not sourly, harshly. 'Lord, what a fool you are, Marie!' he declared. 'And myself also. Like bairns, we are!'

'A bairn – the great Lord High Chancellor of the Realm! The Master of the King's Wardrobe...'

'Aye, there you have it! Think what you have just said, girl. Does it not sound strange in your own ears? For I am *not* the Chancellor, but I *am* the Master of the Wardrobe! There is a great difference, is there not? I could be the Chancellor – yes. I act the part, for the moment. But I do not seek to be the master of Scotland, see you – merely of the royal wardrobe! James has offered me an earldom, but I have refused it. I am well content to be Master of Gray. I do not seek any of these things. Aye, the Wardrobe suits me very well!'

She turned to look at him. 'What signifies the name?' she asked. 'You *are* the master of Scotland. You have made yourself that – and by no accident, I think. Does it matter what they call you, so long as all men do what you tell them? Even the King?'

'You dream, Marie – you dream!'

'It is true. Has not James shut up even Arran at your behest – his own favourite and familiar?'

'Only as a gesture towards Elizabeth.'

She said nothing.

Patrick sighed. 'I would, at least, that the women did as I told them – one woman in particular!'

'Enough do, I believe, to keep you from ... discomfort!' She looked away again. 'And yet you ... you deny me even George Ogilvie!'

It was the man's turn to be silent. He began to pace the garden path, and quite naturally she fell into step beside him.

'George tells me,' she went on, in another voice, 'that the Master of Glamis is back in Angus, at his castle of Aldbar. That my lord Bothwell has been seen in Dundee, and the Earl of Mar is said to be on Donside. None of them without your knowledge, I am sure?'

'Your George would seem to be notably well informed for a heather lairdling!'

'He says that the whole north country buzzes with it. All the Ruthven lords are back – and to some purpose, no doubt.'

'And does your knowledgeable Ogilvie suggest what these purposes may be?'

'He says – he but repeats the clash of the countryside – that it is *your* doing, Patrick. That you have brought them back, in order to constrain the King ... without your hand seeming to appear.'

'Lord, was ever a man so detracted! Whatever ill is done in Scotland, it must be my doing, for some deep and sinister motive! And do you believe all this, Marie?'

'I do not know. I have long since given up trying to know what to believe of you, Patrick. Save that you will go your own gait, always.'

'And would have you go it with me, my dear. That, too, you know.'

'George Ogilvie notwithstanding?'

He shrugged. 'As you say, George Ogilvie, or the Devil himself, notwithstanding!'

'But this . . . this is most generous of you!' she exclaimed, though her voice broke a little. 'Am I to be almost as privileged as you are? Permitted the magnificent freedom of a man, plucking fruit by the way where I will?'

'Aye,' he said, heavily for Patrick Gray. 'If needs be. If that is how you would have it. For have *you* I must, Marie.' Wryly he smiled. 'You see how much means your talk of me being master of all!'

She was moved – but hardened herself. 'You conceive this as the only way to master me, perhaps?'

'I think that I shall never master you. I do not know that I wish to. Only to marry you, woman – and that is different.'

'Yes, Patrick, marriage is different, as you say. But you know my views on marriage, to be sure.'

'Aye. That is why I came here with some hopes tonight, Marie. Perhaps foolishly. But tonight I am a free man – save for *your* toils. Today, I had word that my marriage to Elizabeth Lyon is no more.'

He heard the catch in her breath, as she turned to him. 'Patrick!'

'Aye. Or better than no more – that it has never been. It is annulled, as void and invalid.'

'Annulled . . . ?'

'The Kirk, in its wisdom, finds this the better course. And who am I to question it? Moreover, I think that you will take it kinder than a divorcement . . .'

'Oh, yes, yes! I do! I do! Patrick – you did not tell me . . . ! This is . . .'

'You are happy, my dear?'

'Of course. Of course. Can you doubt it?'

'Then . . . does it mean . . . can I believe . . . that you will indeed wed me now? At last, my love?'

Brokenly she laughed. 'I cannot see . . . how I can refuse, any more! Can you?' Abruptly she swung round, to bury her face against his chest, clutching him convulsively. 'Oh, Patrick! It has been so long! A very lifetime. I can hardly understand it. That at last there is nothing to stand between us . . .'

'Save the Master of Gray?' he asked, holding her fast. 'This . . . monster who must rule Scotland and all men! The satyr who uses all to serve his own wicked ends?'

She looked up at him. 'Even he does not stand between us,' she said. 'Perhaps he should. Perhaps I am a fool, weak, sinful. But I love you, Patrick – all of you, the good and the bad. I am not so very good, my own self, And I will wed you as you are. Once I told you that, a free man, I would give you an honest answer. There you have it.'

'My beloved! And . . . your door that was to stand wide open for me, one day?'

She raised a hand to his hair. 'It stands open, my heart. I could not hold it shut, any longer. I am but a weak woman. But . . . I would esteem you the more if you would bear with me, and wait . . . a little longer. Until we are wed. Or is that too much to ask of the Master of Gray?'

He drew a long breath. 'I' faith, Marie Stewart, you drive a hard bargain! Is life with you going to be this way, always?'

'I think not, Patrick. But . . . if it is?'

'I will wed you, just the same – God help me!'

They were married on a grey November day, with great pomp and ceremony, at Holyroodhouse, in the presence of the King – who indeed gave away his cousin – and all the great ones of the land. Mariota saw her father there, for the first time since Patrick's earlier marriage; the Bishop was prepared to be affable, but his daughter was not.

James once more suggested that to celebrate the occasion he should make the happy couple earl and countess, but again Patrick declined. He was the Master of Gray. Let that stand. One day, God being merciful, he would succeed his father as sixth Lord Gray; until then he would serve his King very well as he was. He did, however accept the Commendatorship of the prosperous Priory of Culross as a small mark of his monarch's esteem – which at £5000 Scots a year, was always a help to a man taking on the burdens of matrimony.

Actually, Patrick had another and personal request to put to the King, that he humbly ventured to suggest might fittingly mark this joyful occasion. He pleaded that James might, of his royal goodness and clemency, see fit to transfer the unfortunate Earl of Arran from durance vile in St. Andrews Castle, to less rigorous ward in his own house of Kinneil – under due and strict guard, of course. He had had a word with Wotton on the subject, and he agreed with him that Queen Elizabeth was not likely at this stage to differentiate between the two forms of imprisonment. His Majesty was of course graciously, indeed eagerly, pleased to accede to this generous request on the part of the bridegroom. Indeed, everybody was pleased – fond monarch; Arran, who had himself written to Patrick suggesting the move and offering as inducement to his friend the great and influential Commendatorship of Dunfermline, the wealthiest church lands in all Scotland, which he had held for some time; and the returned Ruthven lords, who now knew where they could lay hands on Arran's person, that had been hitherto safe from them behind the impregnable walls of St. Andrews Castle.

Altogether it was an auspicious wedding-day, even though somewhat less dramatically celebrated than had been its predecessor eleven years before.

Patrick Gray had now reached the mature age of twenty-seven years. The bridal pair were still delectably engaged in the discovery of each other, in one of the remoter Gray castles of northern Perthshire, when the reunited and assembled Ruthven lords, with a following of almost eight thousand men, struck without warning at Stirling, where James was in residence. The move was well planned, the royal defence half-hearted in the extreme, the town fell, and the great castle surrendered with scarcely a blow struck. James, in dire agitation, and vowing that this could never have happened had his good Master Patrick been on hand, nevertheless found that his former harsh captors had adopted a new attitude towards him. Instead of hectoring and bullying, they knelt at his feet, swearing devotion and allegiance, and assured him that only His Grace's true good and the weal of the realm had moved them to act thus drastically in order to remove the traitors and scoundrels with whom the unprincipled Arran had surrounded his liege lord. For themselves they had no claims nor ambitions – only the triumph of the true Protestant faith and the King's gracious goodwill. In token of which they did not claim any hand in the government for themselves, suggesting instead that James chose some faithful, well-tried and experienced minister of his own whom his loyal Reformed subjects might support and serve in the interests of all Scotland – for instance, the Master of Gray, if he could be persuaded to exchange his present blissful dalliance for the burden of state affairs.

Nothing loth and mightily relieved, James sent forthwith for the innocent Master of Gray with pleas, indeed imperative royal commands, to come quickly and take control of the rudderless ship of state.

Arran, warned, bolted from Kinneil, the royal guards conveniently looking the other way, and fled the country.

Patrick sighed, complained that they might at least leave a man alone to his nuptial exercises – and returned to duty, resolutely refusing to admit that he was now indisputably the master of Scotland, even to his wife.

Happy Scotland, that seldom in her long history can have known a ruler at once so able and so devoid of personal ambition.

Chapter Twenty-eight

FOR the best part of a good, peaceful and prosperous year, that of our Lord 1586, Patrick Gray largely controlled the destinies of his native land – whatever the names and titles of the nominees who carried out his policies, for he still rigidly refused the office of Chancellor, or indeed any other save that of simple Master of the King's Wardrobe, the holding of which seemed to tickle his fancy. For that year, the bribery of underlings all but faded from the life of Scotland; corruption, in the major courts at least, became a rarity; and the King's law, however uncertain and curious, prevailed in all but the wildest Borders and remoter Highlands. For one year even the great lords held their hands, sheathed their swords, and waited. For one bare year.

Then on the fifth of August, Walsingham reached out his long arm and arrested Anthony Babington, in Harrow Woods, and the peace of Scotland, the *pax Patricius!* was shattered quite.

Babington was a hot-blooded young Derbyshire squire and a Catholic. In concert with some companions of like outlook, he devised one more project for the dethroning of Elizabeth, the elevation of Mary in her place, and the re-establishment of the True Faith in England and Scotland. Unfortunately perhaps, he was more effective than most of his predecessors, more thorough-going and vigorous. His plans were not in the clouds, but realities. Unfortunately, too, he communicated the gist of them, by letter, to Mary the Queen, though taking the precaution to sign them with a cipher.

Warned, through Giffard the Jesuit counter-spy, Walsingham laid hands on Father Ballard, another Jesuit agent who was in touch with Babington. Tortured, he at length revealed the identity of the leaders of the plot. Babington and his colleagues were apprehended, and put to the rack. Their confessions, and the progress of their plans, shook England. The ports where Spanish, French and Papal troops were to be landed were listed; estimated numbers of local supporting forces were given; arrangements for the rescue of the Scottish Queen were detailed; and, worst of all, the identity was revealed of six gentlemen who were conjointly responsible for the assassination of Elizabeth, without which the invasion could not be assured of success – the names including Babington himself and even one, Charles Tilney, of the Queen's own Gentlemen Pensioners.

Mary was taken to Fotheringay, now under closest arrest, while Parliament screamed for her blood. It mattered not now whether she knew of the proposed assassination or no. The new Act naming as guilty any in whose favour a plot might be hatched adequately covered her position, from the point of view of England's law.

Babington and his companions died horribly, on the 20th and 21st of September, as a public spectacle and warning, Elizabeth's own commands insisting that their agonies be extended for as long as humanly possible, after mutilation and disembowelling.

Parliament, in London, set an early date for Mary's trial, and, prejudging the issue, vociferously demanded the death penalty.

The trial, held in indecent haste at Fotheringay, was a farce, a mere formality, and intended to be nothing else, the judges including even Walsingham himself. Mary, denied an advocate, defended herself with vigour and dignity, but Walsingham could produce letters to prove all that he wanted, genuine or forged. Although the judges held that it was legally unnecessary now to prove Mary's knowledge of and condoning of the assassination attempt, Walsingham produced a letter addressed to Babington from the Scots Queen, plainly supporting this course. Mary, whilst admitting the authenticity of most of the other intercepted letters, swore by all that she held to be holy that this was false, a forgery, that never could she countenance the violent death of her sister-queen, that the assassination of an anointed monarch was a crime against the Holy Ghost, the assenting to which would damn her own soul to everlasting torment.

The thirty-six judges, under the Lord Chancellor, the two Lord Chief Justices and Burleigh himself, were not impressed. They adjourned the Court for a week, and on the 25th of October found Mary Stuart, daughter and heiress of James the Fifth, late King of Scots, guilty, and sentenced her to death by execution at such time and place as appointed by the Queen's most excellent Majesty. God save the Queen!

Scotland boiled into a ferment. England could not do this to her Queen – even though many Scots had called her a whore and an idolatress for years, well enough content for her to linger a captive. Imprisonment was one thing, but death by execution quite another. Moreover, this was a national insult, since no English court assuredly had jurisdiction to try and condemn the Queen of Scots. Demonstrations and near-riots broke out all over the country. The Kirk itself was moved to protest against this unwarrantable attack on the sovereignty of Scotland. The Catholic north and the Highland clans blazed alight with ire. The Estates of Parliament met and demanded the anullment of so iniquitous a trial and judgment.

All this might seem strange in the circumstances, if not positively ridiculous, but it could be argued that the Scots were always a particularly thrawn, awkward and disputatious race, and wickedly proud. Moreover, despite their determinedly dour and matter-of fact façade, they are sentimentalists, romanticists, almost to a man. But perhaps still more to the point is the fact that the Reformation had come late to Scotland. At this time, therefore, the majority of the population had been born Catholic, whatever faith they opted for later. If the Gaelic Highlands were taken into account, as was not always the case, probably more than half the Scots people still belonged to the Old Religion.

Scotland did not seethe alone, either. France, Spain and the Vatican, as might have been expected, sent vigorous protest, combined with dire threats, to London; but apart from these, practically every crowned head in Europe, every princeling even and petty ruler, sent envoys or urgent written representations to Elizabeth. All saw only too clearly, in Mary's sentence, a shocking and unthinkable threat to their own order – the judicial execution of a monarch. Accept that, and the entire principle of the divine right of kings was jettisoned, lost, their sheet-anchor gone.

Elizabeth neither confirmed nor rejected the death sentence. Elizabeth, indeed did nothing.

Not that she was entirely alone in that. Two others who might have been expected to be markedly active in this crisis seemed in fact to be almost entirely supine, passive. They were James, King of Scots, and his trusted mentor and minister, Patrick, Master of Gray.

James's state was, to say the least of it, curious. He made little comment on the situation, keeping his own counsel. When public opinion forced him to speak, he deplored the grievous assault on the idea of kingship, the injury done to Scotland's pride, the invalidity of the court and its judgment. He did not allow himself the luxury of a more personal statement – and certainly not once did he unburden his soul of the anguish that a son must feel for a mother in such dire straits. Not for kings was the exhibition of private griefs and anxieties, he asserted – and quoted a Latin tag to prove it.

Patrick Gray's attitude was as disciplined, and more calmly assured. Elizabeth would not endorse the death sentence, he declared firmly, unshaken by all urgent demands – David's and his own wife's in especial. She could not, without disastrously weakening her own throne, endangering her own crown. She would not put another queen to death – she dare not. There was no need for alarm, therefore. No move was better than a false move in a delicate situation.

From this considered attitude Patrick would not budge, in public or in private utterance.

Alas for statesmanlike calm and discipline. These admirable qualities were at all times somewhat scarce amongst the Scots nobility, and in a crisis of national sentiment such as this, they were notable for their absence. Indeed, they were even more unpopular than the idea of unity, which is saying something, in Scotland. Adversity, they say, makes strange bedfellows. This death-sentence on an eighteen-years-imprisoned queen did likewise. Sworn enemies made common cause, Catholic and Protestant lords spoke with almost the same voice, and men who had cursed and abused Mary for years suddenly became her vocal friends.

Patrick Gray, for once, had miscalculated.

The extent of his miscalculation was brought sharply home to him when, on the last day of October, he was abruptly commanded into the royal presence from his house in the Lawnmarket of Edinburgh. With David at his side, he strolled unhurriedly down the steep mile of tall lands and tenements to the grey Palace of Holyroodhouse, frowning occasionally. He was unused to such brusque summonses.

They found the palace in a state of considerable commotion, and thronged with men – the supporters of many great lords.

'Huntly's Gordons and Bothwell's Hepburns mixing – and not at each others' throats!' David commented. 'Here is something new in Scotland!'

Wondering, they made their way to the Throne-room. It was as thronged as was the courtyard. One swift glance was enough to establish that this was not just a spontaneous coming together of sundry lords that happened to be in Edinburgh at the time. This was an assembly, summoned and arranged.

That Patrick's sources of information had not advised him of it was interesting. The Ruthven lords, Angus, Johnny Mar, Bothwell, Home, Lindsay, the Master of Glamis and the rest, now the dominating force on the Scottish scene, were very much to the fore; but so were also the Catholic leaders – Huntly, Herries, Montrose, Erroll – along with men of neither faction, such as Atholl, Wemyss, Crawford, Seton and the Lord Claud Hamilton. The King himself, as so often the case, stood nervously in a far corner, a hunched shoulder turned against Sir John Maitland, the Secretary of State, who seemingly sought to convince him to some course.

At sight of Patrick, James's young but woebegone and sagging features lit up. He came across the floor at an ungainly run. 'Man Patrick!' he cried. 'You've been ower long. Where have you been? Could you no' have come quicker than this? Man, it becomes you ill – ill, I say! to treat your prince's summons thus. They have all been at me, Patrick...'

'Sire, I was so deep buried in the affairs of your realm that I fear I took a deal of digging out. It is a toil that I would be quit of, I do declare.' He smiled reassuringly, as James gripped his arm. Then his genial regard circled the entire great room, and he laughed pleasantly, amusedly, and waved a welcoming hand. 'I see many friends of mine here gathered, Your Grace – a great many. I applaud the happy circumstances that brings us all together, thus.'

'They've been at me, I tell you, man – all at me. Like hound-dogs!' the King declared. 'About ... about ... her! About Mary – my mother.' It was not often that James was brought to enunciate that word. 'They are all at it. They'll no' let me be. I have told them what you said, Patrick...'

'Master of Gray,' the brash young Earl of Bothwell interrupted. 'We fear that His Grace is not fully apprised of the danger in which our Queen is placed...'

'*Our* Queen, my lord?' Patrick commented, but mildly. 'I do not think that I have heard you name her that, before!'

The high-coloured, bold-eyed nephew of Mary's former paramour bit his lip. 'Nevertheless, sir, our Queen she is. Scotland's Queen,' he asserted strongly. 'Her life is sore threatened, and Scotland's name and honour with it. We are here to urge that His Grace take immediate and sure action.'

A strong chorus of Ayes came from the assembled company.

Patrick bowed his head to the strength of expression rather than to the fears expressed. 'I applaud your concern, my lords' he said. 'We all feel deeply for Her Highness. But I believe your dread to be ill-founded. I have said before – I do not accept it that Queen Elizabeth will endorse this sentence of execution.'

'*You* may not accept it, but Archie Douglas does!' the Earl of Angus declared. 'He writes to me that all about the Queen believe that she *will* sign the decree, that the bishops have advised that it is her duty, and that Leicester has sworn that he will have Mary slain in her cell if the execution goes not forward.'

The King and Patrick had received a like account, of course. Archibald Douglas, the Scots resident ambassador in London, was a sort of cousin of Angus, as of the late unlamented Morton.

'Master Douglas is a notable correspondent, my lord, but his judgment has been proved to be at fault ere this, where Queen Mary is concerned!'

None failed to detect a barb in that. The Reverend Archibald had been one of the principal parties to the murder of Darnley.

The Earl of Huntly spoke up – to James, not to Patrick. The Cock o' the North addressed no one less than his monarch. 'Your Grace's fair name demands that you protest in the strongest terms at this outrage against your royal mother. And more than protest . . .'

'But I have protested!' the King cried. 'Have I no' sent Sir William Keith to make protest against the wrongous trial . . . ?'

'Keith!' Huntly exclaimed scornfully. 'Think you, Sire, that Elizabeth will pay heed to such as Keith?'

'What else can I do, man Huntly?'

'You can annul and cancel your country's participation in the infamous Protestant League!' the Catholic Gordon chief roared. 'It is a work o' the devil, anyhow!' And he glared at Patrick.

There was a shuffling of feet and a murmuring, there. Unity might cost too much.

Another Douglas, George of Lochleven, the same who had once proved Mary's friend indeed and aided her escape from his own father's fortress, now raised his voice for her once more, and boldly. 'Your Grace would be well advised to listen to the promptings of your own heart, rather than the honeyed words of some who constantly counsel you,' he said. 'Some there are close to you, no doubt, who are but the pensioned slaves of Elizabeth! Their aim, I will swear, is but to create bad blood between Your Grace and your royal mother . . .'

'Quiet, man!' James squeaked, his eyes rolling and darting. 'How dare you speak me so!'

Patrick laid his hand on the King's arm. 'Sire, perhaps Lochleven will give us the names of these dastards whom Elizabeth has bought?' He smiled. 'It may be that in his remote tower, he hears whispers which pass over us here! And the House of Douglas, as all men know, has its, h'm, its own channels of information.'

The Earl of Angus, for his part, laid a hand on his kinsman's shoulder. George Douglas swallowed, but met Patrick's amused gaze squarely.

'Let it suffice, now, that His Majesty knows that such men there are, and in whose service they labour. The rest can wait.' He turned back to James. 'Your love for your mother must instruct you, Sire.'

The King frowned, staring at the floor. 'How is it possible for me to love her, man? Or to approve her proceedings? Did she no' write to the French ambassador here, that unless I conformed mysel' to her wishes, I should have nothing but my father's lordship o' Darnley? Has she no' laboured to take the crown off my head, and set up a regent? Is she no' obstinate in holding a different religion, man?'

There was a considerable stir at the King's outburst. Men, hardened men who had never hesitated to decry any cause but their own, to name Mary harlot and Messalina, to savage any who stood in their way, looked askance at each other in discomfort at the expression of these unnatural sentiments of a son towards his mother. Half-a-dozen lords began to speak at once. Strangely, it was the calm and measured tones of Monsieur de Courcelles, the French ambassador, that prevailed.

'My master, the Most Christian King, is gravely perturbed, Sire,' he said. 'He urges that you make the most vigorous, the most stern representations, the most vehement of which Your Grace is capable. Even to the moving of an army to your borders. I would remind Your Grace that the lady your mother is also Queen-Dowager of France. This threat to her life and affront to her name and state, is equally an affront to my royal master. I am to say that any failure on Your Grace's part to uphold her honour and assure her safety, must be looked upon as an attack upon His Most Christian Majesty – and indeed upon all Christian princes.'

Strangely enough, even the Protestant lords growled fierce

345

commendation of these strong sentiments.

James gulped, and looked unhappily at the Master of Gray, seeming even younger than his twenty years. 'But . . . but what can I do, sirs?' he gasped. 'She'll no' heed me. She's a hard, hard woman, yon Elizabeth. I canna put soldiers at her. She has more o' them than I have, Monsieur. What can I do, sirs?'

'You can denounce this shameful alliance!' de Courcelles said briefly.

'But, man – the cost! The cost o' such a process! I canna suffer it.'

Bothwell snorted. 'If Your Majesty suffers this other process to proceed, I think, my liege, that you should be hanged yourself the day after!'

A shocked silence fell upon the Throne-room. Only the slightly crazed young Hepburn, who was also James's cousin, could speak in such fashion – but even so, he had gone too far. Patrick judged that it was time to take a hand, a decisive hand.

'My lord of Bothwell is carried away, Sire, by his new-found love. You must forgive him. He misjudges more than the occasion, I think. Far be it from me to suggest that these good lords, His Excellency of France, and the most Christian King are all mistaken. Such would be unthinkable. This matter is all no doubt a question of degree, a question not of right and wrong, of statecraft or government – but of understanding character. One woman's character. I flatter myself that I can read Queen Elizabeth's character as well as any here present – even my Lord Bothwell and Lochleven! – having talked with her, debated with her, even danced with her. And I do believe that she will not warrant another Queen's death. It is not a matter of her hardness of heart, nor yet her anger and fear. It is much more than these – her whole life and outlook and situation. She is Queen of England. Dog, they say truly, does not eat dog. Queen does not execute Queen. Elizabeth will commute the sentence.'

'We know that is your opinion, Monsieur de Gray,' the Frenchman demurred, 'Others think otherwise. Is this lady's life – possibly the fate of Europe : to hang on so slender a thread as one man's opinion? Your Highness – is it, *mon Dieu?*'

Patrick answered quickly. 'No – indeed no. I would be the last to suggest it. I could be mistaken. His Grace would be unwise, wrong, to ignore the advice of so many good councillors, so great a weight of wisdom and experience.' He turned to the

King. 'Your Highness must send forthwith another envoy to Elizabeth.'

'Another envoy will win the same reception as the first – as Keith!' Angus objected. 'Elizabeth will not even see him.'

'I think that she will. More particularly if that envoy is myself, my lord.'

No one spoke for a few moments – a silence that was at length broken by James himself.

'Aye, Patrick – that's it, man! That's it!' he exclaimed. 'You go. You tell her. You tell Elizabeth of our feelings. That we are much perturbed. That we canna be unmoved by our royal mother's fate...'

'My God – you will have to tell her more than that!' Bothwell burst out. 'Tell her that if she does not denounce this monstrous sentence, we sound the call to arms!'

'Aye – tell her that I myself will lead five thousand lances across her march!' the Lord Claud Hamilton cried.

'Tell her that I will burn Carlisle!' Bothwell declared. 'Thousands shall die!'

'I suggest, my lords,' Patrick intervened, with his faint smile, 'that what I tell Queen Elizabeth is for His Grace's Privy Council to decide.'

'But when, man? There must be no delay.'

'Fortunately, with so many of the Council here present, we can meet forthwith. Today, if it is His Grace's pleasure.'

'Aye, aye, Patrick...'

'And when will you go to the south? The matter is of great urgency...'

'This very night, if it is the Council's wish.'

'Tonight, yes. That is straight talking.'

'To this Council then, gentlemen...'

Patrick Gray did not miscalculate twice.

After the Council, the King, with much secrecy and gesticulation, beckoned Patrick, and David with him, into a private room. Locking the door behind them, he listened at it for a few moments, and even went poking behind the hangings and tapestries of the walls.

'Ears,' he muttered. 'Ears everywhere. Aye, and eyes too. They're aye listening, aye watching me, Patrick. I've none I can turn to, but you. They took Cousin Esmé from me, and Captain Jamie. We'll have to watch that they dinna take you, man...'

'I think that Your Grace need not fear for me...'

'Aye, you've aye got Master Davy to look after you. Man, there's times I thank the Lord God for Master Davy – so sure, so strong! Never let him frae your sight, man Davy – d'you hear me? That's a command, mind – my royal command. Or they'll get you, Patrick . . . !'

'Do not fear. Your Grace is overwrought . . .'

'I'm no' overwrought. And I ken fine what I'm saying. Davy's to go with you to yon London, mind – to watch over you. The man Walsingham . . . and Leicester . . .'

David cleared his throat. 'I will see that my brother is enabled to fulfil his mission. Your Grace – God aiding me!'

Patrick smiled sardonically.

James shambled about the small room, throwing uncertain glances at the two brothers. 'After you have seen Elizabeth,' he said in a different voice. 'You must seek a private audience. Private, see you. Could you do that, Patrick? Think you could you win her ear, privily?'

Gravely Patrick nodded. 'I think that it might conceivably be arranged, Sire.'

'Aye, good. Good. Then, in her privy ear, man, you must tell her that this is a bad business and I must have my amends. My amends, see you. You'll tell her that?'

'Amends, Your Highness? You mean . . . ?'

'Aye – amends, man. Compensation. As is only just and suitable. The woman has laid a great insult upon me and my kingdom. A monarch canna do the like to another monarch, and no' pay for it! Na, na – she will have to recompense me. And richly. You will insist on that, Patrick. In her private ear, mind.'

Patrick stroked mouth and chin thoughtfully.

David was less controlled. He could not hold himself in. 'You mean *money* Sire?' he gasped.

'That would be best, aye. It is a matter o' principle. Just and fair indemnity for hurt done. Without the like there would be no decent commerce between realms and princes. It will need to be a goodly sum, mind – for our honour isna to be lightly spat upon. Or maybe an increase to our pension – a substantial increase.'

Patrick's glance flickered over to his brother. 'I shall essay what may be achieved, Highness,' he said solemnly.

'Aye, do that. And another matter. It is time that there was an Act of her Parliament naming me Second Person to Elizabeth, and successor to her Throne. High time. Tell her privily, that if she will have siklike an Act passed, I will overlook yon other ill Act they passed. You have it?'

'M'mmm. I do not know, Sire, that Queen Elizabeth will bear with talk of that kidney – even privately. She is a woman of notable spirit. But . . . I will do what I may.'

'This is an opportunity, man Patrick – a great opportunity. And I have great faith in you. Aye, and in you, Master Davy, to look after him. There's no others that I'd trust with an errand o' siklike delicacy. No' a word o' this to Sir Robert, mind. He's gey thick in the head, yon soldier-man.' Sir Robert Melville, brother to Sir James and Sir Andrew, was the second envoy whom the Council had chosen to accompany Patrick on his mission, one of an honest family, and an uncompromising Protestant.

'It shall be as you say, Your Grace . . .'

Chapter Twenty-nine

THE Master of Gray's second embassage to Queen Elizabeth was a very different affair from his first. There was no pomp and ceremony, no splendid gifts, no ladies, no impressive escort; only the two principals, David Gray, and two or three armed servants. They made the four hundred miles to London, in consequence, in little more than half the time that it had taken the previous entourage.

Elizabeth made much play about not receiving them, keeping them hanging about for days in the ante-rooms of various palaces, while demonstrations of popular wrath against the imprisoned Mary were staged for the envoys' edification, undoubtedly on Elizabeth's own instructions, decapitating the Scots Queen in effigy with gruesome realism, with the help of buckets of ox-blood. Sir Robert Melville blustered and swore, David fretted, sick with anxiety, but Patrick was an example of all that such an envoy should be, imperturbable, courteous, amused even. Play-acting, he asserted, should be enjoyed, not taken seriously.

When, at last, at Greenwich, the Scots embassy was admitted to the royal presence, Elizabeth interviewed them, flanked by a glittering array of her nobles and ministers, including Leicester, Oxford, Essex, Burleigh, Walsingham and Hatton, and treated them, while they were still bowing their entry, to a full and stirring ten minutes of impassioned oratory, brilliant dialectic and vicious vituperation such as few of her hearers had ever experienced, and which left them all dumbfounded and almost as breathless as the Queen herself.

All, that is, except Patrick Gray – and perhaps old Burleigh, who had weathered so many storms in his Queen's service. The former bowed low again, and into the gasping hush spoke pleasantly, admiringly.

'Such eloquence, Your Majesty – such brilliance, such lucidity of utterance, leaves all men abashed and wordless. None may hope to prevail against such a tide of logic, wisdom and wit – least of all this humble spokesman from the north, with but a few uncouth words to jingle together. Yet speak I must, on behalf of your royal cousin, James, King of Scots, and his

Council, if all unworthily.'

'If you do . . . you waste . . . your breath, sir!' the Queen panted, her own breath all but gone, her superstructure of blazing gems heaving alarmingly. 'You . . . come to plead . . . for mercy for . . . that self-confessed murderess . . . Mary Stuart! You waste your time . . . and mine, sirrah!'

'Fair lady, can it be that you misapprehend?' Patrick asked, wonderingly. 'That you have been misinformed in this vital matter?' He cast a comprehensively reproachful glance on the serried ranks of England's advisers. 'We had thought Your Highness better served than this! For such is not the burden of our mission. I plead for nothing – save Your Grace's patient hearing. It is not mercy that we seek. Only justice.'

'Justice, sir!' Elizabeth cried. 'Have you the effrontery to stand before me and say that my courts do not dispense justice? In the presence of my Lord Chief Justice, who himself presided over that woman's trial! You can be too bold, Master of Gray – as I have had occasion to warn you ere this!'

'I speak but what I am commanded, Your Grace. Is it not one of the very elements of justice that the court which holds trial on a cause shall have due authority and jurisdiction so to do? Can your Lord Chief Justice, or any other, show that he had jurisdiction to try the crowned and anointed monarch of another realm – or even of *this* realm, indeed!'

'God's Passion, man – have a care!' the Queen exclaimed, jumping up from her Chair of State. 'Watch your tongue, sirrah, or you yourself will taste the power and authority of my courts!' Imperiously she waved aside the Lord Chief Justice who had stepped forward to speak. 'I myself will answer your ill-judged question sir. Mary Stuart is no longer Queen of Scots, nor crowned monarch of any realm. She abdicated eighteen long years ago, and voluntarily entered *my* realm as a private citizen, thereby placing herself under my authority and the laws of England.'

'Does not Queen Mary deny such abdication, Madam? And if an anointed monarch denies abdication, who shall declare her abdicate? How may you prove otherwise?'

'But . . . good God, man, if Mary did not abdicate, then your James, in whose name you speak, is a usurper! You have no authority to be here, troubling us!'

'Would you deny Scotland a ruler, because you have shut up her Queen these eighteen years, Highness? James and his mother are both anointed sovereigns of Scotland.'

'Lord, this is but wordy dissembling! Words, words, words! Mary, in England, has conspired the violent death of the Queen of England. And plotted the invasion and overthrow of the realm. For that she must pay the penalty required in law. That is all there is to it, sir. Tell you your prince that same.'

'But, dear lady, that I fear is not all that there is to it. I fear . . .'

'By God, it is not!' Sir Robert Melville burst out, unable to contain himself longer. 'If we tell that to our Prince and Council, Ma'am, Scotland marches! Hamilton leads five thousand lances against Newcastle. Bothwell burns Carlisle. The Scots, the Kerrs, the Turnbulls ride. Your border flames from end to end, and the clans march south! Is that nothing to you, Ma'am?'

An outburst of growling wrath and consternation arose from the great company – an outburst that was speedily silenced, however, by Elizabeth's own high-pitched neighing fury.

'Christ's Holy Wounds!' she shouted. 'You . . . you threaten *me*! Threaten me with force, with swords, with bloody attack – here in my own house! Fiend seize you, fellow – how dare you!'

Blinking a little at the storm he had unleashed, the blunt soldier yet held his ground. 'I but warn you what the Council declared . . .'

'God's curse on your Council, then! Think you they can speak so to me – Elizabeth? Yapping curs! Penniless savages! Lord – what insufferable insolence . . . !'

'Madam – good lady,' Patrick intervened – and it took courage indeed to interrupt Elizabeth of England in towering rage. 'Sir Robert may have used injudicious words, but he only intended to indicate that passions in Scotland are much roused in this matter. It would be wrong, improper, for us not to have you know it. The people *here* are roused, as you have rightly shown us. If the two realms and peoples are so equally roused, then, alas, blood may well flow, innocent as well as guilty. It becomes but the simple duty of all in whose hands are affairs of state, to act not only by law and rule, but with mutual care and compassion . . .'

'Shrive me – is that the Master of Gray preaching me a sermon, now!' the Queen broke in, impatiently. 'Are you seeking to teach me my business, sir? Have the pair of you come all this way but to insult and to preach? Have you nothing better than that to say? If not, 'fore God, you may go whence you came – and swiftly!'

Patrick, who indeed had but talked to gain time and a change of tune, nodded now. 'We have indeed, Your Grace. The compassion and care I spoke of, we do not seek only from yourself, noble as is your reputation. Our Prince suggests that his mother, if she were to resign her rights in the succession to your English crown to himself, would no longer endanger you, and so all might live in peace. He will vouch that she will so do.'

'What rights, man – what rights? Mary has no rights. She is a prisoner. She is declared "inhabil", and can resign nothing, convey nothing to her son.'

'If she have no rights, Your Majesty need not fear her. If she have, let her assign them to her son, in whom then will be placed the full title of succession to Your Highness ...'

'What – by the Living God!' Elizabeth's voice actually broke, in her passion. 'Get rid of one, and have a worse in her place! Nay – never! That were but to cut my own throat, no less. For you – yes, *you*, Master of Gray – for a duchy or an earldom to yourself, you or such as you would cause some of your desperate knaves to murder me! And so secure your prince on my throne. No, by God, your master shall never be in this place!' And she banged her white fists on the wooden arms of her throne. 'The sentence stands!'

Patrick took a long breath. 'Even, Madam, if the League, the Protestant League which we so sorely wrought, were to be quite broken ... through the passion of the Scots people?'

Tight-lipped Elizabeth nodded.

Patrick looked away from her, then, all round the rows of watching, hostile faces, and from them to Melville, and back to David who stood half-a-pace behind them. And one shoulder faintly shrugged.

David swallowed, noisily.

Sir Robert, at his colleague's gesture of failure, sank his grey head on wide old shoulders. 'Ma'am,' he mumbled, 'I beg of you ... give us respite. Spare Her Grace ... if only for a little. For fifteen days even. That we may have time to seek other instructions from our Prince.' The Melville brothers had always loved Mary.

'No,' the Queen declared.

'Then ... for a week, lady. Eight short days ...'

'Christ-God – no! Not for an hour!' Starting up, Elizabeth stood trembling. 'This audience is at an end!' she cried, and turning about without another glance at envoys or hurriedly bowing lords, she stormed out of the presence-chamber in a swirl of skirts and a glitter of diamonds.

*

353

'The woman is a monster!' David declared. 'Crazed with her power, and without human feeling, without sympathy or even conscience. This realm is ruled by a mad-woman, puffed up with belief in her own greatness, her invincibility. Lord – and for her blind pride, our Mary must die ... !'

'Not so, Davy,' his brother denied. 'On the contrary, this realm is ruled by a very frightened woman indeed! A woman driven near to distraction, I believe. There lies the danger of it – and the doom of our hopes, I think. For there is no goad like fear, no surer barrier to break down than mortal dread. With aught else, I might yet achieve much – in private. But with this fear ...'

'You think ... ? You really believe that, Patrick? That it is fear that makes her thus? Not damnable pride? Hatred? Myself, I believe that Elizabeth hates Mary, envies her, and always has done. Envies her for her beauty, her grace, her motherhood, her way with all men – and her legitimate birthright to her own crown. All the attributes which she herself lacks. For that, I believe, she would send Mary to the block. Yet you say it is fear? Fear for her own life? Fear of assassination? Or of losing her throne?'

'Not for herself, no – not directly, that is. For she is a courageous woman. They both are that, these two queens. No, it is fear for her realm, Davy. Elizabeth believes that she alone can save England – and England is in grave danger, God knows. Indeed, she believes that she *is* England. Blame her if you will, for that – call it outrageous pride – but there is truth in it too. And she loves this England, I think, that is another form of herself, with all the passion that a woman has to give – and that our Mary has squandered on worthless men! She is the Virgin Queen – and England is her true lover. She sees that lover in dire danger, threatened within and without – and will do anything, everything, to save her love. Mary she sees as the heart of the danger. So long as Mary lives her crown is unsure. Therefore Mary must die.'

'I' faith, man, you sound as though you do believe that your own self!'

Patrick frowned. 'I believe that is what governs Elizabeth. I do not say that it need be so. I shall indeed seek to convince her otherwise. But ...'

'She will never see you, Patrick. It is crazy to imagine that she will.'

'I think that she will, Davy. I have besought Raleigh to

approach her. He has her ear these days, I am told. Philip Sidney would have assured it – but Raleigh may serve . . .'

'But to what end, man? She is set in her wicked course. You say yourself that you do not think to move her. Better surely that we should spur back to Scotland with all haste, and set forward a march over the Border! Before it is too late. Perhaps she will pay heed to that, if not to your words.'

'Would you be for war, Davy? Bloodshed? Houses, towns, aflame? Rapine? The innocent dying? For one woman's life?'

Heavily his brother answered him. 'For right, truth, justice, the sword must be drawn, at the last. When all else fails. Scotland has drawn it oft in the past for less worthy cause.'

'Thus, sober Davy Gray! Thus, no doubt, noble Philip Sidney, at Zutphen! And so men die – and women and bairns – the many for the few. Myself, in this matter of dying, I'd liefer it was the few for the many, Davy! The rulers for the people – not the people for the rulers. But I may be mistaken. It seems an unpopular creed!'

Patrick was not mistaken in one instance. Late the same night, Sir Walter Raleigh rapped on the door of the Scot's lodging. The Queen's Grace would see the Master of Gray forthwith, secretly and alone, he announced. A brief private audience. Only the Master of Gray . . .

Elizabeth, crouched over a great fire, received him in a dark-panelled sitting-room, clad in a bed-robe, and looking older than her fifty-four years. She huddled there in silence, while Raleigh closed the door behind him, and Patrick straightened up.

'Well?' she said. That was question, challenge, reproof, all in one – and something else as well, something warmer, something that might even have been the glimmerings of hope. But she sounded weary – nevertheless – and looked it.

'Very well, dearest lady,' Patrick agreed, smiling. 'First of all, in that you have graciously consented to this meeting. Then, in the felicity of your warm and womanly presence. Also in the anticipation of your understanding. Aye, very well indeed!'

'God, Patrick, do you never tire of it?' she interrupted. 'Tire of such talk, such empty flattery and fulsome praise? I swear it oozes out of you like wind from a bladder!'

'Your Grace jests – for here is no flattery. Is gratitude flattery? Or a man's appreciation of a woman? Or recognition of intellectual worth? If these be empty things, then Patrick Gray is but a bladder indeed.'

'Very well, man – let it be. Let it be. I confess I am too weary to debate it with you! I am glad that I give you so much satisfaction, for it is more than I give myself, I promise you!'

He stepped forward to take her unresisting hand and press it to his lips. He had never seen Elizabeth like this. 'My satisfaction is beyond poor words,' he said. 'Would that I might translate it into deeds! And the more so that, tonight, neither of us need act a part . . . unlike this afternoon!'

Swiftly now she looked up at him. 'You think then that I acted a part, this day?' And, before he could answer, 'Was it so evident, Patrick?'

He schooled his features to calm understanding, and no hint of surprise. 'We both had our roles to fill, Your Grace, before the eyes of men. But now, please God, we may be done with dissembling, and speak plain.'

'Do you ever speak plain, Patrick? And to what end?'

'I do, Highness. As now. To the end that folly and weakness and confusion shall not always triumph, even in affairs of state!'

'Plain speaking indeed, sirrah!' Elizabeth's eyes flashed momentarily. 'Folly, weakness and confusion, forsooth! So that is what you think of my policies?' Even as his hand rose in protest, the Queen's turbanned head sank again. 'But it is true – God knows it is true, man. I knew this afternoon that you saw it – aye, and your precious bastard brother too! I watched you, you devil, even as I stormed and raved. I saw it in your eyes. You knew that I could not, dare not, sign Mary's death-warrant. The Master of Gray *would* know that, if none other did! And so you mocked me – and I hated you, man. I do not know that I do not hate you now – only, tonight, I fear that I am too tired for hate. I knew that you would seek this private audience, to tell me what no others are bold enough to do. And I . . . I granted it, lest I dare not face myself in a mirror again!'

Patrick Gray stood very still, but his mind was furiously active. For a long moment there was silence. 'You say . . . that you cannot sign? Dare not sign the death-warrant?' he got out, at last.

'Not without cutting my very throne from under me – as well you know! Not without executing my own queenship as well as hers! Think you that I do not recognise that to execute an anointed monarch is to destroy my own authority – the divine authority vested in all Christian princes? Christ-God – was ever a woman so trammelled, so enmeshed! Mary will have my

356

life and my throne if I let her live – and I endanger my throne, all thrones, if I take her life! You did not need to come to tell me this, Patrick!'

'I did not come to tell you this,' he said, even-voiced.

'I have thought of it and thought of it – beaten my wits!' Elizabeth went on, tensely. 'Some way out of this toil there must be. Do not mock me with your talk of sending Mary to France, or of her resigning her rights to her son! You know that to be utter folly, as well as I do. Mary, while she lives, will resign nothing of her claims. And even if she would, or could, others would not, on her behalf. Every Catholic in Christendom would continue to plot to put her on my throne. You know that, man.'

'I know it,' he said.

'Why do I talk thus to you?' she demanded, heatedly. 'Admit my fears, my impotence – to you, of all men? A devil – and my enemy!'

'I am not your enemy, but your friend. I have been your friend since the first day that I saw you, in yon barge. Have we not acted friends, since then? Have you not supported me, in Scotland? And have I not done there what I said I would do?'

Eyes narrowed, suddenly she interrupted him, not listening to what he was saying, but recollecting. 'Patrick, you said . . . a little ago, you said that you did not come to tell me this. That I could not sign the warrant. What did you mean? Why then did you come?'

He spoke slowly. 'I came because I am indeed your friend. I came to bring you . . . this.' And drawing a folded parchment from his doublet, he handed it to the Queen.

Taking it, her eyes widened as she saw the scrawled signature at the foot, the cracked Great Seal of Scotland. As she glanced at the heading, the brief wording, already fading with the years, she gasped.

'But . . . man, this is . . . this is beyond belief!'

'It is true, nevertheless, Your Grace. You will know what to do with it!'

'But why, Patrick? Why? This is the key to all. Why give me this? You? I had heard that there had been such a document – a deed of abdication. But I never thought to see it. I was assured that Mary would have destroyed it, long since. Yet it is her signature – I know it only too well! Or . . . is it a forgery, man?'

'It is no forgery. Mary was . . . careless in such matters, shall we say?'

357

'This is the true deed of abdication, then? Signed by her own hand at Lochleven. In July 1567. Twenty years ago. And all these years this has existed – the proof that I needed! That she had indeed abdicated – signed with her own hand!'

'Under unlawful pressure, as she ever claimed,' Patrick observed dryly. 'Not that I think that need concern you now!'

'No. No – not with this in my hands! I have her now!' Elizabeth rose to her feet. 'I can prove that she abdicated her crown twenty long years ago. None may claim that she is any longer a crowned monarch. She has not been for twenty years, whatever she has claimed. God – what a notable writing is this! That signature is her own death-warrant!'

'I thought that you would perceive its value!'

'Where has it lain all these years? Where did you find it, man?'

'Amongst the ordinary state papers. Amongst her bills for silks, and appointments of sheriffs!'

'Lord! And to think . . . !' Elizabeth paused, parchment in hand, to search Patrick's handsome features. 'But why, man – why? You have not answered that. Why have you given this to me? Delivered your Mary into my hand, thus? After what you declared before all, this afternoon? What is the meaning of it, Master of Gray?'

He shrugged one shoulder. 'This afternoon, I said what I was commanded to say – played my part as you played yours. Scotland's envoy. Tonight I am Patrick Gray and my own man. And yours. I give you this, now, for good and sufficient reason – in addition to my love for Your Highness. You have declared that reason with your own lips. Whilst Mary lives, your life is in danger, your throne also. England is threatened, within and without, and all Europe stands on the brink of war – bloody war. It is too high a price to pay for one woman's life. There is no other issue from the tangle. Mary must die.'

For seconds on end Elizabeth stared at him in silence, at all the grace and beauty of him. Then her eyes fell before his calm, even compassionate, regard. 'Lord . . . !' she muttered.

'I told you,' he went on. 'Folly, weakness and confusion. It was not *your* policy that I condemned thus, but our own. Scotland's policy. Stupid maudlin sentiment instead of clear thinking. Scotland needs peace – not Mary Stuart, strife and war!'

'But, you said yourself that there would be war if Mary was

executed. That Scotland would march. Carlisle would be burned...'

'That was Melville. Tut – a few Border caterans may cross your March, yes, burn a few thatches, steal a few cattle. Nothing more. I know them – wind-bags, slogan-shouters all! In a month all will be forgotten.'

'But . . . but not by me!' The Queen sank down again. As though all of a sudden she seemed to realise what the paper in her hands meant for *her*, meant in personal decision. Her way was cleared, but she still had to travel that way. 'Not by me,' she repeated, her voice uneven – so unlike the voice of Elizabeth Tudor. 'If I sign that death-warrant, I shall see it before me for the rest of my life!' she whispered.

Brows puckered he looked down at her. 'At least Your Grace will be alive!' he said.

'Mary will haunt me,' she insisted.

'You have signed other death-warrants, Madam, in plenty!'

'Aye.' She raised her head. 'God pity me, I have! I perceive that you are a harder man than you seem. You see only a weak woman before you now, but perchance tomorrow I shall be Queen of England again – and hard as my name and reputation!'

'Just, say, dear lady – never hard.'

'It will require hardness to sign that warrant.'

He fingered his chin. 'It might just be possible, Madam, that fate might overtake Mary other than by the headman's axe?' he suggested. 'With no need of a warrant signed.'

'Think you that I have not considered that, man? But, with my court's sentence of death hanging over her, would the world acquit *me* of her death by other means?'

'Still, with proof of her abdication in your hands, the world's censure would be tempered. If you are so averse to signing the warrant.'

'I . . . I shall think of it. But, oh – if it did not have to be . . . death!'

'The dead do not bite, Highness. That is worth remembering, also.'

'Aye. I thank you for reminding me, sir!' The great Elizabeth, this strange night, was like a weathercock, blowing this way and that. 'And what of James?' she demanded. 'What of your master? How will he take this? He, who sent you to speak so otherwise!'

Patrick smiled faintly. 'I think that you need not fear for my Prince's fury, Madam! James is an indifferent warrior, but an excellent huckster. He would have his amends. A fair sum, he said, for the insult done to his realm by the trial and sentence on his mother – no doubt a slightly larger sum for her actual death! A small matter of adjustment between himself and your good Lord Treasurer!'

'Fiend seize me – money! Is this the truth, man?'

'Aye. He commanded me to seek a secret audience, especially to impress this upon Your Grace. May I assure him that his pension will be increased?'

'God be good! And this is the creature who would follow me upon England's throne!'

'No doubt he will nurture England's trade to unheard-of heights, Majesty!'

She stared at him. 'Does he know of this paper, then?'

'No. No one knows of that paper, save only ourselves. I pray you that you do not reveal whence and when you obtained it.'

The Queen smiled thinly, for the first time in that interview. 'I can understand your concern on that matter, Master Patrick,' she said. 'I can keep a secret better than most women, I believe.'

'So I judged – since it puts my life into your hands!'

'So it does, Patrick! So it does. And *that* you judged also, I have no doubt. Knowing something of weak women. Indeed, you know women too well, I think.' With a somewhat laboured return to her favourite coquettish pose, Elizabeth blinked weary eyes and simpered. 'Some day I shall perhaps consider how suitably to handle that life you have put within these hands of mine. Eh, Patrick? But . . . not tonight. Ah, no – tonight I am tired. Tonight I would sleep, not dally – if I may. Go now, Master of Gray – your mission well accomplished. Poor Walter will be asleep out there, I do declare – if he is not already bedded down with one of my Sluts of Honour!' She yawned elaborately. 'Off with you, man. I do not know whether to thank you, or no!'

He kissed her thin hand. 'Thanks I do not seek. Only and always, your esteem, lady.'

'M'mmm.' At the door, she touched his arm. 'Tell me, Patrick, what says your honest and beloved brother to this matter?'

Her visitor's whole visage, even carriage, seemed to change before her, his handsome features hardening strangely as though into stone, his fine eyes going almost blank, flintlike. 'A good evening to you, Madam,' he said, gratingly, and turning, without so much as a bow, he stalked out.

For long the Queen looked after his striding upright figure.

It was almost morning before Patrick Gray arrived back at

his lodgings. David, who had lain more or less awake and waiting all the night, heard him come in, reeling drunk. Never before had he seen his brother thus. It was, he adjudged, the final proof and evidence of the failure of the mission. Sick at heart, he got him to his bed, with difficulty but with a great sympathy.

The very next day, the Scots ambassadors, silent, depressed, rode north again for their native land. It was the first of February.

Chapter Thirty

THAT same first day of February, Elizabeth Tudor signed the death-warrant of Mary, Queen of Scots, in her Palace of Greenwich, in a state of near-hysteria. After snatching at her pen and signing, she dropped the paper on the floor beside her chair, and refused thereafter even to acknowledge its existence. Bitterly she compained that surely somewhere amongst her supposedly loyal and loving subjects was one with enough true affection for her to spare her the odium of this necessary task, to settle the matter of Mary without this unhappy warrant being needed? Davison, her Secretary, stooped to pick up the fatal document thankfully, even gleefully, and conveyed it with all haste to Walsingham.

There followed some delay. Walsingham, knowing his mistress only too well, to cover his own head put to Sir Amyas Paulet, Mary's gaoler at Fotheringay, Elizabeth's expressed wish that, now that Mary's fate was sealed, it would save a deal of trouble if her death could be achieved quietly, without fuss, and without further involving the Queen. As the only man with access to the prisoner, it would have to be done by himself – Sir Amyas – or at least with his connivance and arrangement. Undoubtedly, the Queen's gratitude would be very substantial for any such loyal help.

Paulet, however, could not be brought to see that this was his duty. Hard and unsmiling Puritan as he was, he insisted in putting private morals into public practice. The very qualities which made him a sure and incorruptible gaoler now turned him quite against this other service. He claimed stubbornly that he had lived an honourable life to date, and that though his heart was the Queen's and his head at her disposal, he did not propose to turn assassin at this time of his life.

That, however, was enough for Walsingham. Two men now stood between him and any monarchial second thoughts or scapegoat-making – Davison and Paulet. His own position was well secured. He gave the necessary orders for carpenters, witnesses, headsman and the like.

Mary of Scotland was executed on February 8th, the day that Patrick Gray and his colleagues rode across the Border into their own country. She died as she had lived for these last eighteen years, courageous, dignified, with spirit, even a trace of humour, professing the Catholic faith and her hope in God's mercies for her undoubted sins. The headsman made something of a botch of the first stroke – it was said, owing to tears in his eyes – but managed to sever her lovely neck at the second.

The church-bells pealed out joy and triumph all over England, thereafter; in London crowds sang and danced in the streets; bonfires were lit, largesse was distributed, loyal addresses were delivered, and Parliament sent a deputation to congratulate the Queen on her blessed and God-sent deliverance.

Elizabeth took to her bed and would see no one.

In Scotland, the Master of Gray and Sir Robert Melville reached Stirling and conveyed their fears to their royal master and his Council, informing that Elizabeth was sore set on carrying out her terrible intent, each ambassador vouchsafing for the other that all that could have been done to save the royal prisoner had been done – Sir Robert even pointing out that he believed them fortunate to have escaped with their own lives, such was the violence of Elizabeth's wrath. In private, Patrick assured the King that while utterly determined, Elizabeth was not quite so wrathful as she must seem publicly, and had listened with patience to his royal demands for amends; he thought that he could promise an increase to the pension, and possibly even an additional lump sum, but that, unfortunately, there was still no great probability of an Act naming James as Second Person and official successor to the English throne.

Scotland waited, therefore, and though James did so in nail-biting agitation, and members of his Council may have fretted in some alarm, by and large the country lay quiet, seemingly almost apathetic – readily explainable in the sheer disbelief of ordinary people that one queen could cold-bloodedly order the death of another.

Exactly one week after the ambassadors' return, another traveller, weary and unescorted, galloped over the Border – one Roger Ashton, an extra Gentleman of the King's Bedchamber, who had been in London on routine state business. He sought the King in private audience at Stirling. Mary, His Grace's royal mother, was dead, he reported.

Suspense over, James put a brave face on it. After ordering that, since this was a purely private and unofficial intimation, no word of it was to be publicly announced, he conferred with Patrick and Maitland about suitable steps to take, consonant with proper dignity and filial duty. Patrick had his advice ready, and Maitland agreed sardonically that it could hardly be bettered in the circumstances. Lord Maxwell Kerr of Ancrum, and young Ferniehirst, son of the late unfortunate Warden of the Middle March, were sent for, as two suitably fiery yet accessible and therefore disciplinable Border leaders – with orders to muster their clan.

Six days later Sir Robert Carey, son of old Lord Hunsdon, Elizabeth's own cousin-german, arrived at the Border at Berwick-on-Tweed, as official courier and envoy of his Queen. On the King's orders he was halted there, and required to answer whether or no it was true that the King's mother had been cruelly done to death. On his admission that Mary was dead indeed, but that he had a letter from the Queen explaining all, he was told that the King of Scots would on no account receive him, and was kept kicking his heels at Berwick until Sir Robert Melville and Home of Cowdenknowes were sent south to interview him and relieve him of his letter. Seldom had an official English ambassador been so scurvily treated.

Elizabeth's letter amazed even Patrick Gray. In terms of heartfelt sorrow and sympathy, it mourned Mary's death as a miserable accident that had befallen, far contrary to her own royal meaning. It was all the fault of her Secretary Davison, she declared, who had wickedly outstepped his responsibilities and given orders in her name, for which grave fault he was now confined to the Tower of London, dismissed his office, and his property confiscated. For herself, she was prostrated by this unfortunate incident, was overwhelmed with excessive grief, indeed had been made very ill and had eaten nothing for days. James would understand full well the problems of a monarch with untrustworthy underlings, of which she judged he had had rich experience. Suitable and tangible expressions of regret and recompense naturally would be forthcoming, but meanwhile would James accept the deep and sincere condolences of his devoted sister in God, Elizabeth R.

King James's first reactions, that this was a very suitable and proper letter, were rudely upset by the much less understanding and charitable reactions of his councillors and nobles. Bothwell, Angus, Mar and the rest of the Ruthven lords seemed to have lost all their previous fondness for Elizabeth. The Catholic leaders, of course, made a great outcry. On Patrick's advice, a strictly limited foray of Kerrs was dispatched over the Border, in a flag-showing gesture which was straitly enjoined to avoid large centres of population and not to burn any important castles. A suitable letter of protest was also concocted, for transmission to Elizabeth – sufficient to show the deep hurt sustained, without of course disturbing international relations – and prayers ordered for the soul of the departed in Scottish churches, however contrary to Calvinist principles. More than this seemed scarcely feasible in the circumstances.

As the news leaked out, however, and spread abroad through the land, the Scottish people, lacking any understanding of statecraft or the predicaments of rulers and princes, blazed out into elemental and extraordinary fury. Without more than a rumble or two of warning, almost the entire country seemed to erupt in wrath. Highlands and Lowlands both gave tongue. Mobs formed in the cities and towns, demanding vengeance. The lesser lords, barons and lairds, insisted on the calling together of the Estates in Parliament. The Kirk was almost split in twain. Scotland, as distinct from the Scots nobility, seethed up as it had not done for centuries.

If the King and his immediate advisers were surprised, so, to some extent, were the great lords and the Council. It did not take these latter long, however, to grasp their cue. Soon they were heading up the popular clamour, arming men, demanding action. Every pass and road into England was closed by armed and angry companies. Six quite spontaneous and independent raids were made over the Border, causing the Kerrs' careful foray to seem like a puppet-show. Young Bothwell did indeed descend upon Carlisle, with nearly three thousand men, and while he did not manage to burn it, he created considerable havoc and alarm. Other raids by Home, Angus, Hamilton and others, penetrated much deeper into Cumberland and Northumberland, spreading terror and death, one particularly audacious joint effort by Scott of Buccleuch and Kerr of Cessford going the length of assaulting the English Warden, Sir Cuthbert Collingwood, in his own fortress of Eslington, burning him out, putting his men to the sword, and taking himself and his sons prisoner. Well might the English commander in the north write a piteous letter to Walsingham, describing the country as having been reduced to a desert, wasted with fire and sword and filled with lamentation and dismay.

All this, though stirring, did not satisfy Scotland – more especially as England, with highly unusual patience, refused t be drawn, and refrained from making any counter-moves worthy of the name. The King and his advisers were abused as faint-hearts, cravens and worse, and demands for outright war resounded. The name of the Master of Gray, in especial, came to be spat upon, as the King's closest adviser.

That man of peace, however, continued to smile confidently, imperturbably, even when he was hooted at in the streets of Edinburgh. He had never had any high opinion of the populace anyway, of course. The fact that his brother David sided rather with the popular clamour, seemed only to amuse him. His advice to the King remained the one stable and predictable element in a maelstrom of emotion, tumult and confusion.

Unfortunately or otherwise, all this was the ideal forcing-ground for that most fatal of all Scots weaknesses – the preference for fighting each other instead of a common foe, that has been the comfort and stay of the English from time immemorial. Gradually, as Patrick had foreseen that it would, the clamour for invasion, reprisals, war, faded – or was at least metamorphosed into internal dissention. The strong urge to violence, since James refused to go to war – recognising the end of all his hopes of the English succession if he did – found outlet in turning upon the King himself, on his ministers and Council, on the symbols and servants of authority. Near-anarchy gripped the land – not for the first time in such circumstances, nor the last. Terrified, James cowered in Holyroodhouse, afraid to show himself to an angry people, who named him matricide, coward, Elizabeth's toy and hireling. Patrick, who had been trying, since he attained authority, to build up a national army, so that the Crown should not have to rely upon the unpredictable levies of arrogant lords, had only sufficient men as yet to protect the royal person and palaces. The country at large he could not attempt to control.

The Catholic lords saw their opportunity, and sent out a call to arms, Huntly, Erroll and Herries sending an urgent demand to Philip of Spain for soldiers and support.

Three short months after the execution of Mary Queen of Scots, her mourning realm was on the verge of civil war.

It was in these circumstances that England decided that the time was ripe for playing a somewhat more positive role – but not blatantly or too obviously. Walsingham wrote a lengthy and interesting letter – not to the Master of Gray, but to Sir John Maitland, the Secretary of State. It was a very important letter indeed, nevertheless, for Patrick Gray.

*

Conditions made Patrick almost something of a prisoner in Holyroodhouse, along with his royal master, when in the capital, since his beautiful but unpopular features were only too readily recognisable wherever he went. He and Marie had therefore taken residence meantime in the palace itself, now considerably overcrowded.

Nothing of these complications, of course, applied to David, whose aspect and apparel were ordinary enough to escape notice anywhere. He continued to live with Mariota and the children in their lofty eerie in the Lawnmarket, and in consequence heard much of what went on in the city of which his brother remained ignorant.

David came to Patrick's quarters in the palace rather urgently one night in early May – an unusual procedure. Marie, who greeted him, remarked on it.

'How good to see you, Davy,' she declared warmly, taking his hand. 'You are as good as a stranger to me, this while back, I do declare. I believe that you avoid me, do you not? Confess it. Sorrow that it should be so – whatever the cause.'

He shook his head. 'Not so,' he declared. 'No, no. You I would never avoid, Marie.' But he looked away from her, out towards the dim bulk of Arthur's Seat, rising huge in the gloom.

'It is Patrick again, is it not? You are at odds with Patrick, Davy? Seriously at odds. Oh, I always know it, when you are. Patrick shows it, plainly enough . . .'

'Patrick!' his brother jerked. 'As though Patrick could care for any opinions of mine!'

'He cares more than you think. He considers your opinions more than those of anyone else – mine own included! Always I can tell when *you* are strongly against what he is doing, however little he cares for the opposition of others.'

'If he considers, then that is all that he does! Never has he let an opinion of mine change his course . . .'

'I would not be too sure, Davy. But . . . you are against what he is doing now? You have been against his policies for some time?'

'I believe that he is in the wrong road, Marie. That is nothing new, of course! It has been my croaking plaint for years, as he seldom fails to declare. But this time it is different. Usually I have been afraid for the hurt that he might do to others. Now, I fear that he himself it is who will be hurt.'

'Hurt, Davy? How mean you – hurt? In himself? Not in his person . . . ?'

'That is what I fear. I think that he is in danger. I have told him, warned him, that the country has turned against him . . .'

'He cares nothing for what the people say, I know. But it could be that he is right, in that. They are so ignorant, he says – unthinking, swayed by gusts of emotion. Like a ship without a helm . . .'

'Aye – perhaps they own to emotions like love and loyalty and faith and trust!' he asserted bitterly. 'And Patrick, with his statecraft and clear wits, is above all these! But . . . it is not such poor honest fools that I fear. Not in themselves. It is the lords, their masters. They are frightened. The King is frightened. The Council is frightened at the way in which the country has risen. And I fear that all are going to turn on Patrick.'

'Turn on him? But why?'

'As the author of the King's policies. As the chief minister. As the man who can be blamed for their fright. As a scapegoat.'

'As the man who would not have bloodshed! Who refused to lead the country into war!' Marie added loyally.

'Perhaps. Though I think that there are two sides to that. But whatever the reasons, I believe Patrick is in danger. Not from the mobs who hoot him in the streets, but from men closer, much closer.'

'And you have told him, Davy?'

'Aye, I have spoken of it in a general way, many times – to his amusement. But tonight I have had more sure, more definite word. The danger is closer than I had feared. I must see him, Marie. Where is he?'

'Where else but as always – at his papers. Through in the small room, with Sir William . . .'

'With Sir William, aye – always with William Stewart, now!'

'You do not like him, Davy? Patrick says that you are jealous of him! Can men be jealous, thus? I do not know . . .'

'I do not trust him, anyway – and with reason.'

'But, then, you do not trust Patrick either, do you!'

Their grey eyes met, and held, for seconds on end. Then David shrugged.

'I must see him,' he said. 'But I do not wish to see Stewart.'

'I will fetch him for you,' Marie told him.

In a few moments she was back, with Patrick, a furred house-robe over his silken shirt.

'Here is an honour indeed!' he declared. 'Davy gracing my humble abode unbidden! To what mighty conjunction of the stars do we owe this felicity?' That was heavy, laboured, for

Patrick – presumably indicative of strain or preoccupation.

'Davy fears for your safety, Patrick,' Marie said urgently. 'He believes that you are in danger.'

'That Davy has been fearing all his life, and mine!'

'This is new. Only tonight have I heard of it,' David said evenly. 'And I beg you to spare me your mockery, this once. I have heard that you are to be impeached.'

'Impeached! Lord, man, are you crazy? Who would impeach the Master of Gray? Who *could*?'

'Many, it seems. Most of the Council, indeed. But specifically, one Sir William Stewart!'

'What! Save us, Davy – have you taken leave of your senses? Stewart is my own man. I trust him entirely. I have been working with him all this evening. He is but newly gone back to his lodging . . .'

'That may be. But none of it means that Stewart cannot impeach you tomorrow!'

'But . . . why should he? All that he is, I have made him.'

'He is Arran's brother.'

'What of it? What reason that for doing me injury?'

'Well may you ask! For the same reason, perhaps, that you have advanced him so notably, singling him out for preference – since his brother's fall.'

Patrick frowned. 'What nonsense is this, now? William Stewart is a man of talent. He has been of much service to me – and to Scotland. To what tales you have been listening, Davy, I do not know. But any talk against Stewart is manifestly ridiculous, close as he is to me. The work of enemies . . .'

'He is close to Maitland also, Patrick.'

'What do you mean?'

'I mean that Maitland sees more of Stewart even than you do. He is Secretary of State and Vice-Chancellor – and he has never loved you. As I heard it, he is behind this matter.'

'What matter, man? Out with it. Speak plain, for the good Lord's sake!'

'Very well. One of Maitland's own clerks, to whom I once did a favour, told me. This night. At tomorrow's Convention of the Estates, called in answer to this clamour, you are to be impeached on a charge of treason. The accuser being Sir William Stewart, acting on the instructions of Sir John Maitland of Thirlstane and the Council.'

Patrick stared at his brother. 'I do not believe a word of it!' he declared. 'The thing is absurd. And impossible. James himself is to preside at this Convention. He would never permit it – even if the rest were true.'

'The King will permit it. He has been informed and persuaded, and has given his agreement.'

'Tush, man – this is beyond all belief! Which is the greater fool, I know not – Maitland's precious clerk for concocting it, or you for crediting it!'

'They are frightened, Patrick – frightened. All of them. Even if you are not. James most of all. The country is torn with strife, the people are out of control, the Catholic lords are openly preparing to strike – and this Convention called for tomorrow is going to demand that heads fall, in consequence. It will be the most unruly of the reign, you yourself said. And yours is the head that has been chosen to fall! Maitland and your friends the Ruthven lords have selected you as scapegoat, that their own heads may remain. I have feared something of the sort for long . . .'

'And I have seldom listened to such folly!'

'Patrick, pay heed to him!' Marie cried, in agitation. 'You cannot be sure that it is not as he says.'

'Think you that I should believe the maunderings, or worse, of a knavish clerk, against my own wits and the words of my closest associates, Marie? Have I not been working all this night with Stewart, preparing the arrangements and agenda for tomorrow's Convention? Think you that he would be doing that if he intended to do this thing tomorrow? The man who is but new back from my business in France – for whom I have gained the appointment of Ambassador to King Henri? It is nonsense even to consider it.'

'Yet Davy believes it – and despite what you say now, you have never thought Davy a fool! At the least, you must enquire into it. Take precautions . . .'

'Enquire into it? What would you have me do? At this late hour? The King is retired to his bed, long syne. Stewart is away to his lodging in the town. Maitland is not in the palace. What precautions would you have me take, woman?'

'*I* would counsel you to leave this place forthwith – tonight,' David said heavily. 'At Castle Huntly you will be safer . . .'

'Fiend seize me – this is beyond all! To bolt like a coney because some grudging clerk whispers deceit . . .'

'You will not deny, Patrick, that Maitland has never loved you? With you out of the way, he can be Chancellor, not Vice-Chancellor, and rule the kingdom.'

'Maitland is not of that sort. He is not one for adventures – a canny able man who knows his own place. Besides, what has he to impeach me on? A charge of treason against such as myself demands much and damning evidence. What have they? Nothing. I have . . .' Patrick stopped himself there, shortly.

'That I cannot say,' David admitted. 'But was such necessary for Arran's fall? Or Lennox's? And you have taken many . . . risks, have you not?'

'These were, h'm, different. They were not impeached. Morton was – but there we had the proof, the evidence . . .' Patrick paused. Clearly some new notion had struck him. 'If there is anything in this clerk's tale at all, then it might be that Maitland, or others, may desire this very thing to happen – that I should take fright and run. A gobbledygowk to scare me away from tomorrow's Convention. Maitland could then steer the meeting, under the King. If he, or others, had some project afoot, which they believed I would oppose. It might be that. In which case, this whisper of Maitland's clerk in your ear, Davy, would be readily explained! Aye, that bears thinking on.'

David could not deny it. Just as he could not think of a charge of treason that could stand proven against his brother. He recognised that Patrick's suggestion made sense – a manoeuvre to keep the acting Chancellor away from the Convention. Stewart's name might have been taken wholly in vain. 'It could be,' he admitted reluctantly. 'Yet, even so, it smacks of trouble, of danger, with enemies moving against you . . .'

'Small men intriguing, mice nibbling! Of such is statecraft all the time, man – as you should know. Think you that, placed as I am, I can pay heed to such?'

'Pay heed, yes. At least you are warned. It may be more than this, as I still fear.'

'I am warned, yes. For that I thank you. At the Convention tomorrow, I shall be ready for any untoward move. But I still believe it nonsense . . .'

'You will attend then, Patrick, still?' That was Marie. 'Is it . . . wise?'

' 'Fore God – could I do otherwise? Have you joined the mice, Marie? I have not, I promise you! But enough of this. Davy – late as is the hour – some refreshment?'

'No. Mariota awaits me, anxiously. And the children. Ready to ride forthwith. For Castle Huntly, or otherwhere!'

'Lord – so seriously do you all take my poor affairs! The kind Mariota...'

Next morning, in the Throne-room of the palace, Patrick from the Chair had only just managed to still the noisy assembly of the specially-called Convention of the Estates of Parliament to welcome decently the King's entry, and had begun to read out the form of the day's business, when Secretary of State and Vice-Chancellor Maitland of Thirlstane stood up and in a loud voice addressed the Throne directly. He declared, into the hush, that before the important debate of the day should commence, it was proper that a matter which demanded the immediate attention of His Grace and the whole Convention should be brought to their notice. It concerned the fitness of the Master of Gray, in the Chancellor's seat, further to speak in their name. Sir William Stewart indeed accused the said Master of Gray of highest treason.

As Patrick, brows raised, lips curling, began to rule this out-of-order without due notice and warning, James from the Throne raised a trembling hand. They would hear his trusty and well-beloved Sir William Stewart, he declared in a falsetto squeak.

Stewart, a good-looking man though less boldly handsome than his brother Arran, rose, and in unimpassioned tones announced that out of his love for the King and the weal of his realm, he was in duty bound to declare that he knew of treason committed against the Crown by the Master of Gray. On no fewer than six counts. To wit: Having trafficked with France, Spain and the Pope for the injury of the Protestant religion in Scotland; having planned the assassination of Sir John Maitland, the Vice-Chancellor; having counterfeited the King's royal stamp; having worked for the alteration and troubling of the present estate; having sought to impede the King's marriage; and having, in England, failed in his duty in the matter of Queen Mary's death.

James hardly allowed him to finish before he stood up – and all men must needs stand up with him. They would not hear more of this just then, he stammered without once looking towards Patrick. This was not the time nor the occasion. The matter must be duly investigated. He repeated the word investigated. The Convention had other important matters to deal with. Sir William Stewart should have full opportunity to substantiate these serious charges, and the Master of Gray to answer them. He hereby fixed the diet of trial for four days hence, the tenth of May, until when both principals to the charges would be confined in strict custody, as was right and proper for the safety of the realm. He therefore ordered his leal Captain of the Guard to take and apprehend the said Patrick, Master of Gray and the said Sir William Stewart, convey them forthwith to his royal castle of Edinburgh, and to hold them both straitly there until the said day of trial, on pain of his life. Meanwhile his right trusty and well-beloved Sir John Maitland, Vice-Chancellor, would act as Chancellor of the Realm and look to the good ordering of this Convention. This his royal will. The Captain of the Guard to his duty!

The paper from which the King had gabbled this peroration slipped from his nerveless fingers to the floor, as the assembly erupted into uproar.

David, from the clerk's table, watched his brother led from the seething Throne-room under substantial and ungentle guard. The fact that Sir William Stewart was marched off with him deceived none.

Chapter Thirty-one

THE trial of the Master of Gray took place in the Council chamber at Holyroodhouse, not before any mere panel of professional judges, but in front of a very specially selected section of his fellow Privy Councillors – Angus, Bothwell, Mar, Hamilton, Home, the Master of Glamis and so on – in fact, the Ruthven lords, almost to a man. The King was present, though looking markedly ill at ease. David Gray sat amongst the other clerks and secretaries as was his wont, none ordering otherwise.

Patrick, though led in under guard, to find his accuser and supposed fellow-prisoner esconced comfortably beside the president and acting Chancellor, appeared to be quite the most coolly assured and confident person in the room, even though his clothing lacked something of its usual excellence.

The atmosphere, from the first, was strained, unreal. In all the company none seemed willing to catch the sardonic eye of the man who had so often presided over this same company in this same chamber, and who was now the accused. Unease and uncertainty clothed them all in an uncomfortable garment, which some wore with nervous posturings, some with brash noisiness, and some with glum silence. No single Catholic lord was present.

Maitland, sitting in the chair that formerly had been Patrick's, opened the proceedings as acting Chancellor, craving the King's permission to proceed. He at least spoke in the dull clipped pedantic voice that was his normal.

'Your Grace, my lords,' he said. 'I declare to you that Patrick, Master of Gray, Master of the King's Wardrobe and Commendator of the Abbey of Dunfermline and of many other priories and benefices of Christ's Reformed Kirk, stands before you charged with the most heinous and monstrous of all crimes, that of treason against his King and liege lord, in that, while he was himself accepted leader and preses of this most high Privy Council, did conspire to the injury of the realm, of the King's peace, and of Christ's holy Kirk. Sir William Stewart, whom all know to be an honourable and true servant of His Grace, has been the means of discovering for us this evil and base traitory. He has acted for the said Master of Gray in many close matters, as all here are aware, and has but lately come to perceive that much of the said Master's works were and are contrary to the good of the kingdom and the King's honour. For the weal of His Grace, therefore, and the greater comfort of his own conscience and soul, the said Sir William came to myself, as His Majesty's principal Secretary of State, with the matter, that His Highness might be apprised and informed. Hence these proceedings, taken upon the command of our gracious liege lord. I therefore call upon the said Sir William Stewart to speak to his charges.'

Patrick, from the other end of the great table, intervened pleasantly, quite conversationally – for no air or impression of court or trial prevailed, what with the lounging confident attitude of the accused, the discomfort of his judges and, despite the grave wording of the charges, the unimpressive aspect and manner of the speaker.

'Your Grace, my lords and friends all,' he said, smiling. 'Interested as I am, but naturally – nay, agog to hear what poor doings of mine have so inconvenienced the conscience of my good familiar and assistant, Sir William Stewart, I would nevertheless seek to spare the time of this noble and notable company, by pointing out that any findings of this court of enquiry are already invalid, the presiding judge having thus early prejudged the issue by declaring my conduct to be evil and base traitory. You will note, gentlemen, that he did not specify that the charge was such, but that Sir William – whom God succour – had discovered such to be the case. In consequence, Your Grace, I request that this enquiry be dismissed, and the charges with it, or else a new hearing fixed.'

Various emotions chased themselves across the features of his hearers – astonishment, consternation, wrath, even relief.

Maitland hurriedly leaned over, stooping, to murmur something to the King, who blinked rapidly, pulled at his ear, wagged his head, and then nodded.

'Aye. A slip o' the tongue just, my lords. Och, nothing mair. Sir John but meant that the charges were thus, no' the deeds. No' the deeds, my lords. Aye. Let Sir William proceed. He has . . . he has our royal attention.'

Stewart rose, bowed, and addressed himself to a pile of papers. 'This first charge, Your Grace and my lords, refers to the traffic of the Master of Gray with the King of France, the King of Spain, the Duke of Guise and the Pope of Rome, for the injury of our true Protestant religion. I testify that he wrote letters – I was indeed the bearer of sundry of them – to these princes, proposing the invasion of certain portions of the realm of England by the forces of the said princes, to the hurt of the Protestant faith.'

Patrick nodded agreeably. 'That is not a charge, but a statement of fact,' he averred. 'It was done with the full knowledge of the King and of Sir John Maitland, to the end that it might weigh against Elizabeth in the matter of her sore oppression of our beloved Queen Mary, mother of the King. If most of the noble lords present do not know of it, that is because they were at the time unfortunately banished this realm and Court on a charge of treason, and dwelling in the said realm of England under the protection of the said Elizabeth. If charge there be here, surely it should be preferred by the Queen of England, whose realm was threatened, not by the King in whose name the threat was made!'

'Ummm,' James said. 'Och, well.'

Stewart cleared his throat, and went on hurriedly. 'The Master of Gray further sought to persuade His Grace to allow liberty of conscience and worship, in the matter of religion, to the admission of wicked heresy and contrary to the laws of the Kirk and the statutes of this realm.'

'Lord – is that treason? To seek to persuade! I am a traitor self-confessed, then! As, of course, are you likewise, Sir William – who sought to persuade the King, with my assistance, to alter the law passed forfeiting the estates and property of your unhappy brother the Earl of Arran! Indeed, each of you noble lords committed treason, in such case, when you pleaded with the King, through my own self as mediator, to overturn the sentence of banishment passed upon you all after yon ploy at Ruthven! Certes, when a minister of the Crown may not advise the King to alter a law, then there will be no more Ministers, and soon no more Crown!'

Angus cleared his throat loudly. 'Here is a minor matter, i' faith. Let us to the greater evils,' he declared.

'Indeed, yes,' the prisoner agreed affably.

Stewart, after a glance at Maitland, went on. 'Secondly, I charge that the said Master of Gray planned and intended the assassination, for his own ill purposes, of certain of His Grace's Ministers, to wit, Sir John Maitland, Vice-Chancellor; Sir James Home of Cowdenknowes; and the Collector-General, Master Robert Douglas, Provost of Lincluden. This was to be done at Lauder ...'

'Wait a bit, wait a bit,' Patrick urged, actually laughing. 'Did I hear you to say planned and intended, Sir William? Man, man – have I not taught you better than this? This will never do. What a man may plan and intend is no crime – only what he does or attempts to do. Will Sir William tell us of any occasion on which I attempted, or occasioned to be attempted, the assassination of the good Sir John, Sir James and the Reverend Master Douglas . . . since it seems apparent, most happily, that the attempt lacked something of success?'

'I heard the plotting of it. In a room of this palace . . .'

'Heard, friend? With whom did I plot this intention, I wonder?'

'That I could not see. It was done secretly, behind a closed door.'

'Ah – you did not see! Then how do you know that it was I who spoke?'

'By your voice. I ken your voice full well . . .'

'Through a closed door, sir, you *thought* that you heard me expressing the intention to do way with these three gentlemen? A slender charge, my lords, is it not? Heigho – I can give you a better, here and now – and through no closed door! I say, may the devil roast and blister one, Sir William Stewart, who owes me the sum of 4,000 pounds Scots, which I intend to recover even if I have to wring his neck to do so!' Patrick's smile was wide, utterly inoffensive. 'There, my lords, you have plan, intention and dire threat in one! Yet I dare assert that none here will charge me with having committed any offence – much less a treason. So much for Sir William's testimony!'

Out of the involuntary laughter and comment, Bothwell spoke. 'You deny, then, that you plotted against Maitland's life?'

'There is no need to deny anything so flimsy, my lord. A charge based on the length of Sir William's ears, the depth of his pocket, and his interpretation of a supposed conversation with somebody unknown, represents no charge at all. Even Even if it was a crime to intend.'

'You will not deny that you have ever misliked me, Master of Gray,' Maitland interposed stiffly. 'That you have worked against my endeavours, and spitefully used me?'

'I do not deny, sir, that there are others of the King's Ministers for whom I have more personal esteem, with whom I would sooner spend a night! But do not take it to heart, Sir John – it is all a matter of taste, is it not?'

377

The Lord Home guffawed loudly, and not a few of his companions grinned or covered mouths with hands.

'Proceed with the charges,' the acting Chancellor snapped.

'Yes, do,' the accused nodded. 'Now that we all know why this peculiar impeachment has been brought!'

Stewart fumbled amongst his papers uneasily. 'It is thirdly charged, that the Master of Gray did counterfeit the King's royal stamp, and did employ the same to stay the King of France from his intention of sending an army of soldiers to Scotland on King James his royal mother's behalf.'

Patrick looked straight at James, who kept his head down. 'I have been using the King's royal stamp for many months, with the King's full knowledge and agreement – as must any of the King's Ministers . . . not least Sir John himself. I had a new stamp made, yes – since the old one was much worn and the imprint scarce to be made out. Do not you all, my lords, do the same with your seals as they wear out? But do you name the new a counterfeit of the old . . . or just a replacement?'

'It was done without the King's authority,' Maitland declared.

'Certainly. I conceive His Grace to have more important matters to attend to than the replacing of his stamps! As for the staying of the King of France his soldiers, my letter was to suggest that His Most Christian Majesty use his men for the invasion of England rather than land them upon this realm. It occurred to me, perhaps wrongly, gentlemen, that with the Catholic lords entreating the said King of France, Philip of Spain, and the Pope, to send troops here for their own purposes, it might be less than convenient to have some thousands of his Christian and Catholic Majesty's soldiers already secure on Scottish soil! Was I mistaken?'

There was no doubt as to what the Protestant Ruthven lords thought of that, however anxious they might be to dissemble their feelings.

'The next charge, man,' Angus jerked.

'It relates, my lords, to His Grace's proposed marriage to the Princess Anne, the King of Denmark's daughter,' Stewart went on. 'The Master of Gray, consistently and without due warrant, has sought to impede such marriage, to our liege lord's injury and the ill of his realm, in order that a Papist and idolatrous woman be chosen instead.'

'And the name of this Papist idolatress, sir?'

'What matters her name . . . ?'

'Much. Since you have named the one lady, you must name the other.'

'You cannot gainsay that you have been against the Danish match?' Maitland challenged.

Patrick shrugged. 'I have seen the lady's portrait, and conceive that His Grace might do better!' he answered lightly. 'Moreover, I have not heard that His Majesty of Denmark is so well endowed with possessions as to provide a dowry which will, h'm, paint the said portrait fairer! If such well-wishes for our dear prince's future happiness add up to treason, then condemn me out of hand, my lords. Off with my head!'

'You have other charges yet, I think, Sir William?' the young Earl of Mar said, impatiently. 'Let us have done with this play-acting.'

'Aye – enough o' this. Let us to the heart o' the matter.'

'Speak up, man.'

Stewart stroked his scanty beard. 'To be sure. There is my assured knowledge, through long and close working with the Master of Gray, that he has laboured for the alternation and troubling of the present estate of Scotland, in many matters which might have destroyed the King's realm. Which works, if they had taken effect, might have endangered His Majesty's person, thereby committing the crime of treason . . .'

'Might have . . . ! If . . . Might have . . . !' Patrick scoffed. He snapped fingers in the air. 'That for your further evidence! In your generalities, sir, you are as enfeebled as in your particulars. No word that you have spoken would convince of my guilt the most heather-toed sheriff in all this land – much less the lords of His Grace's Privy Council. Indeed, I am ashamed for you, man – I had thought that I had trained you in statecraft better than this!' He turned a scornful shoulder on his accuser, and squarely faced the ranked Council. 'As for you, my lords,' he said with easy authority, as though he still presided over them. 'I need not tell you that your time has been wasted quite, this day. Nothing that has been put before you represents other than the fact that at sundry times Sir John Maitland has disagreed with my policies for His Grace's realm. But disagreed within himself, mark you – not, as was his plain duty in such case, before this Privy Council. I submit that all that you have before you here is the evidence of the spite and spleen of a small and twisted mind. The mind not of Stewart, my lords, for he is but a poor paid creature, unworthy of your attention – a mere jackal where his brother once was something of a lion!

379

But of Secretary Maitland himself, who now presumes to sit in presidency over your noble lordships . . .'

The acting Chancellor's gavel beat loudly on the table, but the Master of Gray spoke on, without so much as a glance towards the Chair.

'This dismal clerk, this knight of the scratching quill, now seeks to rule His Grace's Scotland! Mark it well, my lords! We have had many bonny masters in this realm, 'fore God – but never, I swear, such a gloomy piddling notary as this . . . !'

'Highness! Your Grace . . . !' Maitland cried, his creaking voice cracking indeed. 'This is intolerable! I protest! You must . . . I pray . . . I pray that you silence this, this scoffer, this mountebank! To speak thus, in Your Majesty's presence . . . !'

James, who had been alternately drawing off, sniffing at, and pulling on his heavily scented gloves, licked slack lips, and seemed to have difficulty in getting his tongue, once out, back into its due place. 'Ooh, aye. Just that, aye,' he said thickly. 'Belike it's no proper, Sir John. You must speak otherwise, Patrick man . . . er, Master o' Gray. In our royal presence. Aye.'

'Sir, I intend to speak no more. I have nothing to answer in these paltry accusations. They do not merit the name of charges! I deny any and every suggestion that I have worked to other than the best interests of Your Grace and your realm. I never sought the office of Chancellor – indeed I have refused it time and again – but while I have been Your Grace's Minister it has been my duty to advise on sundry policies. If these policies have been mistaken, then it was for this Privy Council to decide and pronounce thereon. There was no need for this absurd impeachment. I rest content in the assurance of Your Grace's and your lordships' wise judgment.'

'Wait a bit, man – no' so fast! Wait you,' the King mumbled. 'We are no' finished yet, Patrick. Are we, Sir John?'

'We are not Your Grace!' Maitland declared tightly, and smiled, actually smiled.

David Gray, at the clerks' table, sat forward, as indeed did most others in that great chamber. He had never before seen Maitland to smile, and the effect was somehow ominous, chilling, in the extreme. Hitherto his brother had dominated the entire proceedings. David had recognised it, better than any other, as a brilliant performance, perceiving all the innuendoes, the side-blows, the playing on weaknesses and prejudices of his hearers, the thin ice over which Patrick had skated with such apparent confidence and authority. David indeed had almost begun to believe in the possibility of an acquittal, despite the fact that he knew that this was a trumped-up trial, arranged beforehand not only by Maitland and Stewart, but by the King and the Council also; that Patrick had been selected for the role of scapegoat. The Master of Gray's personal ascendancy and consummate skill might have achieved, if not complete triumph and a reversal of the situation, at least a modified success. But, of a sudden, the entire atmosphere seemed to change at Maitland's thin smile and the King's unusual assurance and obvious knowledge of something vital yet to come.

'Aye, out with it!' Johnny Mar exclaimed. 'The matter o' the Queen.'

'Proceed, Sir William,' Maitland ordered.

Stewart leaned over the table, and raised a hand to point at Patrick. 'I further charge that, for sumptuous reward in England, the Master of Gray did, while especial ambassador for the release and saving of the King's royal mother, conspire, advise and consent to the death of Queen Mary of this realm!'

For long moments there was complete silence in the Council Chamber, broken only by James's heavy, throaty breathing.

Patrick's voice, when at length he found it, was strangely uncertain, almost breathless. 'That is ... a lie,' he said.

'We have ample proof that it is not!' Stewart assured. 'From the most lofty and certain sources. I hereby charge the Master of Gray, not only with compounding the death of the Queen, but of urging it and working for it, in foullest treachery and treason!'

Patrick stared at his accuser, seemingly all but mesmerised by the still pointing hand. The difference in his aspect and attitude from heretofore was markedly evident to all.

The stout goose-quill pen which David held, snapped broken in his hand with a crack which sounded through the room, as he gazed at his brother.

'The proofs, Sir William – let us have the proofs,' the Master of Glamis demanded, into the hush.

Stewart held up a paper. 'I have a letter here, written to Sir John Maitland as Secretary of State, by Sir Francis Walsingham, principal Secretary of State to Her Grace of England. In it he declares that after making public protest against the sentence of death, before the Queen and her Council at Greenwich Palace, the Master of Gray did privately seek audience of Queen

Elizabeth, and there did urge and persuade her to the signing of the death warrant, which Her Grace was in doubts as to doing. He told her the words. "The dead do not bite!", and declared that while Queen Mary lived, Queen Elizabeth's own life must be in danger, thereby persuading Her Grace to the death. Moreover, he counselled that some other means might be found to encompass our princess's bloody fate, more secret and convenient than the headsman's axe, if this puked Her Grace. And he assured Elizabeth that there would be no uprising or commotion in Scotland over the said death, but only a few slogans shouted. That the folk cared not for their Queen, that the lords were hypocrites and windbags all, and that naught need be feared of fury from the King . . .'

'It is untrue!' Patrick cried. 'Lies – all damnable lies!' Curiously, he had turned around, so that it was at the clerk's table that he looked, not at his accuser, his King nor his judges. 'I tell you, it is false. Walsingham lies. He would divide us. He fears the invasion of his realm. He would have us fight each other, not England! It is ever the English way . . .'

David sat, eyes wide but unseeing, motionless, as though turned to stone.

'Do you deny that you had this private audience with Queen Elizabeth?' Stewart demanded, notably confident now.

'No. That I sought on our prince's direct command.' He turned to look at James. 'It was for another purpose, as His Grace knows well.'

'But you used the opportunity to press for the death of your Queen!'

'No! I deny it. I would never do such a thing. You have no proof – save the accusation of Walsingham who hates me, who hates Scotland.' That was said with violence but a certain lack of assurance, and Patrick's eyes now rested on the pile of papers in front of his accuser, tensely, as though his allegation of lack of proof held a question-mark behind it, and out from those papers one might materialise which would answer his question.

'We have clear proof, other than Walsingham's word,' Stewart nodded grimly. 'Is it your wish that it should be produced, Master of Gray?' In his hand, now, was a faded folded parchment, discoloured by years.

For seconds on end there was no sound nor movement in that chamber. Patrick Gray moistened his lips, but no words came. The silence became almost unbearable. That parchment, the accursed Deed of Abdication, had been Mary's real death warrant; now, it could equally well be his own. It could condemn him, utterly. Elizabeth had played false, in the end. But . . . why was Stewart not reading it out? Why this asking him if he wished it to be produced? Because, of course, if it was proof of his guilt, it was also proof that Mary at her death, and for eighteen years, had been no longer true Queen of Scots – thus lowering his offence from highest treason to something less. That reluctance to publish this lost and forgotten document might yet save him . . .

As Patrick hesitated, on the horns of this dire dilemma, Maitland shook his head at Stewart, almost imperceptibly, and looking along at the King, nodded.

It was James, therefore, who broke the throbbing silence, less than willingly it seemed. Swallowing loudly twice, he licked his lips, and after a false start, spoke. 'I . . . we ourself can testify to, to this matter. That the Master o' Gray willed our royal mother's death. He . . . he advised us that it would be best. Best for our Crown and realm. Mair than once, aye.' The King kept his lolling head down, looking at none.

Swiftly Maitland took him up. 'Your Grace – we are beholden to you. My lords, what need have we of further evidence? The King's testimony is final and cannot be overturned or questioned. The Master of Gray stands condemned of advising and contriving the death of His Grace's royal mother. If nothing else is accepted against him, this is sufficient indictment. How say you, my lords?'

'Aye, he is guilty!' Bothwell exclaimed. 'Guilty as Judas Iscariot!'

'After our command that he take sure and immediate action to save her, yon time!' Angus cried. 'He didna believe that Elizabeth would sign the warrant! *He* misnamed Archie Douglas for saying that she would! And all the time – this!'

The Master of Glamis spoke gratingly. 'Always the man was a dastard – have I no' told you so? A forsworn rogue. Away with him!'

'Aye, his guilt is assured. Manifest.'

'My lords,' Maitland began, primly correct. 'If this Council is duly . . .'

Patrick interrupted him urgently. 'My lords – hear me. Since His Grace has spoken, my lips are unsealed. Hitherto I could not speak you plainly, owing secrecy to the King's privy affairs. But now . . . ! You have heard His Grace's own testimony. How that I advised him for the good of his Crown and realm. I did so advise him, yes. That for Scotland's sake and his own, his mother would be better dead. I admit it. Indeed I tell you, assure you, that it is so. While Mary lived, she would not abate one jot of her claim to this throne. To her, His Grace was but a child, a princeling, usurping her Crown. No King. And you, my lords, therefore, no true Council. While she lived, Elizabeth's life and throne were in danger, and there could be no peace between Scotland and England. While she lived, our prince could never be named successor to Elizabeth's throne. While she lived, Philip of Spain stood heir to Scotland – she had nominated him so. With all inducement to invade and take, in Mary's name, what she had given him. While she lived, therefore, the Protestant cause, in which I was born and reared, stood menaced. It was Mary or war, my lords.'

'Away with him! He is a Papist rat himself!'

'Heed him not. He lies, as always.'

'It is the truth. Think, my lords – use the wits God has given you. You are of the Kirk, all of you – Protestant. You raised no hand to free Mary, all the years of her captivity. You were content. You called her the Whore of Babylon, the Pope's Harlot! You would have none of her. Why – if I am wrong . . . ?'

'Master of Gray,' Maitland said, hammering with his gavel. 'What you say is nothing to the point. You are impeached on a charge of treason in that, contrary to the express and solemn instruction of the King and this Council, when sent to strive and treat for the life of Mary the Queen, contrariwise you did advise and contrive her shameful and bloody death. Which infamous and treasonable deed you have admitted . . .'

'Not treasonable – no, sir. Since Mary was abdicate, and no longer Queen of Scots, how can it be treason?'

'Any act contrary to the King's interests and given command is treason, sir.'

'Even if His Grace knew and approved?'

'Silence, sir! How dare you drag His Majesty into your base treacheries!' Maitland exclaimed. 'Sire, we have had patience enough, have we not?'

'Aye. Oh, aye,' James agreed hurriedly.

'My lords, you have found the Master of Gray guilty of treason. The penalty of treason is death. Can any of your lordships state reason why the said penalty of death be not passed upon the said Master of Gray?'

'No! None!'

'Away with him! Send him after Mary!'

'If any man deserves to die, Gray does!'

James half-rose, and leaned over to tap the acting Chancellor's arm, hesitantly.

Hastily Maitland spoke, feigning not to notice the King. 'You judge well, my lords. Anything less than death, and our own heads would be forfeit, I do declare! The folk are roused, as I have never known them. They will have their vengeance on their Queen's murderer, that is certain. If we fail in our plain duty, they will not deal lightly with *us* – nothing is surer. With any of us!' He glanced at the King now. 'The Crown itself might not survive. A people roused is no' a thing to gainsay, I tell you.'

James subsided into his Chair of State again plucking at his lip.

Maitland stood up. 'I declare the findings of this most high Privy Council to be, then, that Patrick Master of Gray is hereby found guilty of the heinous and monstrous crime of treason against his sovereign lord King James whom God protect, and is in consequence worthy and deserving of the punishment of death. Which punishment shall be achieved, according to the law of this realm, by cutting off the said Master of Gray his head from his body, at such hour and place as the King's Grace shall command. And this is pronounced for doom. God save the King!'

'God save the King!'

'God save the King!'

'Captain of the Guard, to your duty. Take the prisoner away, and ward him in the castle of this Edinburgh, secure on peril of your own life!'

Patrick Gray was marched from the Council Chamber, looking neither to left nor to right.

Chapter Thirty-two

THE brothers faced each other at last, in a dim, damp, vaulted cell of Edinburgh Castle, with the heavy door locked upon them and the clank of armed men pacing outside.

'Thank God that they have let you come, at length, Davy!' Patrick cried. 'I feared that they were not going to allow you to visit me, for all my pleading. Man, it is good to see you.'

David stood stiffly, just inside the door, looking stonily ahead of him. 'No man prevented me from coming to see you, save my own self, Patrick,' he said evenly, his voice flat.

The other searched his face urgently in the gloom. 'So-o-o! That is the way of it, is it, Davy? I am sorry. But at the least, you have come now, at last.'

'Only because I heard that the day of your your execution has been set for Thursday. I take it that there will be matters which you will wish to be arranged? Charges which I may be able to carry out for you . . . ?'

'By God, there are! A-plenty! And but three days to do it in, curse them! The folly of it – the utter senseless folly! Frightened bairns, scared of their own shadows! It is hard, hard, to be so trammelled by fools and paltry knaves, Davy. And now they have left me so little time - so much to be done in so short a space. They would let me see no one, Davy, ere this – not even Marie. How is she, man? How does she take all this . . . ?'

'She is well enough. She bides with us in the Lawnmarket.'

'Good. That is well. But . . . why have they let you in, Davy, and not Marie?'

'I do not know. I came, and none hindered me.'

'They have not sent you with some message for me? Some proposition, perhaps?'

'No. I came of my own accord. I have seen none in authority.'

'Ah, well - it matters not so long as you are here.' Patrick began to pace up and down his restricted floor. 'Listen well then, Davy, here is what is to be done, and quickly. You must win your way into the King's presence, and seek a royal pardon – annulment of this ridulous death sentence. Have it reduced to imprisonment, forfeiture banishment - anything. Any of these I can deal with well enough, in my own time . . .'

'I cannot, Patrick.'

'Och, man, I know it will not be easy for you to gain James's presence, as matters lie. They will keep you from him, if they can. But it must be done, and it can be done. You must get one of the great lords to convey you in – one who has the King's ear. It will have to be a Catholic – for none of the Protestants will oblige you, I swear. It had better be Huntly – he is a far-out cousin of ours, and as Lieutenant of the North, the most powerful. Our Ruthven friends cannot prevent Huntly from seeing the King – and you with him. Not yet . . .'

'It is of no use, Patrick . . .'

'Tut – do not be ever so damnably gloomy! Huntly will do it, I promise you – if suitably induced. He is no different from other men, Cock o' the North though he be. Offer him, in my name, the Abbey of Dunfermline. It is the richest plum in all Scotland. George Gordon of Huntly will accept it, never fear.'

'That is not what concerns me, I tell you . . .'

'If it is the King, Davy, I think you need have no fear either. James's heart was not in yon business. He is not set against me, and cannot wish my death. He would have spoken against the death sentence, yon time, had not Maitland silenced him with fool's talk about the folk's wrath. Indeed, I cannot think what they used to turn him thus far against me. It was not the business of his mother, or Walsingham's letter, I swear . . .'

'*I* can tell you what turned him,' David said grimly. 'If your own conscience does not. The Ruthven lords told him who was truly responsible for Esmé Stuart's downfall and death.'

'Tcha – that! An old story, and no proving it. He was but a bairn then . . .'

'But James has never forgotten it. He loved his Cousin Esmé, Patrick, as he has never loved another. James never forgets anything.'

'Then he does not forget Ruthven either! He loves not these bullying Protestant lords, you may be sure, for what they did to him there. By the same token, he will not forget who delivered him out of their hands, yon time. He owed *you* his freedom then, and much service since. He will pay heed to you, Davy. If you plead for a pardon, he will not withhold it. They cannot stop him – the Protestant lords – from signing a royal pardon. And once in Huntly's hands, and given by him to Erroll the Constable, that will put all well. Secretly mind – for I do not doubt that they would have me despatched privily here in this cell, if they feared that their execution was going awry.

Poisoned food, or a slit throat . . .'

'Exactly as you proposed to Elizabeth for our Queen Mary! Pretty justice would it not be?'

'Tut, man – must you still harp yon tune? What's done is done. Here is no time for such talk, for recriminations and arguments on policy and statecraft . . .'

'As you say, Patrick,' David interrupted levelly, but strongly. 'Such time is past. As I have been trying to tell you. I did not come here to argue or to recriminate. Not any more. Only to take any last messages . . .'

'So be it. I am glad to hear it, Davy. Now – you have it about Huntly, and the Commendatorship of Dunfermline? That should be enough, and more . . .'

'No. It is no use, Patrick. You might as well save your breath. I will not see Huntly. Nor yet the King.'

'Eh . . .?' The other stared at his brother. 'What in God's name do you mean?'

'I mean that we have come to the parting of the ways, at last, Patrick.' Slowly, heavily, David brought out the words one by one his tone so flat as to be almost expressionless, his features as though carved. 'Too long I travelled your shameful road with you – God forgive me! It is finished now.'

'You mean . . . ? Good Christ – you mean that you will not do this thing for me?'

'This – or any other that might save you from the judgment that you have so richly so terribly, earned'

'Merciful Heaven – it cannot be! You jest Davy – aye, you but jest?'

'Think you that I could jest at such a time? Was I a jester ever? You were the jester, Patrick – not me!'

'Then . God Almighty – it is beyond all belief!' Patrick strode forward and grabbed his brother's shoulders all but shaking them, staring into the grey steady eyes. You to do this! You Davy Gray to desert me to turn traitor at the end! After all – you to betray me! My own brother. I'll not – I tell you I'll not believe it!'

Unwinking, unflinching, David's level regard held the other's blazing eyes. 'Betray . . . ?' he repeated quietly. 'I wonder that you dare form that word, brother!'

'Brother! And *you* dare call me brother? You that could save me, but prefer to throw me to my enemies! You, who would have me die rather than lift a hand to save me! Brother, for-sooth!'

'Perhaps you are right in this, Patrick. Perhaps never were we true brothers – only suffered under the accident of the same heedless sire! For 'fore God, I would not wish to be brother to the man who sent Mary Stuart to the scaffold!'

'As you would send me now!'

'As I . . .' David swallowed. 'As I would send you now!'

The other whispered. 'You . . . you want me to die, then?'

Stiff-lipped, slowly, David nodded. 'I . . . want you . . . to die.

'Christ God – this then is . . . murder! The crime of Cain.' Glittering-eyed Patrick gestured towards his brother's head. 'Watch you your brow, for the mark coming! Cain's mark . . . !'

The other gazed straight ahead of him. 'So be it, if it be God's will.'

'God's will . . . !' Patrick flung away from him, to go pacing about the cell again. '*You* prate of God's will. Lord – this is not possible!'

'I warned you, Patrick. Have you forgotten? I told you, yon day after Wotton left, that if ever you acted to betray Mary the Queen, as you had betrayed so many others I would stand by no longer. I would act. I would forget that we were brothers. And you would never betray another. Do you not remember?'

'That woman! She was a witch, a devil! She turned your head, man. About her, you are crazed. What was she, man, to set above your own brother? A woman whom you saw for a few moments, once – near old enough to be your mother!'

'She was my Queen, and yours – and a helpless, sorrowing, gallant woman whom we had vowed to free and serve and cherish . . .'

'Tush – what is that but callow sentiment! And for such youth's dreams such pap you would have me die under the axe?'

'For more than that. I would see an end to your destruction. For that is what you are, Patrick – a destroyer. All your life you have worked for destruction, setting up only that you may drag down, enticing and fascinating that you might betray. You betrayed Mariota, seducing her and then abandoning her with child. You betrayed *me*, to your father, asserting that the child was mine. So that you could have Elizabeth Lyon and her riches. You betrayed *her*, on her very wedding-night. Then, rising higher, you betrayed your faith, the Protestant faith in which you were baptised and bred, going over to the Romans – not for conviction, but for gain only, and that you might betray them in turn. You betrayed Esmé Stuart, your friend, to the death, after raising him high. Then Gowrie, your own uncle, also to the death. Arran you betrayed and brought low over yon business of the Redeswire, and Ferniehirst you threw to the dogs. Your King you betrayed to Elizabeth - and no doubt Elizabeth to de Guise and Philip of Spain. Mary Stuart was only your final and crowning infamy, dear God!'

Patrick had stopped his pacing to stare at him, mouth forming words but no sounds. He seemed to shrink in on himself, as he stood there, and for perhaps the first time in his life there was no beauty, no attractiveness, visible in those delicately moulded features. 'Are . . . are you finished?' he got out, at last, from ashen lips.

'Aye.' David sighed wearily. 'Finished, yes.'

'Finished your smug, hypocritical, self-righteous litany!' That was a gabble.

'Aye. And making sure that you are finished your tally of betrayal, at last, also. Would to God that I had had the courage, and found the way, to do it sooner.'

Patrick was silent. He turned and went over to the bench that was his couch, and sat down heavily.

'So this is the end?' he said. 'I had never envisaged it . . . thus.'

David said nothing.

'I can see now why they sent you in to me - you, and only you!'

'They did not send me. I tell you, I came of my own accord.'

The other did not seem to hear him. 'I trusted you, Davy. I never thought that you would go over to my enemies even though you found fault with me. Ever you have done that. Is there nothing I can do, man - nothing that I can say to soften your heart? If you have a heart? No amends I can make?'

'None. Even if I believed you capable of amend.'

'Marie . . . ? And the bairn to come? For her sake . . . ?'

'I shall look after Marie as best I am able. You can rest assured of that. As for the bairn, it will be heir to Gray. My lord will see that it suffers nothing.'

'Aye. So. It is all decided. So simply. So nicely. And I thought that you loved me . . . !'

'Simply!' David's stern armour seemed to crack. 'Lord, man - think you that aught has been decided simply, nicely? That I have not worn out my knees with praying, deeved the good God's ears to guide me, to help me to my duty? Think you that all these years I have not fought and struggled with this evil thing, cursing myself and my weakness - aye, and my love for you - as much as your fatal . . . '

'Aye – so you prayed your iron Calvinist God – and He sent you here to comfort my last hours thus! My thanks, brother – my thanks! *I* pray now – pray that you will spare me more of your pious hypocrisy.'

The other seemed to bite his lips into stiffness again. 'I came . . . I did not wish to come. I came, as I told you, but to see if there were any last messages, final charges . . .'

'Ah, yes – fond farewells! You touch me deeply, Davy – i' faith you do! But I think that I can do without your loving services in this! Marie knows me well enough, without grave-yard messages. Mariota also. My beloved father never knew me – no words will change him now. Only . . . only young Mary, sweet small Mary, will, will . . . oh. for God's sake, get out! Go, man – go! If you have any heart left in you, leave me alone!'

'I . . . I am sorry.'

For moments brother looked at brother, starkly, nakedly, unspeaking, their tormented, searching, anguished eyes saying the goodbyes which their lips would not form. Then slowly, Patrick raised his hand and pointed, urgently, pleadingly, to the door.

Blindly, David turned on his heel and strode thereto. He had to rattle on the iron latch for it to be unlocked from outside, waiting wordless.

The door opened, and he stumbled out without a backward glance.

David Gray had taken only a few almost drunken steps along the stone-flagged corridor, when his arms were gripped strongly. ungently, from either side. He looked up, blinking the tears from his eyes, seeking to see clearly. Two men in breastplates and morions, men-at-arms presumably, held him. Two more levelled halberds at his chest. Beyond them another man stood, of a different sort, seemingly richly dressed. Shaking his head to clear the weak tears away, David perceived that it was Sir William Stewart.

'Master Gray. you will come with me,' he was told curtly.

They led him out across the cobbled square. up a flight of steps cut in the naked castle-rock, and into another wing of the fortress – the Governor's quarters. In a richly furnished apart-ment therein, he found himself thrust before the presence of Sir John Maitland.

The Secretary of State and acting Chancellor eyed him with his usual dyspeptic and disapproving stare. 'You have taken some time to visit your brother, Master Gray,' he said, without explanation or preamble, in his dry lawyer's voice. 'It is eight days since he was imprisoned. I adjudge this to mean either that you have singularly little of brotherly affection for the said base and wretched traitor, or else that you oppugn and condemn his wicked treasons - as indeed must all His Grace's loyal servants. In either case, it seems likely that you will not fail in your duty to your King, now.'

David looked from the speaker to Stewart, to another who seemed to be an officer of the royal guard, and sought to jerk his arms free of the men-at-arms who still gripped him. 'I do not understand you, sir,' he said, frowning. 'Nor why I have been roughly handled and brought here thus. I have committed no offence. What means this, sir . . . ?'

Maitland ignored the other's protest entirely. 'Your duty to King James is plain. You will do well to remember it. By what means does the Master of Gray plan to circumvent the King's justice?'

Astonished, David gazed at the man. 'You mean . . ?'

'Tut, man - do not play the fool! You are not dealing with fools I assure you. Your precious brother is a nimble-witted rogue. He will not fail to take such steps as he may to save himself and overturn the true course of justice. And undoubtedly he has friends amongst the disaffected and the disloyal. He cannot achieve much in a prison cell without a go-between. You are the only one who has been permitted to visit him.'

'I see!' David's grey eyes smouldered, now. 'So that is why you permitted me to see him, without hindrance! You must have a poor opinion of me, I think, sir! You name him traitor - and adjudge me to be a traitor likewise, in that I would betray my own brother!'

'We give you the opportunity to prove that you are *no* traitor, rather, Master Gray,' Maitland said, but sourly. 'Less merciful and patient Ministers of the Crown might consider that since you were your brother's close confidant and secretary, you must be equally implicated with himself in his treasonable activities. You might well be in the next cell to the Master of Gray at this present, sir! You would do well to remember it.'

'If I am not, sir, it is not because of your love for me, I swear!' David returned. 'Rather, because you have no evidence which would condemn me - for I am as loyal to King James as I was to his gracious mother the Queen. As I have proved.'

'I rejoice to hear it. In that case, you will tell us what steps your wretched brother intends in this pass – since it is inconceivable that he will not strive to save his neck, contrary to the King's decree.'

David looked steadily at his questioner, and said nothing.

Maitland frowned. 'Master Gray, I would remind you that we have the means to loose halting tongues in this castle!'

'No doubt, sir. But they would avail you nothing. For though I would not reveal my brother's plans to you if I could, the truth is, there are none. I bear no messages from him, am committed to no projects.'

'Think you that we shall believe that, fool!'

'Whether you believe it or no, it is the truth ...'

That ended in a wheezing gasp, as David reeled back and would have fallen had not the two men-at-arms held him upright. The officer had struck him hard full across the mouth with a gloved fist, at Stewart's nod.

Maitland went on primly, as though nothing whatsoever had occurred. 'We require the truth, Master Gray, and shall have it. Your brother is not one to accept his fate without lifting a hand. we have known that from the first, and have taken due precautions. He has already tried to bribe his guards. Your visit offered him his greatest opportunity. What would he have you to do?'

David licked the blood from his lips. 'I would not tell you – even if I knew.'

His head snapped back with a sickening jolt as the captain jabbed two vicious blows at him, to nose and eye, in swift succession.

'Yes, Master Gray? We are waiting.'

'Curse you ... !' David, dizzy, reeling, yet struggled desperately with his captors, striving to free his arms. But the men-at-arms held them fast, indeed twisted them behind his back until the agony was excruciating. Even so, as the officer lunged forward again, David lashed out with his foot, to catch the man strongly below the knee-cap.

A hail of furious blows fell upon him, and the weight of his own body sagging against those twisted arms had him half swooning away.

Dimly, as though through a thick red mist, he heard Maitland's dry voice droning on. '... obstinacy is the attribute of a fool, Master Gray. I had not esteemed you that, ere this. Come, man – enough of this folly. What are your brother's wishes? To whom does he send you?'

Slowly David's swollen and bleeding lips moved, sought to form words, 'Do . . . your . . . worst,' he got out, at length, only just intelligibly. 'You . . . cannot . . . make me . . . speak. You cannot . . .'

He choked to silence then, as the edge of a hard hand slashed at the front of his neck, his adam's apple. The torment was exquisite. His throat filled with bile. Blind with pain and nausea, David was convulsively sick.

It was a little while before he realised that it was a new voice that was speaking through it all – presumably Sir William Stewart's voice.

'. . . that this is all we can do? That there is not the rack and the boot, the wheel and the thumbscrews? Och, we are well provided with such niceties here – my lord of Morton saw to that! You have a long way to go, fool, before we are finished with you!'

David sought to raise his splitting head. He did not know whether he achieved it or no, even whether the words which he so sorely formed were indeed enunciated. 'I'll . . . no' . . . speak,' he muttered. 'You've . . . got . . . the wrong . . . man!'

The hails of blows which followed that made but little difference.

For how long David Gray's tribulation lasted, he never knew. Looking back, it seemed an endless purgatory of searing pain. But at the time he was almost more obsessed, undoubtly, by a furious anger, an all-consuming rage of hatred at his persecutors, and an overwhelming ache of anguish, not for himself and his plight, but for his inability to hit back, the wicked injury to his pride in that he could not give as good as he got. The Gray in him undoubtedly was far from latent.

And presently there crept upon him a warm and grateful awareness that things were not quite as they had been, that blows were no longer really hurting him, that savage pain was ebbing, that nothing mattered so much. It was a good, an excellent feeling. A great and overpowering relief began to enfold him, and he embraced its warm drowsy comfort with all that remained of his reeling consciousness.

The final descent into blessed insensibility held no single lingering echo of hurt.

Chapter Thirty-three

THE ascent to pain and tribulation was gradual, also. Reluctantly, indeed, David came to himself. He kept his eyes shut, in fact, deliberately, out of sheer shrinking unwillingness to accept the grievous burden of it all, for quite some time – until, indeed, he discovered that he could scarcely open them anyway. One eye was in fact completely closed up; out of the other, presently, he decided that he could see, after a fashion.

What he saw out of it took some time to register, for it had to compete with other and very pressing perceptions and impressions, mainly of multiple and comprehensive hurt, of dizziness, sickness, stiffness, and general physical misery. But at length his eye told him, with some insistence, that the people standing watching him not only were not belabouring him in any way, but were not so inclined, at all. They were, indeed, small children.

This knowledge, when it sank into his bemused brain, aroused him. His mind suddenly began to function with a strange clarity, even while his aching body remained inert, anxious only to escape back into blessed oblivion.

He perceived that he was lying on the ground, out-of-doors. Moreover, he recognised that it was raining. He seemed to be in a narrow, confined place amongst damp stone walls – undoubtedly one of the wynds or closes that opened off the main city streets. And only the children watched him, and a small sniffing dog. He was no longer in the castle, then . . .

As David lay there, eyes closed again, seeking to understand this strange circumstance, his nose, though battered and very sore, kept transmitting to him a message of its own. At length he attended to it. Malt liquor – whisky – that is what it was. He stank of it. Gingerly he opened his eye again. All the torn front of his doublet was soaking wet – indubitably with whisky.

Groaning involuntarily, David stirred, sought to raise himself, got to his knees, staggered to his feet, leaning against the wall for support .The children stepped back warily, but hooted their merriment. Obviously he was thought to be drunk, very drunk indeed.

Testing his joints, his muscles, cautiously, painfully, the man decided that no bones were broken. He took a tentative step or two, clinging to the wall – and though he winced with the stounding hurt of it, he perceived that he could walk. The dog began to bark, loudly.

Feeling his way, hand never leaving the masonry, and with the children chanting in his wake, he began to edge along. A dark archway opened ahead of him – no doubt the pend from the wynd leading out on to the street. Through its echoing vault he limped, tottering.

At the other end he paused, breathing deeply, trying to focus his unco-ordinated sight. Even so, it did not take him long to recognise his whereabouts. He was in the Lawnmarket, not far from his own house – even on the same side of the street. Thankfully, if with great care, he began to stagger up the cobble-stones. The children and dog deserted him.

How he managed to drag himself up the many steep stairs to his lofty eerie of a house, David did not know. Undoubtedly it took a long time. But one part of his mind was busy through-out, despite the physical stress – that clear, active part which pain indeed almost seemed to sharpen.

They had not put him into a cell, like Patrick, as they had threatened, then. Nor had they resorted to the rack and the thumbscrews. Why? They had brought him down from the castle, spilling whisky over him to make him appear to be drunk – to account for his unconsciousness and battered condition. Brought him near to his own house. Why?

Not out of any remorse or pity, that was certain. It could only be policy. What then? Why trouble thus? They wanted in-formation from him. Presumably they had decided that they would not get it in a cell or under torture – nor from an un-conscious man. They must still hope to get it out of him some-how, then, or they would merely have locked him up, or dis-posed of him out-of-hand. They must be going to watch him, therefore – keep him under observation, and hope that he would lead them to the information that they sought. No doubt they were watching him, now. The fools! If only they knew the truth, the terrible, incredible truth! Not that they would have believed him if he had told them ... !

David Gray lurched into his own house, and collapsed part upon a settle, part against the table. Consternation gripped the little household. Fortunately both Mariota and Marie, who had stayed with them since her husband's arrest, were practical-minded women, not given to hysteria. However vocal their distress and urgent their demands for explanation and information, however vehement their denunciation of whoever was responsible for his state, they set about the loving care of David's injuries and provision for his comfort and needs, without delay. They both knew him too well to be impressed by the smell of liquor. Mary, now thirteen years old, stared in wide-eyed horror, whilst seeking to keep young Patrick quiet.

Speaking with difficulty through cut and swollen lips, David told them briefly what had happened after leaving Patrick's cell, dwelling mainly upon the fact that his assailants had but used him as a bait, allowed him unhindered access to his brother merely so that they might question him afterwards, and stressing that they undoubtedly would be watching him still, watching the house, hoping that he would lead them to what they wanted to know.

'The brutes!' Mariota exclaimed. 'The dastardly brutes! To think that they could sink so low – Maitland, Stewart! Men you have worked with ... !'

'It is but what Patrick would name statecraft, I suppose!'

'It is savagery! Barbarity ... !'

'It is shameful! They are no better than brute beasts!' Marie said. 'But ... but ...' Her voice faltered. 'If you are to be watched, Davy, as you say – then what are we to do? It is but three days until ... until ...' She bit her lip.

David cleared his throat, but said nothing.

'We shall find a way, never fear,' Mariota asserted stoutly. 'We shall win Patrick free.'

'But how? Oh, how can we? If they watched David thus, they will watch me also, Patrick's wife, without a doubt. And you too, Mariota ...'

'My lord – he would help. They would not dare to treat *him* so!'

'I would not be so sure. But Lord Gray is at Castle Huntly, still. He has not come – he has not come, though he must know well that Patrick is taken and condemned. I wrote to him, but ... he has not come! Anyway, to ride to Castle Huntly and back would take too long – four days.'

'The King, then. You must try to see the King again, Marie. He is your own cousin.'

'They will not allow it. I have tried – you know how I have tried. But they surround James – guard him like a prisoner himself. They will not allow me into the palace. Davy – what did Patrick say? What did he tell you to do?

397

David moistened damaged lips. 'He . . . I . . . ' He swallowed sorely. 'I cannot do it, Marie. I told you before. I am sorry – but I cannot do it. Would not, even if I could.'

'Davy! You do not . . . you cannot mean that! Not really mean it . . .'

'Aye. As God is my witness, I do!'

'But . . . your own brother!'

'Aye. My brother.'

'No, Davy – no! Oh, I know how he is at fault. That he has done shameful things. I know that you blame him – I blame him also. But . . . but not this, Davy. Not to . . . the death!'

'Has he hesitated at the death of others?'

'Perhaps not. But . . . that does not make us his judges.'

'You would have me to forget all the evil that he has wrought?'

'Not forget – but forgive!'

'Who am I to forgive him? The ill was not wrought against me. But I . . . I could have saved some of the ill from happening, had I been stronger, truer to my conscience, of a better courage. Do not talk to me of forgiveness, for I do not forgive myself!' David had sat up in his bed, in his vehemence, and now swayed dizzily with the effort, his features contorted with pain. 'Only . . . only of this I am sure,' he declared thickly, uncertain only in the enunciation of his words. 'It must not, it shall not, happen again.'

'Davy, lie down,' Mariota commanded. 'You distress yourself. Lie back, Rest – you must rest. You are not yourself. We shall speak of this again . . .'

'If you mean that I will think differently in the morning, woman, you are wrong,' he told her, sinking back.

'Tut, now, In your right mind, Davy, you would never condemn your brother to death! No, no. I tell you . . .' Suddenly Mariota turned, recollecting her great-eyed, watching children. 'Mary, take your brother ben the house. Quickly, now – off with you. Here is no talk for bairns . . .'

'I am sorry, Mariota,' Marie said, low-voiced, after the door had closed on them. 'I had forgotten the children. I hardly know what I am doing, or saying. I think that I shall go mad – if we are not all mad already!'

'Hush you, my dear. It will be better in the morning. Davy will think differently then, I swear. He is hurt, sick . . .'

'That is nothing to the point,' the man said, wearily. 'My mind is made up.'

'Oh, Davy! If not for his sake – for mine!' Marie besought

him, brokenly. 'We have understood each other, been good friends, always.'

Slowly, painfully, David turned his head away from them, to face the wall.

'Leave him, Marie – let him be,' Mariota counselled. 'He needs rest, sleep. We must let him be . . .'

David did not sleep, nor scarcely rest. Tossing and turning on his bed, despite the hurt of it, he wrestled with himself, his faith, his conscience and his love, and knew no peace of body, mind or spirit.

Some time, how much later he knew not, he heard the door of his bedchamber open and shut. But he did not turn towards it, did not open the eye that was less painful closed. Indeed he had forgotten it when, after a while, some faint stir of movement near him penetrated the turmoil of his mind. Reluctantly he turned his head and looked.

Young Mary sat on a chair beside his bed, gazing at him silently. In her hand she held a cup.

'I have brought you a posset,' she told him. 'It is to help you to sleep.'

'It will require more than a posset to make me sleep this night!' he said. 'But . . . thank you, lass.'

She helped him drink it down, so that he need not sit up. Then, still unspeaking, she sat down again at his side, to watch him, her eyes fixed on him, unwavering.

David would have turned his head away once more – but somehow could not. He would have shut his eye again – indeed did shut it often enough, but always opened it again. He could not keep his gaze away from her, avoid her eyes. It was those eyes that held him, burned in on him, ravaged him – deep, dark, lustrous, lovely eyes, so damnably like Patrick's. They never left his face, considering him, reproaching him . . .

Mary Gray had more than fulfilled the promise of her early childhood. She was small still, but perfectly made and already well developed, thus early on the threshold of most lovely young womanhood. Always she had been a dainty, exquisite creature; now she was of an elfin beauty to take the breath away and catch the heart-strings. Only one other had David ever seen who touched her in beauty – and that her namesake Mary of Scotland.

He stood it for as long as he could. 'Why do you stare so,

child!' he exclaimed at length. 'Lord knows, I cannot be a pretty sight!'

Gravely she shook her dark head, but her great eyes never left his ravaged features nevertheless. 'Father,' she said, gently, but thoughtfully, 'Mother and the Lady Marie are weeping. Because my Uncle Patrick is to die, is it not?'

Swallowing, the man nodded dumbly.

'And you could save him, could you not, if you were well and able?'

David started up, aches or none. 'No, I could not! I could not, I tell you!' he cried, almost shouted. 'It is impossible, child.'

'Oh yes, you could,' she asserted, quietly, assuredly. 'You can do anything that you set your hand to. Uncle Patrick told me that, himself. Long ago. He told me that you were the finest, strongest man that he knew, and that he would wager you against any man or set of men in all Scotland. It is true. I know.'

David groaned. 'It is folly, girl – sheer arrant folly. I am weak, helpless, a broken reed . . .'

'Only because you are sick and injured and beaten, by those evil men. But you *could* save him, if you were well.' She nodded decidedly. 'So *I* must do it, in your place.'

David choked, and the blood came trickling from a corner of his mouth. 'Lord child, – what . . . what are you saying?'

'That I must do it, for you, Father. You will tell me what to do, and I will do it.'

'Och, Mary lass, Mary – you do not know what you say . . .'

'I do, Father. These wicked men must not gain the mastery. And it is right that I should do it, I think – for Uncle Patrick is my true father is he not?'

Dumbfounded David gazed at her, peering from his watering eye. 'You . . . you . . . who told you that, child?' he got out at last, thickly.

'Many have said it. Often. Children about the Court. My grandfather, once, when he was drunk. I am so like my Uncle Patrick – all can see it. It is the truth, is it not?'

After seconds, wordlessly he nodded his head.

'So, you see, it is right that I should do it – for my own father. I love you best, of course. But I have always loved my Uncle Patrick, too.'

David drew a long breath. 'My dear,' he said. 'There is nothing that you can do. Nothing. I am sorry . . .'

'I can go to the King. If you will tell me how I may win in to him. The King will hear me. He likes me well. He told me that I was a bonny lass. He thanked me, mind, for being kind to Vicky that is Duke of Lennox. He would pay heed to me.'

'But, lass, it is not so easy as that. Even if I could bring you into the King's presence.' He paused. 'Do you know for what your, your Uncle Patrick was judged and condemned?'

'That I do. Everybody knows that. It was for not saving poor Mary the Queen, when he went to London.'

'Aye – just that. For not saving Mary the Queen! A heavy charge, my dear.'

'Poor Mary the Queen! I hate that Elizabeth for killing her – hate her! But it *was* Elizabeth who killed her, was it not? It was not Uncle Patrick?'

'No, Yes. But, you see . . .'

'And you went to London with Uncle Patrick to try to save her too, Father, did you not?'

'Yes. I went also. But not as Patrick went – only as a secretary . . .'

'But to try to save the Queen. But you did not save her, either of you.'

David looked down, away from those glowing, searching eyes, at last. 'No,' he said. 'Neither of us.'

'But you did try – which is the main thing, is it not? Mother says that you did all that you could to save the poor Queen. Tell me what you did, will you? Did you try to save her, the way that you saved the King, at Ruthven?'

He did not answer.

'As you saved Uncle Patrick and Vicky's father in France, that time – with the cattle-beasts?'

He stared at the floor. 'No,' he muttered. 'It was not possible.'

'Then, Father, if you tried all to save her, and could not do it – how could Uncle Patrick? Always he told me that you could do anything that you set your hand to – and I know that it is true. Did you not set your hand to saving the Queen?'

He met her eyes now, and strangely his swollen lower lip was trembling. 'God help me, child – I do not know!' he burst out. 'I do not know.'

Gently she reached out to touch his clenched bruised fist. 'Do not worry, Father – do not worry,' she said. 'I am quite sure that you did your best. Like Uncle Patrick – whatever they say. Is that why these evil men beat you so cruelly?'

He made no reply, did not seem to hear her.

'They had no right,' the girl declared. 'Even though they loved the Queen, they had no right. For she said that all were to be forgiven. She said that all, all who encompassed her death, even the horrid man who cut off her head, and Queen Elizabeth who told him to do it – all were to be forgiven.'

'Eh . . . ? What was that? What did you say?' The man turned slowly, to lean towards her, as though hard of hearing. 'What did you say?'

'Have you not heard? Everyone speaks of it. The speech that she made. They have made a broadsheet of it. Mary the Queen spoke it before she died. She said . . . I mind not all that she said. But this she did say – might God, who alone can judge the thoughts and acts of men, forgive all those who have thirsted for her blood. Was she not good, Mary the Queen? Kind. I am glad that I am named Mary, too. She said all were to be forgiven. So, the King cannot be angry with Uncle Patrick, any more – nor with you either, Father. Can he?'

David Gray was not listening.

'If I go to him, I am sure that he will say that Uncle Patrick is not to die. So, will you tell me how I can come to the King, please?'

There was silence in that bedchamber for long moments, as Mary Gray waited, serious, intent. Only the man's deep breathing sounded.

Then abruptly, he brought his open hand down upon the quilt that covered him. 'Amen! So be it!' he said, and turned to her urgently. 'Child – you know my lord of Huntly's great house down the Canongate?'

'Huntly House – over the street from the Tolbooth? Aye, I know it fine, Father.'

'They will never think of you, a child . . . with a basket, maybe. Aye, a basket on your arm, when you go errands to the booths for your mother. In the morning. That is it . . . See, Mary – fetch me paper and quill and ink-horn from my desk. You know where they are – paper, quill, ink-horn. And quickly!'

Eyes alight, the girl ran to do his bidding.

Chapter Thirty-four

GEORGE, 6th Earl of Huntly, Chief of Clan Gordon, Cock o' the North, principal Catholic of the realm – and now, curiously, to be the Kirk's Commendator-Abbot of Dunfermline – red-faced, haughty, arrogant, leaving his tail of five-score mounted Gordons stamping and clattering in the forecourt of Holy-roodhouse, strode past all wary-eyed and circumspect guards and officers in the various palace doorways and corridors without so much as a glance. Behind him his five bonneted and plaided Gordon lairds were scarcely less proudly overbearing, hands on their broadsword hilts, so that the sixth, David Gray, wrapped in Gordon tartan and with bonnet crammed hard down over his brow, stiff and sore as he was, had great difficulty in keeping up with this fierce Highland stalking. And, Heaven knew, he did not want to fall behind, to become in any way conspicuous, to become other than just one plaid-wrapped supporter amongst six, for keen-eyed watchers to consider. It was a blessing that these Highlanders always kept their bonnets on, save when actually in the royal presence; also that his face was still swollen and discoloured enough to be barely recognisable.

Huntly's shouted demands as to the whereabouts of the King brought them expeditiously to the library of the palace – Huntly always approached his sovereign in this fashion, as a matter of principle, considering himself practically a fellow-prince. In the ante-room, the young Earls of Bothwell and Mar sprawled at ease with tankards of ale, and deliberately did not rise to their feet at the Gordon eruption. The older man snorted loudly as he passed, but otherwise ignored them. Their mocking smiles were discreetly kept below the level of laughter which might reach Gordon ears. They did not bother to look at Huntly's following.

At the door of the library, an officer of the guard stood on duty. He made no attempt to halt the oncoming party, but on the contrary threw open the door and announced that the noble Earl of Huntly, Lieutenant of the North, sought audience of His Grace. Reinforced by a growled pleasantry from the noble suppliant himself, the party swept inside, David in the midst. It was as easy as that. The last Gordon in, turned to close the door with something of a slam in the face of the officer.

The King was sitting alone at a table in the musty-smelling, booklined room, surrounded by open volumes, pen in hand, scratching away at a paper. Next to the hunting-field James was happiest when in a library. He looked up, frowning, with no relish for being disturbed. Moreover, he had always been a little afraid of the potent and fiery Huntly.

'Ha, y'Grace,' the latter cried, doffing his feathered bonnet at last. 'At your books again, I see! Man, I would not let the books take a hold of you, see you. They are worse than women or the bottle for sucking the marrows out of a man!'

James rose, trembling with his earnestness. 'My lord, books are the finest gift of Almighty God to men!' he protested. 'Without them, we should be as the beasts that perish.'

'Bah!' the Gordon snorted. 'Without them, many men would be the happier. Many men now dead would be alive. Mother o' God – show me a bookish man and I will show you a rogue ... with due respect to Your Grace! Yon Maitland, for instance. William Stewart. The bladder o' lard, Davidson, whom you miscall a Bishop! George Buchanan, that fount o' bile – aye, and most of the rest of his Bible-beating kin!'

'My lord, you speak amiss! Och, man – yon's no way to talk. You should think shame o' yoursel' to speak o' godly men so. I'll no' have it. I'll no' listen to such ill speech. What ... what do you want with me, Lord Huntly?'

'For myself – nothing, Sire. Save maybe that you get rid of the pack of yapping lap-dogs of the Kirk that yelp around you, these days! No, no – for George Gordon – nothing. It is Davy Gray, here, who seeks your ear. Eh, Davy?'

David stepped out from behind his protective screen of Gordon lairds. 'Yes, Your Grace,' he said.

'Master ... Davy!' the King gasped. 'Man – is it you? Waesucks – your face! Man Davy, how ... what ... what has become o' you?'

' 'Tis nothing, Sire. The methods of your new Chancellor Maitland, that is all! In search of ... information, on Your Majesty's behalf! Heed it not. I seek Your Grace's ear on a much more important matter. In clemency ...'

'Na, na – I canna do it, Master Davy!' James interrupted him, pulling at his ear in agitation. 'It's no' possible, man. I canna do anything for Patrick – for the Master o' Gray. Dinna ask me to ...'

'But I do so ask, Your Grace. I ask you, of your royal clem-

404

ency, to pardon him. Or, at the least, to commute the sentence of death.'

'No. I canna do it, I tell you.'

'You can, Sire – if you will. For you are the King. You can sign a pardon if you will – and none can gainsay it.'

'They'd . . . they'd no' allow it. They'd no let me. And they'd no' let him go, man.' James babbled, slobbering copiously in his distress. 'They watch me, all the time. I canna do it.'

Huntly growled. 'You are afraid of a coven of upstart clerks and lawyers, Sire – you, the King of Scots?' His scorn was undisguised.

'They need not know – not until it is too late to stop it,' David declared hurriedly. 'Keep the matter secret, Highness. Your signed pardon, in the hands of my Lord Erroll, the Constable, and presented to the Governor of Edinburgh Castle . . . ! He could do no other than release Patrick. Then my lord of Huntly's men would escort him to a ship at Leith, within the hour. None could challenge them.'

'Challenge Gordon?' Huntly hooted. 'The Saints defend them, if they did!'

The King plucked at his lower lip. 'But . . . treason is no' a thing I can pardon, man. Conspiring the death o' my royal mother . . .'

Set-faced David eyed him. 'The Queen was sentenced to death, Sire, before Patrick ever went to London.'

'Aye. But you'll no' deny that it was an ill thing to do, Davy – to aid Elizabeth to the death . . .'

'I do not deny it, Sire. It was a shameful and wicked deed. I only cast myself and Patrick's life upon your royal mercy.'

'Ummm. Ooh, aye – do you so, man?' Always, any implication that James was all-powerful and in a position to grant or withhold life or death, was apt to be well received. And clearly the frank admission of guilt left him at something of a loss. 'Well, well, now . . .'

David sought to pursue his advantage. 'I do not ask for more than his life, Highness. He deserves to suffer much, I do not deny – though it may be true that he believed that he did what he did for the benefit of this realm. Punish him, yes – forfeit him, take away his offices and estates, banish him the realm. But spare his life, Sire, I beseech you.'

James moved round the littered table at his shambling walk, touching papers, frowning, darting, glances here and there. 'I . . . I . . . no, I canna do it, Master Davy,' he declared. 'Can

I, my lord? As ambassador o' this my realm, Patrick betrayed his trust. To pardon that would never do – never do, man. My ambassador speaks for me – he is my royal voice, see you. If thy tongue offends thee, cut it out, the Good Book says . . .'

'It also says forgive, until seventy times seven, Your Grace. Moreover, has not your own mother, Mary the Queen, ordained forgiveness on all concerned with her death, even with her dying breath? You would not have her noble wish made of no avail, Sire? You wrote kindly enough to Queen Elizabeth, who ordered the execution; can you not at least spare the life of him who but advised it?'

'Och, that is altogether different, Davy. Dinna harry me, man – I'm no' to be harried. You shouldna do it . . .'

'Sire, he is my brother. I will do much, say much, even that I should not say or do, to save my brother! *I* failed Queen Mary also, in England. I could have attempted her rescue. I spoke of it, once, but allowed myself to be dissuaded. I was weak. I believe, had I been strong, that I could have saved her. At Wingfield. I shall never forgive myself . . .'

'Mercy, man – what havers is this? How could you have saved her . . . ?'

'The way that I saved you, Sire, at Ruthven. By force and guile and fast horses. By deeds and not words . . .   '

'Waesucks, Davy – are you crazed? Yon would never have done – never. Dinna speak o' it. In Elizabeth's England! Yon would have meant war!'

'I wonder. Now I look back on it, I think not. Sire. But . . . it is done now, past. I failed the Queen. My eyes are open to it, at last.'

'Never say it,' the King told him. 'Violence and swordery – yon's no' the way to conduct the affairs o' the realm, man.'

'It gained you your freedom, Sire, once.' David took a step forward. 'I pray you now, not to forget it. If it meant anything that I saved Your Grace then, spare Patrick now! I have asked for nothing – would have accepted nothing. But now, Sire, I do so ask. For Patrick's life.' He paused. 'It was a long time ago, but surely you owe me something for that? And for other services, since.'

Even Huntly frowned. 'Davy – here's no way to speak to your King!' he protested.

'I know it, my lord. I said, did I not, that I would do and say things for my brother – things that I should not do?'

James was biting his finger-nails. 'Aye, Davy – I was beholden

to you for yon business. And for others, aye. I should have
rewarded you. I've thought o' it, man – more than once. Oh,
aye – it was featly done. A . . . a knighthood, man Davy? Eh?
Aye, I could knight you. There's many a bastard been knighted.
I could do it here and now – with my lord's braw broadsword,
there. Sir David Gray, Knight . . .' James was almost eager, for
the first time.

'No, Sire – I am not of the stuff of knights. Save that for Sir
John Maitland and Sir William Stewart and their like! I have
tasted their knightly prowess, and want none of it. I am just
plain Davy Gray, schoolmaster . . .'

'A grant o' lands, then? Estates? An office under the Crown . . .

'Thank you, no, Sire. Nothing – save my brother's life.'

'A curse on you, Davy Gray!' the harassed monarch exclaimed. 'Hard, stubborn as a Hieland stot! I told you – it's no'
possible. The folk, the people, would decry me, if I did. They
would have my mother avenged.'

'Forfeiture and banishment would be vengeance enough for
them.'

'Who rules in Scotland, then – people or King?' Huntly
scoffed. 'Besides, Sire, the people will have other matters to
think on! Very shortly.' That was grimly said. 'Good Catholics,
in especial. And what did the other sort care for Mary?'

James's jaw dropped. 'You're, you're no' meaning, my
lord . . . ? You wouldna, wouldna . . . ?'

'. . . Say that I would advise Your Grace not to fash your
head about what the folk will say. They will be a deal too busy
shouting for Christ's true religion!'

David frowned. He drew out a paper from his doublet within
the plaid, and smoothing it out, laid it on the table before the
King. 'Here is a pardon, all written out ready, Highness,' he
said. 'It declares the Master of Gray forfeit, dismissed all
offices, and banished from Your Grace's realm. But his life
spared. These provisions may be amended with a scrape of your
pen . . .'

'Master Gray, you exceed yoursel' – you greatly exceed
yoursel'!' James declared, drawing himself up with a pathetic
dignity.

'No doubt, Sire,' David nodded, and fixed the huge, limpid,
royal eyes with his own direct grey ones, however red-rimmed
and bloodshot. 'But you will mind that I was in yon small
room, not so far from this, when you gave my brother his
instructions, his secret instructions, as to what he was to say

in private audience with Elizabeth! You mind? About the terms on which you would overlook certain matters relating to your royal mother?'

'Hey, hey – what's this, Davy?' Huntly demanded. 'What's this, in the name of God?'

James sat down abruptly on his chair.

'Just a small matter, my lord, that His Highness may have forgotten. That may lead him to think more kindly of my brother on the matter of his amends . . .'

The King croaked something unintelligible.

'Amends? What mean you, man? About Mary the Queen, you said?'

'Small matters, yes – but which perhaps were not irrelevant to Patrick's behaviour. If I had thought to mention it at his trial, perhaps His Grace might have judged . . . differently. I blame myself.'

'No!' James got out, in strangled voice, 'No.'

'What of the Queen, man? Stop speaking in riddles,' Huntly commanded. 'Are you seeking to say . . .?'

'Only that, if His Grace will not sign the pardon, at least he may grant a stay of execution. So that this matter may be brought before the Council. You, my lord, might consent to bring it?'

'Not, by the Powers, until I know what it is, fool!' the Gordon cried.

James reached out his hand for his quill, dipped it tremblingly in the ink, and scrawled JAMES R. at the foot of David's paper.

'My God . . . !'

'My sincere thanks, Your Majesty!'

Huntly looked hard at David. 'This matter was none so small, I think!' he said. 'Do not tell me that the King . . .?'

'It is not for me to tell you anything, my lord – unless the King so will it.'

'I do not!' James cried, his voice cracking. 'Nothing, do you hear? It was a, a private matter. Between Queen Elizabeth and mysel'. A matter relating to my privy purse. Expenses, just . . .'

'M'mmm,' the Gordon said.

'No' word o' this will be spoken – by any!' the King declared breathlessly, staring from Huntly to his five perplexed-looking lairds, and back to David. 'This is my royal command. D'you hear – my royal command? No' a word. And as for this . . .' James pointed a quivering finger at the signed pardon. 'It is for life. For life, d'you hear? Banishment for life. Put that in, man – put it in. And no' to England. I'll no' have him in England, making trouble. I never wish to see his face again. Nor yours either, Davy Gray! You are an ill graceless breed, and I'll be quit o' you both! Begone, now – and mind, never let me set eyes on you again.'

David bowed stiffly, and picked up the paper. 'Your command shall be obeyed, Sire – most explicitly,' he said.

'Aye. See to it, then. And you, my lord – you have my permission to retire.'

'No doubt, Sire,' Huntly nodded. 'No doubt. And I shall not linger, for I do not like the smell o' this, by the Mass!'

'Go, then . . .'

So the tartan-clad party backed perfunctorily out of the royal presence, clapped on bonnets, and went striding through Holyroodhouse again, David Gray anonymous once more in the midst. Huntly exchanged no word with any of them.

Indeed he did not speak until, at the head of his mounted retinue, he drew rein outside his great mansion in the Canongate. He turned to David, at his back.

'It is done, then,' he said.

'Aye.' David drew out the pardon from within the folds of his enveloping plaid. 'Relays of your fastest gillies to get this to the Constable, my lord – riding day and night. We have less than forty-eight hours. When my lord of Erroll rides up to Edinburgh Castle, the deeds and charters of Dunfermline Abbey will be ready awaiting you.'

The Earl took the paper, but his eyes never left the younger man's battered face. 'Davy Gray,' he said slowly. 'You are a hard man to cross, I perceive. I'd liefer have you as friend than enemy, by the Rood! I vow you should turn Catholic!'

The other shook his head. 'You are wrong,' he returned. 'I am not a hard man, at all. Would to God that I was! It is just that . . . my, my daughter believes that I can do anything that I set my hand to. I had to prove it. Heaven forgive me, I had to prove it! A good day to you, my lord.'

Leaving Huntly to enter at his front door, David, with the rest of the clattering horsemen, rode down the side vennel to the stable entrance in the South-Back Canongate. There, dismounting, discarding plaid and bonnet and clad as just plain David Gray again, he slipped away by back-courts and wynds, to approach his own house in the Lawnmarket up the hill.

No song of triumph lightened his heart.

HUDDLED in shawls and plaids, the Grays sat their horses, all
four of them, in the shadow of the dripping trees, waiting. The
morning mists still rose from the Nor' Loch below them, and
wreathed the battlements of the great fortress high above them,
with the blue plumes of Edinburgh's breakfast fires beginning
to add their daily veiling. They waited each in different fashion –
young Patrick excitedly restless, vociferous, forever twisting
and wriggling in his saddle; Mary in still quiet eagerness;
Mariota flushed, strained, not far from tears; David set-faced,
silent. All gazed in the same direction, up over the steep slope
of grass and rocks to the high ridge-like causeway, outlined
against the morning sky, which climbed up from the outer
gate at the head of the Lawnmarket, right to the main frowning
gatehouse of the castle, the lofty slender catwalk which formed
the quarter-mile-long approach to the fortress, open to the eyes
of all men and all the winds that blew. Sometimes, admittedly,
David's glance turned elsewhere, making a swift survey of the
broken slopes below and around them, and the window-pierced
ramparts of the nearest tall houses – so many windows, so many
eyes to watch them.

The high defensive causeway was some two hundred yards
above them. Nearer than this, under the last of the scattered
trees, they dared not go. They were taking all too great a risk
even to be here, though probably only David considered that
aspect of the matter. The pacing guards up on the castle battlements could hardly fail to see them, just as would a myriad
eyes that might peer from all those windows at the other end of
the causeway. Undoubtedly they would have been better,
wiser, to have left Edinburgh before the city gates shut the
night before. Waited somewhere on the road to Leith . . .

The dense mass of horsemen that could be seen waiting up
there outside the portcullis gatehouse was reassuring, of
course – even though they had no interest in, represented no
security for the little family, bunched, all packed and ready
to ride, beneath the trees. They were armed Gordons, save
for the few of Erroll's Hays, and the sound of their confident,

laughing, north-country voices came clearly down to the anxious group, so that David, beneath his breath, cursed all arrogant boastful Highlanders, who must thus draw attention to themselves and what was toward so early in the morning.

Would they never come? Had anything gone wrong, in there within the castle, where so much might well go wrong? Was the Governor refusing to release his prisoner, despite the royal pardon? Was he trying to get word out to Maitland or the lords – though how could he achieve that, past the barrier of Gordons? It could not be that they were, in fact, too late? That James had resiled, gone back on his signature – or revealed the whole matter to his Ministers? And Patrick already disposed of, in his cell? Surely, if that had been so, he himself would have been arrested and silenced before this?

Apparently stolid, steadfast, but inwardly seething, David wondered for how long he could prevent himself from snapping at his small son to be quiet, to be still; how far they might already have progressed on the long road to Stirling and Perth and Castle Huntly, had only Erroll and Huntly not lain so late in their noble beds? The city gates would have been open now for well over an hour ...

For all his seeming inattention, young Patrick's keen eyes first perceived the increased agitation and stir up amongst the horsemen by the gatehouse, and his voice proclaimed the fact shrilly. The eddying of the riders around the end of the draw-bridge must surely mean that somebody had just crossed it, emerged from the gatehouse archway. The press of Gordons hid any actual view of this.

'There is the Lady Marie,' Mary's quiet but vibrant voice announced. 'See – her red cloak.'

Above the noise and commotion up there, a great laugh sounded clearly – Huntly's laughter.

'They have come out,' Mariota whispered. 'Is ... is Patrick there?'

David did not answer her.

The mass of Gordons was now circling round, manoeuvring, forming up into some sort of a column, all with infuriating leisureliness and lack of urgency. To see them, one would have said that nobody up there had a care in the world – or that it lacked only three short hours until the appointed time of Patrick Gray's execution.

Then, as the cavalcade began to string out, to ride slowly down the narrow causeway, not even at a trot, a great banner rose at the head of them – the three golden boars' heads on blue, of Gordon – and, to the horrified eyes and ears of David Gray at least, the reason for this deliberate and unhurried progress became evident, as a couple of strutting, puffing pipers came pacing out in front of all, blowing their shrieking, skirling instruments to the ears of all Edinburgh, and thus, to the challenging triumphant strains of *The Cock o' the North*, led the long procession down towards the city. A less discreet and expeditious rescue operation could scarcely be conceived.

They could see Patrick now, riding alongside, Marie slighter-seeming than most of his burly, plaided escort, hatless, his dark curls blowing in the breeze. A lump rose in David's throat at the sight. He seemed to be laughing and chatting vivaciously with Huntly, who rode just in front.

Slowly, in time to that most insolent Gordon march, they came on. Young Patrick was now singing his own monotonous version of the song at the pitch of his lungs.

As they came nearer, Marie could be seen to be pointing down the steep slope towards the little waiting party, drawing Patrick's attention. They saw him gazing, and then a hand rose in salute.

The boy shouted, Mary waved vigorously, Mariota's hand rose to her throat, her mouth.

They came on. Again Patrick raised his hand, looking down.

Mariota this time whipped off the kerchief that bound her hair. and flapped it. Her son all but fell off his horse in his enthusiasm. Mary was smiling, moist-eyed.

The cavalcade was at the nearest point of the causeway to the watchers, now, no more than a couple of hundred yards away. Patrick was half-turned in his saddle, leaning over, his eyes fixed on them. It seemed almost as though he was going to rein in his horse, to turn down to them – but the causeway had a vertical stone ramp, and was moreover protected by a formidable *cheval-de-frise* of iron spikes. The arm that had remained raised in salute, slowly sank.

Mariota sobbed in her throat, and turned to David. He sat still, immovable.

Patrick could not delay. All the Gordon cohort pressed on at his back. His mount, inevitably, moved on, away. He had to turn ever further round in his saddle. At his side Marie was waving and waving. He shouted something, and his hand half-rose again, but his words were indistinguishable against the bagpipes' shrilling and the beat of hooves.

'Davy – oh, Davy!' Mariota whispered.

Patrick was carried onwards, his whole slender body now twisted to face the rear. His handsome features were only a blur at that distance, but his entire posture and bearing were eloquence itself. In a few moments the riders behind him would block the line of vision between him and the group below. He raised both hands, not up as before but out, back behind him, open-palmed, towards his brother – and so rode.

David sat like stone, although the knuckles of his fists, clenched on his horse's reins, gleamed whiter than ivory. Then, gradually, one of those fists loosened, relaxed its grip, and slowly, quiveringly, lifted. It was as though it rose of its own volition, but hardly, against the man's will, until it was high above his head, open, no longer a fist, and so remained.

There was no drowning Patrick's shout, then, high-pitched, ringing, exultant, as his own hands shot up above his dark head, to clasp there, and shake, and unclasp and clasp again. They saw Marie's arm reach out, to her husband's shoulder. And then the horsemen at their back came between to hide them both.

In silence the family group sat now, watching as the front of the cavalcade reached the end of the causeway and was swallowed up amongst the high frowning tenements – or not quite silence, for Mariota was sobbing frankly, openly.

David moistened his lips twice, thrice, before he could find words. And even then his voice was curiously uneven, broken, for so stern-faced a man. 'Why . . . why are you crying, my dear?' he asked. 'What is there to weep for? All is . . . well, is it not?'

The strangled choking sound that Mariota produced might have signified anything or nothing.

David reached out his equally uncertain hand, to stroke her hair. 'Very well, is it not?' he repeated. 'He is safe, now. None will snatch him from Huntly's care, before Leith. He has his life. He will do very well in France . . . will the Master of Gray!

She nodded, blowing her nose.

'And we . . . we shall do very well, too. At Castle Huntly, my dear. Very well. No more cities and courts and statecraft for us! You were right. I should never have left Castle Huntly. We shall do finely – leading our own life, at last.' His voice strengthened. 'Rob Powrie is past stewarding. I shall steward Castle Huntly hereafter. My lord promised it. We shall be very happy, Mariota my dear – the four of us. It is what was meant to be – for we are simple country folk, you and I.'

413

A sniff – but she put her hand out to grasp his.

'Whatever Mary Gray may be! Very well so – on our way to Castle Huntly, before anyone can say us nay. To the West Port with us . . . and . . . and no looking back!'

'Yes, Davy . . .'

Postscript

THAT was not the end of Patrick, Master of Gray, of course – not by a long chalk. Indeed, he was back again in Scotland within two years, and suing the Crown for damages – and winning! But that, and a further catalogue of typical and highly doubtful endeavours is, for the moment, another story.

Enough for the day . . .

N. T.

MORE TITLES AVAILABLE FROM
HODDER AND STOUGHTON PAPERBACKS

NIGEL TRANTER

☐	17838 8	The Courtesan	£4.50
☐	17837 X	Past Master	£4.50
☐	40572 4	The MacGregor Trilogy	£5.95
☐	49485 9	Rough Wooing	£3.50
☐	21237 3	The Wallace	£4.50
☐	38636 5	Lord of the Isles	£3.50
☐	50826 4	Columba	£4.50

All these books are available at your local bookshop or newsagent, or can be ordered direct from the publisher. Just tick the titles you want and fill in the form below.

Prices and availability subject to change without notice.

Hodder & Stoughton Paperbacks, P.O. Box 11, Falmouth, Cornwall.

Please send cheque or postal order, and allow the following for postage and packing:

U.K. – 80p for one book, and 20p for each additional book ordered up to a £2.00 maximum.

B.F.P.O. – 80p for the first book and 20p for each additional book.

OTHER OVERSEAS CUSTOMERS INCLUDING EIRE – £1.50 for the first book, £1.00 for the second book, plus 30p per copy for each additional book.

Name ....

Address ....

....